There was a ga
chests, but so i.
with Bastiano's every move that
she felt as if their bodies touched.

It was time to stay or go. Sophie knew that. Even at this stage she could smooth it over and make her farewells.

Or she could meet those lips and discover bliss.

'Come here,' Bastiano moaned, and his hand came up and pulled her head down to his.

Always she had avoided such contact, and yet now she craved it.

His mouth was soft, and the dark shadow of his skin did not make her skin crawl with its tickle; instead it was rough and delicious and matched the building desire in her.

Now, instead of resisting, she opened her lips, wanting and willing.

His tongue felt like a reward as it coiled around hers. They tasted each other, and they inflamed each other—and not just with their mouths. He was stroking her breast through the fabric of her dress and Sophie ached for bed.

His bed.

Billionaires & One-Night Heirs

Secret babies they are determined to claim!

Raul, Alim and Bastiano—
three billionaires renowned the world over
for their charisma and commanding ways.

Lydia, Gabi and Sophie—three innocents
who cannot resist their seductive appeal.

And when sizzling nights lead to nine-month
consequences there is no other option—
these billionaires *will* claim their heirs!

The Innocent's Secret Baby

Bound by the Sultan's Baby

Sicilian's Baby of Shame

Available now!

You won't want to miss this addictive new trilogy
from Carol Marinelli!

SICILIAN'S
BABY OF SHAME

BY
CAROL MARINELLI

MILLS &
BOON

First Published in Great Britain 2017
By Mills & Boon, an imprint of HarperCollins*Publishers*
1 London Bridge Street, London, SE1 9GF

© 2017 Carol Marinelli

ISBN: 978-0-263-92528-9

Printed and bound in Spain
by CPI, Barcelona

Carol Marinelli recently filled in a form asking for her job title. Thrilled to be able to put down her answer, she put 'writer'. Then it asked what Carol did for relaxation and she put down the truth—'writing'. The third question asked for her hobbies. Well, not wanting to look obsessed, she crossed her fingers and answered 'swimming'—but, given that the chlorine in the pool does terrible things to her highlights, I'm sure you can guess the real answer!

Visit the Author Profile page
at millsandboon.co.uk for more titles.

For my wonderful editor Flo Nicoll.
Thank you for being you.
Carol xxx

PROLOGUE

BASTIANO CONTI HAD been born hungry.

And born a problem.

His mother had died giving birth to him and had never disclosed who his father was. All she had owned had been left to him—a ring.

It was Italian gold with a small emerald in its centre and some seed pearls dotted around it.

Bastiano's uncle, who had four children of his own, had first suggested that the nuns raise the orphaned baby who'd lain crying in the small maternity ward in the Valley of Casta. There was a convent that overlooked the Sicilian Strait and orphans had usually been sent there.

But the convent was on its last legs.

The nurses were busy but occasionally one would take pity and hold Bastiano a little longer than it took to feed him.

Occasionally.

'Familia,' the priest had said to his uncle. 'Everyone knows that the Contis look after their own.'

The Contis ruled the valley to the west and the Di Savos held the east.

Loyalty to their own was paramount, the priest told him. And so, after a stern talk from the priest, Bastiano's *zio* and his reluctant wife had taken the little bastard to their house but it had never, for Bastiano, been a home.

Always Bastiano had been considered an outsider. If something had gone wrong, then he'd been the first to be blamed and the last to be forgiven.

If there had been four brioches for lunch, they had not been split to make five.

Bastiano had done without.

Sitting in school next to Raul Di Savo, Bastiano had started to understand why.

'What would your parents save in a fire?' Sister Francesca had asked her class. 'Raul?'

Raul had shrugged.

'Your father,' she prompted, 'what would be the first thing that Gino reached for?'

'His wine.'

The class had laughed and Sister Francesca, growing more exasperated with each passing moment, had turned her attention from Raul.

'Bastiano,' she snapped. 'Who would your *zia* save?'

His serious grey eyes had lifted to hers and Bastiano had frowned even as he'd given his response. 'Her children.'

'Correct.'

She had turned back to the board and Bastiano had sat there, still frowning, for indeed it was the correct answer—his *zia* would save her children. But not him.

He would never be first.

However, aged seven, Bastiano was sent to collect the brioches and the baker's wife ruffled his hair and so unused to affection was he that his face lit up and she said that he had a cute smile.

'You do too,' Bastiano told her, and she laughed.

'Here.' She gave him a sweet cannoli just for brightening her morning and Bastiano and Raul sat on the hill and ate the gooey treat.

The boys should have been sworn enemies—for generations the Contis and the Di Savos had fought over the vines and properties in the valley—yet Bastiano and Raul became firm friends.

The small encounter at the baker's was enough for Bastiano to learn that he could get by better on charm.

Oh, a smile worked wonders, and later he learnt to flirt with his eyes and was rewarded with something far sweeter than cannoli.

Despite their families' protests, Bastiano and Raul remained friends. They would often sit high on the hill near the now vacant convent and drink cheap wine. As they looked out over the valley, Raul told him of the beatings his mother endured and admitted that he was reluctant to leave for university in Rome.

'Stay, then.'

It was that simple to Bastiano. If he'd had a mother, or someone who cared for him, he would not leave.

And he did not want Raul to go, though of course Bastiano did not admit that.

Raul left.

One morning, walking down the street, he saw Gino storm out of Raul's house, shouting and leaving the front door open.

Raul was gone and, given what his friend had told him, Bastiano thought he ought to check that his mother was okay.

'Signora Di Savo…' He knocked on the open door but she did not answer.

He could hear that she was crying.

His *zia* and *zio* called her unhinged but Maria Di Savo had always been kind to Bastiano.

Concerned, he walked inside and she was kneeling on the floor of the kitchen, crying.

'Hey.' He poured her a drink and then he got a cloth and ran it under the water and pressed it to the bruise on her eye.

'Do you want me to call someone?' he offered.

'No.'

He helped her to stand and she leant on him and cried and Bastiano did not know what to do.

'Why don't you leave him?' he asked.

'I've tried many times.'

Bastiano frowned because Raul had always said that he'd pleaded with her to leave yet she'd always refused.

'Could you go and stay with Raul in Rome?' Bastiano suggested.

'He doesn't want me there. He left me,' Maria sobbed. 'No one wants me.'

'That's not true.'

'You mean it?'

She looked up then and he went to correct her to say that what he had meant was that he was sure there were people who wanted her...

Not him.

She put a hand up to his face and held his cheek. 'You're so handsome.'

Maria ran a hand through his thick black hair and it did *not* feel like when the baker's wife had; this felt more than an affectionate ruffle and, confused, Bastiano removed her hand and stepped back. 'I have to go,' he told her.

'Not yet.'

She wore just a slip and her breast was a little exposed; he did not want Maria to be embarrassed when she realised that she was on display, so he turned to leave.

'Please don't go,' she called out to him.

'I have to go to work.'

He had left school and worked now in the bar that was a front for the seedier dealings of his *zio*.

'Please, Bastiano…' Maria begged. She reached for his arm and when he stopped she came around so that she stood in front of him. 'Oh,' she apologised as she looked down and saw that her breast was exposed to him, but Bastiano did not look. He was still pretending that he had not noticed.

And she would cover herself now, Bastiano thought, yet she did not. In fact, she took his hand and placed it on her plump, ripe skin.

He was good with the girls but in those cases he was the seducer. Maria was around forty, he guessed, and, for heaven's sake, she was the mother of his best friend.

'Signora Di Savo…' Her hand pressed his as he went to remove it.

'Maria,' she said, and her voice was low and husky. He could feel and hear her deep breathing and when she removed her hand, Bastiano's remained on her breast.

'You're hard,' Maria said, feeling him.

'Gino might—'

'He won't be back till dinner.'

Bastiano was usually the leader and instigator, but not on this hot morning. Maria was back on her knees but this time by her own doing. It was over within minutes.

As he left, he swore he would never return there.

But that very afternoon Bastiano made a trip to the pharmacy for protection, and an hour later they were in bed.

Hot, forbidden, intense—they met whenever they could, though it was never enough for Maria.

'We're getting out,' Bastiano told her. He had been paid and, if all else failed, he had his mother's ring. He could not stand the thought of her with Gino for even a moment longer.

'We can't,' she told him, even as she asked to see the ring and he watched as she slipped it on.

'If you love me,' Maria said, 'you would want me to have nice things.'

'Maria, give me back the ring.'

It was all he had of his mother but still Maria did not relent. Bastiano left.

He walked up the hill to the convent and sat looking out, trying to figure it all out. All his life he had wanted a taste of this elusive thing called love, only to find out he did not care for it. It was Bastiano who now wanted out.

And he wanted his mother's ring.

He stood, walking with purpose to the town below, where he saw it unfold.

A car driving at speed took a bend too fast. '*Stolto*,' he muttered, and called the driver a fool as he watched him take another bend...and then the car careered from the road.

Bastiano ran in the direction of the smoking wreck but as he approached he was held back and told that it was Gino's car that had been in the accident.

'Gino?' Bastiano checked.

'No!' a woman who worked in the bar shouted. 'I called Maria to say that Gino was on his way home and angry. He had found out about you! She took the car and—'

Maria's death and the aftermath had not painted Bastiano in a very flattering light.

Raul returned from Rome and on the eve of the funeral they stood on the hill where once they had sat as boys.

'You had your pick of the valley!' Raul could barely contain his fury.

'I went to check on her—'

But Raul did not want to hear that his mother had been the seducer. 'And you turned on that fake charm…' Raul had seen him in action after all. He knew how Bastiano could summon even the shyest woman with his eyes and melt restraint with a smile. 'I was a fool to trust you,' Raul said. 'You as good as killed her.'

Yes, he was the first to be blamed and the last to be forgiven.

'Stay away from the funeral,' Raul warned him.

But Bastiano could not.

And the next day things went from bad to worse. After a bloody fight at the graveside, it later transpired that half of Maria's money had been left to Bastiano.

Raul, once his friend, now accused Bastiano of engineering Maria's death and swore the rest of his days would be devoted to bringing him down.

'You're nothing, Conti,' Raul told him. 'You never have been and, even with my mother's money, you never will be.'

'Watch me,' Bastiano warned.

It is said that it takes a village to raise a child.

The Valley of Casta had never really been kind to Bastiano, but when the entire population considered you a cheat, a liar, a seducer, a bastard…that's what you become.

So, when a drunken Gino came to confront him, instead of taking it on the chin, Bastiano fought back, and when Gino called Maria a whore, Bastiano saw red and did not stay quiet. Instead, he gestured with his hand in the sign of horns and tossed Gino the biggest insult of all.

'Cornuto!'

Cuckold.

Bastiano, the villagers agreed, was the worst of the worst.

CHAPTER ONE

Some nights were hell.

'Bastiano!'

He heard the familiar, syrupy call of his name and knew that he must be dreaming, for Maria was long dead.

Unusually, he was alone in bed and as dawn sneaked over Rome, Bastiano fought to wake up.

'Bastiano!'

She called his name again.

When he reached his hand down and felt that he wasn't hard for her, it was a triumph, and Bastiano smiled a black smile as he silently told her she didn't do it for him any more.

Maria slapped his cheek.

She wore his mother's ring on her finger and he felt the cold metal as she delivered a stinging slap, one that had his hand move to his face for the wound was gaping. His cheek was sliced open and there was blood pouring between his fingers.

Bastiano fought with himself even in sleep. He knew that he was dreaming, for the savage fight with Raul had happened at the graveyard; the wound to his cheek had come *after* Maria had been lowered to the ground.

Everyone had said that it was Bastiano's fault she was dead.

And it was the reason that he was here, some fifteen years later—lying in one of the presidential suites at Rome's Grande Lucia hotel.

Raul Di Savo was considering its purchase, which meant that it had been placed on the top of Bastiano's must-have list.

Bastiano forced himself to wake up. He lay there in the darkness and glanced over at the hotel's bedside clock. Reaching over, he switched off the alarm. He had no need for it. He would not be going back to sleep.

Bastiano knew the reason that Maria was back in his dreams.

Well, she had never really left them, but that dream had been so vivid and he put it down to the fact that he and Raul were staying at the same hotel.

He heard the soft knock at the main door to his suite and then the quiet attempt to wheel in his breakfast trolley.

'*Puzza!*'

Bastiano smiled when he heard the small curse as the maid knocked into something and knew from that one word that the maid was Sicilian.

The door to the master bedroom had been left open but she quietly knocked again.

'*Entra,*' he said.

Bastiano was more than used to room service. Not only was he considering the purchase of this hotel but he was the owner of several premium establishments of his own. He closed his eyes, indicating, as she came in, that he wanted no conversation.

Sophie could see that he had made no move to sit up so she did not offer him a 'Good morning'.

The rules were very specific at the Grande Lucia and the staff were well trained.

Sophie loved her job, and though she did not usually do the breakfast deliveries she had been asked to do this one before her night shift ended. She had been called in to work late last night and so had missed the handover where the staff were told of any important guests, their idiosyncrasies and specific requests. Sophie, of course, knew that any guest staying in one of the presidential suites was an important one, and she had checked his name on his breakfast order.

Signor Bastiano Conti.

Being as quiet as she could, Sophie opened some heavy drapes and the shutters behind them so that the guest, when he sat up, would be greeted by the stunning view of Rome in all her morning glory.

And *what* a glorious day it was turning out to be!

It was as if the theatre curtains were opening on a beautifully set stage, Sophie thought.

There were a few clouds high in the sky that would soon burn off, for it was going to be a warm summer's day. The Colosseum was picture-postcard perfect and its ancient beauty gave her goosebumps.

Oh, it was a good day indeed for had she not made difficult choices and declined her family's desire for her to marry Luigi, today would have been the eve of her first wedding anniversary.

For a moment, Sophie forgot where she was and stood there simply taking in the view as she reflected on the past year. Yes, hard choices had been made but she was completely sure that they had been the right ones.

Oh, she was curious about men, of course she was, and though her mother would never understand it, she could readily separate that thought from marriage.

When she had tried to picture her wedding night and sleeping with Luigi, Sophie's blood had run cold. She had been out with a couple of younger men during her time in Rome but Luigi's wet, whiskery kisses had left their legacy and, though curious, Sophie had found herself ducking her head from any male advances.

Her parents imagined she was living a sinful life here in Rome.

Sadly, that couldn't be further from the truth!

Sophie was naïve, she knew that, but she was strong too.

Strong enough to say no to a man and a marriage she hadn't wanted.

'Buongiorno.'

A deep voice snapped her to attention and Sophie turned around as she realised that she had just been caught daydreaming, and by an important guest in his own suite!

She went to apologise but her flustered breath was literally taken away for there, lying in bed and idly watching her, was possibly a sight more arresting than the one she had just been feasting on. He was tall—she could see his length in the huge bed. His hands were behind his head and the sheet low on his stomach revealed his naked torso.

He really was magnificent, with olive skin and jet-black hair. The only blot on perfection was a jagged scar on his cheek, yet it only seemed to make him more beautiful. Most of all, it was his eyes that drew Sophie's. They were grey and piercing and as she met his gaze she found that her breath hitched in her chest and that she could not tear her gaze away. That was rare in itself for Sophie. In her job, she was very used to rich and beautiful men but with this one, with *this* one, she found that her eyes did not divert and, instead of an apology, her cheeks went a little bit pink.

'I was just preparing the view for you, Signor Conti,' Sophie said, and he gave a small smile in return as she made a little joke—as if she had been arranging the scenery outside specifically for him.

'Thank you.' He glanced towards the window and the million-euro view. 'You did a good job.'

And then he looked back at her.

When he had thought her to be taking her time Bastiano had opened his eyes to tell her to hurry up and leave, but there was something about her that halted his usual impatience.

And she mesmerised him now.

The eyes that met his were a very dark brown. He already knew from watching that she was as slender as a blade and wearing a pale green dress and flat shoes, both of which looked to be a little too big for her. Now he examined her face and saw that her thick black hair was worn up in a messy bun with a few long strands escaping.

She looked tired, Bastiano thought, and he guessed that her shift was just finishing rather than starting.

She had made him smile, just a little, but that was a surprise in itself given the dream he had so far failed to banish from his mind. The bedroom was rather messy and he was quite sure that the very sumptuous lounge was not much better; no doubt it was a stray bottle of champagne in the floor that had caused her small expletive on the way in.

'Would you like me to serve your breakfast?' she offered, still a little flustered and not just from being caught staring. Sophie made her way over to the breakfast trolley and lifted one of the silver domes.

'No, thank you,' Bastiano said. 'Actually, if you could bring me coffee that would be fine.'

'Would you like some water, or juice, too?' she offered, and then he saw the slight twitch to her lips and a certain knowing tone in her voice as she spoke on. 'Or perhaps you would like both?'

Again he smiled as she revealed her suspicions of his crashing hangover.

'Please.'

She brought over two glasses and Bastiano drank the cold water as she went back to the trolley and poured his coffee from the pot.

Usually Bastiano poured his own coffee for he did not like attempts at idle conversation, yet it was he who was pursuing it now.

'Sicilian?' he asked as she carried the cup to his bedside. She nodded and then, as she placed it on the table, she gave a little grimace, realising that he must have heard her swear.

'Me too,' he said calmly, and something in the delivery of his words told her that he got it, for the air was a touch bluer back home.

'What is that?' he asked, gesturing to the trolley, for despite the fact she had replaced the dome and covered the food there was now a rich, spicy scent mingling into the air.

'*Shakshuka,*' Sophie said. 'Middle Eastern baked eggs.'

The gorgeous guest screwed up his nose and Sophie was worried that the kitchen had got the orders mixed up so she quickly checked the paperwork on the trolley but, no, it was correct. 'You ordered it.'

'What was I thinking?' he drawled.

'I've heard that they're amazing,' Sophie said, and if the smell was anything to go by then her recommendation was bang on. 'Would you like me to take them back down and have something else sent to you?'

'It's fine.' He gave a shake of his head. 'Just leave it.'

'I hope you enjoy your day,' Sophie offered, and he gave a slight mirthless laugh and then nodded.

'You too.'

She went to close the bedroom door but he told her to leave it open.

As she left, Sophie picked up the bottle she had tripped over on her way in and put it on a tray. The room was a disaster and she would love, right this minute, to set about straightening things up, but it was not her job today and it was far too early to service a suite.

Anyway, as of now, she was off duty and so she headed to clock off and collect her things.

'What are you doing, delivering breakfasts?' Inga asked as Sophie retrieved her jacket from her locker. Just to be polite, Sophie had made a casual comment as to why she was a few minutes late coming off duty but Inga had, in her usual critical way, pounced. 'That is for the more senior chambermaids.'

'I just do as I'm told,' Sophie said, and poked her tongue out at Inga's departing back.

They did not get on.

Inga liked to deliver the breakfasts, especially to the very rich men, and though turning tricks was strictly forbidden, Sophie was quite certain that was the reason it was a designer bag that Inga had just put into her locker.

It wasn't for Sophie to judge and she tried not to.

Her dislike for Inga was simply due to the frequent disparaging comments and the endless digs that were sent her way. Sophie did her best to shrug them off but it was difficult at times. She didn't even know what she had done to incur Inga's wrath.

Still, she chose not to dwell on it. Sophie was more than ready for home—she was tired, hungry and ached for bed. Instead of heading out of the side entrance, Sophie, as she often did, decided to exit through the kitchen.

The reason was twofold.

It took her out to the alley, which was closer to the small flat she shared with two others.

And her little diversion would hopefully mean a free breakfast!

There were several chefs that worked in the kitchens, of course, but her favourite was Sicilian and he was just taking a batch of brioches out from the oven as she made her way over. Not the French brioche or even the sweet pastry those here in the north referred to; instead, these were the most delicious plain-baked buns of home. And he had made *millefoglie* too—also a bun, but with raisins mixed in and sugar on the top. Sophie guessed it was exactly the breakfast this morning's guest might wish that he had chosen.

Apart from Inga, Sophie was very well liked and popular at the Grande Lucia. She was a very good worker and always went the extra mile for guests. Signor Conti's mirthless laugh had stayed with her and so, instead of sneaking a brioche for her walk home, she spoke with the chef. He arranged a plate of freshly baked pastries and she put a small silver dome over it and then took her jacket off and, placing it over her arm, she headed back up to Signor Conti's suite.

She knocked and let herself in and then called out.

'Room service.'

After the maid had left, Bastiano had got up, taken one look at the eggs and replaced the dome.

His friend Alim, the current owner of the hotel, had always suggested he try them when they met for brunch and last night as he'd squinted at the selections it had seemed a good idea.

Not now.

There was no point him even being here.

Last night Alim had told him that his plans had suddenly changed and that he would not be able to show him through the hotel today as planned.

That wasn't all that irked Bastiano.

For once—in fact, for the first time in his life—a woman had turned him down.

In recent weeks, Bastiano had decided he would like a wife, and one with a castle in England and money problems had appeared to fit the bill.

It had seemed a decent solution at the time.

Lydia Hayward, with her breeding and porcelain looks would, he had decided, be the perfect trophy wife. It would be mutually beneficial, of course, and for his part he would help with her family's dire financial situation. He had flown her and her stepfather, Maurice, over to Rome so that he could kill two birds with one stone—view the hotel and put in an offer that would blow Raul out of the park. And maybe return home to Casta having secured a bride.

The more he had thought about it, the more he had decided that it might just be enough to rattle Raul—for Bastiano was more than financially secure, but settled... not so much.

But his plans hadn't exactly worked out that way.

Lydia had decided she would spend the evening catching up with friends and had left him hanging with the appalling Maurice.

Bastiano hadn't even attempted small talk with the man; instead, he had come back to his suite, and with his mood too dark to hit the clubs he had hit the bottle instead.

A foolish choice, in retrospect, for it had not been Lydia who had crept into his mind as he'd slept.

It had been Maria.

Fifteen years on and he could not fathom that he had ever cared for another person, for he cared for no one now.

No one.

Bastiano had a reputation for cold-hearted ruthlessness that ran from the boardroom to the bedroom.

Beating Raul Di Savo was the only thing that interested him.

He heard a knock at his door and a voice that was too cheerful for his black mood announce that room service was here.

Again!

Bastiano put a towel around his hips and walked out, more than ready to tell her to get the hell out and that, had he wanted a second delivery, he would have picked up the phone himself.

Yet she smiled so nicely as she took the lid from the plate she carried and held it out.

'Better?' she asked, as his eyes went to the plate.

Now, *that* was breakfast.

And his eyes went back to hers. No, they were not simply dark brown, they were the amber of a fox, and her smile was so bright that Bastiano could not bring himself to chide her. 'Much,' he rather reluctantly replied.

'I thought so too. Would you like another coffee?'

'That would be good.'

He got back into bed with the towel still round his hips and breakfast was served for the second time.

'You didn't have to do that,' Bastiano commented as, once in bed, she handed him the plate.

He guessed she must know that he was the potential new owner, for all the staff were walking on eggshells around him.

'I know.' She smiled 'But I also know that we have the best Sicilian chef here at the Grande Lucia. I was going to sneak a brioche for the walk home and it made me think of you.'

Perhaps she did not know that he might soon be the new owner? Bastiano could not care less about her sneaking a pastry. His staff all got meals on their shifts anyway, he made sure of that, but many owners were strict about such things.

'What's your name?'

'Sophie.' She saw him glance at the jacket over her arm. 'Really, it's not a problem—I am at the end of my shift.'

'Then would you like to stay and have some Middle Eastern eggs?' he offered, teasing her by replaying her words. 'I have been told that they're amazing.'

'No, thank you.' Sophie let out a small laugh as she shook her head. She wasn't unused to suggestions from businessmen and had declined her share over the last year. Sophie was no Inga!

'Enjoy.'

'I am.' He had torn open the brioche and as she left, the scent that reached him was the one of home and he spoke, really without thinking. 'I used to collect these from the bakery.'

'Ha!' Sophie said, turning around. 'Until I came to Rome I used to work at a bakery.'

'For how long?'

'Seven years,' Sophie said. 'Since I left school.'

And it was very easy—too easy—to speak of home. She missed it.

Oh, Sophie loved the life she had made here in Rome, but there was an ache for home at times, so for a moment they chatted, really just about the food and the stunning

Strait of Sicily. He guessed that she was also from the west. He was about to ask her exactly where but then Sophie yawned.

'Excuse me,' Sophie said. 'I really do have to go, all this talk of…' And she stopped because he had invited her to eat already and it might seem that she was angling for him to ask her again if she said just how hungry she felt.

Maybe she *was* angling?

Later she would look back and try to remember exactly how she had felt at that moment.

Happy and relaxed. It felt nice to be in his company.

'Have breakfast,' Bastiano said.

There was no motive.

That in itself was beyond rare for Bastiano, for he lived by motive, he did nothing without motive, yet all he saw this morning was that she was tired and probably hungry after a long shift.

And she heard, absolutely, the kindness in his offer and so, with just the briefest hesitation, she nodded.

'Thank you.'

Sophie could not know that kindness in Bastiano generally did not exist.

CHAPTER TWO

IT WAS AS natural as that.

The conversation between them came readily and it was simply pleasant to be with him. Sophie put her jacket on a chair and poured herself some chilled water and placed it on a tray. To that she added the plate of *shakshuka* and then looked around, wondering where she should take it to eat. First she glanced over at the chair where she had placed her jacket but it was rather full as his was there too. It was inside out so she could see the deep aubergine lining as well as a crumpled white shirt on the floor beside it. She looked at Bastiano, who was moving more to the centre of the bed, as if to make room for her to sit there, and so, instead of the chair, she made her way over to the bed.

Yes, it was as natural as that to walk over and sit on the edge of the huge bed, not too close, but alongside his thighs. She placed the tray on her lap.

The cloche had kept warm the eggs that were nestled in a rich-looking sauce, and she took her first tentative taste. It was a little spicier than expected and Sophie missed his smile as she reached for her water.

'Nice?' Bastiano asked.

She turned and looked at him and her eyes moved briefly to the scar on his cheek—Sophie would have loved to know its source—but then she looked back to his eyes. 'You know when you have wanted to try something for a very long time and then finally you do…'

Her words were not meant as provocative and they were not taken as such, for he was waiting for her to screw up her nose and to say that it was not as nice as she had thought it would be, but then she smiled. 'It is better than I expected.'

It was then that her words were provocative, though only to Sophie—for the pleasure of his company had her thoughts taking her mind to places they had never been.

He was stunningly attractive, yes, and she was no fool as to her situation, yet as Sophie looked at him her throat seemed to close in on itself and she could feel the pulse beat in her neck.

She was innocent from the lips down, and those lips had determinedly stayed as closed as they could when she had kissed her fiancé.

She had never shared a meal in a man's bedroom, or sat on a bed with a man and chatted so easily.

And neither had she ever stared so readily into another's eyes.

It truly was better than expected.

Was it the hot Baharat mix in the *shakshuka* that made her cheeks suddenly redden, or was it the first stirrings of desire?

Sophie did her best not to dwell on that thought. She tore her gaze from his and spoke on quickly. 'Apparently Sultan Alim has put a lot of new things on the menu since he took over the hotel.'

'Sultan?' Bastiano asked. He and Alim were friends. The Grande Lucia was Bastiano's favoured hotel when in Rome, and he and Alim often painted the town a rich shade of red but, despite lavish spending and wild ways, as far as Bastiano knew, Alim had always kept his royal status under wraps as best he could.

'We only found out that he was royal a few months ago,' Sophie revealed. 'His family came to stay and so of course the desk staff soon worked it out.' She thought for a moment. 'He's a good boss.'

'In what way?' Bastiano asked. He liked to hear the things that were important to staff, and knew that that sort of information could not readily be gleaned from a questionnaire or an appraisal. He didn't want to admit it, but he also just liked hearing her thoughts.

'He knows all of his staff by name,' Sophie said. 'And he is fair and kind. There was a Christmas meal and gift for all the staff who were working over the festive season.' She was silent for a moment as she thought back to that lonely day—coming to work had been the brightest part.

'How long have you worked here?' Bastiano asked.

'For nearly ten months. I've been in Rome for just over a year.' Sophie thought back to when she had first arrived and how nervous she had been, for she had never spent so much as a night away from home until then. 'It took a few weeks to find a job. I would have taken anything, but then I came for my interview and I wanted to work here so badly. I never thought I would get it as there was two months' training involved, but Benita took me on.'

'Benita?'

'The head of housekeeping,' Sophie explained. 'It is so much better than my old job.'

'I guess working at a bakery would have meant many early starts?'

'So early!' Sophie nodded and rolled her eyes. 'The shifts here are much better and the staff are really friendly. Well,' she added, thinking of Inga, 'most of them are.'

'Most?'

'There is always the odd person that you don't get on with in any workplace.' Sophie shrugged. 'I enjoy working here; I can't believe my luck really. It is, for me, the perfect job.'

'Why?'

'I like order,' Sophie said. 'I like things to be neat and tidy. When I see a suite such as yours, I itch to have it back as it should be.'

'Really?'

'Yes, really.' She nodded her head in the direction of the chair. 'I would have that jacket hanging up and that shirt put away.' Then she looked back at him. 'I would have that bed made, even with you in it...' And she hesitated. It was something that she often said as a joke to guests, usually the ones on the twelfth floor when she shooed them out to service their room.

It was not something that would ever be said to a guest such as Bastiano; he would never be shooed out, even jokingly.

It was not just that thought that had her pause, it was more a sudden awareness of their situation that silenced her.

Yet she had let the words out, and they were how she felt.

Not so much a neat bed, of course, more the thoughts that were there—an emerging awareness that made the room feel a little warmer.

Bastiano said nothing, just held her unblinking gaze until she spoke on.

'It really is the perfect job. Sometimes people ask me what I want to be, or they ask if I am working while studying, but I want only this—I'm happy now.'

'That's a very good place to be,' Bastiano said, though he couldn't fathom it for himself. The more he had the more he wanted, the more he achieved the further the goal seemed to stretch. 'Do you miss your family and friends?'

'I've made some friends…' She thought of her flatmates and though they were not particularly close she got on well with them. And Sophie thought of Gabi, a wedding planner, who she had met on her first weekend here and had got on with straight away.

Usually Bastiano would leave it there. In fact, usually it would never have reached this point, for sitting in bed and chatting with a woman was not something Bastiano did regularly.

Regularly? Ha! Ever.

Yet he found he wanted to know her better.

'Do you miss home?' Bastiano asked, carefully rewording his question.

'Sometimes,' she admitted. 'But if I was still there…' Sophie stopped what she was about to say and put down her cutlery, even though her meal was not finished. The conversation was edging towards topics that she usually kept closed.

Her newly made friends knew little about her. To them she was Sophie, twenty-four years old and happily single.

They had no idea how hard she had fought and how much she had given up to achieve such a small victory.

'*If* you were there?' Bastiano pushed, and now he *was* fishing—he really did want to know more about her.

She was about to stand, to end the conversation and get on with her day. Return to the real world.

Surprisingly, she found she liked this one.

Sophie liked the peace in his bedroom and the ease with which she spoke with this man.

She thought of his kind smile when she had realised he'd heard her swear. It had been a smile that had spoken of mutual understanding and a familiarity with the ways back home.

Something told her that he would…understand.

And though she had in the main been happy, it had also been a lonely twelve months.

'I was engaged to be married,' Sophie admitted. 'Had I stayed, tomorrow would have been my first wedding anniversary.'

'Had you stayed?' Bastiano verified. 'So it was you who ended it?'

'In a very mature and thoughtful way.' Sophie nodded and then she gave a small laugh that told him she was joking about handling things in an adult fashion. 'I ran away, if it is possible to run away from home when you are twenty-three. A month before the wedding I took a train to Rome and when I got here I called my parents and told them that I would not be marrying Luigi.'

He laughed at her explanation, although not un-kindly—it was a deep, low laugh that was almost enough reward in itself for that awful phone call she had made to her parents.

Something told Sophie that he did not laugh easily, that what was happening this morning between them was both delicious and rare.

And then that low laugh faded, like a roll of soft thun-der moving through her.

Lightning had already struck, Sophie realised.

She was here alone in his room and it was exactly where she wanted to be.

'Have you been back home since?' he asked, seem-ingly unaware of the dance in her mind. Sophie was ter-ribly grateful for the resumption of conversation, and answered hurriedly for her thoughts were all over the place.

'No, it was a big disgrace. I expected them to be cross but when it came to my birthday and my mother would not even come to the phone I realised just how bad things were.'

'When was your birthday?' he asked.

'A few months after I ran away.' She told him the date. 'It was pretty miserable.'

Birthdays had always been about family and standing around a cake while having a hundred photos taken.

Not this time.

It had been the same at Christmas—and the reason she had been so grateful that Alim ensured his staff celebrated also. Her flatmates had all gone home to be with their families and so the meal and gift from work had been the only Christmas that Sophie had had.

'They must miss you,' Bastiano said, but Sophie shook her head.

'I'm not sure that they do. I come from a big family; they wanted me married so that there would be one less. You know how things are back home.'

He nodded. Bastiano did know how things were for many but then he looked at Sophie and was still sure of one thing—they *must* miss her, because from the moment she had opened the drapes it had been as if an extra ray of sunshine had been let in. 'Will you go back?'

'I'm their only daughter…' She shrugged but it belied the pain behind the inevitable decision. 'If I return then I am to abide by their rules. I don't know what will happen. For now, though, I live my dream.'

Even if it was lonely at times.

'What about you?' she asked.

'I don't have any family.'

'None?'

He shook his head and he saw that she waited for him

to elaborate. 'I was raised by my mother's brother and his wife.'

'What about your mother?'

'She died.'

'How old were you?'

He didn't answer.

'What about your father?'

'You know as much about him as I do—nothing.'

'Not quite.' Sophie smiled. 'I know that he was good looking.'

Yes, she was like sunlight because until now, when he had revealed that his father was unknown, it had either terminated the conversation or resulted in averted eyes or a derisive comment. Not with Sophie, for she turned the awkwardness around as she smiled—and possibly flirted—and the conversation was far from closed.

'What happened with your *zia* and *zio*?' she asked.

'I see them on occasion but we don't really speak,' Bastiano said, peeling off some brioche and handing it to her to mop up the last of the spicy sauce. 'They threw me out when I was seventeen.' He thought of the row they had had after the affair had been exposed and it had come to light that he had slept with the enemy—a Di Savo. 'Deservedly so.'

'So what are you doing here in Rome?' Sophie asked. 'Business?'

'In part,' Bastiano said, but knew that he was being evasive. Sophie obviously had no clue that he was considering purchasing the hotel. He didn't want to enlighten her for he knew that it would put a wedge between them. So to avoid speaking of work he told her something rather personal. 'I got dumped last night.'

'Oh!' She smiled at his revelation. 'I cannot imagine anyone dumping you.'

'Neither could my ego,' Bastiano admitted, and then he told her a bit more. 'She's English and lives in a castle.'

'Nice,' Sophie said, and he shrugged.

'It would have been a lot of work.'

Sophie frowned, not sure what he meant by that.

'What was your fiancé like?' he asked, curious about the man she had left behind.

'He was a lot older than me, more than forty years old,' Sophie said, and screwed up her face.

'Is that why you ended it?'

'Not really.' She shook her head. Looking back at that time, she remembered that moment when she had felt as if she could see her life spreading out before her, and not liking what she saw.

Sophie had never discussed it with anyone and perhaps she should not now but there was nothing regular about this morning. She had never met anyone who felt less like a stranger before. Bastiano knew more about her than her flatmates and she had lived with them for a year. More about her than Gabi, for she had been a touch elusive of late and their catch-ups had petered out. And he knew more about her than her parents, for they had never once asked for her take on things.

'Luigi came over to my parents' for dinner, as he often did…'

Bastiano said nothing, he even fought a slight eye rise, but at forty shouldn't the guy have at least been entertaining her?

Sophie glanced at him—the truth was a touch personal, but his eyes were patient and finally there was a person to whom she could speak her truth.

'That night I felt a little sick and didn't really eat much. When my mother took away the plates and my brothers and father left us alone he asked what was wrong with me. I told him that I had gone on the Pill.' She blushed just a little as she said it but far less than she had when she had told her fiancé. In fact, Bastiano seemed completely at ease with the sensitive topic.

Unlike Luigi.

It hadn't been up for discussion. Sophie had had to find everything out for herself. Even the village doctor hadn't been particularly friendly. In the end, it had been her friend at the bakery who had told her that she could skip her period entirely if she chose.

'What was his reaction?' Bastiano asked.

'He seemed cross. He said, "Why would you go on that?" Then he told me that he wanted children straight away and a lot of them!'

She pulled such a horrified face that Bastiano laughed.

And there was that thunder again, only this time she was counting the minutes, for the delicious storm drew closer with each revelation and with each passing word.

'I said that we needed my wage from the bakery and my mother came in from the kitchen. She didn't hear the part about the Pill, of course, just me saying I would put off having children so I could work, and she said she would look after them. It's not that I don't want children...'

He halted her when she tried to further explain for there was no need.

'Sophie,' he said in that rich voice of his, 'well done for running away.'

Bastiano was the first person she had really told about it and his reaction made her feel warm with pride for her choice, rather than sick with shame as her family had.

'Thank you.'

Oh, they were as natural as that, for Bastiano, who rarely bothered with conversation, was telling her some more about himself.

'I flew Lydia over from England with her stepfather, Maurice, under the guise of business. We were supposed to be meeting in the bar and then going out for dinner but when she turned up she said that she was going out with friends instead.'

Sophie gave him a quizzical look, because she really couldn't imagine declining dinner with him, but Bastiano read her frown as curiosity.

'I think she had worked out it wasn't just dinner.' He saw her cheeks darken in a blush and he further clarified that it had not been sex he was after. Bastiano had no trouble at all finding that. 'Like your fiancé, I had got it into my head that maybe it was time to settle down.'

Though his main reason had been simply to beat Raul to it.

Bastiano had everything money could buy and so too did Raul. The only thing neither had was a family.

He had decided that he would be first.

It had been as simple as that.

'Had you been going out with each other for long?' Sophie asked.

'We'd never been out.' Bastiano yawned and it really was a relief not to have to explain that romance and love were not always prerequisites for marriage back home. 'It just seemed like a good idea at the time, though not so much now.' He shrugged. 'Easy come, easy go. On reflection, I think I'm far more suited to the single life.'

'Well, with your looks and…' she looked around the lavish suite and stated the obvious '…your money, why not have fun?'

'Oh, I do,' Bastiano said.

Though lately he wouldn't describe it as fun.

He lay back on the pillow, but as their eyes met the silence was heavy. She wore no make-up, not a scrap, Bastiano noted as he took in her dark lashes. He felt her gaze move to his mouth and for once he was unsure where they were going, for usually when a woman was on his bed there was no question as to what was about to happen.

Come here, he wanted to say.

Sophie knew that.

Her perfect storm had now gathered and it would be so terribly easy to be swept into it, but she really was no Inga, even if he perhaps thought of her as such.

There was a reason the maids were told not to accept gifts.

Yet there was no air of expectancy from Bastiano.

Sophie felt no pressure as she put down her cutlery, took a drink of water and then stood.

She gave him a polite smile and effortlessly she was back to being a maid. She put her plate neatly back on the trolley.

'Thank you,' Sophie said. 'That was delicious.'

'You're more than welcome,' Bastiano said. 'So were the pastries.'

She came over to collect his plate.

It rested on his thigh and, though covered by the sheet, Sophie thought it was better that he be the one to retrieve it for she could see a black snake of hair on his stomach—as much as she tried not to look. There was desire pitted low in her stomach and an itch to pull the sheet down. Her hands shook a little and just like that she was no longer a maid. Their fingers met for a little too long and rather than pull back she lingered for his skin was warm and even that slight touch had her aching for more.

'I have to go,' she said as she fought for control.

'Of course.'

Yet still she stood there and instead of turning away

she put the plate down on the bedside table. She was not so much uncertain, more nervous of her own curiosity.

'Thank you,' she said again.

Bastiano could not read her, for he could feel her desire and yet sense her reticence so he moved things along a fraction. His index finger came up and he tapped it twice on the cheek nearest to her, the one that was not scarred.

A kiss to the cheek was still okay, Sophie thought, for she would kiss her friend Gabi on the cheek when they said farewell after sharing a meal. But even as she tried to convince herself, Sophie knew that this situation was nowhere near as innocent as that.

It wasn't even a conscious decision. It was more that she might as well have been standing on a conveyer belt, for it was as if she glided towards him.

She bent forward and moved her mouth to where his finger had tapped, the place where his rough morning shadow transitioned into smooth skin. The contrast sent shivers down her spine. The warmth of him on her lips was enticing and her tongue fought not to taste as her lips lingered.

Sophie sensed him holding his breath and hers now came a little too fast in response. She pulled her head back and moved to kiss the other cheek.

Bastiano jerked his head a little, for he did not like anyone touching his scar. He would by far prefer her mouth to meet his and usually he got what he wanted.

Not this time.

She misread the small signal and her mouth moved to his other cheek. Once on his scar, her lips lingered there, kissing him softly as if she didn't care about the damage beneath.

CHAPTER THREE

THERE WAS A gap between their chests, but so in tune was Sophie with his every move that she felt as if their bodies touched.

It was time to stay or go, Sophie knew. Even at this stage she could smooth it over and make her farewells.

Or she could meet those lips and discover bliss.

With Luigi, she had dreaded a kiss, let alone sex.

Not now.

When she had left home at twenty-three, Sophie had been considered a disgrace for her failure to commit.

She was twenty-four now and there was no disgrace to be had here.

It was better than her dreams. And so much better than the reality she had run from.

'Come here,' he moaned, and his hand came up and pulled her head down onto his.

Always she had avoided such contact, yet now she craved it.

His mouth was soft, and the dark shadow of his skin did not make her skin crawl with its tickle; instead, it was rough and delicious and matched the building desire in her.

Now, instead of resisting, she opened her lips, wanting and willing.

His tongue felt like a reward as it coiled around hers,

and then he slowly suckled the tip. They tasted each other, and they inflamed each other and not just with their mouths. He was stroking her breast through the fabric of her dress. His thumb was teasing her nipple and Sophie ached for bed.

His bed.

She pulled back, and knew that even now she could walk out having shared no more than a kiss.

'You taste spicy,' Bastiano said.

'And you taste sweet.'

'But I'm not,' he warned her.

'I'm working,' she told him, for she would get into the most terrible trouble if anyone found out.

'You finished an hour ago,' he reminded her, and then he stretched out an arm and she heard the click of a button that would turn on the Do Not Disturb sign outside.

'I'm in my uniform…'

'Good,' he said.

He thought her experienced, Sophie suspected.

Perhaps now would be the time to tell him she was not. That this morning was, in fact, a most irregular occurrence for her.

But Sophie knew that would change things. And there was nothing about this man and this morning she would change, even if she could.

Sophie wondered if she was on that conveyer belt again, for she moved so easily to be closer to him and when he guided her so that she sat on his stomach, she went readily.

Bastiano looked up as his fingers undid the buttons to her uniform and revealed a threadbare bra so sheer that her nipples could almost part the fabric and he could see the dark of her areolae. His hands cupped her breasts and he wanted her to shrug off the dress, to discard the bra and to lower her head, yet she closed her eyes in bliss as he toyed with her breasts.

'Take down your hair,' he told her, for he wanted the curtain between them when she took him in her mouth; he guided her back so that she sat on his thighs and the sheet moved with her.

She saw him erect, and since it was the first time she had seen, let alone touched, such a thing she held him in her hands.

'Sophie,' he said, for he did not want hands and tentative fingers even as he grew to them.

He was mesmerised, though, watching as she stroked.

Simply touching him was compelling. The feel of soft skin was a contrast to the strength in her palm and there was a coil of want that seemed to tighten within him as she gripped him more firmly.

'Take down your hair,' he said again, yet Sophie did not care for his orders, for the pleasure that grew was not just his. Her knickers were damp and she ached to feel him there. She wanted to stand and remove them, yet her legs felt clamped to his thighs.

She ran a finger over the tip and teased out a silver drop; the moan he gave had her rise to her knees.

He lifted the skirt of her dress, taking his own thick length and running it over her covered mound.

Sophie knelt up with her hands on his chest, biting on her lip at the exquisite pleasure he delivered. Oh, it was wrong! If she examined it, then she knew that was the only conclusion that could be drawn.

Yet there was so much that she had not even known was missing and she felt like a colourblind person able to see a rainbow for the first time.

She had for a long time dreaded sex and that dread had now completely gone. Sophie was turned on like she had never been in her life. Even in her imaginings there had never been desire such as this.

Despite the barrier of fabric he pushed in just a little way, enough to incite and make her ache for more.

He reached into the bedside drawer for condoms while she hovered and teased, and then he held a condom out for her once she had peeled off her knickers.

'Put it on,' he said, his voice ragged as his fingers met the pink lips that would soon enclose his length. 'Sophie…' His impatience was building for he had to be inside her. 'Put it on.'

And then she spoke and the words that she said stilled him.

'I don't know how.'

Bastiano's conscience had left him a long time ago.

He had thought it buried alongside Maria, for he cared nothing for anyone, but when it hit that he would be her first, his conscience made itself known once more.

Bastiano knew very well how things worked, especially in hotels, and often he didn't need to go out or even pick up the phone for sex to drop into his lap.

Sophie wasn't his usual style—an innocent conversation and a breakfast.

Sophie really was sweet.

'What the hell are you doing here, then?' he asked.

'The same as you,' she told him, and his lips pressed together as he got first hand a taste of her defiant streak.

'I think you should go.' His conscience seemed to stand in the wings and, like a prompter, told him the words he should say. 'I'm not looking to get involved with anyone. I'm back to the single life, Sophie.'

'You already told me that,' she said.

'You've been saving yourself, and a one-night stand in a hotel room—'

'It's morning,' Sophie interrupted, but Bastiano was having none of it and he tipped her from his lap and pulled up the sheet.

'Go.'

There was no air of negotiation to his tone but still she sat there.

'Out,' he told her, and Sophie climbed from the bed.

Humiliated, she stuffed her knickers into her uniform pocket as Bastiano looked at the ceiling, or rather anywhere than at Sophie.

And again she could see her life spreading out before her.

Regret.

Utter regret that her first time had not been with someone as beautiful and sensual as him.

She was twenty-four and she ached to know such intimacies.

Bastiano was exquisite.

He was male beauty personified, expensive yet raw too, with a visceral undercurrent that finally matched hers.

That was why she had waited—to find someone who was her match.

Maybe later she would finally give in to her parents' silent demands and return home. Perhaps someday she would settle and marry and pretend that it was her first time, while holding the secret that it had been him all along.

Almost.

'You're right,' she said, and went to do up some of the buttons on her uniform. 'I *have* been saving myself—for a time and a person of my choosing.'

'You can do better.'

'Please...' she scoffed.

Now he looked from the ceiling and at her as Sophie spoke.

'This time last year I was told I could do no better than the man they had lined up to take my virginity.'

'But he would have been your husband.'

'Do you think it helped to know that?' she asked, and her question was both important and urgent.

'No,' Bastiano admitted, and there was a flicker of guilt that flared because of his own quest for a trophy wife. He looked at Sophie, still doing up her uniform; in the bedroom he usually didn't need to think, yet she was clever and strong and knew her own desires.

'It doesn't matter,' Sophie said. She was starting to think of all the professional consequences of this current humiliation. He was, after all, a guest, and she was desperately trying to get back to being a maid. 'I am sorry for any misunderstanding...'

Bastiano loathed her apology.

There had been no misunderstanding.

'Sophie.'

She ignored him and headed for the bedroom door. This time she would not be returning. Her cheeks were on fire and, rarely for Sophie, she felt on the edge of tears.

He was doing her a favour, Bastiano told himself.

Yet it was a favour that neither of them wanted.

'Sophie.' This time he said it as he got out of bed.

Bastiano had never run after anyone but he called her name again just as she walked through the door. Sophie paused and turned around.

He was entirely naked; he hadn't even attempted to bring the sheet with him. The sight of him standing naked caused her to breathe as if she had taken the stairs all the way up to his suite.

He was tall, so tall that as he stood right in front of her

she was at eye level between his clavicle and one dark mahogany nipple.

'You forgot your jacket.'

She didn't look up and neither did she look down; the chair near the window seemed like a very long way away. 'Could you fetch it for me, please?'

'Are you sure?' His hand came to her chin and gently but firmly he forced her head up so that she looked at him.

'I don't understand the question.'

'Yes, you do.' For his words had nothing to do with the jacket that lay over the chair, and they both knew it. Still, he clarified. 'Sophie, I leave tomorrow morning. Maybe we could have dinner tonight...?'

And that in itself was a concession by his standards, for it was usually dinner and then bed, rather than the other way around.

Yet with his hands holding her chin she shook her head and surprised herself when she did, in fact, turn down dinner with this stunning man. 'I'm working tonight.'

And so he asked her again. 'Are you sure this is what you want?'

Not once in her lifetime had she been so certain. She wanted this man.

Decisions had all too often been made by others on her behalf.

From the friends she kept to the clothes she wore.

On her thirteenth birthday she had said that she would like to go shopping for clothes. There was a skirt she had seen and a top too, and instead she had come home from school to be told there was a surprise for her in the bedroom.

On her bed lay a new dress and sandals.

They were pretty enough, though best suited to a ten-year-old and not what she would have chosen. Even Sophie had not fully understood the disappointment and even anger that had welled inside her as she had thanked her smiling parents.

And she could well remember being told that it was time to leave school as her father had found her a job at the baker's.

And though she had smiled and worked hard and been proud to bring home a wage to help take the pressure from her family, she had always felt as if she were somehow not living her own life.

Being told that it was time to marry had proved to be the final straw for Sophie.

"He's twenty years older than me," she had said when they had told her whom she would marry.

"Then he's steady," her mother had replied. "Reliable."

The man Sophie looked at now was none of those things, yet Bastiano had not only asked if she was sure this was what she wanted, he had paused to have her confirm it.

It was indeed potent to be asked.

For once the choice was hers.

And so she made it. She would have him.

'Very.'

CHAPTER FOUR

IT WAS BASTIANO who closed the shutters and then the drapes and turned on the bedside lights.

The breakfast trolley he pushed out of the bedroom then he closed the door.

She had expected a fierce kiss, and to resume where they had left off, but Bastiano had decided that this should not be rushed.

'Are you nervous?' he asked, walking over to her.

'No,' Sophie said.

Her response was unexpected but, then, so was everything about this morning, Bastiano thought.

'Not at all?' he checked, for he could see the pulse leap in her throat as he stood in front of her and, more slowly this time, started to undo the buttons.

'I get nervous when I call my parents.' She smiled at his serious face and moved her own closer to his. 'And I get nervous when I go to pay for my groceries because I am not sure if I have enough money to cover...'

He smiled and she moved in and stole a kiss from his cheek, a kiss that moved to his ear. 'I don't feel like that now.'

He moved the dress down over her shoulders and watched it fall to the floor. Then he walked behind her and she felt his fingers unclasp her bra. Her knickers she had dispensed with earlier, and this was all that was left before they were naked together. His hands were warm over her arms as he moved the straps down slowly and then removed the flimsy garment.

He made her feel dizzy, her eyes closing as he ran a finger the length of her naked spine.

Now he turned her around and it felt as if every pore pleaded for his touch, for it was like being painted with fire as his eyes roamed her body.

'I feel like I know you,' she told him.

It made no logical sense for they had never so much as met before, yet she was not even close to feeling shy, and when he lifted his eyes to hers he made no promise with his reply.

'No one could.'

He led her to his bed and it was very different from before, for he gave no instructions. There was no point because Sophie would not follow them—that much he already knew.

'Aren't you going to ask me to take down my hair?' Sophie asked as she climbed between the sheets.

'No,' Bastiano said, for now he wanted no curtain between them.

Still she did not get the fierce welcome of his kiss; instead, she sank into a mattress that felt like a cloud and sheets and a pillow that were still a little warm from his body.

He lay on his side, propped up on one arm and looking down at her.

'Nice?' he asked as she closed her eyes in bliss.

'So nice.'

And so was the light touch of his hand on her breast. Less than a tickle and more than a brush, it made her breathe in sharply through her nostrils. His face came over hers and the kisses she had stolen as he had undressed her Bastiano now returned.

Each time his mouth met hers it was like a teasing glimpse of summer: warmth on her skin and the bliss of more to come, then the cool tease of distance.

The light touch of his fingers had her nipples harden like studs and he could read the need that spread through her. Each slip of his tongue coiled her tighter and the heat from his palm on her breast was a gentle torment. As his fingers squeezed her nipple hard she moaned, and was rewarded with a kiss.

So focused was she on the bliss that his lips delivered, she had barely registered the downward movement of his hand until it slipped between her thighs; he adored that they did not tighten but instead parted softly.

She tasted of all that was good, and he of all that was illicit.

His mouth moved down to her neck and the kiss on her tender skin at first was gentle but as skilled lips moved down his kisses deepened.

Sophie's hand pressed into his shoulder, feeling his warm skin as his mouth sought her breast. There he toyed, slowly at first, licking and teasing her nipple with his tongue. The scratch of his jaw was sublime and Sophie found her fingers digging into his shoulder when he sucked deeply.

Bastiano heard her soft moans, and he wanted to hear more of them so his fingers explored and pushed inside her.

She felt as if every nerve in her body was on fire with the source at her centre, as if she might fold over if he did not stop or that she would surely die if he did not go on. His mouth came back to hers and now his kiss was fierce as he teased and stroked her below.

She arched to his palm, her mouth opening wide, her jaw tensing as Sophie lost contact with the earth.

Bastiano wanted to kiss her all over and savour slowly each inch of skin, but feeling her beneath his fingers, slick and pouting, he felt himself driving closer to the point where he would be neither slow nor tender.

He reached for a condom, as he had before, but her words halted him. 'I'm still on the Pill.'

Bastiano would lecture her later, he decided. He knew he was safe, for he always wore protection—he trusted no one.

It was a first for them both, for he had never made love without one.

Not once.

There was slight trepidation in Sophie as his weight came over her, but it was quickly overridden by yearning.

'Nervous?' he checked.

'Never.'

Bastiano was.

The emotion caught him by surprise as he looked down into amber eyes, for she was so willing and wanting and he was so loath to hurt her.

For some reason he could not readily define, there was rare caution in him as he entered her a little way, and though he met resistance there was a warm willingness swallowing him in.

No, Bastiano did not rob Sophie of her innocence; she gladly relinquished it as she embraced the sensation of pain edged with bliss.

He moved up on his elbows and kissed her tense lips, fighting his own need.

Sophie squeezed her eyes closed for each slow movement from Bastiano delivered fresh trauma and her hand moved to his chest. It was a silent plea to take his time, but as he drew back the ache turned to need and her hips rose to him as he filled her again.

'Slowly,' she whispered, and she watched the tension in his features as he did his level best to honour that request.

She could feel him fight to keep the delicious, unhurried paced she demanded. And when the pain had left, when each stroke had her frenzied and thick desire filled her loins, Sophie removed her hands from his chest, ready to meet his fierce need to possess.

Their rhythm was intense, and he looked her right in the eyes. Her hands moved down his back to his taut buttocks as Bastiano dictated the pace.

He took her leg and wrapped it around him, positioning himself carefully with a patience her body could not return.

'Bastiano...' Sophie was suddenly frantic, her head slipping between huge pillows, but Bastiano flicked them away and rescued her head with his hand; he held her taut body, and only as she started to come did he cease his restraint and give her a glimpse.

Just a glimpse of Bastiano unleashed, but it was enough to harness the energy that built within; the ripple of her orgasm deepened and she shuddered as it swept fast through her.

In the throes of her cry, he knelt and thrust in deeper, his muscled arm scooping behind her back and lifting her body. Taking her hard, she was utterly open to him.

Sophie did not know where it ended, but she knew she came again to the final bucks of his desire.

He was looking down at the point of their joining, delivering those last precious drops deep within as she pulsed to him.

And it faded, for it had to.

As he released her, as he withdrew, Sophie knew that Bastiano had given her everything she could have wanted for her first time. He had taken care and brought her pleasure, he had opened her mind to her body, and it was in those dying seconds that she felt robbed.

Not of her virginity—she had been more than willing in that.

But of time.

There was so much more to Bastiano that she now ached to see.

CHAPTER FIVE

SOPHIE AWOKE MIDAFTERNOON, wrapped in Bastiano's arms.

If bliss was a place, then she had found it.

She lay there examining her needs and wants, only to find she was entirely content.

Oh, she needed the loo, but apart from that there was nothing, not a single thing she required. Sophie did not want to get up because she did not want to wake him, and because she did not want reality to impinge just yet.

Today, she decided, was her day and she intended to make it last!

She wriggled out of his arms, picked up her uniform and underwear and headed into the bathroom. It was sumptuous indeed, themed like a Roman bath with stone walls and a deep alabaster soaking tub that took centre stage. The windows were designed so that the guests could lie in splendour and gaze out on Rome with their privacy assured.

Only Sophie wasn't here for that—lazy days spent lying in an alabaster bath were not for the likes of her.

Turning on the tap and with a somewhat mischievous smile she threw her clothes in the sink. Not just to be sure that her uniform would be fresh for tonight but to make certain she would not be leaving any time soon!

Then she looked again at the bath that seemed to beckon and asked herself, Why not?

At her flat there was a small shower, and more often than not a flatmate waiting their turn.

Sophie knew she would never get a chance like this again.

And so, once she had hung her clothes over the towel warmers, rather than clean the bath, as Sophie so often did when she serviced a suite, instead she ran the deepest one and added everything that she possibly could to it—oils, salts, bubbles. All the lovely bottles that she usually replaced each day were now tipped into the steaming, fragrant water and then she climbed in herself.

This, she decided as the warm water engulfed her, was indulgence at its finest. As she lay there feeling utterly pampered, and with a body sated by his touch, Sophie knew that she would never look at this view again and not think of this wonderful day.

And that was how he had made her feel—simply wonderful.

There was no guilt about this morning's events, though perhaps that would come.

Had she done the right thing by her family's standard, her first time would have been a year ago and it would have been something to forget rather than remember. This was how it was supposed to feel, she knew that now.

She lay there and smiled, and closed her eyes to picture Bastiano better.

And that was how he found her when he came in, up to her neck in bubbles and half dozing.

'Why are there clothes hanging everywhere?' he asked. 'It looks as if the gypsies have arrived.'

Sophie opened her eyes and smiled, for he stood there

gorgeous and naked, frowning at her dripping uniform and underwear.

'If you must know, I washed them because you are a gentleman and I know that you would not send me out in wet clothes.'

'I admire your cunning,' Bastiano said. 'However, I am not a gentleman and if I wanted you gone then, wet clothes or not, you would be.'

'Nope.' She did not believe it of him, for in Sophie's eyes he was perfect.

She held out her hand for him to join her, but he hesitated because he generally didn't really care for such tender intimacies. He told himself that it was the fragrant, foaming water that seemed so inviting before climbing in at the opposite end, with his back to the view. Sophie rested her feet on his chest.

Certainly, Bastiano thought, if he did get into the bath with a woman then it was not to lie there half dozing, but that's exactly what he found himself doing.

For a while, at least.

But then her heels pressed into the wall of his chest.

He ignored her.

'What?' he asked, when her heels nudged him again.

'Rub them.'

He was too relaxed to decline, and so he got right into the soles with his thumbs, enjoying her moans of pleasure.

'Your posh English girl does not know what she's missing,' Sophie said.

She assumed him the kindest, most thoughtful person, Bastiano realised, and he chose not to enlighten her.

'Are you sore?' he asked, not meaning her feet.

'A little bit,' Sophie admitted, and then her lips twitched

provocatively as she met his eyes. 'Though not sore enough not to do it all again.'

Yes, Sophie decided, Lydia really did not know what she was missing because Bastiano massaged her calves as if he knew how they ached, and he made her feel as if there was nowhere else he wished to be.

'For skinny legs,' Bastiano said, 'you have a lot of muscle.'

'Because I am on my feet all day, climbing stairs.'

Not today, though.

Sophie accepted that they only had this day, but for the times ahead when she thought about these precious moments and her mind drifted to this intriguing man, there were things she would want to know.

And she was curious enough to ask.

'What happened to your cheek?'

It was rare that he was relaxed enough with anyone to answer.

'I got into a fight.'

'How old were you?'

'Seventeen.'

'Was the fight with your uncle?' she asked, because he had told her it was at that age he had been kicked out.

'No.'

'Seventeen was a busy year for you, then!'

'I guess.'

'Who was the fight with?' Sophie asked, and she ignored the warning in his eyes to leave it because she was too immersed in the sensual feel of his hands, though they stopped working her calves as he answered her.

'A man I hate to this day.'

Sophie looked over at the change to his tone. It did not unnerve her in the least; she just waited for him to go on, yet Bastiano revealed no more.

Always that type of conversation was marked out of bounds, yet he had opened up a touch and he found himself curious about her.

'What were you doing at seventeen?' he asked.

'I told you, I was working at the bakery...' And then she thought back to that time and she let out a small laugh. 'I was in love. Or at least I thought I was.'

'With whom?'

'A man who used to stop in on his way to work.'

'Did he stop by to see you?' Bastiano asked, assuming that to be the obvious case. 'I'd have been stopping by morning and night and again for cake at lunchtime.'

'Ah, but then you'd have become as fat as the baker.'

'I'd have worked it off,' Bastiano said, taking her legs and pulling her closer so that they both sat up and her legs wrapped around him. Together, they made an alternative reality where it *had* been Bastiano who'd stopped by in the mornings, and between teasing kisses she told him how it had been.

'It was nothing like that. He was married! I just had a crush and he very politely ignored it.'

And Bastiano wondered what her reaction would be if he told her his sins. Not that he had any intention of doing so.

She lay back down and closed her eyes, looking utterly at ease, as if she had not a care in the world.

Sophie didn't.

Not a single care.

'Usually I am cleaning this bath,' she sighed. 'Once I had to bring into this very bathroom a bucket of ice and its stand along with a bottle of champagne. That in itself is not uncommon, but on this occasion the couple were sitting in the bath.'

'Well, it wasn't me,' Bastiano said, his response dry.

'Of course not, you are too polite for that.'

He was about to correct her and say he really didn't give a lot of thought to sparing the maids' blushes—more that he tended not to indulge in romantic baths.

Yet here he was.

'What else have you seen?' he asked.

'So much.' Sophie smiled and leant back on the head-rest, closing her eyes as she recounted. 'There are lots of weddings here and I enjoy them the most. There is always something wonderful going on. I don't often deliver the breakfasts, but some mornings I do, and some couples have champagne at seven a.m....' She had questioned it the first time, but now she smiled at the romance of it. 'I've seen so many different sides to life, working here. I've never even tried champagne, let alone first thing in the morning.'

'Would you like me to call for some?' he offered.

'No,' Sophie said with her eyes still closed but then, as she had done when waking in his arms, she examined her wants. There were no needs—they had been more than taken care of—but there *was* a tiny want. 'I thought I wasn't hungry,' she said.

'And are you?'

'Not really,' Sophie admitted, but she was determined to make use of the good life while she had it. 'But I could *just* manage a gelato with a shot of hot espresso...'

He groaned as another of life's simple pleasures now became a necessity and Bastiano reached out for the bath-side phone. He gave his order, telling them they could override the Do Not Disturb sign on this occasion and leave the dish in the entrance to the suite.

Ten minutes later, Sophie lay in the bath with her hand clapped over her mouth, trying not to laugh as Inga wheeled their treats through to the lounge.

Bastiano was in a towelling robe and he didn't even close the doors so his conversation with Inga drifted through from the lounge and Sophie could hear every word that was said.

'Is there anything else I can do for you, Signor Conti?' Inga asked, and Sophie knew that she was not speaking out of turn because the suite looked as if they had visiting rock stars *in situ* and was in serious need of a full service.

'That is all,' Bastiano responded.

He came back into the bathroom and Sophie screwed up her nose. 'I cannot stand her,' she admitted.

'Why?'

'Just…' Sophie shrugged, suddenly a little awkward, for after all, wasn't she doing the same as Inga?

No, she decided, for this had nothing to do with money or designer bags. Instead, it was a promise that she had made to herself long ago—that her first time would be because she wanted it and was ready for it— and that promise to herself had been fulfilled. Still, Inga and thoughts of home were soon forgotten when she re- alised that he had come into the bathroom empty handed. 'Where's my gelato?'

He didn't answer. Instead, Bastiano came over and lifted her out of the bath, carrying her dripping wet back to the bed. She laughed and protested and he found him- self smiling as he dropped her onto the bed.

'Here.' He propped her up on the pillows and poured a shot of hot coffee over the gelato and then handed her the dish. Sophie had a taste and gave a purr of pleasure. It was deliciously cold after the warm bath and the fla- vour, both sweet and bitter, was perfection.

She looked over as Bastiano took off his robe and then picked up his own dish but he did not add the espresso.

'Where's your coffee?' she asked.

'I don't think you'd like it,' Bastiano said, and then took a large scoop of ice cream and held it in his mouth, so that his tongue and lips were almost blue with cold.

'What are you doing?' Sophie asked as he knelt on the bed and parted her legs.

'Kissing it better.'

Yes, she had found bliss.

It was a day in bed spent hidden from the world.

A day spent making love, dozing, laughing and talking, and Sophie never wanted it to end, though of course she knew that it must.

Wrapped in his arms, Sophie woke and did not want to look at the bedside clock.

The drapes and shutters were heavy enough to block out every chink of light, but there was a certain stillness to the air and she knew that it was night.

Sure enough, when she lifted her head from Bastiano's chest and read the time, she saw that in less than an hour her shift would commence.

And they would end.

She slid out of his arms and went back to the gorgeous bathroom. This time she had a shower and then did up her hair and dressed in her dry clothes.

She walked back into the master bedroom and there lay Bastiano, asleep.

No, she would never regret it.

She had heard her friends speak of their first time and some of them had sounded dismal, some had been described as good at best.

This had been perfection. He had taken such care of her, both in and out of bed.

For the first time in her life she had been spoiled and

adored but she knew that the world they had built this day had not been one designed to last.

Sophie ached to wake him, but she did not know how to say goodbye without tears and that certainly wasn't a part of the deal they had made.

And so, instead of waking him, instead of fumbling through a goodbye that she did not want, Sophie went to the bureau in the lounge, took out a piece of paper and wrote him a little note.

Mai ti dimentichero' mai.

I will never forget you.

And if it was too sentimental for Bastiano, she didn't care, for she never would forget, Sophie thought as she quietly let herself out of the suite. Though sad to leave, as she headed to the elevator and awaited its arrival, there was the complete absence of guilt.

Her mother, if she knew, would never forgive her and that was no idle thought—it was fact. And neither would Benita, the head of housekeeping, if she were ever to find out.

Yes, to others it might seem wrong, but to Sophie everything felt right with the world and she hugged the memory of them close to her chest.

It had been the best day of her life without a doubt, and if it were possible to float in an elevator, then that was just what Sophie would have done as she made her way down to the foyer.

She actually didn't start work for another ten minutes but knew that her friend Gabi was working on the plans for a wedding being held tomorrow.

No, she wouldn't tell even Gabi about what had happened—some things were too precious to share. But she couldn't find her friend; Sophie put her head around the ballroom doors and saw that she wasn't there.

In fact, there was no sign of her.

It felt as if Gabi might be avoiding her because usually they caught up all the time, but for the past couple of months Gabi had always been too busy or tired.

Sophie headed through the foyer and to Reception, where Anya was on duty.

'Have you seen Gabi?' she asked.

'Gabi!' Anya said, and gave a dramatic eye-roll. 'I have more than seen her! I had to call an ambulance earlier on. She went into labour.'

'What do you mean?' Sophie asked, unable to take in what she was being told. 'Gabi's not pregnant…' But even as Sophie said it, Gabi's avoidance of her in the last few months and the new distance between them was starting to make sense.

'She's more than six months gone,' Anya said. 'I had no idea either until her waters broke. I think the baby will come tonight.'

'Is there anyone with her?' Sophie asked, while knowing that there was nothing she could really do.

'I think she was going to call her mother once she got to the hospital.'

It was a rather distracted Sophie that went in for the evening briefing. Here she would be told where she would be working tonight, though it didn't really matter to Sophie. She just wanted to know what was going on with her friend.

'Are you listening, Sophie?' Benita checked.

'Of course,' Sophie said, and forced herself to at least look as if she was paying attention.

'Could you help with the set-up of the ballroom for the wedding tomorrow? Things have fallen rather behind.'

Sophie nodded and wrote the instructions down in

her notebook as Benita spoke on to the rest of the gathered staff.

'Sultan Alim has had to fly home unexpectedly,' Benita continued, 'which makes things a little easier on this busy night. Laura, you and I shall service his floor when there is a moment to breathe. Now, in Presidential Suite B we have Signor Conti…'

Sophie felt her heart soar and her cheeks warm at the sound of his name.

'He's an important guest at the Grande Lucia,' Benita carried on. 'Today he has declined to have the suite serviced. However, should he change his mind, Inga and Laura, could you see to it promptly, please?' Benita's voice was sharp and sometimes Sophie was rather sure that Benita knew what Inga got up to. 'Please remember that Signor Conti is a serious contender to purchase this hotel. He may well be your boss in the future, so please be on your best behaviour. Remember that he is here to observe the staff and glean as much information as he can about the running of the hotel.'

Sophie felt as if the floor had shifted beneath her. The handover continued but Sophie heard not a word. She wanted to call out, to ask Benita to explain further about Bastiano. Still drenched in horror, she could not quite take in what had just been said, but Benita was wrapping things up and gave her team a smile. 'Let's get to work, then.'

It was a shaken and tearful Sophie who did her best to work through the night.

Gabi's boss, Bernadetta, had been called in to accomplish overnight all the work to be done. She was a poisonous woman at the best of times, and on this night she worked the fragile Sophie hard.

The ribbons she had her tie over and over, the chairs

she had her lug and move, and she screeched at Sophie
to concentrate as for the umpteenth time she had to lay
the place cards according to the table plan.

Finally, *finally*, around two in the morning, Benita
popped her head in the ballroom and told Sophie it was
time for her break.

'Is everything okay?' Ronaldo, the doorman, asked
as Sophie stepped outside the kitchens for a breath of
air. Ronaldo was also on his break and having a ciga-
rette.

'I'll be glad when it is morning,' Sophie admitted. 'It
is awful working with Bernadetta and there is all this
talk of the hotel being taken over.'

'I know! Let's hope it's Di Savo,' Ronaldo said. 'He
has a hotel here in Rome.'

'What about the other one?' Sophie fished.

'Conti?' Ronaldo said, and raised his eyebrows. 'He's
a risk taker, a loose cannon.'

'In what way?'

'In every way. He and Di Savo are sworn enemies.
Security was told to be on high alert, what with the two
of them staying here at the same time.'

'Really?'

Ronaldo nodded. 'Especially because last night Di
Savo was entertaining Conti's guest.' He gave a knowing eye raise. 'We just have to hope that Di Savo wins
the bid as well as the girl. Bastiano Conti's a cold-hearted
bastard—that much I know.'

'How do you know?'

'I'm the doorman,' Ronaldo said. 'He often stays here
as he and the sultan are friends. Believe me when I say
I see all that goes on. I wouldn't let my sister within a
mile radius of him.'

'They're friends?' Sophie checked, recalling Bastiano's skilled questioning—he had acted as if he was surprised that Alim was a sultan.

'Good friends.' Ronaldo nodded. 'Though I thought the sultan had better taste.'

It was bad enough that she had slept with the potential new boss, but it was utterly humiliating the way she had been taken in by him. Bastiano had had her opening up and speaking to him as if they were lovers.

That was what she had thought they were.

What had taken place had for Sophie been so wonderful, but now it was tainted.

She had thought he'd been asking all those questions to find out about her, but instead he had been playing her all along.

Thank goodness she hadn't told him that she thought Inga was up to tricks. Sophie did not like her, but neither did she want to get her into trouble—it was a dismissible offence.

And one that she herself had committed.

Oh, whatever way she looked at it, she was in trouble.

Her job was the biggest and proudest achievement of her life. Sophie loved coming to work each day, she loved her colleagues and the friends she had made.

And at any moment now it might all be taken away.

By morning, the ballroom was somehow ready for the upcoming wedding but Sophie was no less frantic. When Benita asked if someone could go and help out with the breakfast service, Sophie did not put up her hand.

She simply did not know how to face him.

Bastiano was more than ready to face Sophie, though.

He had woken at around midnight having had the best sleep he had known in a very long time.

It had taken a moment to register that she had gone. Bastiano had even gone to the bathroom, half hoping to find her lying up to her neck in bubbles as he had earlier in the day.

Recalling what Sophie had said about liking order, he had called the butler and asked that he send someone to service the room.

To his disappointment it was Inga, the woman who had brought the *gelato*, who'd arrived, along with another chambermaid.

'You were working this afternoon,' Bastiano commented.

'They asked me to do a split shift.' Inga smiled.

He placed his breakfast order.

Shakshuka for Sophie and Sicilian pastries for him, only this time he asked for summer berries and a bottle of champagne to be served with the juice.

Finally morning arrived and there was a knock at the door; he heard the trolley being wheeled in and then another soft knock on his bedroom door.

'Entra,' Bastiano said.

He had been in the industry long enough to know Sophie would have no say where she was assigned, yet as he sat up to a soft *'Buongiorno...'* he lay back down when he realised that it was not Sophie.

The curtains were opened and the shutters too, but Bastiano deliberately closed his eyes.

'Can I serve you breakfast?' Inga asked, when protocol dictated she should leave rather than speak.

'No.'

'Is there anything else I can do for you, Signor Conti?'

He opened his eyes and though imperceptible to many, Bastiano knew the ropes well and could both hear and see the veiled offer; yes, Inga would love to be in bed with the boss.

'You can leave.' His voice was curt and with a flick of his wrist he dismissed her.

Inga left and the minutes dragged by ever more slowly as Sophie failed to appear.

It edged close to seven and still Sophie did not arrive. Bastiano knew only too well how bad it would look if he were to call down to the front desk and ask after her.

There was nothing he could do except wait.

And, when the morning was already misbehaving, Bastiano got up and poured his own coffee, but by then it was far too cool. He flicked open the newspaper and suddenly his day got a whole lot worse.

There was an image of Raul Di Savo, his nemesis, sitting in a café, one Bastiano recognised as being opposite the hotel. And he was holding hands with Lydia Hayward.

So she hadn't been catching up with friends after all.

Bastiano and Raul both had colourful reputations and both knew how the other worked.

Raul must have found out that Lydia was a guest of his, Bastiano surmised. Hostilities had just increased tenfold, and he screwed up the paper and tossed it to the floor.

His phone rang. It was Maurice, spluttering his apologies that Lydia remained unavailable and asking when they might meet to speak about the castle.

But Bastiano had no interest in Maurice's draughty old building now.

'We shan't be meeting, Maurice. And when you see your stepdaughter, tell her that the reason for Raul Di Savo's interest in her is simply to get back at me. There is no more to it than that.'

He was in no doubt that Maurice would indeed pass

the message on and, he hoped, at the very least, that it would cause Raul and Lydia to have a major row.

Next he called down to the front desk and asked that his bags be packed and his transport arranged.

Forget Rome! Forget fragrant baths and spiced Sicilian pastries! And most of all, forget Sophie!

Bastiano was back to being a bastard.

CHAPTER SIX

SOPHIE HAD SIMPLY not known how to face Bastiano.

It wasn't just that she was frightened for her job, Sophie felt angry and humiliated—sure that he had been silently laughing at her all along.

And so, after the longest night at work, instead of heading to his suite she headed for home. Once there, she called the hospital to find out what she could about Gabi but they gave out little information.

'Can I visit?' she asked. After learning the hours when she could see Gabi, she decided that she would go in the evening, before the start of her next shift.

She felt sick at the thought of walking into work and positive that she was going to be in deep trouble.

Perhaps he wouldn't buy the hotel, Sophie thought as she tried to sleep. Though there was little solace that that would contain things, for she now knew that Bastiano was a personal friend of Sultan Alim.

And as nice as Alim was, he had a fierce reputation with women too.

Sophie lay there with visions of Bastiano thanking Alim for the *nice surprise* sent to his suite.

And yet for all her worries there remained the absence of regret.

Today, Sophie knew, could so easily have been her first wedding anniversary.

And so that evening, as she walked onto the maternity ward to visit her friend, she knew full well that it could easily have been her sitting pale in the bed, having just given birth, with Luigi by her side.

No.

She might have to suffer the consequences work-wise, but her first time would always be as she had wanted it to be.

Even if she lost her job.

'Sophie…' Gabi started to cry as soon as Sophie walked in.

She had bought her a bunch of flowers and a little lemon-coloured bear for the baby, who was nowhere in sight.

'It's okay,' Sophie said, taking her friend in her arms and not really knowing what to say. 'Is the baby okay? The nurses wouldn't tell me anything.'

'I had a little girl,' Gabi said. 'Lucia.'

'And how is she doing?'

'She's in the nursery. She's very early but they say that for her size she is doing really well.'

'I bought this for her.'

Sophie handed over the little bear and Gabi smiled when she saw her baby's first toy.

'I can't believe she's here,' Gabi said.

'Believe me…' Sophie's eyes widened '…neither can anyone! All the staff are in shock. Why on earth didn't you tell me that you were pregnant?'

'It seemed wrong to be telling everyone when I haven't even told her father…' Gabi admitted.

Sophie waited, but Gabi shook her head; clearly she still wasn't ready to reveal who the father was.

It didn't stop Sophie from trying to work it out, though!

'Ronaldo?' Sophie asked, because she often saw them chatting.

'Oh, please,' Gabi said, and then through her tears she started to laugh. 'Ronaldo?'

'Well, he is good looking.' Sophie shrugged. 'And you two are friendly.'

'I talk to Ronaldo because he knows all the gossip,' Gabi said.

Not *all* the gossip, Sophie hoped.

She stayed for a little while and promised to come in and visit again, but all too soon she was heading to work, terrified of what awaited her yet conflicted, for she knew she secretly hoped to see Bastiano again.

Benita gave her a smile when a blushing Sophie joined the group for the briefing.

'The wedding is in full swing,' Benita said, and took them through the plans for the night ahead. 'Signor Conti checked out early this morning.'

Nobody heard as Sophie's heart dropped.

She stood, staring at her pencil poised over her notepad, and there were tears in her eyes as Benita spoke on.

'The staff have been busy all day and have not been able to service the presidential suite. Sophie, could you make a start, please, and I'll come and help you as soon as I can, then you can go and help with the clear up once the wedding guests have left.'

The workload was so heavy that Benita suggested she didn't stay for the rest of handover and so, with a heavy heart, Sophie made her way up in the elevator, the same one in which she had once floated back down to earth.

Each presidential suite had its own butler's pantry and its own cleaning supply room so there was no trolley to collect. She let herself in and saw that it was a lot neater than when she had left it.

Sophie walked through the vacant lounge to the master bedroom. On a silver trolley stood an untouched breakfast. She lifted the domes and saw the pastries and *shakshuka*, but there were summer berries too. What brought tears to her eyes, though, was that there was an unopened bottle of champagne standing in a bucket of water, and she knew he had ordered it for her.

It was the most romantic thing that had ever happened to her.

Or, rather, that had never happened.

Maybe she had been too hasty, Sophie thought.

There was the expensive scent of him in the air and the memory of them in her mind.

Sophie was quite sure she was going to be fired anyway and so, just for a moment, she lay on the bed where he had slept and tried to tell her heart to slow down.

Please, let her job be safe!

Which meant she had better get on and do it, for Benita might well be here soon and so she peeled herself from the bed.

First she wheeled out the breakfast trolley and did a little pick up of rubbish. There was a screwed-up newspaper on the floor and when she smoothed it out there was a photo of Raul Di Savo and a pale blonde beauty, sitting together in the café opposite the hotel.

It was Lydia, Sophie was sure.

This must have been the reason that Bastiano had checked out early.

His rapid departure had nothing to do with her—Sophie knew she didn't wasn't so much as a pawn in his games.

She had been nothing more than a diversion—that was all.

Sophie scrubbed the bath where they had lain smiling and chatting; it hurt to recall him joining her and then carrying her through to the bed that she now stripped back and remade.

To service a presidential suite to standard took ages. Benita had said that she would come and help but, of course, she was too busy and so it was Sophie who had to make sure that it was done to perfection.

And it hurt.

It was some considerable time later that Benita arrived with her check list and together they went through the suite.

Ornaments, decanters, glasses, furniture, all had to be gleaming. Every feature down to the last detail was checked and ticked off.

Two pairs of eyes were needed as generally, though inadvertently, something was missed.

Not on this night.

She had erased every last detail of them.

'All ready for the next guest.' Benita smiled. 'Very well done, Sophie—Signor Conti always leaves a storm behind him.'

'Really?' Sophie couldn't help but fish for details.

'He likes the women and knows how to party.' Benita gave a tight smile. 'You have done an excellent job,' she said as she flicked off the lights. 'You would never know that anyone had been here.'

Now Sophie just had to tell her heart the same.

CHAPTER SEVEN

REALLY, HER BIRTHDAY was just another day.

Sophie got up late and had coffee with her flatmate, Teresa, who then headed off to her waitressing job.

It had been Teresa's birthday last month and Sophie had stopped on the way home from work and bought a cake.

It shouldn't hurt that Teresa made no mention of the date.

She made too much of things, Sophie told herself. She pulled on a top and skirt and left a little earlier than usual for her twilight shift at the Grande Lucia.

She unlocked the mailbox in the foyer of her building and there was a small wad of mail; Sophie found that she was holding her breath as she flicked through it.

Nothing.

There had been no phone call this morning from her parents and now not even a card.

Her oldest brother had called the other week and told her that Luigi still came for dinner each week, only now he hit the wine.

'Do you think that makes me want to come home and marry him?' Sophie had said and ended the call.

They didn't get it.

Bastiano had.

Even after all these months just the thought of him could stop Sophie in the street.

Just the memory of that day was enough to make her smile—a little gift she could open and treasure on a day when she felt forgotten and small.

There was still a little while before her shift commenced and Sophie decided that she would drop in on Gabi and see how she and little Lucia were doing. It had been a while since they had caught up. Gabi had only been back at work for a couple of weeks and had already been on an international trip to help organise Sultan Alim's upcoming wedding while her mother cared for Lucia.

It all sounded terribly glamorous to Sophie.

'Sophie!' Gabi gave her a tired smile as she opened the door. 'It's good to see you!'

Little Lucia was crying and Sophie was more than happy to hold her as Gabi made them a quick lunch. 'What time is your shift?' Gabi asked.

'I start at two,' Sophie said. 'How was your trip overseas?'

'It was…' Gabi gave a tight shrug. 'It was hard leaving Lucia.'

'But what was it like?' Sophie asked. She had never been out of Italy, let alone flown to the Middle East! But then she remembered that Gabi had had a bit of a crush on Alim and guessed her questions might be insensitive. 'How was Alim?'

'I didn't really see him.'

'So you don't know who's buying the hotel?'

Gabi shook her head.

'Everyone is worried for their jobs,' Sophie sighed.

'It should be okay,' Gabi tried to reassure her. 'Raul

Di Savo has many hotels, one of them is here in Rome. I am sure there wouldn't be too many changes.'

'What about if the other one gets it?'

'God help us all then,' Gabi sighed. 'Conti takes over old buildings, guts them and then modernises them…' She pulled a face. 'Sultan Alim has spent the past two years restoring the hotel. Conti will ruin all that…'

'He might not,' Sophie countered, though she recalled him talking about Lydia and the castle that she lived in and how much work it would have been.

Was it all just business for him?

'Apparently, he turns all his acquisitions into upmarket rehab facilities,' Gabi said. 'I can't imagine there would be many weddings being held at the Grande Lucia if that is the case.' Then she gave a tight shrug. 'Not that it will matter much to me. I am not sure I can hold on to this job.' Gabi explained things a little better. 'My mother wants me to get a job with more regular hours.'

'Is she still cross about the baby?'

Gabi nodded. 'She has started to come around—at least we're finally speaking. In truth, I wouldn't be able to work without her support.'

'What about Lucia's father?' Sophie asked.

'I'm not ready to talk about him,' Gabi admitted.

'Fair enough,' Sophie said, and glanced at the time. 'I'd better go. I'll come and see you both soon.'

'Make sure that you do.'

And so her birthday went unnoticed again, and of course Sophie didn't blame her friend. Gabi had enough on her mind as it was.

Sophie walked the back streets, down the alley and entered the hotel via the side entrance, then walked through the kitchen and to the locker area.

There was a pile of clean uniforms with her name

on that were freshly starched and uncomfortably tight and scratchy when she put one on; quickly, she re-did her hair.

The hotel was very full, they were told at the briefing.

There was a high turnover of rooms to make up and no time to waste if they were to get everything done.

Benita gave out assignments for the day. 'Sophie, you are on the twelfth floor, odd numbers.'

Sophie nodded. The twelfth floor housed the cheaper rooms, all without any landmark views and were just plain hard work.

'Oh, and, Sophie,' Benita added, and Sophie waited to be told that when she had finished she was to go and help out Inga, who always seemed to be running behind, but instead there was some surprising news. 'You have a delivery to pick up at Reception.'

'A delivery?'

'Yes. Is it your birthday or something?'

Sophie nodded and her heart started to beat fast, wondering if maybe, just maybe, her parents had sent her something here.

She was almost bouncing on the spot for the briefing to finish and when it did, instead of heading straight up to the twelfth floor, she went straight to the reception desk.

'There is a delivery for me?' Sophie said to Anya.

'Indeed there is,' Anya said. 'Lucky girl.'

Even as she came out of the cloakroom, Sophie knew that the flowers Anya held were not from her parents, for this was not the type of gift they would ever give.

It wasn't a big bouquet; in fact, it was a small posy that Anya handed to her, wrapped in cream tissue paper and exuding understated elegance.

The flowers really were exquisite.

Perhaps a hundred miniature roses in the softest

creams, all edged in the palest green. Each one looked as if it had been individually painted with the most skilled brush, and the scent when she drew the bouquet close to her face was like inhaling summer.

'It's stunning,' Anya sighed. 'All the staff have been coming in and out for a peek.'

And as if to prove her point, Inga came over.

'They're nice,' she said.

'I think Sophie has an admirer,' Anya teased. 'Come on, open the card.'

'Who are they from?' Inga asked, but when Sophie opened the card it was blank.

'I don't know,' she lied.

Or was it the truth?

For the Bastiano Conti everyone spoke of did not send flowers and was guaranteed to forget.

Had he remembered?

Or was this an elaborate gift from Gabi?

Even an expensive gift from a stressed, broke, new mum made rather more sense than it coming from Bastiano, yet her heart knew they were from him, and each bloom felt like a tiny kiss to her soul.

'They need to go in water,' Anya told her. 'I can do that for you and you can collect them when you go home.'

'Thank you,' Sophie said, but she was reluctant to let them go and so she selected one and coiled it into her messy bun.

Oh, the twelfth floor had never seen such a smiling maid, for even if the roses weren't from Bastiano, it was simply nice to know that someone had remembered.

And yet the flutter in her heart told her that that someone was him.

'Benita's looking for you,' Laura told her. 'She wants to see you now in the staffroom.'

There was still that slight edge of dread, Sophie thought as she took the elevator down. Still that fear that she was about to be found out.

But it had been months ago, she consoled herself.

Three months, in fact.

And, Sophie knew, Bastiano had stayed a couple of times at the Grande Lucia since then, though never when she had been working. Sadly, she wasn't privy to the guest list and tended to find out about these things after the event.

But surely, Sophie thought, if word was going to get out then it would have happened by now.

Her palms were just a little slippery as she opened the door to the staffroom.

'Buon Compleanno!'

'Happy birthday' was being called out to her and there was even a cake with candles and jugs of soft drink.

'Your favourite chef made this for you,' Benita told her. 'He says next year a little more notice would be nice. You should have told us!'

The chef had made her *torta setteveli*, or seven veils cake. Layers of chocolate mousse, hazelnut, praline, cream and sponge, all topped with a chocolate glaze.

It was the last thing that Sophie had expected. To have her colleagues gather and wish her a happy birthday meant everything and she thanked her lucky stars for the day she had been given a job at the Grande Lucia.

The cake tasted like chocolate silk and was a mouthwatering slice of home.

'Actually,' Sophie admitted, 'this tastes better than any I have ever had.'

'Well, don't have too much,' Benita teased, and gave a little pinch to her waist as Sophie went for a second slice. 'Or you will be asking for new uniforms.'

Sophie laughed; the cake was decadent and rich indeed but that would not stop her from having a second slice. Soon, the staff who had gathered drifted back to their responsibilities and the remains were left in the fridge for Sophie to take back to her flat.

She sailed through the rest of her shift. The flowers and cake had lifted her, yet home would have to wait for as her shift neared its end she was offered an hour of overtime.

'Sophie,' Benita called her, 'we have an important guest arriving. Are you able to stay back?'

'Of course.'

Overtime was always welcome, and it was also nice to be asked.

They raced up to the presidential suite—though cleaned, it had not had the finishing touches for an important guest.

It was always hard to be up here, but Sophie did her best not to show it, to carry on as if it was just another room that she was preparing, rather than the site of her magical day with Bastiano.

'Why don't these stars give a little more notice?' Sophie asked as the champagne and flowers were brought in and she and Benita turned back the vast bed.

'Because they don't have to; they know we will always jump to their tune,' Benita said as she turned down the silk sheets. 'Anyway,' she added, 'it's not some famous rock star coming to the Grande Lucia tonight, it is Signor Conti, the soon-to-be...' She paused, because the news had not yet been confirmed.

And Sophie just scrunched the sheet in her hand as, unwittingly, Benita let her know that not only was Bastiano due to arrive tonight but that soon he would be taking over the hotel.

'I should not have said that,' Benita admitted.

'It's fine,' Sophie answered. 'It shan't go any further.'

'Make sure it doesn't. The contracts have not yet been signed and Alim wants to leave any formal announcement until they are.' Benita let out a long sigh, but now that Sophie knew, Benita admitted to a little of what was on her mind. 'Really, I wish it had been the other. Conti is bad news.'

'Bad news?' Sophie said, and while she usually acquiesced to Benita, suddenly she saw red. She was sick of hearing everyone bad-mouth Bastiano.

'I doubt he got to be a billionaire by accident,' Sophie said tartly to her senior. 'I think the Grande Lucia would be very lucky to have someone as astute as Signor Conti as its new owner.'

Benita raised an eyebrow as Sophie sprang to his defence but decided against saying anything further about her potential new boss!

'The room looks perfect,' Sophie said, blushing a little at having spoken her mind to her senior.

She put a slip of paper by the bed, informing him about the weather tomorrow—she wanted to add a heart.

Benita went to close the shutters and drapes so that all the esteemed guest had to do was peel off his clothes and drop into the sumptuous bed.

It seemed a shame to block out the view but that was how things were done during turndown.

The lights were dimmed and the room ticked off on the service sheet, and then Benita did one more sweep of the drawing room and lounge before exiting to the corridor.

And Sophie stood there, her heart hammering, uncertain what she should do.

Oh, she wanted so badly to speak to him—she simply had to find out if she was about to be in trouble, but more than that she needed to see him again.

And then Sophie knew how to let Bastiano know that she was thinking of him.

She walked over to the drapes and opened them, pushing back the shutters, and remembered that moment when her heart had found him.

It truly felt as if it had.

Not the man everyone spoke of so ominously, more the man who had smiled and made her melt.

She looked out on Rome at night and recalled turning to his smile.

'What were you doing?' Benita asked when Sophie joined Benita in the corridor.

'I was just checking that I had written the weather down for tomorrow. Everything is looking perfect.'

'Then you can go home now, Sophie. When are you back on?'

'In the morning, at six.'

'Well, go and get some sleep.'

Sophie walked slowly down the corridor and, instead of taking the elevator to the basement, she went to the foyer, hoping for what, she did not know.

A glimpse of Bastiano perhaps?

But he had not arrived.

Benita had already told her that she would be on house duties tomorrow and working in the foyer. Certainly she would not be up in the presidential suites.

Sophie knew she had to speak with him.

But how?

Her voice might be recognised, or perhaps he would not take the call.

As Sophie reached Reception she thought about hanging around to wait for his arrival.

'Sophie?' Inga stopped as she walked past. 'What are you hanging around for?'

'I had some overtime,' Sophie said, 'but I think I dropped my notebook…'

And in that moment she made up her mind and turned for the elevators.

It was wrong; she could well be fired for what she was about to do, and Sophie's heart was hammering as she pressed the buttons that would take her to the floor from which she had just come.

She had to use her staff pass as the presidential suites had limited access.

He might bring a woman back with him, or a friend, Sophie suddenly thought in panic. The butler would be there, and also there would be the bellboys delivering his luggage. There were a million things that could go wrong, but she simply had to speak to him, to thank him for the beautiful roses.

If Bastiano was to be the new owner, then she was probably about to lose her job anyway, so she let herself into the suite.

The lights were dimmed and there was soft music playing to welcome him.

She touched nothing.

Sophie sat on a chair by a writing bureau and waited as the moments ticked by, but then finally there were voices.

Voices!

She stood from the chair and went into a small alcove where the staff would be unlikely to venture.

Sophie stood in the dark, her heart hammering, realising the foolishness of her actions and anticipating his anger…yet there was also excitement curling in her stomach for finally she would see him again.

'I have no luggage…' She heard his deep voice tell the butler that there was nothing to unpack, and then a terse, 'I can pour my own drink!'

Bastiano simply wanted the man gone.

The butler closed the door and finally there was silence.

What the hell was he doing here?

What was he doing, putting in an offer for a hotel he didn't even want, just to score a point over Raul?

Raul didn't want it either.

He had paid Bastiano a visit the other day. At first Bastiano had assumed he had come to argue over the hotel.

Instead Raul had asked for Lydia's address.

Bastiano's price?

The return of his mother's ring.

This morning, just as he had finished speaking with the florist to arrange Sophie's birthday surprise, a packaged had arrived.

Bastiano hadn't yet opened it.

Now, all these years on, he gazed at the ring, remembering Maria trying it on and holding it up to the light.

Yet memory was not kind.

Now that he held the ring in his hand, long-buried memories were starting to come back.

'Give me back the ring, Maria.'

He could hear his younger voice attempting to hold on to his temper as she had claimed his mother's ring as her own.

A couple of hours later, still wearing it, she had died.

He placed it on the gleaming table, for holding it kicked up black dusty memories that were best left undisturbed.

Bastiano stood and poured a cognac. Looking around the suite, he remembered the last time he had been here, reading the paper, finding out about Raul and Lydia, but then he remembered the hours before that, the bliss of a day away from the world, and so clear were the memories that for a moment he was sure he could recall the scent of Sophie.

He could.

Bastiano opened his eyes and wondered if it was Sophie who had prepared the room; as he filled out the breakfast order, he wondered if she might be the one to serve it.

He hoped so.

And then he heard a movement.

Her intention had been to call out, to step out, but now she stood in the dark, terrified by the predicament that she had placed herself in.

'Sophie?'

She heard her name, he knew she was here and she knew she had to reveal herself.

'I didn't know how else to see you…' she started as she stepped from the shadows and walked towards him.

Her presence was enough for Bastiano to know that this was the real reason he was here in Rome. Sophie was the reason the contracts were unsigned, and that he'd had his lawyers stringing things along, for while he did, there was a chance to see her again.

'If you had wanted to see me then you should have come back that morning,' Bastiano said.

'I was scared I was about to lose my job!' She could hear that her voice was raised. There was fear mixed in with desire for, yes, the months that had passed had dimmed her recall of his absolute power. 'You never told me you were thinking of buying the place. Why did you lie?'

'I never lied.'

'You did.' Sophie raised an accusing finger. 'I would have never told you the things that I did—'

'And I knew that,' Bastiano hotly responded. 'I wanted to keep us the same.'

'We're not the same.' She came right up to his face, and all the hurt and anger she had held in these months flooded out. 'You're the rich man and I'm the maid, how could we ever be the same…?'

'You know that we are.' He too was nearly shouting. 'In here we are.'

Weeks and months of denial and anger met now and she loathed his absolute beauty, that, even now, had absolute power over her. And in turn he loathed the chink in his armour that bore her name, because he could not forget and he could not move on.

He kissed her hard and she fought with herself not to kiss him back.

'What happens when you own it?' she asked. 'My job is everything to me…'

'I'm not buying the hotel.' He stole more kisses and when she pulled back her mouth he simply found it again.

'So why are you here?'

For this.

He didn't say it, but now his mouth did.

Today had been hell and he craved oblivion. Their teeth clashed as their mouths met once again, and his tongue tethered her fury as she returned his fierce kiss.

Bastiano went for her uniform and she heard the rip of the buttons and she was kissing him back and crying as she tasted him again.

'Now we are the same,' he told her as very deliberately he removed her uniform, pushing it down her arms and then past her hips so it fell to the floor.

'No.'

For he was still the rich man in his expensive suit and she stood in drab underwear, but soon he was removing that too.

He turned her and kissed her so that her back was to the wall and his suited body pressed against her naked flesh.

Sophie closed her eyes and drank in his scent, recalling her silent desire to know this man less restrained. And now she knew, for the sound of his zipper and his ragged breath in her ear turned rage to desire, and it was she who held his head now, kissing him back hard as he wrapped her leg around his waist.

'Never let me down,' she begged, and her words were nonsensical for even as he drove into her, even as he consumed her, Sophie knew she was opening herself to hurt, and that tomorrow the countdown would resume and abstinence must surely start over again.

He placed one hand on the wall behind her while the other dug into the cheek of her buttock. He was as coarse in delivery as her violent need required. She did not understand how the woman who had trembled and hidden only a matter of moments ago now coiled naked around him.

Now they were the same.

Matched in desire and lost in lust.

'I thought of you…' he told her, and whether or not she believed him those words tipped her.

He felt the shift and lifted her other leg, so she was wrapped firmly around his hips and their kisses were intense as he spilled deep inside.

'You're going to get me fired,' Sophie whispered as their bodies began to relax and now, slowly, he let her down.

'Never,' Bastiano said. 'Are you supposed to be working now?'

'Not until morning.'

'Good,' he told her. 'Then we have all night.'

CHAPTER EIGHT

'YOU PREPARED MY SUITE,' Bastiano said as they stepped into the master bedroom and he saw the gorgeous night view of Rome.

'I did.'

Sophie did not feel disadvantaged at being the one who was undressed, for indeed she got to slip straight into bed and to lie watching as Bastiano got undressed.

'I wanted you to remember me when you came in.'

'I don't need a view to remember you.' It was undoubtedly the most romantic thing he had ever said but she appeared not to notice its significance. In fact, Sophie thought she was being fed a line and lay there sulking as he went and had a quick shower.

'You got my flowers.' He could see the tiny rose that was now knotted in her hair but as beautiful as her flowers had been, Sophie was not going to let him off that easily.

'Three months late.'

'You were the one who didn't come back,' Bastiano pointed out, taking his time to dry himself.

'And you were the one who failed to tell me you were thinking of buying the place. Can you imagine how it felt to find out?'

'I meant to tell you before you left for work,' he admitted.

'I was scared for my job and I kept thinking of all the things I'd told you.'

'Sophie, I was hardly sitting taking notes.' He got into bed and the soapy clean scent of him was divine. 'I wasn't even thinking about the hotel, I was just…' And it was he who was quiet then because now he allowed himself to look back properly at that perfect day.

'I thought you were staying for another night,' she said. 'You were booked in until the Monday.'

'I left angry,' he admitted. 'I found out…' Bastiano shook his head, not wanting to bring up the feud with Raul.

He was tired of it.

But Sophie had long since guessed the reason he had walked.

'You found out about Raul and Lydia?'

He looked over and gave her a slow smile. 'Nothing gets past you.'

'With the right education, I'd have ruled the world.' Sophie smiled and then told him how she knew. 'I saw their picture in a screwed-up newspaper, I guessed you had seen it.'

'I had.'

They lay together and he pulled her close so that she lay in the crook of his arm, and it was such a nice place to be.

'He came to see me the other day. We hadn't spoken for fifteen years. I thought it was to argue over the hotel but he wanted to find out where Lydia lived.'

'Did you tell him?'

'For a price,' Bastiano said, and thought of the ring.

'Why do you two hate each other so?'

'We always have,' Bastiano told her. 'Our families have always been rivals.'

It was the easy version of the story.

It was too complex a conversation for ships that passed in the night, yet they lay there and stared out at the view, Sophie nestled in the crook of his arm. This was more than a casual encounter, Bastiano knew.

Sophie had arrived with no warning.

She had stepped onto the stage of his life, but there was so much debris, so much damage, and he did not know how to clear it. He told her a little of the complicated version.

'We used to be friends,' he admitted. 'When we were growing up our families frowned on it but we didn't care, and as teenagers we thought we could take on the world. Then Raul left for university.'

'What did you do?'

'I worked in my uncle's bar.' There was no point prettying it up—he and Raul had been enemies for a reason. 'After he left I slept with his mother.' He awaited her recoil or the uplift of her head and narrowing eyes but she just lay there. 'We had an affair, and when it was exposed she died in a car crash.'

'How old were you?' Sophie asked.

'Seventeen. I wasn't exactly innocent before that, though. In the end I tried to persuade her to leave her husband and come away with me but she refused. Raul believes I as good as killed her.'

'Were you the one driving?'

He frowned at Sophie's question.

'No.'

'Well, then, how could it be your fault?'

Sophie lifted herself up on her arm and he glimpsed again her absolute refusal to simply acquiesce.

'Her husband had found out about us.'

'How old was she?'

'Thirty-four,' Bastiano said. He had thought Maria closer to her forties at the time but really she had not been much older than he was now.

Sophie's lip curled. *'Poutana.'*

'Hey!' He rose to Maria's defence, as he always had. 'We were in…' Bastiano halted but a little too late, for Sophie knew what he had been about to say.

'In love?' she sneered, and then shook her head. 'That's not love.'

'How would you know?' he demanded.

'I know what love isn't,' Sophie responded hotly. 'I left home because, for all my lack of experience in the matter, I believed that love should make you smile.'

'Perhaps—if you live on the cover of a chocolate box.'

'So, if it was love, why didn't she leave her husband?'

'She was very religious,' Bastiano said. 'When Maria was growing up she wanted to be a nun.'

Sophie gave a derisive snort. 'Why wasn't she one, then?'

'Because at sixteen she got pregnant with Raul.'

Bastiano reached over and turned out the light but, far from annoyed at her scathing assessment of Maria, he was actually touched that somehow, on rather black evidence, she was defending him.

They lay in silence but far from sleep.

It was difficult to speak of that time but it was also hard to hear.

'It was Raul you fought with?' she asked.

'After the funeral.' Bastiano nodded. 'That was the easy part—the next day we found out she had left money in her will to be divided between him and me. He thinks I knew that she had money…'

'Did you?'

'No,' Bastiano said. 'Raul told me he'd watch me go under, he said I was nothing without her money.'

'So she left you enough to buy the Grande Lucia?'

'No.' He gave a low laugh at the thought. 'I bought a derelict building...' He thought of how the Old Convent had been then. 'There were no roads to access it. There weren't many tourists then in the west and I bought it for a song. I've bought a few more since then.'

'You could have blown that money,' Sophie said. 'Instead, look at all you have done.'

She did not know the scope of his wealth, just that he could consider the purchase of this hotel, which told her how much Bastiano had done with the start he felt he had not deserved.

In Sophie's mind he had earned every cent.

'Last month,' Sophie said into the darkness, 'when I called home, my brother told me that Luigi had taken to drink.'

Bastiano said nothing.

'It's my fault apparently.' She turned and saw his strong profile and that his eyes were open but he did not look at her. 'As I said to my brother, I'm quite sure there was a problem long before he had me to blame it on.'

'You certainly take no prisoners.' He looked at her then and she heard rather than saw his smile. 'Were you always tough?'

'I had to learn to be,' Sophie told him, 'and fast. I have five brothers and all of them would be perfectly happy to have me pick up after them. I pick up after myself, unless, of course, I am being paid.'

Bastiano slept, but Sophie lay there awake, troubled by her own words on the subject of love.

He made her smile.

Oh, not in a chocolate box way.

Just the thought of him, and the memory of them, had elicited more smiles in the last three months than she had collected in a lifetime before that.

And the world turned too fast when they were in bed, for when she reached for water, Sophie could make out the outline of the Colosseum when before it had been wrapped in darkness.

As she lay back down he pulled her in so that her head lay on his chest and she watched the sky, willing morning not to come.

His hand was on her arm and she toyed idly with the snake of black hair that had entranced her when she had gone to reach for the plate that first morning.

There was no reason now not to move the sheet, no reason left to be shy, and so she slipped her hand lower, feeling him grow hard under her fingers.

Her face felt warm on his chest and his hand was still on her shoulder as she slid down.

She had no real idea what she was doing, but he rose to her palm as if to greet her. She felt the warmth nudge her cheek and as she kissed just the tip and then knelt and ran her tongue down the side, he grew to the length of her face. This she knew, for she worked her tongue up and down, absorbed in the task at hand.

Bastiano moved the hair from her eyes.

And then as she ventured deep he took her hair and coiled it around his hand, just so that he could see her.

Usually he preferred a curtain of hair, but with Sophie he liked watching the stretch of her jaw and then the tease of her tongue.

He liked watching while she closed her eyes and they were lost to each other, utterly oblivious to a world waking up outside.

So oblivious that the sound of the main door opening went unheard.

Bastiano moaning her name did not.

'Sophie…'

One hand was stroking her bottom, the other wrapped in her hair, and she was lost in the moment as he came to her mouth.

And Inga stood there, jealousy rising like bile as she saw Sophie's uniform a puddle on the floor.

Sophie, always sweet and smiling, and yet so judgmental of Inga, was at it too.

And with their soon-to-be boss—Bastiano Conti.

Oh, the two of them were not quite finished yet and remained oblivious to her arrival in the suite, but Inga's eyes lit on a ring, and she knew exactly how she would punish Sophie for her hypocrisy.

She slipped the ring into the pocket of Sophie's discarded uniform and quietly wheeled the trolley back out, then she took out a pen and changed his breakfast order to seven.

'Hey.' Inga wheeled the trolley back to the kitchen and spoke with the chef. 'Signor Conti's breakfast is not due for another hour. Luckily I noticed.'

Very lucky.

For some.

Explain that, Sophie!

CHAPTER NINE

'I'M GOING TO be late,' Sophie warned as they showered together.

'Don't go to work today.'

'You might have some sway if you were the new boss…' She laughed. 'No, I am going in so I can be guilt-free on my days off.'

'How long are you off for?'

'Two days and two nights.'

She quickly dressed and, yes, she was going to work but with conditions attached.

'This time you're to come back,' he warned, taking her in his arms. 'Tonight we'll go out, somewhere nice.'

And she frowned because, yes, it was an age-old problem but Sophie truly had nothing suitable for a date with Bastiano Conti. Luckily, he read her concern.

'I'll take care of everything.'

As she left, Bastiano was ready to plan their evening.

More than that, he was considering flying her home.

Never had he had any inclination to bring anyone back to the Old Convent, but telling her his history, finally having someone on his side, for the first time he wanted to explore his past…

With her.

Bastiano cared for no one and had been raised not to do so, yet he knew now the real reason he was back in Rome.

Sophie.

Maybe the return of his mother's ring was a sign that things were starting to turn around. For the first time he believed that maybe, just maybe there was more to life than revenge.

He walked out and looked over to the table where he had placed the ring last night, yet there was no ring there. He had left it there, Bastiano was sure.

In fact, he could remember precisely the moment he had put it down for it had been then he had become aware that Sophie was near.

And he tried not to think that she too might have seen him with it.

He looked at the floor beneath the table.

Unlike the last time he had been here, the room was immaculate and after a few minutes of fruitless searching it was very clear that the ring had gone.

He recalled her expression when he had told her they would go out tonight.

Perhaps Sophie had decided that she needed something to wear.

Had she taken some notes from his wallet he would not have cared, but he'd only just got his mother's ring back.

Bastiano was still scanning the floor and the surfaces as he dressed, still going over last night's details in his mind as he pulled on a shirt and impatient fingers did it up, but he didn't even attempt to tuck it in.

And that was how she saw him.

Sophie had just come from the morning's briefing and instead of house duties she was to work in the foyer, ensuring that all surfaces were gleaming, including the brass revolving doors.

It wasn't her favourite job but it was not an unpleasant one. She could observe the guests and chat with Ronaldo the doorman. It was not an easy shift either, for there were many lounges and there were always guests leaving coffee rings and crumbs. But today she could have been anywhere, she was so happy.

They had shared something so precious last night, Sophie knew it.

And then she saw him and it was not the Bastiano she knew.

Immaculately dressed or deliciously naked, she knew only those two.

Now he looked dishevelled, his clothes thrown on, his shirt barely done up and he wasn't even wearing shoes.

'Sophie...'

His hair was tousled, his jaw unshaven but most disconcerting was his impatience, for she could feel it as he strode up to her.

'Can we speak?'

'I can't.' She tried to smile and address him as if he were just another guest. 'Bastiano, not here...'

'Yes, here!' His voice was low but so clipped that Ronaldo and a couple of guests turned their heads. 'Do you have something of mine?'

'Bastiano...' She was nervous. His eyes were blazing, his lips were pale and tense and she could feel his anger. 'I don't know what you're talking about.'

'Just give it back now and we'll say no more about it.'

Yes, he got that he had never paid her, and he got that she probably thought she deserved something after two nights in a rich man's bed but, hell, *not his ring*!

'Problem?'

Inga perked up and came over. Sophie found she was holding a tense breath but she forced herself to speak. 'No, there's no problem.'

'Sophie…' Bastiano was livid, even his scar seemed to be jumping to the pulse in his cheek, but he waited until Inga had turned around before he spoke again. 'Give me back the ring.'

'I don't know what you're talking about, Bastiano,' Sophie said, relieved that Inga had walked off. 'Can we please speak when my shift ends?'

Only Inga had not merely drifted off but had fetched Benita, the head of housekeeping.

'Can I help you, Signor Conti?' Benita asked.

'It's nothing,' Bastiano said, and he did all he could to rein his temper in. This was her job after all.

But things were already out of hand.

'Signor Conti seems to think that Sophie might have his ring,' Inga said.

'I am sure there is a misunderstanding.' Benita smiled. 'Did you drop it?' She looked around the foyer. 'It might already have been handed in.'

'No, I didn't *drop* it,' Bastiano answered curtly with his eyes firmly fixed on Sophie. 'I'll go to my suite and check again, I'm sure it must be there.'

'Sophie only prepared your room,' Benita patiently answered. 'You weren't even in residence when she did…' And then her voice trailed off as she looked at Sophie's flaming cheeks and then Bastiano, who had clearly just come from bed. And as realisation hit, Benita's eyes briefly shuttered.

It happened, everyone knew that, but Benita had expected better from her, Sophie knew.

'Could you come to my office, please, Sophie?' Benita smiled at Bastiano. 'I shall get to the bottom of this.'

It was awful.

Occasionally staff were caught stealing and Sophie knew only too well what would happen.

'I have to go through your locker with you, Sophie,' Benita said. 'These are very serious accusations, though I'm not just concerned with theft. Have you had any dealings with Signor Conti since he checked in?'

'I did not take his ring.'

'That doesn't answer my question, Sophie,' Benita said, though Sophie's flaming cheeks had already done just that—of course she had had dealings with him.

'You won't find anything in my locker.'

'Then you won't mind me checking.' Benita was firm. 'And if there is nothing to worry about then you will be more than willing to turn out your pockets for me now.'

Bastiano had decided he would be the one to best deal with this. Although he now had no intention of buying the hotel, Benita didn't know that so he walked into the office, ready to take control, just in time to see Sophie pulling from her pocket his mother's ring.

'I don't know how it got there...' She shook her head at the impossibility and then turned and there was Bastiano. 'I didn't take it,' she pleaded.

'Are you saying that you've never seen this ring before?' Benita checked, though there was a slightly mocking edge to her voice, for the evidence was clear.

'Yes,' Sophie said. 'I've never...' And then she halted for to say she had never seen the ring would be an outright lie. Last night, as she had stood nervous and trembling in the alcove she had, after all, watched as Bastiano sat staring at the small piece of jewellery for the longest time before putting it down.

And he would know that she had seen it.

She turned to him and her eyes implored him to believe her. 'Bastiano, I didn't take it.'

Bastiano said nothing.

He wasn't even disappointed in her.

Instead he was disappointed for *them* and scornful of himself—for a moment there he had started to believe in the possibility of them.

Not now.

'Could you wait outside, Sophie?' Benita said, and though her request was polite her voice was pure ice.

Sophie did as she was told.

She leant up against the wall and heard snatches of the conversation; she heard Benita mention the police and knew he was being asked if he wanted formal charges made.

'No,' Bastiano said, but he could see that Benita was tempted to so he pulled rank. 'It would cause more trouble for me than the ring is worth. I have it back now.' His head was pounding; he did not want to be standing here, speaking with the head of housekeeping, though he did so, for one reason only. 'There is no need for Sophie to lose her job, it was a one-off—'

'Signor Conti,' Benita broke in, 'I think we both know that I have more than one reason to fire Sophie.' She gave him a tight smile. 'You own plenty of establishments yourself, you will know that liaisons between staff and guests are an ongoing issue.' She shook her head. 'I will deal with Sophie and, of course, I shall brief Sultan Alim…'

'There's no need for that.'

But Benita wasn't just cross with Sophie.

She was cross with the very esteemed guest for the havoc his libido had caused.

'Unlike Sophie,' Benita tartly responded, 'I value my

job so I shall deal with things by the book. I trust you accept that from the head of housekeeping?'

'Of course.'

He walked out and there Sophie stood, pale in the face with her back against the wall, but she still met his eyes with confidence.

'If you needed money you should have just said…'

Sophie hurt.

Unbearably.

'I was never there for money, Bastiano,' she said, but he was walking off and that incensed her. 'It was about more than that, you know it was.'

'Please…' He raised one hand and flicked it in the air, dismissing her absolutely. Sophie was incensed.

'Why did you send me flowers for my birthday, then?' she called out.

Bastiano halted and then turned and walked back to her.

She had only ever known him nice.

Oh, she'd been warned he could be otherwise, but the Bastiano that other people painted so darkly was one she had never seen.

Until now.

'Your birthday?' He frowned. 'Who said anything about your birthday? I sent flowers so you would know I was in residence and would know to come to my suite. Accordingly, you did.'

Bastiano waited—for an angry slap perhaps, or for Sophie to tell him that she'd always known what a bastard he was, and how he had finally proved it.

Her words cut far deeper though.

'I don't believe you,' Sophie said. 'You're better than that.'

Benita came out then. 'I've got this from here, thank you, Signor Conti.'

She waited until he had walked off and then turned to Sophie.

'Signor Conti doesn't want the police brought in, but I'm left with no choice but to fire you.'

Benita was not cruel in her dismissal—her disappointment was the part that hurt Sophie the most.

'I didn't steal the ring.'

'Sophie, what were you doing to even give him the opportunity to think that you had? We serviced the room and left together, long before Signor Conti arrived.'

She had no answer to that.

'I thought you were better than that,' Benita said. 'It would be bad enough with any guest, but he is the future owner of this very hotel.'

'I didn't know that when we first—'

'So there were other times?' Benita said, and shook her head. 'Come on.'

It was not a pleasant morning.

Her room pass was handed over as well as her uniform. All she had in her locker were some shorts and a strappy top. Having dressed, she emptied it out entirely.

'You had a good job here,' Benita told her. 'You know what this industry is like and how word spreads. You will struggle to find work in a good hotel...'

It was true.

Everything Benita said was true.

But as scared and upset as she was, that was not what hurt.

It was the look he had given her, the black smile that had told her he had expected no less.

No trial by jury.

There wasn't even a trial.

Dario, the head of security, had been summoned and she did not get to leave by the trade door but was escorted out the front to serve as a warning to all staff what happened if caught.

And Bastiano saw it all unfold. He watched as the staff on Reception, the doorman and the maids all paused and turned to watch a rather dignified Sophie walk out.

'Sophie,' Anya called out. 'Your flowers…'

And she almost crumpled.

Sophie looked at the perfect blooms and remembered the joy in her heart when she had received them, and then she glanced over to where he stood. 'I wish I'd never laid eyes on them,' she said, while meeting his dark gaze.

'Likewise,' Bastiano mouthed for her eyes only.

He headed up to his suite but everything he touched turned black. He thought of her, feisty and sunny and smiling when they had met, and how much she had loved her job.

And now she had been fired.

He looked at the ring in his palm and it felt as if it scalded his skin; he was pocketing it when there was a knock at the door.

'Room service.'

Not the type he wanted.

It was Inga with breakfast, and she lifted a silver dome and offered to serve.

'No.'

'Would you like—?'

'Out!' he barked, and when the door closed he picked up the dome himself and saw those bloody baked eggs he had ordered last night while, yes, secretly hoping for Sophie.

He hurled the plate and it slid down the wall.

No, there were no rock stars in residence at the Grande

Lucia, but when the staff came to service the room a few hours later and saw how it had been trashed, it was decided that there might just as well have been.

CHAPTER TEN

THANKFULLY HER FLATMATES were at work when Sophie arrived home and she was able to let go of the tears she had been holding back.

Yesterday had been the happiest day of her life.

Today felt like the worst.

For three months Sophie had lived with the knowledge that she might lose her job over what had happened between her and Bastiano. But the scenario had evolved in the most humiliating, painful way imaginable. And still she had no explanation for how the ring had got into the pocket of her uniform.

She had been branded a thief and a whore, not just by her boss and peers but by Bastiano himself.

Worse, though, even worse was the damning look in his eyes—almost as if he had expected nothing less from her.

It had been her first glimpse of the man that everyone said he was—ruthless and cold—but it was not the Bastiano she knew.

As Sophie stripped off her clothes and pulled on a T-shirt in which to sleep, she flicked out her hair and felt something knotted amongst the strands.

A flower.

The stem was bent and twisted, yet somehow the tiny bloom was still perfect.

Recalling his words—how the flowers had been left to let her know that he was in residence—Sophie was tempted to screw up the rose and toss it into the trash, yet she could not.

It was all she had left of them, the only tangible reminder of a time when life had felt very close to perfect. And so, instead of discarding it, Sophie put it in her journal, pressing the pages together and then placing the journal under her mattress and doing what little she could to preserve the fleeting beauty.

Things did not look any better in the morning.

If anything, in the days ahead, things started to look considerably worse.

The Grande Lucia had been an amazing place to work and Benita was right—getting a job in a hotel of its calibre was going to prove difficult, if not impossible.

The phone calls she made went unanswered or she was told to provide a résumé and references. Sophie knew she had to get to the library and use a computer but even that felt daunting.

'Any luck?' Teresa her flatmate asked when Sophie returned after another fruitless search for work.

'No.' Sophie shook her head. 'Even the cafés aren't hiring.'

Summer really was over.

'You have a message,' Teresa told her, 'from a lady called Bernadetta. She asked you to call her—maybe it is about some work?'

Bernadetta?

Sophie frowned as she read the message and then made the call. Bernadetta was Gabi's boss and the one who had run her ragged in the ballroom that night.

Maybe she had heard and was calling to offer her work.

It was a futile hope and a very fleeting one because two minutes into the conversation it became apparent that Bernadetta had indeed heard the news about Sophie being fired and was speaking to her only because she had to.

'Sultan Alim has asked me to contact you,' she explained tersely. 'I told him that I'm not sure you can be trusted with something so confidential but he insisted.'

'I don't understand.'

'Matrimoni di Bernadetta has been asked to organise his wedding.'

'His wedding? Who is he marrying?'

'Gabi. She just doesn't know that yet.'

Sophie stood there gripping the phone, completely stunned.

'Gabi?' Sophie checked, but Bernadetta had already moved on.

'The wedding is to be this Saturday at the Grande Lucia. As Gabi's close friend, the Sultan wants you there. He also needs you to ensure that Gabi is home on Saturday when he calls her.'

'She doesn't know?'

'It's a surprise.'

Sophie's heart was beating terribly fast. Gabi, *her* Gabi was about to be proposed to by Alim. 'Does that mean Alim is Lucia's father?'

But Bernadetta wasn't calling for a chat. 'Are you prepared to ensure that Gabi is home on Saturday?' she asked.

'I'll do my best,' Sophie said, her head spinning as Bernadetta relayed instructions. Alim, it would seem, had thought of everything, even down to providing an outfit for Sophie that was suitable for a royal wedding.

'You are to go and see Rosa. She is making Gabi's dress, and will put something together for you as well.'

'Rosa?' Sophie swallowed. Rosa might be a friend of Gabi's but her designs were completely out of Sophie's league.

'It's all covered,' Bernadetta practically whistled through gritted teeth. 'If there are any problems please let me know and I must reiterate that you are to say nothing to Gabi.'

'Of course I shan't.'

It was the most exciting, breathtaking, happy news and there was no one to share it with.

First she called Gabi who, after offering her commiserations about Sophie losing her job, then asked if there was anything she could do to help.

'Could you help with my résumé?' Sophie asked. 'I don't have a computer and I tried at the library but I don't know how to make margins.'

'Of course. Come on over.'

'I'll come on Saturday,' Sophie said, and then she remembered something. 'I have to go to the doctor's at nine, I'll come after that.'

It wasn't a lie. Sophie did indeed have to go to the doctor's for a prescription for her Pill. With a royal wedding to go to on Saturday, she rather wished she had been a little bit more organised and had some more Pills so that she could avoid having her period that day!

The wedding should prove a wonderful diversion from her current problems but her heart felt heavier with each passing day. Even walking into an exclusive boutique for a private fitting, it was an effort to smile.

Still, her smile did come a little more readily as Sophie found herself for once spoiled for choice.

'This one would be perfect on you,' Rosa said as she held up a dress that seemed little more than a slip.

It was a gorgeous silver-grey and it actually reminded her of Bastiano's eyes.

'Try it on,' Rosa said. 'And slip on the shoes so you get the full effect.'

Sophie went into a very lavish changing room and pulled off her skirt and top and then tried to put the dress on over her head before discovering a concealed zip.

'Is it on?' Rosa asked.

The dress was amazing. It hung beautifully and gave Sophie curves when she usually had none, but for Sophie there was a concern.

'Isn't it a bit much for a wedding?' she asked as she stepped out, but Rosa had thought of that.

'Indeed, but I have a light overdress that goes well with it in a sheer chiffon. I'll just get it. What size shoe do you take?'

Sophie told her and, left alone, she lifted her hair and was trying to decide whether she should wear her hair up or down when she turned and looked at her silhouette.

She had a bust.

Oh, there was no doubt that Rosa was a miracle worker with fabric but there was also no denying that her small bust was a touch fuller.

It was because of the Pill, Sophie told herself.

'Here,' Rosa said, holding out a sheath of pale fabric that Sophie slipped on over the dress before adding the shoes. It was gorgeous and worked amazingly well, although it did dim the beauty of the dress just a fraction. 'You look wonderful.' Rosa smiled. 'I cannot wait to see Gabi's face when she finds out all that Alim has arranged.'

'Are there many guests?' Sophie asked a little later as, for the first time in her life and long overdue, she splurged on some gorgeous underwear.

'Just family and close friends.'

It was her first inkling that Bastiano might be there. Sophie knew that he and Alim were friends.

She watched as Rose wrapped her new silver knickers and lacy bra in tissue paper, and Sophie vowed to herself that Bastiano wouldn't be seeing them.

Yet, though the thought of seeing him would usually have consumed her, Sophie awoke on the morning of the wedding with more than the possibility of seeing Bastiano on her mind.

In the bathroom, having showered, she tried to quash the gnawing of anxiety in her stomach, for her period still had not arrived.

Stress can delay things, Sophie told herself.

Not that she really knew, but she had heard it said amongst friends, and so at her appointment at the doctor's that morning she suggested the same.

The doctor just handed her a jar.

'I've taken my Pill every day,' Sophie said when she returned with her specimen and the doctor ran the test.

'Do you take it on time?'

'Always…' Sophie said, and then swallowed as she thought back to the other morning when she had been fired. 'I had an upset the other day, I might not have taken it until lunchtime.'

'The other day?' The doctor frowned. 'Sophie, you are pregnant.'

'I don't think so.' Sophie shook her head. She had come here to be reassured, to be told she was mad to worry, but the doctor just looked at Sophie as the news started to sink in. 'I can't be.'

As the doctor examined her Sophie's fear only increased.

'I would say that you're more than twelve weeks.'

'How could I not know?' She started to cry, but this doctor was far kinder than the one back home and took some time to gently explain that not all women had symptoms.

'People have commented that my uniform was getting tight,' Sophie said. 'I just never gave it much thought.'

It was a lot to take in, an awful lot to take in, and Sophie left the doctor's more bewildered than she had ever been in her life.

But she had to get to Gabi's.

'Hey.' Gabi gave her a smile and then when she saw Sophie's puffy eyes she drew her inside. 'You'll get another job.'

'I loved that one, though,' Sophie said. It was easier to let Gabi think that her tears were about losing her job and Gabi soon set to work, typing up her friend's résumé.

'You really need a reference,' Gabi said. 'Why don't you put me? I can say you've helped me organise some weddings.'

'That's stretching it,' Sophie sighed.

'Well, why don't you put me as a personal one for now?'

Gabi made it all look so easy, and soon she had printed off several copies of Sophie's résumé, but as she handed them over, curiosity got the better of Gabi and she asked what Sophie had been doing in Bastiano's room.

'Oh.' Sophie was immediately on the defensive. 'So now you think I stole his ring?'

'Of course not!'

'I would never steal,' Sophie said. 'But if I did, I would not steal some stupid emerald and pearl ring. It would be diamonds.'

Gabi laughed and just as she did the phone rang and she went to answer it. Sophie watched as her friend's face paled and she excused herself and went into the bedroom.

It must be Alim!

A few minutes later Gabi emerged, declaring that she had a migraine.

'That came on quickly,' Sophie said as she was ushered out.

'Yes, they tend to.'

They promised to catch up soon but as Sophie walked off, though happy for her friend she felt terribly lonely too. Gabi had struggled with being a single mother, yet she had a job and her mother lived here in Rome.

And now she had Alim.

Sophie couldn't help but wonder what hope there was for her when she had none of those things.

She had nothing, save for her Sicilian pride, though even that was going to be hard to find today.

Sophie tried, though.

She got ready and she wore make-up through necessity rather than choice. Just a little, but enough to ensure that no one could guess she'd been crying. And for once she wore her hair down, though more because it would hopefully hide some of her blushes when she walked into the hotel.

The dress was a dream but, now that Sophie knew she was pregnant, it seemed terribly obvious, for her bust was certainly fuller and there was a soft curve to her stomach. Sophie was very grateful to add to her outfit the sheer fabric that hid even a tell-tale hint that her body had changed.

And so to the Grande Lucia.

She took a cab, which was a treat in itself for Sophie, and as it pulled up Ronaldo jumped forward to let the passenger out.

'*Benvenuto...*' he said, but then Ronaldo's warm welcome petered out as he realised who it was, and now his greeting was both awkward and curt. 'Sophie.'

'Ronaldo.'

She climbed out of the cab and took a second to seemingly fiddle with her dress, though really she was trying to summon the courage to walk inside.

Through the brass revolving doors she went and into the familiar foyer.

It didn't feel familiar, though, for instead of hearing her name called and the regular smiles and waves as she walked through, her ex-colleagues all pretended to be busy and looked the other way.

All that she could handle, Sophie thought as she stood outside the ballroom and gave her name.

The sly glances and whispers, and even being downright ignored, all hurt, but it was a manageable hurt.

What her heart couldn't deal with, though, as she walked through the entrance doors of the ballroom, was the certain knowledge that Bastiano was here.

Even without sighting him, Sophie knew that he was.

There was a current that ran through her whenever he was close and she could feel his eyes on her as she again gave her name so that she could be guided to her seat.

He was here, she was certain.

Yes, Bastiano was there.

He had withdrawn his offer for the hotel and would gladly never have set foot in the place again, yet business was business, he had told Alim.

And they were still friends.

So, having offered his best wishes to the surprisingly nervous groom, he was just taking his seat as they awaited the arrival of the bride when Sophie appeared.

She looked stunning, Bastiano thought.

He watched Sophie momentarily falter as she was guided to the seats near his.

'I am a friend of the bride,' she said to the woman who was ushering her towards where he sat. 'I should be on the other side.'

But this was no ordinary wedding, and she went where she was guided, away from the side where all the royalty had been seated.

'We commoners sit together,' Sophie said as she took her place beside him and Bastiano gave a tight smile.

'For now,' he responded, looking ahead rather than at her.

As soon as the service was over he would move away, Bastiano decided. She might just as well have spilled a bottle of perfume over herself for her fragrance overwhelmed him, yet he knew she had not. The scent was pure Sophie and for now he had to breathe it in, aware of every flicker as she sat supremely still beside him.

And then as the ballroom doors opened they stood and Sophie turned, seeing her friend but all the time feeling Bastiano's eyes boring into the back of her head.

'You knew!' Gabi mouthed as she caught sight of her, and Sophie smiled for her friend; as Alim kissed little Lucia, Sophie did her level best not to break down.

She wanted to tell Bastiano about the baby, she wanted there to be hope for them.

But there was none.

There never had been, she now knew.

It had never been going to end well.

She wanted to be happy for her friend, yet to stand broken-hearted at a wedding, next to the man who had shattered her happiness, was a very private hell and too much to sustain.

Gabi and Alim were in love, it was plain to see.

It just seemed to magnify the hopelessness of her situation as she stood next to Bastiano.

'How long does the service go on for?' he asked at one point.

'How the hell would I know?' Sophie responded and she felt rather than heard his slight mirthless laugh.

It truly was agony.

Finally, though, Gabi and Alim were husband and wife.

As the chairs were moved away and the guests went to take their seats at the tables for the celebratory meal Sophie looked at the place cards and saw she would be seated by him.

It was a hell she chose not to sustain.

'Gabi…' She kissed her friend and congratulated her and then she struggled how best to say what she had to.

Gabi said it for her. 'You're going to go?'

'I just…'

She felt sick.

Oh, maybe it was all in her head and simply because she knew she was pregnant, but suddenly she felt light-headed and nauseous and utterly out of place.

'I understand, Sophie,' Gabi said, for she had heard all the rumours and could have thought of nothing worse than being forced to sit next to Alim when her own world had fallen apart.

'I'm so happy for you,' Sophie said. 'I honestly am. I wouldn't have missed the wedding for the world.'

It was the reception that she could not tolerate.

'Here.' Gabi swiped Sophie's place card from the table and wrote something down. 'That's Alim's private number. Put him down as a reference.'

'I can't.'

'Yes, Sophie, you can.'

'I'll only use it if I'm desperate.'

Desperate was how she felt, though not about work.

She wanted to walk right up to Bastiano and plead her case. She wanted to tap him on the shoulder right now and tell him that she did not take his stupid ring. And she wanted to tell him what she had found out just a few hours ago.

Her eyes scanned the room and immediately she saw him—talking to some leggy blonde. Or rather she was talking as Bastiano's restless eyes scoured the room and found Sophie's.

She turned and walked away and headed for the restrooms, but she didn't get that far.

Sophie looked over to Reception, where Anya stood— once they would have chatted, but now Anya could not meet her eyes.

And there was Inga, polishing the brass doors and chatting to Ronaldo.

Everyone ignored her.

Once she had belonged but, like it or not, she no longer did, so Sophie left.

Not just the wedding.

It was time to accept that there was nothing for her here in Rome and to return home.

Her disappearance did not go unnoticed.

'Excuse me,' Bastiano said to the leggy blonde.

He had no idea who the woman was but that was nothing new.

The difference today was that anonymity held no charm.

He wanted to speak to Sophie, to find out how she had fared. He wanted to know that everything was okay in her world and then he could walk away more easily.

Bastiano could not find her.

As he took his seat the place card next to his had gone, though Bastiano being Bastiano had already checked and knew full well that Sophie had been placed next to him.

Perhaps she had asked to be moved, Bastiano decided when the table filled and the space next to him remained empty.

Wise choice, he told himself, though that did not sit right.

But then the lighting dimmed and it became increasingly clear that Sophie hadn't just moved tables, she had left the venue.

'Where's Sophie?' he asked the happy couple, having sat through the meal and endless speeches.

'I expect it got a bit too much for her,' Gabi said, and she looked straight at Bastiano. 'It would be hard to be here, labelled a thief by everyone and the subject of painful gossip. I'm just grateful she made it to the service.'

And later Bastiano could not help but have a word with Alim.

'I think Sophie might have been dealt with a bit harshly.'

'Oh, so you're in the practice of hiring thieves?' Alim asked, raising his brows, but then he saw his friend's concern. 'She'll be okay.'

'She won't get work.'

'Not true. I've just been informed that I'm to act as a reference.'

And with Sultan Alim of Zethlehan as a reference, Sophie would be okay.

Bastiano could relax now and put the unfortunate incident behind him.

Except he couldn't.

There were beautiful guests galore and yet he was in bed before the bride and groom.

Alone.

And he woke, as he always did, before the sun.

'Entra!' he called, when on the dot of six his breakfast was delivered and he closed his eyes to indicate he did not want conversation.

Some things never changed.

Except they had.

'Would you like me to serve?'

He opened his eyes to the pale blue ones of Inga, the maid that Sophie did not like.

'Out,' he told her, and struggled to contain his anger, for Bastiano had worked out what had happened.

It took less than an hour to prove his hunch.

He stood over Dario, with Benita by his side, looking at old CCTV tapes.

'My breakfast is served at six every morning, except on that morning.'

'You ordered it for seven,' Benita said, looking at the paperwork.

'No.'

Of that he was certain.

The only variance to his breakfast order had been the occasional *shakshuka* and that had either been eaten by a sexy maid or flung against the wall.

His breakfast was always at six.

There it was, right on time, being delivered by Inga.

And there it was, not two minutes later, being wheeled back out.

Sophie was not a thief.

Most disconcerting to Bastiano, though, was that he

had cared enough to find out and pursue justice for his little maid.

'She will get her job back now?' Bastiano checked, but Benita gave an uncomfortable shrug.

'Sophie wasn't just fired for stealing.'

'If turning tricks is the criteria for firing maids at the Grande Lucia,' Bastiano responded tartly, 'then the unemployment rate in Rome is about to skyrocket. Would you like me to name names?'

Benita closed her eyes for a moment before responding. 'That shan't be necessary.'

'Good,' Bastiano retorted! 'So you will be rehiring Sophie?' Bastiano checked, and Benita nodded.

An hour later Bastiano boarded his helicopter for home with his conscience clear.

Almost.

Not.

CHAPTER ELEVEN

SOPHIE HATED HER JOB.

She tried not to show it, of course.

But no matter how thoroughly she cleaned the sleazy bar on the edge of her home town, the surfaces did not gleam and the carpets were still sticky.

Still, Sophie far preferred the cleaning duty when the bar was closed to the hours when it was open.

It was a job and a roof over her head, she told herself, though not for much longer. Pino, her boss, had made it clear when he'd hired her that the live-in post was a temporary one. Now, at six months pregnant, she was still no closer to working out where she would live when the baby arrived.

It would not be at her parents'.

Sophie had left home in disgrace, returned in shame, and after a lot of heartache they had asked the priest to speak with her. She had been told of couples who were desperate for a baby and would be able to provide a wonderful home.

An argument had ensued when Sophie had told her family that she would be the one to provide for her baby and she had barely seen them since.

Gabi's mother might have come around once little

Lucia had arrived, but Sophie knew that it would not be the case with her own parents.

And she could not stay there.

Even if Pino did keep her on, she wouldn't want to raise her baby in a room over a bar such as this.

And Pino gave her the creeps.

Which was why, instead of, as she usually did, working through her rare day off, Sophie headed upstairs to her small bedroom.

'Where are you going?' Pino asked. 'It's time to open up.'

'It's my day off,' Sophie reminded him.

'Well, I need you to work.' Pino shrugged and went to open the main door, clearly not expecting a discussion.

'I have an appointment in town today,' Sophie said, 'at the hospital. It's my six-month check. I cannot miss it.'

It was a lie.

Sophie had had just a couple of visits to her old family doctor but she didn't tell Pino that. Instead, she headed upstairs and washed as best she could in the small bathroom she shared with Pino and then pulled on a black dress and boots and a thin jacket.

As she came down the stairs she could hear Pino chatting to one of the regulars and hoped she could slip out unnoticed.

'Sophie!'

Just as she got to the door he called out to her.

'Make sure you're back for five.'

That would be pushing it.

Casta was three hours away and three back, and she had no idea how long it would take to get to the Old Convent from the railway station, or how long the interview would take.

For the first time in months she had hope.

A woman who dropped off some deliveries to the bar had told her about the Old Convent in Casta. It was an upmarket health and wellness facility and they were looking for live-in chambermaids.

'It's gorgeous,' she told Sophie. 'They take only the best produce…' She sneered in the direction of Pino. 'He takes the dregs. You should call them. A woman called Karmela runs the housekeeping. My niece worked there. They took her on when she was pregnant and she carried on working there for two years after the baby was born.'

'She lived there with the baby?' Sophie's heart had started thumping so fast it must have woken her own baby up because she felt its little kicks.

'Yes. She worked hard, mind you, but she loved it. Look your neatest, though, it's very posh.'

The telephone interview had gone very well and now, as the train went through a tunnel, Sophie dug in her bag and found a comb.

Oh, she would love to make more of an effort, Sophie thought, but she had nothing to make an effort with.

She did have Alim's number!

Sophie took the place card from the wedding out of her purse and looked at it for a long moment.

She hadn't used it yet. The type of jobs that she had been able to find had not required a reference, certainly not one from a sultan, and she would not use this gift lightly.

Yet she needed it today.

Sophie couldn't wait to meet her baby, but she was nowhere ready to. Her parents' suggestion of adoption had very quickly taught Sophie just how much she wanted her baby.

Yes, the circumstances were far from ideal, but her baby was already much loved.

The train pulled out of the tunnel and into the belly of the valley of Casta. It was the first time she had ever been there and the scenery was breath-taking. Ahead was the ocean, with a hill either side of the valley, and now the train turned seemingly on a dime and ran on stilted tracks that hugged the rocky hillside.

Sophie dared not look down so she closed her eyes and rested her head against the window.

She should have stayed in Rome, Sophie thought. At least there she had had friends.

She ached to contact Gabi but did not know what to say—after all, her friend was now married to royalty. Would it sound as if she was begging for help when she told her she was pregnant?

But it wasn't just that.

Alim was a friend of Bastiano's.

With the best will in the world Sophie knew that Gabi would be worried if she found out her predicament and would end up telling Alim.

Would he tell Bastiano?

Sophie guessed that eventually he would and Bastiano's reaction to the news…

Sophie did not want to know.

Oh, he would be aggrieved and cross and no doubt decide she had set out to trap him.

His anger she could deal with.

Almost.

What she couldn't cope with, though, was the sense of duty that would surely ensue.

Bastiano was right—they were the same.

Beneath the glamour of his life, beneath the fearsome reputation and his playboy ways, he was as Sicilian as she.

Bastiano Conti forced into a duty marriage was something that Sophie could not bear to think of.

She had run from one after all.

As she stepped out of the train Sophie breathed in the salty air; the wind whipped her hair and she pulled her jacket tighter.

'I am looking for the Old Convent,' Sophie told a woman behind the station desk, and she was informed that there was a bus due in fifteen minutes.

'Though it only takes you to the base.'

Sophie nodded. She had been told on the phone that there was a gated entrance and once she arrived she had been told to buzz and a car would be sent to collect her.

The bus took her through Casta and then inched its way up the hill, but Sophie was too nervous to take in the view. She was let off, seemingly in the middle of nowhere, but Karmela's instructions were good and soon she pressed a buzzer on the gate and gave her name and said she was there for an interview.

Soon a car arrived and she was driven down a long driveway with overhanging trees on either side, and then they arrived at the Old Convent building.

The grounds were sumptuous. There were fountains and pretty walkways and, far from foreboding, as she stepped into Reception there was a tranquil air to the old building.

'Sophie?' The receptionist was friendly and greeted her by name. After filling in a few forms, she was shown through to her interview.

Karmela, the head of housekeeping, greeted her and asked her to take a seat, wasting no time before getting the interview under way.

'You said on the phone that you had experience in a five-star hotel.'

'I worked at the Grande Lucia in Rome for a year.'

'Can I ask why you left?'

Sophie told the truth.

In part.

'I had some issues with my baby's father.'

'Well, he would have trouble creating issues here. The security is tight, there is limited access and it is gated.'

It wasn't that type of trouble Sophie had been having, of course, but she gave Karmela a smile.

'You would have to sign a confidentiality clause. Some of our guests are very famous and we do not want staff speaking out of turn.'

'We had many famous and titled guests at the Grande Lucia.'

'I understand that.' Karmela nodded. 'Here, though, a lot of our guests are…' She hesitated. 'Shall we say, recovering from a life lived in the fast lane.'

'Oh.'

'Does that concern you?'

'Not at all,' Sophie said.

'You're currently working?' Karmela asked as she read through her paperwork.

Sophie had updated it by hand.

'I am.'

'Would you be happy for me to ring for a reference?'

Sophie's throat went dry and it took a moment before she could respond. 'I think that might make things rather awkward for me.'

'How much notice would he require?' Karmela asked, and she looked up from the paperwork at Sophie and watched as she struggled to reply.

Oh, she did not know how best to put it. 'He would not take it well if I told him I was leaving.'

Karmela seemed to get it immediately.

'What about your previous role?'

'Sultan Alim is my reference—he's the owner of the Grande Lucia. He gave me his private number to use.'

'May I contact him?'

'Of course,' Sophie said, and wrote down the number.

The rest of the interview went very well and soon Karmela was speaking as if Sophie already had the job!

'You will be required to service the rooms and to provide a turndown service. We encourage guests to eat in the restaurant but on occasion you would also be required to deliver meals to their suites. Some of our guests can be rather demanding, but I am sure you are used to that.'

Sophie nodded and decided that now was the time to address the obvious.

'I know that I might only be able to work for a couple of months, but I am very good at my job and when I've had my baby I will work harder still.'

'Sophie, we're very used to single mothers here. There is room in the cells for both a bed and a cot.'

'Cells?'

'We have kept the names of old. The cells are where the nuns would sleep but don't worry, they have been modernised. They are basic but very comfortable. In your case the timing works well—there's a two-month period where you'll be entirely supernumerary and trained to our standard. Signor Conti has a very strict vision for the place that has worked well…'

'Signor Conti?'

'Sì.' Karmela nodded. 'Bastiano Conti. His facilities are world renowned. This gorgeous old building was a dilapidated shell when he first bought it. Now guests fly in from all over the world to retreat here…'

Sophie didn't hear the rest of what was said.

The Old Convent was owned by Bastiano.

There was no way she could work here now, Sophie thought as hope was snatched away.

As soon as he saw that she was pregnant…

Sophie closed her eyes as she pictured Bastiano finding out that the thieving maid who had delivered far more than breakfast was now pregnant with his child.

Sophie simply could not bear to face it.

She was too busy trying not to break down as Karmela wound up the interview.

'The driver will take you directly to the train station,' Karmela told her as she saw her to a waiting car. 'I'll be in touch soon.'

Karmela was as good as her word and the following morning Sophie took a call informing her that the role was hers.

To both women's regret Sophie politely declined.

CHAPTER TWELVE

'Buon Compleanno!'

'Grazie,' Bastiano responded mechanically as his PA wished him a happy birthday.

She was new and from out of town and, of course, did not know that there was no such thing as a happy birthday for Bastiano.

It had been the day his mother had died after all.

He rather hoped she would leave things there, but given that he had been gone for a few days there was much to catch up on.

'How was your meeting in Rome?' she asked.

'Fine.'

He had been back three times since the wedding and though he was no longer vying to purchase the Grande Lucia, he had told his PA to book him in there on business.

Certainly there had been no pleasure.

Rome had felt empty.

There was no sign of Sophie and, given all that had happened, he had been loath to enquire as to her whereabouts.

Bastiano did his best to ignore the date and dealt with the essentials, but by lunchtime he gave in and pressed on the intercom.

'Call for my car.'

A short while later he drove down the private road he had had built when he had taken over the convent and headed into the small town.

He parked by the church and walked down the gravelly side to the graveyard.

He came here rarely now.

He had used to visit Maria's grave, more out of guilt than grief, but he was not here to visit Maria today.

As a child, he would visit his mother's grave on certain occasions, but there were no memories to draw on and there had never been any comfort to be had.

Again, there was none today.

Just guilt.

He had been raised on it.

It was a pervasive guilt that time did not ease, for his very existence had robbed her of life.

Logic tried to tell him otherwise.

His mother had told no one about the baby she carried, and had done all she could to avoid showing—skipping meals until she had fainted one day. She had arrived at the convent hungry and weak.

The Old Convent might no longer be consecrated but for Bastiano those rules of old still applied, hence the policy of support to single mothers who wished to work there.

If only his mother had gone there sooner.

'I have your ring,' he told her, but there was no sudden rustle in the trees and the birds sang just as they had before.

There was no sign that she had heard.

He took it from his pocket and thought back to when Raul had come to visit to ask for Lydia's address, and the opportunity had arisen to ask for the one thing that was precious to him.

It did not feel so precious now.

He stared at the emerald and the tiny seed pearls but instead of beauty he saw only its curse.

Both of the women he'd loved had been wearing it when they had died.

And then he thought of Sophie, turning out her pockets and holding it in her palm, along with the cruel words he had hurled at her.

Of course the flowers had been for her birthday; at the time it had felt easier to lie than admit to caring.

He had lost her for this ring.

What once had been vital was meaningless now. Bastiano took the small ring and tossed it, for it had brought no peace; all it signified was destruction and pain.

He had to know for himself how she was.

Bastiano simply had to know that Sophie was doing okay.

He was the *stulto* now as he drove back up the hill, for he took the bends far too fast and was impatient at the gate, leaving his car with the engine still running.

'Park it,' he told the doorman.

Through the convent he strode, and before he could change his mind he delivered instructions.

'I want to speak with Sultan Alim,' Bastiano said. 'I'll take the call in my office.'

'Of course.'

Zethlehan was three hours ahead of Sicily but even though it was late afternoon there Bastiano knew it might take some time to be put through as Alim would likely be busy.

It wasn't Alim he wanted to speak to, though, but Gabi.

Bastiano just had to know how Sophie was.

It felt as if it was taking for ever to get hold of Alim.

He paced his office and looked out at the view of the strait but it did nothing to soothe him, as it usually it did.

At seventeen, when Maria's will had been read, he had scaled the convent walls just to get away from the toxic gossip in the village.

As Raul had started his ascent in Rome, Bastiano had remained in Casta.

His rise had been slower than Raul's.

Bastiano had seen the potential of the building and his low offer had been accepted; he had taken a loan and renovations had commenced.

The first clients had trickled in and then a B-list actor had moaned to the press about the cost, saying that it was prohibitive.

In response to the best publicity he could have hoped for, Bastiano had tripled the rates.

Now there was a waiting list to get in, though they kept two places on constant reserve should a young royal or such need urgent respite.

Though he had several more exclusive retreats under his belt this was his base and served as his platform to the world. Thanks to his famous guests, Bastiano was a name on the most coveted guest lists. He travelled frequently and partied hard but it was here that he chose to return.

Yet lately these walls no longer felt like home.

'I have Sultan Alim on the line.'

Bastiano picked up the phone.

'How are you?' Alim asked.

'I am well,' Bastiano said. 'Very well. Have you sold that hotel yet?'

'It is off the market,' Alim replied. 'Why, have you changed your mind?'

'No.' Bastiano was rarely awkward. 'Actually, I was

hoping to have a word with Gabi. I wondered if she had heard anything from Sophie.'

'Sophie?'

'The chambermaid…'

'I know who she is. I thought you were back in touch.'

'Why would you think that?'

'Because your head of housekeeping called a while back for a reference. I gave her a glowing one.'

Sophie had been here?

Bastiano made a few noises and said a few words but in less than a minute he had ended the call. He rang Reception and asked that Karmela meet him in his office.

All this time he had been worrying and wondering, only to find out that Sophie had passed through.

'Is anything wrong?' Karmela asked, looking worried as she came in.

'Nothing is wrong,' Bastiano said. 'You interviewed a young woman a couple of months ago…'

'I interview many people.'

'Sophie,' he said. 'She used to work at the Grande Lucia.'

'Ah, yes.'

'She wasn't offered the position?' he checked.

'Indeed she was. Sophie was an excellent candidate and her references checked out, but when I rang to offer her the job she said that she had accepted another position.'

'Where?'

'I didn't ask that,' Karmela said. 'I was disappointed and also cross that she had wasted so much time. I had even told her that there would be no problem when the baby came…'

'Baby?'

'You have always said that so long as their children are kept out of earshot you don't mind if we employ single mothers.'

'I meant, are you saying she was pregnant?'

'Yes, about five or six months along,' Karmela recalled. 'She said she'd had to get out of Rome because she was having some issues with the baby's father.'

The words were like knives.

'Bring me her résumé.'

He was sweating.

Even in the blistering heat of a Sicilian summer Bastiano was so fit that he barely broke a sweat. Even when held by the throat by Raul and accused of causing the death of Maria, he'd stayed cool.

Not now.

He cast his mind back to the wedding and the last time he had seen her. If what Karmela was saying was correct, then Sophie would have been about three months pregnant then.

He would have known. They had made love the night before!

Yet the fast, frantic sex had been the result of pure need and as for the morning…

Karmela brought him the paperwork and though Bastiano wanted to be alone, there were questions he needed to ask.

Most of it was typewritten but her most recent employment was written by hand.

'What is this address?'

'A bar, and not a particularly nice one,' Karmela said. 'I didn't bother to ring them for a reference.'

'Why not?'

'Sophie told me it was a live-in job but she didn't feel particularly comfortable there and it would be made worse if her boss knew that she was considering leaving. I rang her previous employer instead, Sultan Alim.'

Bastiano waved his hand to dismiss her, for he needed to digest all he had just been told, but as she reached the door there was something he had to know, something that could not be gleaned from the pages he held in his hand.

'How did she look?'

Karmela held out her hands and gave a somewhat helpless shrug, unsure what to say. 'Signor Conti, it was a couple of months ago…'

'How did she look?' he asked again. Bastiano did not care if his questions led Karmela to think that the baby was his, for his only concern now was Sophie.

'Tired,' Karmela said.

'And?' Bastiano pushed.

Karmela thought for a moment. 'Relieved. She seemed terribly relieved to have found this place. I got the distinct impression she was struggling where she was, which was why I was so surprised when she turned down the job.'

And Bastiano knew why she had.

Sophie had thought him wonderful when they'd first met—a gentleman who would not have her leave his suite in wet clothes.

She had seen only the good in him.

Until he had proved himself to be otherwise.

In the throes of love making she had pleaded for him never to let her down and he had.

It was time, Bastiano knew, to put things right.

'It's time to open up,' Pino called as he rapped loudly on Sophie's bedroom door.

'I'll be right there.'

It was late on a rainy afternoon and she was exhausted and had a headache to boot.

Lately she had been unable to sleep. She was simply too uncomfortable or too nervous with Pino prowling around, but this afternoon the baby was asleep and Sophie wanted to close her eyes and join it.

It wasn't an option, though.

She hauled herself from the bed and pulled on her shoes. Running a brush through her hair, she braced herself for another long shift behind the bar and then cleaning glasses late into the night.

Sophie knew only too well she could not work for much longer. The baby was not due for another six weeks but her body was telling her that she needed to rest.

Where, though?

She had been so defiant when she had told her parents and the priest that she would provide for her baby but the truth was she had saved little. Her job covered board and meals but the wages after that were tiny.

As she walked out of the bedroom, there in the hallway was Pino.

He gave her the creeps the way he was always hanging around.

'I've been thinking,' he said as she headed down the stairs and he walked behind her. 'You're a good worker, perhaps you can stay on once the baby comes.'

'Stay on?' she turned at the bottom of the stairs and for a second, maybe two, she actually thought that Pino was being nice as he moved past her and unbolted the door.

'You can move your things into the front bedroom at the weekend. It's warmer there.'

It was the middle of January, and not cold as such, but it was wet and the building was damp—though it was not for that reason that Pino would have Sophie move her things.

The front bedroom was his.

Never.

But now the fight was over.

Sophie knew she would have to contact Bastiano.

Oh, she was more than aware that it took two to make a baby and he had responsibilities.

It was the extent to which he might meet them that broke her heart.

Sophie walked into the bar as the patrons trickled in. She knew most of their orders without asking, which was just as well for her mind was too busy for conversation.

Sophie knew that she had to leave.

And soon.

'Sophie!' Her name was being called from several directions and she poured their drinks but did not serve them with a smile.

There was an impatient drumming of fingers coming from the left.

He could wait.

Sophie had perfected ignoring an impatient patron until she was ready to serve.

'Can I help you?' Sophie finally asked the drumming fingers, yet before she had even looked up she was on high alert.

His nails were neat and manicured and there was an expensive scent that in this place was non-existent rather than rare.

Her eyes slowly lifted, taking in the tie and dark suit, and then she met the eyes she had ached to see yet had sought to avoid.

'Bastiano…'

Her mind was moving slowly, trying to tell her that it was possible that he had been passing by and had just stopped in for a drink, while at the same time knowing this place was light years away from anywhere that he would frequent.

'What can I get you?' she asked.

'I'd like to speak with you in private.'

His olive skin was pale and the scar on his cheek was so livid it looked as if it had been freshly seared into his flesh.

Sophie could taste his fury and she felt her chest constrict as his eyes looked down at her swollen stomach.

What she did not understand was that his fury was not aimed at her.

Bastiano had been observing Pino—standing with his arms folded behind the bar and watching Sophie work. Not only had Pino's laziness incensed Bastiano, he had also seen the roaming of his eyes.

He wanted Sophie out of here.

'I'm working,' she told him, playing for time, for, even after many months preparing for a moment such as this one, still Sophie was none the wiser as to what to say, and so, of course, she said the wrong thing. 'What can I get you?'

'Sophie!' he warned. 'I want to speak to you now, outside.'

'She already told you—she's working.'

Bastiano did not even look over as Pino spoke on. 'I think it's time for you to leave.'

The bar fell silent.

Pino's voice signalled danger and, after all, there was a stranger in town.

A slick, suited stranger and she watched as Pino looked out of the window at Bastiano's rather flash car. It was clear to all that he did not belong here.

'I'm not going anywhere,' Bastiano said, and as he did so he looked right into Sophie's eyes. 'Until we have spoken.'

'Bastiano…' she attempted, and her voice came out a little high and strained. 'Not now.'

She wanted to warn him not to make a scene here, for she had seen more than her share of trouble within these walls.

'You heard her,' Pino said, and then made an already tense situation a hundred times worse for he came over and put an arm around her shoulders.

Sophie shrugged him off but the damage was more than done.

To Sophie, apart from on that terrible morning, Bastiano had always been kind, but she saw the other side to him now.

He did not explode; instead, it was far worse. It was as if the bar had been placed in refrigeration.

She could almost see the white of Bastiano's breath when he spoke for his words were pure ice.

'Sophie,' he said. 'Go and wait in the car.'

She would be angry with Bastiano later.

Right now she simply wanted out.

But she wanted him to follow her out because she knew how rough the bar's patrons could be.

'We'll speak outside,' she suggested.

'No,' Bastiano corrected her, though his eyes never left Pino's face. 'You go and wait in the car and I shall collect your things.'

Bastiano lifted the flap of the bar and Sophie walked out. The patrons parted as the one lady present left; when she was inside his vehicle, with a bleep, Bastiano locked her in safely.

He was angry with good reason for he knew she had been too scared to give this man as a reference.

Bastiano knew *exactly* his type.

Uninvited and most unwelcome, he walked behind the bar and into the hallway.

Pino followed him.

Bastiano climbed the stairs and found the cupboard Pino called a room—and no doubt charged Sophie half her wages to live in.

It took two minutes to clear it.

There was an old wooden wardrobe that held a couple of skirts and a bag that felt like it held some shoes. The chest of drawers contained just as little and Bastiano had soon packed her things. He went into the bathroom and picked up her brush and make-up and pulled down all the underwear that dripped over the bath. Not because Sophie would be needing them, for soon she would have much finer things, more because he could not stand that Pino had seen them.

He went back to the room and looked under the bed and found another pair of shoes and then he lifted the mattress and found her purse and a small leather journal. He had been poor once too, and he knew all the tricks.

'She owes me two weeks' notice.' Pino was at the door, watching his every move.

Bastiano said nothing, but as he stuffed Sophie's belongings into the bag the journal fell open and there, pressed between the pages, was a rose. *His* rose.

'I said…' Pino continued, but that single rose was Bastiano's undoing and he pressed the man against the wall.

'You make me sick,' Bastiano told him, and then he told him something else. 'Lucky for you she has her own room because if I find out you have so much as touched her, I suggest you sleep with one eye open.'

Pino seemed to recognise the ferocity in Bastiano's threat, so he put his hands up and Bastiano let him go.

He walked down the steps and out through bar with her bag over his shoulder; there were many fools present but not one game enough to speak out.

Or rather there was one fool.

From the safety of the top of the steps Pino had the last word.

'At least I gave her shelter. Where were you?'

Sophie watched from the car and she waited for the sound of a fight yet it was all eerily quiet and then, to her confusion, as calm as anything, Bastiano walked out.

He unlocked the car and climbed in, throwing her bag into the back and fighting to contain his temper as Pino's words replayed in his head.

'You had no right to charge in—' Sophie started, but Bastiano broke in.

'Is it my baby?'

'You know it is.'

'Then I had every right.'

He wanted to pull off hard, to leave some rubber in his wake, yet he had never driven with a pregnant woman beside him before. 'Why didn't you come to me?' He didn't get it, he truly did not, and was doing his best to contain his temper as he drove. 'You came to the Old Convent looking for work and yet chose to return here. Why?'

'Because I found out you owned it,' Sophie said. 'I didn't want you to know.'

'Why?' Bastiano demanded, but then gave in. Now was not the time for a row. He wanted her in Casta, he wanted her rested and fed.

'We'll talk back at the Old Convent.'

'What will your staff think when I arrive?'

'I have no idea,' Bastiano said, 'neither do I care.'

'Well, I do,' Sophie retorted, and now she too was angry. 'Are you intent on ruining every job I get?'

'Don't worry, Sophie, you will never have to work again.'

'I never used to worry about going to work,' Sophie said. 'I loved my job.'

She had, Bastiano knew that.

'Why didn't you come to me?' he asked again. 'I know I'm a bastard…'

'I never said you were.'

She hadn't.

They were coming to the stretch of road where he had witnessed Maria's crash.

The convent was visible in the distance as they drove in angry silence.

'It's beautiful,' Sophie commented as they passed a humble little church in golden limestone with a small bell tower.

Bastiano glanced over—pretty certainly wasn't the word that came to his mind as they drove past, for behind the church was the graveyard that held only dark memories for him.

'I'm glad you think so, given we'll be there in a couple of weeks.'

'Excuse me?'

'We should marry before the baby is born…'

Should.

That single word said it all.

She would be his wife by duty and nothing more.

It was the real reason that she had chosen not to tell him and had done her very best to go it alone.

Bastiano was right.

They were the same.

She had known exactly what his response would be.

Sophie looked over at him, a man who, when she'd met him, had been considering marrying a woman he had never even dated.

'You would take more care choosing an apple from the tree than in choosing a wife.'

'I don't pick apples.' Bastiano shrugged. 'They come to me peeled and sliced.'

'You know what I mean.'

The car was approaching the entrance to the convent now and Bastiano did not need to buzz. The gates sensed his car and slowly opened as they approached.

'You don't have to marry me, Bastiano,' Sophie said as the car idled, and she did not meet his gaze as he turned and briefly looked at her then offered his response.

'Where we come from, Sophie,' Bastiano responded as the car moved off, 'I do.'

CHAPTER THIRTEEN

THEY BOTH CHOSE to leave it there.

It was dark and late and, though she did not say it, there was certain relief as the car came out from the tunnel the trees provided and the Old Convent loomed close.

The old building really was a comforting sight.

'Where are we going?' Sophie asked as the car veered away from the main convent and took a cobbled path that led towards the ocean.

'Did you think I would put you in the cells?'

A small laugh, which Sophie hadn't known she had left in her, escaped. 'I honestly wouldn't mind.'

'Well, instead you are being sent to seclusion.'

'Sounds good to me.'

The car pulled up at the front of a large sprawling building and she thought of days gone by when the nuns must have come here on retreat. Thankfully nobody jumped out to open the car doors. In fact, Bastiano fetched her bag and carried it to the main door, which he opened.

'This is where you live?' Sophie checked as she stepped in for, even before she had properly looked, it was clear that this was a home.

'It is.'

'I thought you said I was being sent to seclusion.'

'This used to be it,' Bastiano told her. 'It is my favourite space.'

She could see why; it was, for want of a better word, stunning.

The stone walls held all the charm of yesteryear and there were unspoiled views of the ocean from the huge lounge and likely most of the rooms too. The furnishings were modern, though they blended in with the surroundings, and there was a huge leather couch that Sophie ached to simply stretch out on, but she was far from ready to be living with him.

'I want to be alone.'

'I thought you might. In fact, I was thinking of putting you into one of the more secluded suites we keep for royals and such.'

'Then why didn't you?'

Bastiano answered with a question. 'How long until you are due?'

'A couple of months—the end of March.'

'That's only six weeks away.' Bastiano said. 'And time apart doesn't seem to serve us well.'

She was exhausted, he could see, and it was not fair to discuss it tonight.

'I'll show you to your room.'

Sophie eyes widened, just a fraction but enough for Bastiano to see.

'I'm not a complete bastard, Sophie.'

'I never said you were remotely one.'

She never had, Bastiano recalled, as she followed him down a long corridor.

'You really can relax here,' he explained. 'You have your own pool…'

'Did the nuns used to swim?'

'No,' Bastiano said. He was in no mood to smile at one of her jokes, yet he almost did. 'I had them put in.'

It was such a far cry from anything she was used to.

Oh, it might once have been a place for deep contemplation and it would serve as the same now, only with a bed that looked like a cloud and a bathroom so huge that she might need a map to locate the exit.

'Do you want to eat with me?' He offered her a choice.

'No.'

'Then I shall have Karmela bring you supper and come and unpack your things.'

'I think I can manage that,' Sophie said. 'There's not much.'

'We'll sort that out soon.'

'I don't want you dressing me.'

'Fine.' Bastiano shrugged. 'Is there anything you need?'

'No.' Sophie shook her head and then, when she guessed he might feel it was his job to entertain her, she gave a tight smile. 'I might just have a bath and go to sleep.' There was, though, one question that she had for him. 'How did you find out,' Sophie asked, 'about the baby?'

'I told you, I found out you had come here looking for work.' He omitted to mention the frantic feeling that had prompted him to call Alim.

'I wanted something that was live-in.'

'How did your parents take it?'

'As I expected them to. We haven't spoken for a long time but last week they asked me over for dinner...'

'That's good.'

'Not really. The priest was there to tell me about a lovely couple who would give my baby everything that I couldn't.'

He didn't need to guess what her response had been.

'I'm tired, Bastiano.' She really was. Yes, tonight she was supposed to have been working, but now she felt as if she had been unplugged from a fading battery and her energy had simply run out. 'Can this wait until morning?'

'Of course.'

To show Sophie how it all worked, he clicked on the intercom and was put straight through to Karmela.

'Could you send a light supper to the guest room?' he asked.

'Of course,' came the response. 'Anything else?'

'I'll just check.' He looked at Sophie, who shook her head. 'That will be all.'

'She'll be over soon,' he told Sophie.

'Thanks.'

'We can speak tomorrow night.'

'Tomorrow night?'

'I have to work. I lost a day today.'

'Sorry about that.'

Her sarcasm was wasted, for he had already gone.

It wasn't just Sophie who needed to be alone.

Bastiano too wanted to process the events of today. As soon as he had found out about the baby he had jumped in his car. The usual three-hour trip had taken two and he had been more focused on the practical—getting her out of the hell hole where she had lived and, yes, putting things right as speedily as could be arranged.

He poured a drink and lay on the bed, trying to wrap his head around the fact that he would soon be a father.

And that, had he not found out for himself, he might never have known.

He heard a car pull up outside and guessed that Sophie's supper was there.

Bastiano had no appetite.

A baby!

He had never considered fatherhood. When he had vaguely considered taking a wife his thought process had halted there.

In fact, he had heard a few weeks ago that Raul and Lydia were expecting and had silently thanked his lucky stars for the escape.

Bastiano lay there brooding for an hour at least, watching his bachelor life disappear before his eyes.

A knock on the door had him look up and there stood Sophie, her hair wet from a bath or shower and wrapped in a guest robe.

'Did you pack my pyjamas?'

'I packed everything that was there.'

'No, my pyjamas were under the pillow.'

'Well, I didn't go looking under your pillow! Who the hell wears pyjamas anyway?'

'I shared a bathroom with Pino,' Sophie said.

'Fair enough.' He nodded to his wardrobe. 'Take a shirt if you want one, though I've got my own bathroom and I shan't be peeping through the door.'

She smiled.

And not for the first time today.

But, then, that was what she did. Even in the middle of a row, there were some smiles.

And he returned it.

'I meant a clean one,' Bastiano said as she picked up his shirt from the floor.

'This will be fine. I hate starch.' And then she asked him something. 'It's your birthday?'

'How do you know?'

'Karmela said something when she brought my meal. You should have said.' Sophie gave a sweet smile. 'I'd have sent you flowers. But then again it might have given a mixed message.'

'Ha-ha,' Bastiano said, but as she walked off he had a parting shot. 'There will be no mixed messages from me.'

Good, Sophie thought, because sex was the last thing she needed to complicate things.

'Buon Compleanno.' Sophie shrugged and turned for the door, but it was Bastiano who had the last word.

'I still want you.'

No, he didn't deal in mixed messages.

To his own surprise, Bastiano's desire for her remained.

CHAPTER FOURTEEN

SOPHIE HAD NO excuse for not sleeping well.

The supper had been delicious, her bath relaxing and the bed, when she had finally lain down on it, had felt like a cloud.

It was Bastiano who had unnerved her, though in the nicest of ways.

It had never entered her head that this far into pregnancy, and with so much to sort out, there would be such fierce attraction between them.

Sophie swung her feet to the floor and instead of cheap lino she felt the warmth of a thick rug. His home was so warm that there was no need to pull on a robe.

It was early, just before six, and she decided to go and get some milk and bring it back to bed.

She didn't expect to find him in the kitchen, dressed only in trousers and waiting for the percolator to fill.

'I thought you'd have your coffee brought to you in bed.'

'Not when I am here,' Bastiano said. 'I hate conversation in the morning.'

Sophie helped herself to some milk.

'How much prenatal care have you had?'

Always he surprised her. Sophie hadn't thought it the type of question he would ask so casually.

'I thought you didn't like conversation in the morning?'

'Some things have to be checked.'

'Not much,' she admitted.

'We have a doctor that visits daily. I'll get him to call in on you, though I think you should have the baby in Rome.'

'Rome?' Sophie gave an incredulous smile at his suggestion. 'Isn't there a hospital here?'

'Yes but you're not having the baby in Casta.' Bastiano shook his head.

'*I'll* decide where I'm having my baby.'

'*Our* baby,' he countered, but then he halted. He did not want to descend into a row but there was no way she was having the baby here. 'I'll have the doctor visit.'

'Well, let me know when,' Sophie said. 'I want to go into Casta. I need a few things for me as well as the baby. I was thinking of going to the market today.'

'In Casta?' He gave her an appalled look but Sophie just shrugged.

'You're turning into a snob, Bastiano.'

'I turned into one long ago,' Bastiano said. 'You are not dressing my baby from the Casta market. We'll speak tonight.'

He really didn't like conversation in the morning, Sophie thought, because without another word he took his cup and left her alone in the huge kitchen. Sophie headed back to bed and lay there watching the morning arrive over the ocean.

Yesterday's rain had gone, revealing a mild Sicilian winter's day.

Her favourite kind.

It didn't matter that she had hardly anything to wear because the morning was spent wrapped in a thick white robe.

The doctor came and he put her at ease straight away.

'It is busy over there!' He gave an eye-roll in the direction of the main building as he examined her. 'It is nice to have a straightforward pregnancy to take care of.'

'It doesn't feel very straightforward.'

'There is one baby, a healthy mother and a nice-sized baby. That's good news to me.'

She was thrilled to find out that the baby was a good size given her meals had been somewhat sparse.

'What do you deal with over there?' Sophie asked as he took blood to test. Since Karmela had mentioned a confidentiality clause, she had been dying to know what went on over at the Old Convent, but the doctor wasn't about to reveal anything.

'That would be telling tales. Believe me, young Sophie, you don't want to know.'

'But I do.'

After he had taken some blood, they discussed her having an ultrasound.

'Bastiano asked me to refer you to a colleague in Rome.'

'I haven't decided where I'm having the baby yet.'

'Well, without stating the obvious, I suggest you both work it out because babies keep to their own schedules. You could go into labour tonight and then the choice will be out of both your hands.' He gave her a lovely smile. 'Don't worry if you do, though, I've delivered a lot of babies.'

'It would be you who would deliver me?'

'It would be my privilege to.'

Sophie liked him.

He had salt-and-pepper hair and was patient with her endless questions; he didn't make her feel stupid or small.

And he was the first person who seemed genuinely pleased about the baby.

The rest of the morning was spent being pummelled by the resident masseuses, after which she sat on a lounger by the pool, so warm in her robe it was no surprise that she dozed off.

'Hey.'

She woke to his voice and looked up to a suited Bastiano.

'Is there no such thing as privacy?' Sophie asked.

'Privacy is not going to get us very far,' Bastiano said. 'I'm not going to be back until late tonight; work has piled up. What did the doctor say?'

'That everything is going very well.'

'What else?'

'He took some blood.'

'And?'

Sophie knew exactly what he was there for. Bastiano wanted to ensure that his instructions had been carried out.

Well, two could play at that game.

'He said that I am to go for an ultrasound in Casta tomorrow and that he would be thrilled to deliver me.'

She was surprised that he laughed.

So was he.

'You are such a liar.' Bastiano said.

He idly picked up the tie of her robe and as he did, the back of his hand brushed the baby bump beneath and then he turned so that his palm rested on the thick fabric.

'Sophie, please don't have the baby here. I couldn't stand it if anything went wrong.' He could feel the swell beneath his palm and then he looked up at Sophie and knew he simply could not bear it if something happened to either of them. 'If I can wrap things up here we can move into a hotel for a few weeks. Get married there...'

'In a hotel?'

'It's just a formality.' Even Bastiano knew he had said the wrong thing and he cursed himself as she removed his hand. The closeness that had almost appeared slipped back like the tide. 'Okay, we can get married in a church, I'm sure there are a few to choose from in Rome! I just don't want it to be born a bastard.'

'It's the twenty-first—'

'I'm aware of the century,' Bastiano interrupted. 'I want us married before the baby arrives.'

'I don't want to marry you,' Sophie said. 'I don't want a husband who doesn't love me.'

And she loathed that she fished, that she actually threw him a line, one that she hoped would see him pull her into his arms and tell her that of course that wasn't the case.

But Bastiano had long ago decided that his love was a dangerous gift and so he was rather caustic in his reply. 'It stopped being about you when you forgot to take your Pill.'

'Why couldn't I get pregnant by some bastard who just wrote me a cheque?'

'Do you really see us co-parenting, Sophie?' he asked. 'Do you think I am going to smile and nod at your new lover when I pick my child up for an access visit?'

'You could try.'

'If you wanted that then you should have found some new-age guy. I'm traditional. I'm Sicilian, for goodness' sake!'

'I want our child to grow up in a loving—'

'I can be loving.'

'I'm not talking about sex,' Sophie said.

Bastiano was.

He wanted to break the embargo and peel off her robe. Quite simply he was certain this was a dispute best settled in bed.

It was black-and-white to him.

'I want more from marriage,' Sophie said. 'I ran away because it wasn't love…'

'You ran away from a man who relied on your mother to cook for him,' Bastiano said, 'and now you have to settle for a virile billionaire. Boo-hoo.'

He stood and she lay there staring out at the ocean rather than look at him.

They were getting nowhere, Bastiano knew.

He had tried reason, he had tried religion, now he decided it was time to fall back on ways of old.

'How about we go out for dinner tonight?'

'I thought you had work.'

'I'll cancel it. We're going to go out tonight.'

'Are you asking me or telling me?' Sophie checked, and she saw the tightening of his jaw.

She was acting like a sulking princess, Sophie knew.

'We never did have our night out.'

'No,' Sophie said, 'I was too busy stealing your ring…'

'Sophie…' He halted but then he pushed himself to speak on. 'I know you didn't steal it.'

'Do you, now? And how's that?' She desperately wanted him to reply that it was because he knew she would never do that kind of thing. But he didn't.

'We'll speak tonight at dinner. I have a lot of work to get through but I should be through by five so be ready.'

'Five?' Sophie frowned. 'So early?'

'If I could have my PA reschedule the sun I would,' Bastiano said.

'Meaning?'

'I'll see you at five,' he told her. 'And please,' he added, 'do not buy anything from the market to wear! Your regular rags will do!'

He left her smiling.

In her worst mood, somehow he had made her smile.

And, he made her skin prickle.

Oh, the attraction had not faded for her, not a fraction, yet surely it must have for him.

It didn't feel as though it had.

A car drove her down the hill and it was indeed market day, for Casta was busy and it was nice to wander around.

There were signposts for the infirmary, where Bastiano was adamant that their baby would not be born. She passed a school and smiled at the sound of children's laughter.

There was the old courthouse, where Bastiano had told her Maria's will had been read.

It really was gorgeous, with an old hotel that had seen better days and a street lined with shops and cafés.

And it was exciting too because there were a couple of famous faces behind dark glasses in the café that Sophie went into, no doubt on day release from the Old Convent.

The owner greeted her warmly. 'Passing through?'

'No, I'm staying at the Old Convent.' Sophie smiled.

'Ah, a guest of Signor Conti.' The owner smiled. 'Then we need to find you a nice seat.'

He called to a waitress and she was guided to a table near the back. 'For you,' the owner said, and he brought her a large glass of hot blackcurrant without Sophie even looking at the menu. 'It is our house special and good for you,' he told her. 'And don't worry, no one will trouble you here, we'll keep an eye open.'

It took a moment or two to register that they thought she must be a *client*.

Bastiano really had done wonders, Sophie thought, for, unlike home, the town was a buzzing and happy place to be.

Sophie headed over to the church that had caught her eye when she had first passed through town.

It must be here that he had fought with Raul, Sophie guessed, and she slipped around the back to the graveyard and read the inscriptions on the tombstones.

Gino Di Savo.

Raul's father, Sophie knew, and saw that he had died some ten years ago.

Next to him lay Maria, and Sophie wondered about the mind of a woman who would seduce a seventeen-year-old.

And then she turned and Sophie found what she was looking for. There she found out Bastiano's mother's name.

Philomena Conti.

Sophie felt her nostrils tighten when she saw the simple grave.

And then she saw the date of her death and Sophie did not even try to hold back the tears.

Philomena had died on the day that Bastiano was born.

Had Karmela not let on that it was his birthday yesterday, she might never have known. She understood the man a little more, and he was kinder than even she had given him credit for—even in their rows about their baby he had not scared her by telling her that his mother had died giving birth.

It was a sobering thought indeed.

And it was time, Sophie knew, to stop fighting.

She did have something to wear.

One thing.

Sophie stood in the little silver knickers she had purchased on the day Rosa had persuaded her try on the dress.

The over-dress she could not even get over her bust, but the silver-grey underdress slid on.

It clung to every curve, yet somehow it revealed little, for it fell to just on her knee and there was barely even a glimpse of cleavage.

It was incredibly seductive, though.

For the first time in months Sophie added heels and though she had very little make-up to work with, she melted her mascara under a hot tap in order to reach the last dregs and used a pen to dig out some lipstick.

Soon she saw his car approaching and Sophie was suddenly nervous. She felt overdressed for Casta and the small restaurants there.

Hell, she felt overdressed for five o'clock in Rome.

'Sophie!' Bastiano called out.

He wondered if she'd plead a headache to avoid dinner, but instead she stepped out confidently.

Bastiano had thought her like the sun on the day they'd met.

Now a silver star emerged before the sky had even darkened.

Her dress clung tightly to the baby they had made and her legs seemed too fragile.

'Where are we going?' Sophie asked when he bypassed the car.

'We're walking.'

Along the cobbled path on very high heels there was little choice but to take his arm.

It was nice to walk.

'Am I overdressed?' she asked as they approached the convent.

'Perhaps,' he said, 'but only because I prefer you in nothing.'

It was nice to flirt, but as they headed towards the restaurant nerves caught up.

'Will there be a lot of people?'

'I have twenty guests in residence,' Bastiano said as they walked in. 'And on my instruction, all are dining in their rooms tonight.'

Oh, it was heaven.

The tables were all candlelit and each candle had been lit for her. Even the stone walls were softened with thick white pillar candles but Bastiano steered her to the balcony. It had been dressed with care and a single table had been set up just for them.

'It is cool,' Bastiano said, 'even with heaters...'

'You're not eight months pregnant,' Sophie countered as she took a seat. 'I've forgotten what it is to be cool.'

'There's no wine list,' Bastiano said as he ordered bitter lemon for them both. 'My regular guests have no restraint.'

He made her laugh.

And then he made her want to cry.

'I owe you an apology,' Bastiano said, and he was suddenly serious. 'I was wrong to accuse you of taking my ring. I overreacted that morning. It was my mother's ring, it meant everything to me, and I had only just got it back from Raul.'

'From Raul?' Sophie frowned. 'Why did he have it?'

'I gave it to Maria.' He felt uncomfortable admitting it. 'She was wearing it when she died and all her jewellery was left to Raul. I don't think he even knew it was mine.'

'How did he find out?'

'When he asked for Lydia's address I said I would only give it to him if he returned the ring.'

Now she better understood his reaction that morning. It must have been hell to get it back, only to lose it.

'It was Inga who put the ring in your uniform.'

'Inga?' Sophie frowned. 'Did she confess?'

'Please,' Bastiano sneered, 'she has no conscience, she was still blaming you as they escorted her out.'

And he told her how Inga had shouted and sworn as she'd been walked out, remembering Sophie's quiet dignity in the same situation.

'I had Dario and Benita go over the CCTV footage. Inga must have...' He hesitated. He didn't want to embarrass her because he had realised that Inga would have heard them making love so he softened it a touch. 'She would have seen your uniform on the floor.'

It *was* cool outside; despite the heaters there was a chill from the ocean but the air suddenly seemed to blow warm on her skin as she recalled that morning and met his eyes.

'Do you think she heard us?'

'Who cares?'

'I do,' Sophie said, completely appalled. 'Though I shouldn't—she sleeps with guests.'

'That's shocking.' Bastiano pretended to shudder and then laughed. 'Thank God for the Ingas of the world.'

'You're terrible, Bastiano!'

'Oh, indeed I was.'

And instead of being cross, Sophie smiled and then she laughed because her name had been cleared, and it was the best feeling in the world.

Or amongst the best of feelings, because he was looking at her in that way again, a way that made her feel warm, a way that made the tiredness disappear and her body feel sensual and alive.

A waiter came out with a loaf of *mafalda*, which they tore and dipped in oil.

'The Contis and the Di Savos should have focused on making oil rather than feuding over wine,' Bastiano told her as they dipped their bread. 'They would have made their fortune.'

'The Contis and the Di Savos need to stop feuding, period,' Sophie said, referring to him and Raul.

'I agree.'

He was tired of it.

'Lydia is expecting too,' Bastiano told her.

'Your *almost* wife.'

She looked at him and knew that unrequited love was such a curse.

'The bread is fantastic,' Sophie said, to change the subject. She wondered if this would be her life, moving from topics to avoid hurt. Discussing the weather and the food on the table, rather than the hole he had shot through her heart.

'You can't get better than here,' Bastiano responded.

'Not true,' Sophie said. 'The chef at the Grande Lucia made the best…'

'Can I tell you something?' Bastiano said, and leant closer. She met his eyes and she knew she was in the path of a seducer, for his mouth had that smile and his eyes made her burn, and instead of fighting him Sophie let herself be played, for there were worse things she could think of than being seduced by Bastiano.

'Tell me,' she said, and tore another strip of bread.

'I stole the chef from the Grande Lucia. He is the one cooking for us tonight.'

'You stole Alim's chef?' She started to laugh.

A real laugh, because so skilled was she that at times she forgot his game.

'Of course. When I withdrew my offer I had my PA contact your chef with an offer he could not refuse. Now, instead of feeding the hordes in Rome, he has a maximum guest list of twenty-two to cater for. Staff too...'

'Your staff get meals?'

'Of course.'

'Five-star meals?' Sophie asked, as in front of her was placed a dish of *busciate*, Sicily's finest pasta dressed in a light almond sauce.

'Everyone deserves to be looked after,' Bastiano said. 'Not just the guests. That is why my retreats work so well.'

'It's amazing,' Sophie said. 'You should be very proud.'

'I am,' Bastiano said. 'People accuse me of bulldozing treasures but that is because I don't allow the interiors to be photographed—I don't need the publicity. The retreats I offer are for the guests to enjoy.'

And tonight that pleasure was exclusive to Sophie.

Tiny lights started to dance as dusk fell and she found out what he had meant about not being able to reschedule the sun, for it had turned to fire and was mirrored in the ocean.

'Dance?' Bastiano said as soft music came on.

It had been months since they had been in each other's arms, and so much had changed, yet they melded together like they had never been apart. Sophie wrapped her arms around his neck, swaying in his arms.

He looked right into her eyes and then she closed her eyes to his kiss.

She had forgotten the taste of perfection.

How with that mouth he made magic.

How the heat from his palm in the small of her back made her fingers press into the back of his head. And how the feel of him aroused her and could make her forget her cares.

She felt feverish, being held by him, dancing with him, being seduced by him.

His kiss was perfection.

It made her crave him and it made her feel weak.

'Why do you resist us?' Bastiano asked.

In his arms, she didn't know the answer to that.

'Come on,' he told her. 'I'm taking you home.'

CHAPTER FIFTEEN

THEY WALKED IN the dark but the moon was bright and the stars lit the night. They held hands as if they had been lovers for life.

'I love it here,' she said, because it was far safer than saying 'I love you'. She kept things light, determined not to reveal the ache in her heart. 'I went to one of the cafés in town and they thought I was one of your clients,' Sophie admitted, and she started to laugh. 'I'm trying to work out what they thought I was in rehab for.'

'They would have thought you were the partner of an errant actor,' Bastiano said. 'We sometimes have wives and girlfriends take a little holiday while their husbands straighten out.'

'Really?' she asked, as they reached the door and he gave her a light kiss, but one that made her toes curl.

'Really.'

'Who?'

'I can't tell you that,' Bastiano said.

They were stood at the door and she could hear the waves, and she knew that this was the moment.

'At least not until you marry me.'

Bastiano did it by the book.

Well, he didn't go down on bended knee but he took

out a black box and her throat was tight as he opened the clasp.

And there it was.

The proof that he did not love her.

Oh, the ring was stunning.

A diamond so huge that if she reached out and plucked a star from the sky it would surely sparkle just as brightly.

And in that moment she knew she would never matter to him the way she wanted to, because it wasn't the ring that meant everything to him.

'Isn't there something missing here, Bastiano?'

He knew exactly what she was referring to.

'Do you know why people think I'm such a bastard?' he said, and when she didn't answer he told her. 'Because I don't say things that other people want to hear.'

It was a terrible proposal because a big salty tear fell to her cheek. 'Sometimes it's kinder to lie,' she said.

'Not in this.'

If they were going to be honest, she would tell him how much this hurt. 'You gave Maria your mother's ring.'

'And look how that ended up!' He did not understand that she would choose his mother's cursed ring over the diamond he had selected with such care. 'I threw away the old ring,' Bastiano told her. 'It was bad news.'

And he was so cold, Sophie thought, that he could dispose of the thing most valuable to his heart.

Where the hell would that leave her and their child? But then he told her something, something honest and true.

'I will do everything to make our marriage work. I will read every book so that I can be the best father I can possibly be…' Yet still he saw tears. 'Sophie…' He told her the real truth. 'Believe me, you don't want my love.'

With a sob, she brushed past him and rushed straight to her room.

Believe me, she wanted to shout out, *I do*.

Instead, she stood with heart hammering and a body still alive from his touch and his kiss, loathing this one-sided love while knowing it was time to step up.

Of course they would marry.

Bastiano would be a wonderful father and even without his love it could be a wonderful marriage too, for she knew he cared for her.

He had proved it today, for even when arguing he looked out for her—not once had he hinted that his mother had died giving birth.

Bastiano was kinder and fairer than he knew and she knew she loved him.

And there was desire.

Such desire.

So she was stuck with the virile billionaire.

Boo-hoo!

Even with a heart breaking, just the thought of him made her smile. She wanted a slice of that dark, guarded heart, even if it could never be hers to own entirely. Sophie was starting to understand that there was a side to Bastiano she would never be allowed to know.

That privilege had been Maria's and she was through trying to compete with a ghost.

All she could be was herself.

And she would make her own rules.

She kicked off her shoes because they hurt, but it meant that her approach to his room was silent.

Bastiano lay on the bed with his hands behind his head, just as she had first found him, only he was dressed and sulking now.

'If we marry,' Sophie said, and Bastiano looked over to

where she stood at the door, 'it is to be here. If our child is going to be raised in Casta then I want to be married in the church. It is more than a formality to me.'

'Sophie…'

'Let me finish. If we are to marry then there is to be compromise. We can fly out straight after the service. I know it will take a couple of weeks to arrange…'

'I'll sort it,' Bastiano said.

He would.

'You just need a dress and to turn up.'

They would be married in the next forty-eight hours if it meant they could get the hell out of Casta and to the shiny equipment and slick obstetrician he had planned.

'I'll move out tomorrow,' he told her.

'Move out?' Sophie gave a laugh. 'It's a bit late for that.'

'In that case, come here.'

And there was a burn in his eyes that made her both excited and nervous at the same time. 'Should we wait for the wedding?'

'Do I look like Luigi?' he asked.

'No.' Sophie smiled and came over.

She sat down on the bed, as she had on the morning they had met. His hand found hers and then he felt the ripe swell of her stomach.

He could feel the kicks their baby gave and it was both mind-blowing and then calming because while inside her their baby was safe.

'I'm going to take such good care of you both.'

His voice was husky and thick with emotion and even if it wasn't love she knew his words came from the heart.

'I know that.'

Just as she had on that very first day, she leant over only this time she went straight for his mouth.

It was a deep and sensual kiss but an unhurried one, and he guided her so that she sat on his stomach.

'Back again,' he told her.

Only now there was a baby between them and a wedding to arrange. It was both the saddest and happiest night of her life.

Sophie could see the glint of her ring as she undid his tie and opened his shirt. She bent her head and they kissed long and slow, his hands sliding over the silver dress.

'I found out I was pregnant on the day I got this,' she said as he found the tiny, invisible zipper she had failed to spot when she had first tried it on.

He slid the zipper down and then pulled the dress up and over her head. Her breasts were full and encased in lace, and he stroked them through the fabric, then tipped her forward so he could taste with his mouth.

His fingers unclipped it and with it hanging on her arms his mouth met her flesh. It was the touch of a tongue that could make her weep and the nip of teeth that could have her beg.

So wanting was she that her sex was on his hands as he dealt with his belt and zipper and then there was the giddy bliss of him guiding her on.

'You and me,' he said, but did not finish.

Not because he did not want to say things at night that would fade with the dawn but because his love, Bastiano was sure, was a toxic curse.

But when they were together, life seemed to work.

And right now they were together.

Sophie could feel the gentle guidance of his hands as he held her hips and the dig of his fingers in her buttocks as he fought to hold back.

Her thighs gripped him and she ground down, causing a shiver to run through her body, but it felt like fire as she met his eyes.

He thrust up into her softly engorged grip and she leant her hands on his chest. Now there was nothing to hold back, for he knew of her love and so she cried his name when she came.

And he moved her then at whim and shot high into her.

It was deeply intimate and the most intense climax of his life, laced as it was with her name.

They lay there afterwards with his hand on her stomach and she felt it roam across her bump.

'It's asleep,' she told him, and soon so was she.

In the deep of night the baby awoke.

Sophie didn't notice.

Bastiano did.

He felt the wave of movement beneath his palm and then an unmistakable kick and he knew he was holding the future.

Not just the baby's but Sophie's too.

And he would do all he could to give his baby's mother the wedding she deserved.

CHAPTER SIXTEEN

'*BUONGIORNO, SIGNOR.*'

Bastiano did not answer the cheery greeting.

The best room in the best hotel in Casta was nowhere close to the twelfth floor at the Grande Lucia. The maid ignored the flick of his wrist to dismiss her and instead set about opening the drapes.

'It's a beautiful day to get married,' she told him.

Thank goodness it was today!

Bastiano had been away from the Old Convent for two nights and he itched to get back.

Not literally.

The Casta Hotel wasn't that bad!

He missed home.

Only that wasn't right, because as soon as the wedding was over they were flying to Rome and he was looking forward to that.

It was being so close to the street that irked, Bastiano decided.

Bastiano had never missed anyone in his life, so he had not worked out yet that he simply missed his future bride.

The pall that had hung over him for months was back and surely it was not how a groom should feel on his wedding day.

A trophy wife would be easier, Bastiano thought as

he showered in less than sumptuous surroundings. Yes, a nice trophy wife would have demanded a high-class wedding instead of the local church.

He pulled on black jeans and a jumper but found that he was grinning as he wondered how Sultan Alim and Gabi were faring down the hall.

Certainly this was no palace.

Though he had agreed to a low-key wedding, Bastiano had decided that Sophie deserved more than the basics.

Her family would be there but so to would Gabi and Alim.

And it would seem the entire valley would join them too.

Word was out and the joy at the upcoming nuptials was genuine.

As well as that, a couple of A-list guests at the Convent had applied for day leave.

It was turning into the wedding of the year and Sophie had no clue.

He took a walk down to the baker's rather than think about why he was doing all this for her.

The church was dressed for the occasion with flowers and ribbons and, out of sentiment more than habit, Bastiano walked around the side to the cemetery.

Even if it was just a formality, it was, after all, his wedding day.

But as he turned the corner a man looked over and Bastiano felt his hackles rise.

Raul Di Savo.

Here, after all that had passed between them.

But this time Raul did not leap across tombstones to attack him; instead, he stood stock-still as this time it was Bastiano who made his way over.

'I'm guessing that you're not here for the wedding.'

'No, I only just heard about that.' Raul gave a tight smile. 'Today is my mother's birthday.'

'Oh,' Bastiano said, and his first thought was that Sophie might freak if she found out he had arranged that they marry on Maria's birthday.

Bastiano hadn't known, though.

He looked at the tombstone, just as he had many times, and sure enough Maria's birthdate was etched there.

'I hear you are soon to be a father,' Bastiano said, and Raul nodded.

'Lydia is back in Venice. She's due in a few weeks.'

'Sophie too.'

Bastiano turned and walked away and stood for a moment at his own mother's grave.

There was no peace to be had here.

Had she even known she had a son?

Today it mattered, because a few weeks from now he would have a child of his own and there was a sudden need to put things right, to end feuds of old. He could hear the crunch of gravel as Raul walked off, and then the more rapid crunch of his own footsteps as this time it was Bastiano who strode towards him.

'Raul!' he called out, and watched Raul's shoulders stiffen before he turned around.

'Why did you refuse to hear my side?' He stared at the man who had once been a friend. 'Was it because I wasn't family?'

For a moment Bastiano thought history was about to repeat itself, that he would again meet Raul's fist, and he had a brief vision of trying to explain why he had chosen today, of all days, to confront his nemesis…

Except there would be no fighting today.

'Not here,' Raul said. Together, they walked up the hill

and sat on the ground outside the convent, where as boys and young men they had wasted many days.

They sat at first in silence, but it was Raul who finally spoke. 'I didn't *want* to hear your side. It was easier to blame you…'

'I guess,' Bastiano said. He had learned from the cradle that family came first.

'I always covered for her.'

Now the trees rustled, now the bird song seemed to fade as Bastiano learned there had been others.

Many others.

And beneath his feet the earth seemed to shift and then resettle as he chased the thoughts around his mind.

'I know now you didn't go there to seduce her,' Raul said. 'I just wasn't ready to hear it at the time.' And then he looked Bastiano right in the eyes. 'I apologise. When I found out she had taken your ring…'

Bastiano was about to correct him, to say that she hadn't taken it, he had given it to her, but that had been a trick of his mind. A trick Maria had played well.

'If you love me you would want me to have nice things.'

It hadn't been love.

Maria had told him that it was, and with nothing with which to compare it, he'd believed her.

'My mother had many lovers. I don't even know if Gino was my father,' Raul admitted. 'He married her just because she was pregnant…'

'He did the right thing at least.'

'No.' Raul shook his head. 'He resented the hell out of us. No one should marry because…' He halted, perhaps unsure of Bastiano's circumstances.

'I love Sophie.'

He knew he should have told her first, but he had only just realised it himself.

Love *did* make you smile.

Because on the morning of his wedding, as he reshuffled the truths of his past, just the thought of her was a comfort. It was Sophie he missed, Bastiano knew, not the walls of home.

'I'm sorry,' Raul apologised again. 'I wasn't insinuating that you didn't love. I was just saying how things sometimes—'

'No,' Bastiano broke in. 'You're right. I haven't told Sophie.' He looked over to the Old Convent and thought of her preparing for her wedding and not knowing how he felt. 'In fact,' he told Raul, 'I told her that I never could love her.'

'Then you need to call her now.'

'Merda!' Bastiano said as he tossed his phone, and they might have been teenagers again, for Bastiano had his foot in Raul's hands and was trying to get a leg up to scale a wall, but there was glass and wire at the top—his security was good enough to keep out even the hungriest press. He had to get to Sophie.

'You need to get changed,' Raul said, when Bastiano had no choice but to give in. 'You get married soon.'

To a bride who didn't know he loved her.

CHAPTER SEVENTEEN

BASTARD!

Sophie sat in the back of the bridal car with her father and watched as the priest signalled for them to go around.

He was late for his own wedding!!

Perhaps that was why he had been calling, Sophie thought, trying to fight the tears that were threatening.

To call things off.

She took a deep breath as the car slowly drove up the hill and she wasn't sure if it was the tightening in her stomach that made her gasp or the sight of a very dishevelled groom running towards the church with, Sophie was sure, his nemesis beside him.

The priest was now all smiles since the groom had arrived. But as she stepped out another pain hit.

Thankfully both her father and the priest thought it was nerves and that she was merely composing herself when she reached the church door and stood silent for a moment.

The church was full, that was all she saw.

And she was in labour.

If Bastiano could be late for his own wedding Sophie was quite sure he would be only too willing to call the whole thing off if he knew.

And she wanted to be married now, before the baby arrived.

Which meant she just had to grin and bear it!

The pains weren't too bad, and they were ages apart; first babies took a long time, the doctor had told her.

So she walked down the aisle, and blinked as a very famous actress gave her an encouraging smile, and a rap artist too.

What was going on?

And there was Gabi and Alim, and her heart was on fire as she walked towards the man she loved and always would.

She let in the sun, Bastiano thought as she walked towards him.

Here, in this church, where there had been so much darkness and pain, it was awash with colours and smiles.

It was way too late for white, so her dress was cream, with pale mint-green edging, just like the tiny roses she wore in her hair.

She had chosen her dress and flowers as if all this time he had loved her and wooed her.

And so badly he did love her.

And when he said his vows they were heartfelt and right, and Bastiano knew he could never have made it with a trophy wife, for it would have been over with by now.

'I will love you all the days of my life,' he told her, and he stared deep into her eyes, but Sophie's were slightly narrowed with suspicion.

'I really do love you,' he whispered, as he slid the ring on her finger.

Please, don't lie, Sophie thought, for his words sounded heartfelt and she couldn't bear the illusion, not on her wedding day. Her words were the same, though she paused midway as a pain hit and he gripped her fingers tight.

Bastiano knew.

He had seen her standing at the entrance and had read the pain behind her smile. His instinct had been to call off the wedding, but he knew how important it was to her.

'Perhaps,' he said in a low voice to the priest, 'we can do the shorter form…'

It was indeed a quick service and the bells rang out in Casta as the bride and groom emerged.

The past was gone, Bastiano knew.

Almost.

He looked over to the cemetery where his mother lay and he wanted them out of the valley now and into the waiting helicopter.

There would be no cake for the bride and groom.

'Look!' Gabi was holding up a ring. 'Look what I found in the gravel!'

Was it a sign?

His mother's blessing?

Sophie certainly seemed to think so for she slipped the ring on her finger, and though he smiled and shook hands with the guests, Bastiano felt as if he had been drenched in ice.

'We'll go to the chopper,' he told her, but Sophie shook her head.

'I don't think there's time.'

'Sophie…' Fear clutched at his heart and all he could see was that damn ring on her finger, not the wedding band or the engagement ring he had given her but the one that meant death.

'Why don't you go to the infirmary and let them check her?' Gabi suggested. She was used to drama at weddings and keeping things under control. 'If they say there is time to transfer then you can go from there.'

'Good luck,' Raul said, and shook his hand. 'You deserve it.'

A car drove them through the valley and the short distance to the infirmary but Sophie had plenty of questions on the way.

'You were late.'

'I was trying to get to you.'

'How come Raul was your best man?'

Oh, how she wanted to know, but there was so much pain she gripped his hand tight and knew the world was going to have to wait.

The scent of the hospital made him feel ill.

They walked through the maternity unit and past the nursery where babies cried and to a very small delivery suite where it seemed a cast of thousands was gathered.

Well, actually, there were four, Bastiano counted, but he was not about to say what he had to with this audience present.

'Could I speak to my wife alone, please?'

'I'm having our baby here,' Sophie shouted, because she was so pleased to see her salt and pepper doctor and his kind smile. 'I don't want to go to Rome!'

'Signor...' A midwife who introduced herself as Stella asked if she could have a word outside.

She was elderly and kind as she told him there was no question that Sophie be transferred.

'She is soon to have the baby,' Stella said. 'Your wife is ready to push. You need to stay calm for Sophie.'

'I am calm,' he told her.

Bastiano was.

No one knew him.

No one really could.

For he had never allowed anyone to get close. It was a strange and unfamiliar sensation to want to draw Sophie close now.

Bastiano had accepted back in the car that their baby would soon be here and he was not about to add to the drama.

The midwife seemed to think otherwise.

'Bastiano,' Stella said, 'I was here when you were born and so I understand why you are worried for Sophie, but there isn't time to transfer her now...'

'There is time for me to speak with my wife alone, though?'

'For a moment, yes.'

'A moment is all I need.'

Sophie watched as he walked in and the doctors and nurses were called out and then Bastiano closed the door.

'I love you,' he told her.

'Bastiano...' she begged. 'Please, don't do this. You loved Maria.'

'No, she told me that I did and I had nothing to compare it to, and so I believed her. You were right, I was seventeen, and I had no idea what love was.

'I love *you*,' he said. 'Like I never have before or ever could another.'

He would never say such a thing to please someone else, Sophie knew that.

And so she knew it was the truth that she heard.

It was love, and she could feel its fierce embrace, a grip stronger than the pain that engulfed her.

Stella's encouragement was needed, for despite Sophie's slender frame it would seem that she grew big babies.

Bastiano's support was needed too, so he looked not at an emerald and seed pearl ring on her finger but deep into her eyes and told Sophie, when she was sure that she couldn't, that, yes, she could, and that with one more push their baby would be here.

'Make that two,' Bastiano said.

Yes, she grew big babies.

With broad shoulders and a long frame.

And Bastiano watched as his son unfurled and was delivered onto Sophie's stomach, his lusty cries filling the room.

'His father was the same.' Stella laughed as their baby refused to settle. 'I used to stay at the end of my shift to give him a cuddle.' She smiled as she helped Sophie to feed her baby and then there was calm.

He was such a beautiful baby, with long lashes and straight black hair, and finally the shock of his early entrance to the world turned to peaceful slumber in his mother's arms.

The hell of the last few months was gone.

'*Complimenti*, Signora Conti,' a domestic said as she brought in a very welcome meal.

'I can't get used to my name.' Sophie laughed as Bastiano held the baby and she ate brioche and drank warm milk laced with nutmeg.

'There are two names you have to get used to,' Bastiano said, gazing at his son. 'Have you decided on his yet?'

'No.'

She had never known such happiness and later in their little room on the maternity ward they watched the sun set over Casta on their wedding day and the birth day of their son.

'Here.'

Bastiano cracked open a bottle and Sophie had her first, long-awaited taste of champagne, smiling when Stella came in to check on them.

'You have had a lot of phone calls,' Stella informed then. 'There is a big party going on in town.'

'What time do you finish?' Bastiano asked.

'Midnight.'

Sophie handed Bastiano their baby, who was now content, and she watched as he placed him in the little Perspex cot.

'I'm tired,' Sophie said.

'Sleep.'

'You'll stay?'

'Of course.'

It was an exhausted sleep that she fell into and it was after midnight when she woke and there was a frantic moment because neither her baby nor Bastiano was there.

Sophie put on a gown and headed out, past the delivery suite, and she came to the nursery and saw Bastiano sitting there, their baby in his arms, talking with Stella.

She heard a cry from her baby and watched as Stella held out her arms and Bastiano handed him over.

They were talking, deep in conversation, and Stella looked in no rush to go anywhere, despite the fact her shift was over.

Something told Sophie not to approach. For Bastiano to be sitting talking so intently made her certain that Stella was saying something he might just need to hear.

She went back to her room and lay watching the moon drift across the sky and the surf crash onto the rocks. She hoped that there could be some resolution for her husband, for he had made his peace with the past, but there was so much still missing.

'Hey.'

It was a long time before he came back and his face was like marble in the moonlight, his scar vivid, and she could hear the strain in his voice, though he carried on as if everything was normal. 'He is hungry again.'

She fed their not so tiny baby and tried to work out a name for him.

'I can't decide,' Sophie said, when they had nailed it down to the final two. He slept in her arms and made little contented noises, barely murmuring when Bastiano took him and placed him in the cot.

Then he came back to the bed and took her in his arms, breathing in the scent of her hair, and a world that had gone off kilter tipped back to delicious normality again.

'Stella was with my mother when she had me.' He told her of the conversation he had had. 'I always thought she died giving birth but it wasn't until after...'

'So she knew she had had a son?'

She felt him nod and they held each other. 'She chose my name. It means respected man, and that was what she wanted for me, even though she was not married.'

'She chose appropriately,' Sophie said, for Bastiano was very respected in Casta now.

'Apparently, she had a heart attack, her blood pressure kept going up. During the birth she kept calling out for my father...' He was the closest in his life he had ever been to tears, but he fought them, and then he told her the truth he had just learnt. 'He couldn't come, of course, as he had a wife and son. I've just found out that Raul is my brother.'

She peeled herself from his arms and during a conversation where there were no smiles to be had, Sophie found one.

'Half-brother,' she said. 'There is a very important half, for Maria was not your mother.'

'No.' He smiled. 'Certainly not.'

And he told her what he had gleaned, for his mother had cried through the long delivery with the young student midwife.

'She and Gino were dating a little but she wanted to save herself for marriage. Maria decided she wanted Gino and gave him what my mother refused to. Maria got pregnant so he married her, but it would seem he had loved my mother all along. She gave in and slept with him and an affair commenced, but by then he had a wife and a son. He loved her, I think, he gave her this ring…'

'What about you?' Sophie asked. 'Did he love you?'

He let out a long breath. 'He blamed me for her death, and apparently he took one look at me and walked out.'

'Do you think Maria knew?'

'I think she seduced me the same way she seduced my father,' Bastiano said. 'I think I reminded her of him and to get back at her husband for not loving her, she left her money to his son…'

'And look what you did with it,' Sophie said.

For he had fought his way back to respect, and turned ruins into beauty.

They shared a kiss, and there was peace when he lay on the bed beside her. They stayed up to watch the night disappear and light fill the sky.

'Call Raul,' she told him.

'It's too early.'

'I would think this news is thirty-two years late.'

So she lay there and listened to Bastiano as he told Raul the news. That they were more than friends, and even as enemies they had been tied to each other and unable to walk away, for they were brothers.

Which meant there were more questions as they worked their way back into each other's lives.

'Yes,' Bastiano said, 'we have a name.' And he looked over at Sophie as he said his son's name out loud. 'Rafael.'

They had chosen appropriately for it meant God has healed.

He had.

EPILOGUE

THERE WAS NO place nicer for afternoon tea than at the Grande Lucia and Sophie did not have to be asked twice before she said yes.

Lydia and Raul were coming in from Venice and Gabi and Alim were in residence, so what better excuse than to fly to Rome and catch up with friends?

Ronaldo greeted them warmly and Anya waved. What bliss to sink into a leather chair and eat the pretty cakes and to laugh and catch up.

Raul and Lydia had a daughter, Serena, just a few days younger than her cousin Rafael, and little Lucia was a delight, the boss of the babies, they all agreed.

Oh, Sophie loved being back here.

There was a soothing familiarity to the place and she was thrilled that Gabi had persuaded Alim not to sell it.

It was almost a second home.

She looked over at Bastiano, who was holding their son, and to see him laugh at something Raul said made her heart swell.

Yes, Sophie was a thief for she had stolen his heart and she treated it with such tender care, as he did the same for hers in return.

Familia.

Absolutely.

They had been born to love each other, she was certain of that.

'Are you staying?' Gabi asked.

'Of course.' Sophie smiled. 'I just wish they hadn't fired Inga and she could serve me breakfast in bed.'

Oh, that would be perfect, but she could more than live without it.

It was a wonderful catch-up and afternoon tea stretched into dinner, so it was late in the night when Bastiano took Rafael through to the nursery and placed him in his crib while Sophie got ready for bed.

'Sophie,' Bastiano called to her, for she was taking ages and now that the baby was asleep it was time to crack open champagne.

'One moment.'

He poured two glasses and placed hers by the bed. The turndown service had been in and he was just about to get up from bed and open the drapes and shutters for the view when Sophie emerged from the bathroom.

She was wearing her old uniform and her hair was up in a messy bun. She always made him smile.

First she opened the drapes and the shutters and stood a moment to take in the view, and to take in her life, for it was everything she had hoped for and more.

'Get over here,' he told her.

'I'm just preparing the view for you, Signor Conti,' she told him, and turned around and smiled. 'Then I am going to make the bed...with you in it.'

Yes, the words were out, and she had let them out, and they were how she felt.

They loved each other so.

* * * * *

*If you enjoyed this final instalment of
Carol Marinelli's*
BILLIONAIRES & ONE-NIGHT HEIRS *trilogy
don't forget to read the first two parts*

*THE INNOCENT'S SECRET BABY
BOUND BY THE SULTAN'S BABY
Available now!*

Alejandro cradled the glass in his palm, a ghost of a smile curving his lips.

"I do care, Cecily. Hence the situation we find ourselves in. I told you that before I knew about the pregnancy. In fact everything I said to you in Kentucky was true, every emotion I expressed real. The only thing I lied about was my identity, and that I had to do."

Her stomach curled with the need to believe him. To believe *something* in all this was true and real—that what they'd shared had been real. But she'd be a fool to take what he was saying at face value—even more of a fool than she'd already been.

He gestured toward the cream sofa that faced the spectacular view. "Why don't we sit down?"

"I'd prefer to stand."

"Fine." He lowered himself onto the chaise, splaying his long legs out in front of him. "We are keeping this baby, Cecily."

"Of course we are. *I* am," she corrected. "I would never do anything else."

"Good. And just to clarify," he drawled, eyes on hers, "when I said *we* are keeping this baby I meant *us*. We are *both* going to be parents to this child, which means we need to be *together*."

She frowned. "What do you mean *together*?"

"I mean we will marry."

Her knees went weak. She slid down onto the sofa, a buzzing sound filling her ears. "You can't be serious."

"Oh, but I am."

*'I'll wager that not one of you can go two weeks
without your credit cards…'*

The Secret Billionaires

*Challenged to go undercover—
but tempted to blow it all!*

Tycoons Antonio Di Marcello,
Stavros Xenakis and Alejandro Salazar
cannot imagine life without their decadent wealth,
incredible power and untouchable status—but
neither can they resist their competitive natures!

Dared to abandon all they know,
these extraordinary men leave behind their
billionaire lifestyles and take on 'ordinary' lives.

But, disguised as a mechanic, a pool boy and a
groom, they're about to meet the *real* challenge…

Conquering the women they'll meet along the way!

Di Marcello's Secret Son by Rachael Thomas
May 2017

Xenakis's Convenient Bride by Dani Collins
June 2017

Salazar's One-Night Heir by Jennifer Hayward
July 2017

SALAZAR'S ONE-NIGHT HEIR

BY
JENNIFER HAYWARD

First Published in Great Britain 2017
By Mills & Boon, an imprint of HarperCollins*Publishers*
1 London Bridge Street, London, SE1 9GF

© 2017 Jennifer Drogell

ISBN: 978-0-263-92528-9

Printed and bound in Spain
by CPI, Barcelona

Jennifer Hayward has been a fan of romance since filching her sister's novels to escape her teenage angst. Her career in journalism and PR, including years of working alongside powerful, charismatic CEOs and travelling the world, has provided perfect fodder for the fast-paced, sexy stories she likes to write—always with a touch of humour. A native of Canada's East Coast, Jennifer lives in Toronto with her Viking husband and young Viking-in-training.

Visit the Author Profile page at millsandboon.co.uk for more titles.

For my husband, Johan,
who helped me find my perfect ending in a book
that stole my heart. You call life with a writer a
'rollercoaster' but I think you secretly like it!

For Melita and Maria—your help with the beautiful
Portuguese language was so very much appreciated.

And for my co-writers Dani Collins and
Rachael Thomas—it was a joy to work together
and create such a fabulous series.
I can't wait for the world to read it!

XX

PROLOGUE

St. Moritz—February 2017

A 1946 MACALLAN, his three closest friends consuming that exceptional bottle of whiskey with him and a game of high-stakes poker played in a private room at one of St. Moritz's swankiest clubs was a trifecta of such absolute perfection, Alejandro Salazar could not deny it was the ideal ending to a day spent paraskiing in the Swiss Alps.

Cutting a vertical line to the cliff's edge, throwing yourself off a mountainside only to hope your parachute landed you in an equally traversable stretch of snow below required some coming down from—quality bonding time that only this particular male ritual could supply.

It had dwindled down to the four of them tonight after today's challenge—Sebastien Atkinson, his good friend and mentor, founder of the extreme sports club they'd joined in college; Antonio Di Marcello, a giant in the global construction industry and Stavros Xenakis, the soon-to-be CEO of Dynami Pharmaceutical—perhaps the only quartet with the spare change to put up the ante this type of a game required.

Not even the trio of delectable Scandinavian women draped across the packed bar, looking for an opportunity to crash their party had been enticement enough to abandon such a rich moment in time. Friendships forged in fire.

Just last year they had pulled Sebastien off a Himalayan mountainside before it had collapsed in a cloud of snow that had nearly killed them all. The ending to this weekend's challenge seemed tame in comparison.

An intense feeling of well-being settling over him, Alejandro sat back in his chair, rested his tumbler on his thigh and considered the table. There was a different air about the celebration tonight—subtle, but distinct.

Perhaps last year's near tragedy still lay too close to the surface. Perhaps it had reminded them all that their club mantra—life is short—was truer than it had ever been. Or maybe it was because Sebastien had gone and done the sacrilegious in getting married, taking the sampling of the popular ski enclave's wares off the table.

Stavros, as if sensing this new playing field, eyed Sebastien across the table. "How's your wife?" he asked with a curl of his lips.

"Better company than you. Why so surly tonight?"

Stavros grimaced. "I haven't won yet." He lifted a shoulder. "And my grandfather is threatening to disinherit me if I don't marry soon. I'd tell him to go to hell, but…"

"Your mother," Alejandro said.

"Exactly."

The Greek billionaire was between a rock and a hard place. If he didn't play the game, extend the Xenakis line with an heir, his grandfather would follow through on his threat to disinherit Stavros before he assumed control of the pharmaceutical empire that would be his.

Stavros would have called his bluff, walked away with pleasure if it weren't for his mother and sisters who would be stripped of everything they possessed if that happened, something Stavros would never allow.

Sebastien pushed a pile of chips toward the center of the table. "Do you ever get the feeling we spend too much of our lives counting our money and chasing superficial thrills at the expense of something more meaningful?"

Antonio tossed a handful of chips at Alejandro. "You called it," his friend muttered, "four drinks and he's already philosophizing."

Sebastien scowled at Stavros as he added his own chips

to Alejandro's pile. The Greek billionaire shrugged. "I said three. My losing streak continues."

"I'm serious." Sebastien eyed the table. "At our level, it's numbers on a page. Points on a scoreboard. What does it contribute to our lives? Money doesn't buy happiness."

"It buys some pretty nice substitutes," Antonio interjected.

Sebastien's mouth twisted. "Like your cars?" he mused, then moved his gaze to Alejandro. "Your private island? You don't even use that boat you're so proud of," he said, moving on to Stavros. "We buy expensive toys and play dangerous games, but does it enrich our lives? Feed our souls?"

"Exactly what are you suggesting?" Alejandro drawled, pushing a pile of chips into the pot. "We go live with the Buddhists in the mountains? Learn the meaning of life? Renounce our worldly possessions to find inner clarity?"

Sebastien made a sound at the back of his throat. "You three couldn't go two weeks without your wealth and family names to support you. Your gilded existence makes you blind to reality."

Alejandro stiffened. He took offence to that. Sebastien might be the only self-made man among them, older than the rest by three years, but they had all achieved success in their own right.

Leading his family company had been Alejandro's birthright, yes, but *he* had been the one to transform the Salazar Coffee Company from a fledgling international player into a global household name as CEO. He had *more* than paid his dues.

Stavros threw away three cards. "Try telling us you would go back to when you were broke, before you made your fortune. Hungry isn't happy. That's why you're such a rich bastard now."

"As it happens," Sebastien countered with a deceptively

casual shrug, "I've been thinking of donating half my fortune to charity to start a global search and rescue fund. Not everyone has friends who will dig him out of an avalanche with their bare hands."

Alejandro almost choked on the sip of whiskey he'd taken. "Are you serious? That's what? Five billion?"

"You can't take it with you. I'll tell you what," Sebastien mused, gaze moving from one to the other, "you three manage to go two weeks without your credit cards and family name and I'll do it."

Silence fell over the table. "Starting when?" Alejandro queried. "We all have responsibilities."

"Fair enough," Sebastien agreed. "Clear the decks at home. But be prepared for word from me—and two weeks in the real world."

Alejandro blinked. "You're really going to wager half your fortune on a cakewalk of a challenge?"

"If you'll put up your island…your favorite toys? Yes." Sebastien lifted his whiskey glass. "I say where and when."

"Easy," said Stavros. "Count me in."

They all clinked glasses, Alejandro dismissing the challenge as one of Sebastien's philosophical, whiskey-induced rants.

Until he ended up undercover as a groom in the Hargroves' legendary Kentucky stables exactly five months later.

CHAPTER ONE

Five months later—Esmerelda, the Hargrove Estate, Kentucky. Day one of Alejandro's challenge

CECILY HARGROVE TOOK the turn to the final line of jumps at such a tight angle, Bacchus's hind end spun out before her horse regained his balance, smoothed out his stride and headed toward the first oxer.

Too slow. Way too slow. Dammit, what was wrong with him?

She dug her heels into her horse's sides, pushing him forward to give them the momentum they needed for the jump, but Bacchus's hesitancy at takeoff threw their timing all off—only her horse's pure physical power allowing them to clear the fence.

Jaw set, frustration surging through her, she finished the last two jumps of the combination, then brought Bacchus to a dancing trot, then a walk, halting in front of her trainer.

Dale gave her a grim look as she pulled off her hat, the hot summer sun sticking the strands of her hair to her head. Her stomach knotted. "I don't want to know."

"Sixty-eight seconds. You need to figure out what's wrong with that horse, Cecily."

Tell her something she didn't know. With her second mount, Derringer, showing his inexperience in competition, Bacchus was her only chance to make this year's world championship team. Fully healed from their accident last year, her horse was physically sound, it was his mental outlook she was worried about.

If she didn't straighten out his head—this strange hesitancy he was displaying toward jumps he never used to blink at—her dream would be sunk before it had even started.

The only thing in this world that meant anything to her.

"Do it again," Dale instructed.

She shook her head, fury and frustration welling up inside her to spur a wet heat at the back of her eyes. "I'm done."

"Cec—"

She kicked Bacchus into a canter and headed for the barn, fighting back the tears. She had handled all the lemons life had thrown at her and Lord knew there had been a few of them, but *this*, this was not something she could fail at. Not when she'd spent every waking moment since she was five working toward this day.

Pulling Bacchus to a halt in front of the groom who stood lounging against the stable door, she slid off and threw the reins at him with more force than she'd intended. He caught them with a lithe movement, pushing away from the door. Hands clenched at her sides, she spun on her heel and turned to leave.

"You don't cool your horse down?"

The unfamiliar low, slightly accented drawl stopped her in her tracks. Spinning around, she took in its owner. The new groom she'd seen with Cliff earlier, presumably. She'd been so preoccupied she hadn't paid any attention to him. She wondered now how that had been possible.

Tall, well over six feet, he was pure, packed muscle in the T-shirt and jeans he wore. Slowly, furiously, she slid her gaze up that impressive body and found the rest of him was equally jaw dropping. His black hair was worn at a slightly rebellious length, days-old stubble lined a brutally handsome, square-cut jaw, his eyes the most sinfully dark ones she'd ever seen.

Her stomach flip flopped, a moment of sizzling hot, sexual chemistry arcing between them. She allowed herself to sink into it for a moment, to absorb the shimmer way down low, because it was something she hadn't felt in a long, long time, *if ever.*

His blatant stare didn't waver. Unnerved by the intensity of the connection, she sliced it dead. "You're new," she said icily, lifting her chin. "What's your name?"

A dip of his head. "Colt Banyon, ma'am. At your service."

She nodded. "I'm fairly sure then, *Colt,* that Cliff will have explained the finer points of your job to you?"

"He did."

"Why then, do you think it's okay to question how I handle my horse?"

He lifted a shoulder. "It seems to me you were having some trouble out there today. In my experience, spending some bonding time with your mount can help with the trust factor."

The pressure in her head threatened to explode through her skull. *No one dared talk to her like that.* She couldn't believe his audacity.

She took a step closer, discovering just how big he was when she had to tip her head back to look up at him, his dangerously beautiful eyes a rich whiskey fire lighting an inky black canvas.

"And from *which* school of psychobabble does that assessment come from?"

His sensual mouth curved. "My grandmother. She's a magician with horses."

The smile might have taken her breath away if the red haze creeping across her brain hadn't taken complete hold of her now. "How about this, *Colt*?" she suggested, voice dripping with disdain. "The next time you or your grandmother achieves a top one hundred world cup ranking, you can tell me how to handle my horse. Until then, how about you keep your mouth shut and do your job?"

His beautiful eyes widened.

She winced inwardly. *Had she really just said that?*

Shocked at her loss of control, fighting desperately to find some, she clutched her fingers tight around her hat. "He's recovering from torn ligaments on his rear hind leg," she said, nodding toward Bacchus. "Keep an eye on it."

Alejandro watched Cecily Hargrove flounce off, hat in hand, convinced the tiny blonde would be the thing that tested his control in this challenge Sebastien had issued him.

She'd been raising hell around the barn all morning. He was simply the latest in a long list of casualties.

Mucking out stalls, breaking his back caring for thirty horses, twelve hours a day would be child's play compared to dealing with *that* piece of work. She had a mouth on her that would strip the paint off a car and an attitude to match.

Unfortunately, he conceded, studying her fine rear end in the tight-fitting gray breeches as she stalked away, she was also extraordinarily beautiful. Traffic-stoppingly, outrageously beautiful. He would have had to have been fixed like half the horses in the barn not to have appreciated the delicate, heart-shaped face, remarkable blue eyes and honey blond hair that gave her an almost angelic look. Highly deceptive, clearly.

Blowing out a breath, he gathered up Bacchus's reins and took the beautiful bay gelding for a walk along the cobblestoned laneway to cool him off. To cool *himself* off.

It had been damn near impossible to swallow the comeback that had risen to his lips when Cecily Hargrove had thrown her world cup ranking at him. His grandmother had been top three in the world. She would have ridden circles around the superior *Ms. Hargrove* in her day. But exposing his true identity as a Salazar and rendering this challenge null and void wasn't something he could do. Not when Antonio and Stavros had already successfully completed theirs.

Not when his private island in the BVI was up for grabs—one of the few places on earth he found peace.

He led a cooled-down Bacchus into the barn and rubbed him down with a cloth. The therapeutic work he'd always loved gave him a chance to process the last, bizarre, twenty-four hours of his life.

It had not surprised him when Sebastien's jet had deposited him at the Louisville airport last night where he'd been instructed to report to the Hargroves' legendary, hundred-acre horse farm just outside of the city. Nor to find in the rustic cabin he'd been allocated in the staff quarters a couple of pairs of jeans, some T-shirts and boots, as well as a small stack of cash and an ancient mobile phone. It was exactly the same picture that had greeted Antonio and Stavros upon their arrival at their challenges.

The cryptic note that had been left on top of the pile of clothes had been similar as well.

For the next two weeks Alejandro Salazar does not exist. You are now Colt Banyon, talented drifter groom. You will report to Cliff Taylor at the stables at six a.m. tomorrow, where you will work for the next two weeks.

You will not break your cover under any circumstance. The only communication you may have with the outside world is with your fellow challenge-takers on the phone provided.

Why this particular assignment for you? I know you have been searching for the time to provide your grandmother with the proof she desires to right a wrong long-ago perpetrated. To restore the Salazar family honor. Your time as a groom will provide you

with both the means and the opportunity to do so.
I hope it offers you the closure you are looking for.

I wish you luck. Don't blow this, Alejandro. I've
gone to a great deal of effort to provide you with an
airtight identity. If you, Antonio and Stavros success-
fully complete your assignments, I will donate half
of my fortune, as promised, to setting up a global
search and rescue team. It will save many more lives.
Sebastien

Alejandro's mouth twisted as he switched to Bacchus's
other side, toweling the sweat from the gelding's dark coat.
No doubt the idea of him breaking his back shoveling horse
manure for two weeks with a name torn from the pages
of a Hollywood script had provided an endless source of
amusement for his mentor. But if Sebastien had been here,
he would have told him this chance to provide his grandmother with the justice she was seeking was exactly the
kind of closure he'd been looking for.

The feud between the Salazars and Hargroves had been
going on for decades—ever since Quinton Hargrove had illegally bred his mare Demeter to his grandmother, Adriana
Salazar's, prize stallion Diablo while the horse had been
on loan to an American breeder. The Hargroves had gone
on to build an entire show jumping legacy around Diablo's bloodline, one Adriana had never been able to match.

Heartbroken, his grandmother had been unable to at-
tain proof as to what the Hargroves had done, watching as
her fortunes plummeted and the Hargroves' star had risen.
Sebastien, in setting up the elaborate identity he had for
him had put Alejandro in the perfect position to acquire
that proof. Not only did he have the skills to carry out the
subterfuge from summers and holidays spent on his grandmother's Belgian horse farm, he had her touch with a horse.

He ran the towel down Bacchus's hind end. Somehow,

he acknowledged, it seemed almost *too* simple, this assignment of his, given the emotionally complex challenges Antonio and Stavros had been handed.

Antonio had been sent undercover to work as a mechanic at a garage in Milan. No issue there given his skill with a wrench. Far more shocking had been the child the Greek billionaire had discovered, the product of an old love affair. Antonio was still grappling with the considerable fallout of that life-altering discovery.

Stavros had warily gone next, finding himself sent to Greece to pose as a pool boy at his old family villa, a place he had long given a wide berth. Purchased by new owners, the property still held the ghosts of Stavros's childhood, the site of his father's death in a boating accident in which Stavros had survived.

Which undoubtedly left Alejandro the winner in the challenge lottery. Collecting a DNA sample from Bacchus, Cecily Hargrove's prize horse, to prove the Hargroves' crime was as simple as saving a few mane hairs from a brush and sending them off to Stavros to analyze in one of his high-tech labs.

Which left his biggest challenge to find a way to steer clear of Ms. Cecily Hargrove's razor-sharp mouth and perfect behind over the next two weeks.

Cecily's bad behavior plagued her all afternoon and well into dinner in the formal dining room at Esmerelda, a ridiculous indulgence on her stepmother's part when the stately redbrick manor's elegant, columned entertaining space seated thirty and it was only she, her father and her stepmother dining tonight.

She spent most of the insufferably dry meal staring moodily out the window. Her mother, Zara, had raised her to have impeccable manners. She was *never* rude. But Colt Banyon had hit a nerve this afternoon—a guilt she'd been harboring perhaps. A part of her knew this mess with Bacchus wasn't just his fault—that whatever had happened to them in that horrific accident in London was something that still haunted them both.

Dessert was finally served. Her stepmother, Kay, otherwise known as the Wicked Witch of the South, flicked a jasmine-scented wrist at her as a maid served a lime sorbet. "What are you wearing to the party next week?"

Something her stepmother would undoubtedly hate on sight.

"I don't know," she dismissed. "I'll find something."

Kay eyed her. "You know Knox Henderson is coming here specifically to court you. He's number forty-two on the Forbes list, Cecily. A catch if there ever was one."

Her lip curled. "No one uses the word 'court' anymore. And like I've told you a half a dozen times before, I have no interest in Knox."

"Why not?"

Because he was an arrogant jerk who owned half of Texas with his massive cattle ranches and oil reserves, merely looking for a wife to decorate his salon in entertainment magazine photo spreads. Because he reminded her far too much of her ex, Davis—another male who'd been far too rich and far too appreciative of multiple members of the opposite sex—*all at the same time.*

"I am not marrying him." She lifted her chin and stared her stepmother down. "End of story. Stop matchmaking. It's only going to be embarrassing for both of us if you keep this up."

"Perhaps Cecily is right," her father interjected, sweeping his cool, gray gaze over her. "She would do better to focus on the task at hand. Dale said your times today were still subpar. Do I need to buy you another horse to make this happen?"

Her stomach twisted. No, 'I'm sorry you had such a bad

day, honey.' No 'You've got what it takes, just stick with it' from her father. Never any of that. Only the stern, silver-haired disapproval that was her father's de facto response. It made her feel about two feet tall.

Her lashes lowered. "I don't have time to break in a new horse, Daddy. Besides, the committee will expect me on Bacchus."

"Then what do we need to do?"

"I will figure it out."

Suddenly the idea of Knox Henderson's impending visit combined with the vast amount of pressure being heaped on her from all directions vaporized any desire for dessert.

She set her spoon down with a clatter. "If you'll excuse me, I have a headache. I think I'll go lie down."

"Cecily."

Her stepmother put a hand on her father's arm. "Let her go. You know what she's like when she's in one of these moods."

Cecily ignored her, scraping back her chair and leaving with a click of her heels on the hardwood floor. She started toward her bedroom, then changed her mind, taking a detour to the kitchen where she acquired some of Bacchus's favorite breakfast cereal, then headed out the back door to the barn.

She thought she might owe both Bacchus and Colt Banyon an apology. She told herself that was the only reason she was venturing out into a balmy, perfect Kentucky evening when she had a stack of entrance forms waiting to be filled out. It was not, she assured herself, because of Colt Banyon's sinful dark eyes she couldn't forget.

Her bad timing on the course earlier today seemed to follow her as she entered the barn to find the grooms had finished up work. Not about to track Colt Banyon down at the staff quarters, she headed for Bacchus's box.

She pulled up short when she got there, watching with

astonishment as her horse, extremely picky when it came to grooms and highly nerved, blew out a breath and closed his eyes, putty under Colt's hands as the groom massaged his head. She hadn't seen him look this relaxed since before the accident.

Her attention shifted to the two-footed male in the box. Still clad in the close-fitting faded jeans, a gray T-shirt skimming his amazing abs, she found herself transfixed by the ripple of muscle in his powerful arms…by the lean, taut, undeniably ogle-worthy thighs underneath the worn denim.

He was a *man*—unlike Knox Henderson who preferred to preen like a peacock, there was a quiet substance to Colt that held her in its thrall.

He slid his hands down her horse's head and began working his neck muscles, the kneading movement of his big hands making her horse shudder. Her stomach curled, tiny pinpricks of heat unfolding beneath her skin.

Would he handle a woman with such sensual precision? What would those hands feel like? Would they be deliberate and demanding? Slow and seductive? *All of the above?*

Bacchus lifted his head, his soft nicker of welcome causing the subject of her fascination to turn around. She wiped her expression clean, but perhaps not quick enough. Colt Banyon's cool, dark stare made her freeze, utterly disconcerted.

"Why aren't you eating with the others?" she blurted out.

A blast of arctic air directed her way. "Wasn't hungry."

She sank her hands into her pockets. Blew out a breath. "I owe you an apology for my behavior earlier. I was frustrated, I took it out on you. I'm sorry."

A barely perceptible blink of those long, dark lashes. "Apology accepted."

He turned and went back to work. Her skin burned.

He'd clearly formed an opinion of her and wasn't about to change it. Which should have been fine because she was used to people forming false impressions of her. Sometimes she even encouraged it, because it was easier than trying to maintain human relationships, something that never seemed to work out for her.

But for some reason, she wanted Colt Banyon to approve of her. Maybe because her horse had already given him the thumbs up and Bacchus's opinion was never wrong.

Her horse nuzzled the pocket of her dress. She pulled out a handful of his favorite brightly colored fruit breakfast cereal and fed it to him.

Colt eyed her hand. "What is *that?*"

"Breakfast of champions. He'll do anything for it."

"Except jump the course the way you want him to."

Ouch. She winced at the dig. "Are you always this—"

"Impertinent?"

"I didn't say that."

"But you thought it."

"I *think,*" she corrected stiffly, "that you are direct. And that you don't like me very much."

He glanced at her, face impassive. "It doesn't matter what I think. I'm paid to follow orders just like you said."

She bit her lip. "I didn't mean that."

"Sure you did."

Wow. He wasn't going to make this easy for her. She watched as he ran his hand over Bacchus's side and dug his fingers into his trapezoids, key muscles her horse used to balance himself with. "What are you doing?"

"He seemed stiff when you rode him earlier. I thought a massage might loosen him up."

"Did your grandmother teach you that too?"

"Yes. If he's tight, he can't stretch over the jumps properly."

Well she knew that, of course. Jumping was all about form. But she'd only ever heard of equine therapists doing this kind of a massage.

"Is your grandmother a therapist?"

He shook his head. "Just a horse lover with a special touch."

"Does she live in New Mexico?"

A longer glance at her this time. "You been checking my résumé out?"

Heat stained her cheeks. "I like to know who's working in my stables."

"So you can see which 'school of psychobabble' we come from?"

"Colt—"

He started working on her horse's back. She crossed her arms over her chest and leaned back against the stall. "We had an accident," she said quietly. "In London last year. Something in the crowd spooked Bacchus as we approached a combination. His takeoff was all wrong—we crashed through the fence."

She closed her eyes as the sickening thud, still so clear, so horrifically real, reverberated in her head. "I was lucky I didn't break my neck. I broke my collarbone and arm instead. Bacchus tore tendons—badly. Physically, he's a hundred percent but mentally he hasn't been right since then. That's why I was so frustrated today."

He turned around and leaned against the wall. The corded muscles in his forearms flexed as he folded them over his chest, a flicker of something she couldn't read sliding across his cool, even gaze. "That had to have left some emotional dents in you as well."

She nodded. "I thought I was over it. Maybe I'm not."

Alejandro knew he should keep up the brush off signals until Cecily Hargrove walked back out that door—the safest place for her. But there was a fragility that radiated from her tonight, dark emotional bruises in her eyes he couldn't ignore. Perhaps they were from the accident. He thought they might be from a hell of a lot further back.

His heart tugged. Her undeniably beautiful face, bare of makeup, blue summer dress the same vibrant shade as her eyes, she looked exceedingly young and vulnerable. His grandmother had always said showjumping was a mental game. If you lost your edge, it all fell apart. Maybe Cecily had lost hers.

"Maybe you need to take a step back," he suggested. "Take some time for you and Bacchus to fully heal—mentally and physically. Figure out what's missing."

She shook her head. "I don't have time. I have a big event in a month. If I don't perform in the top three there I won't make the world championship team. Bacchus is the only horse I have that's at that level."

"So you make it next year."

"That's not an option."

"Why not?" He frowned. "What are you—mid-twenties? You have all the time in the world to make the team."

Her mouth twisted. "Not when you're a Hargrove, you don't. My grandmother and mother were on the team. I am *expected* to make it. If I don't, it will be a huge disappointment."

"To who?"

"My father. My coach. The team. Everyone who's backed me. They've spent a fortune in time and money to get me here."

That he understood. He'd spent a lifetime trying to live up to his own legacy—to the destiny that had been handed to him from the first day he could walk. Sent to an elite boarding school in America from his native Brazil when he was six, then on to Harvard, the pressure had been relentless.

When he'd moved to New York to run the Salazar Coffee Company's global operations as the company's CEO, that pressure had escalated to a whole other level, driven by a ferociously competitive international marketplace and a father who had never been content with less than a hundred and ten percent from his sons.

He knew how that pressure could rule your life. How it could crush your soul if you let it.

He set his gaze on the woman in front of him. "You know better than anyone what you do is as much psychology as it is sport. Master the course in your head and you're halfway there. Fail to do so and you're dead in the water." He shook his head. "If you push Bacchus before you're both ready, it could end up in an even worse disaster than the one you've already been through."

Long, golden-tipped lashes shaded her eyes. Chewing on her lip, she studied him for a long moment. "Was your grandmother a show jumper?"

Meu Deus. He gave himself a mental slap for revealing that much. He'd thought it an innocent enough reference at the time with Ms. High and Mighty goading him, but it had clearly been a stupid thing to do. Proof he liked to live close to the edge.

"She competed in small, regional stuff," he backpedalled. "Nothing at your level. She gave it up to have a family. But she had a way with horses like no one I've ever seen."

Her expressive eyes took on a reflective cast. "My mama was like that. Horses gravitated to her—it was like she spoke their language. They'd do anything for her in the ring."

Zara Hargrove. Alejandro knew from his grandmother she had died in a riding accident at the height of her career. Which would have made Cecily only a teenager when she'd lost her… *Tough*.

He ran a palm over the stubble on his jaw, hardening his heart against those dark bruised eyes. "You will figure this out. Bacchus will come around."

Her lips pursed. "I hope so."

She fed Bacchus another handful of cereal. He pulled his gaze away from the vulnerable curve of her mouth. *Dio. She was the enemy.* It might be guilt by association, she might have been *trained* to be a Hargrove, but she was one nonetheless. He was nuts to be standing here trying to solve her problems.

He knelt beside Bacchus's hind leg. "Show me where he tore the tendons."

She squatted beside him and ran her hand down the horse's leg. "Here."

"Difficult spot." He wrapped his fingers around the tendons and very gently worked the leg, massaging the sinewy flesh until it eased beneath his fingers.

"Can I try?" Cecily asked.

He nodded and dropped his hand.

She wrapped her fingers around the horse's leg, kneading his flesh. But her touch was too tentative, too light to do any good.

"Like this." He closed his fingers over hers to demonstrate, increasing the pressure. The warmth of her hand bled into his, a fission of electricity passing between them. Heat flared beneath his skin. Her breath grew shallow. He inhaled her delicate floral scent, so soft and seductive as it infiltrated his senses with potent effect. They may have had a rocky start, she might be the enemy, but his body wasn't registering either of those facts, consumed with a sensual awareness of her that clawed at his skin.

She turned to look at him, eyes darkening. "Have you ever thought of doing this for a living? You're very good at it."

"I've thought about it." He responded as Colt Banyon,

professional drifter. "But I like to travel too much. Maybe someday I'll settle down and get my own place."

She didn't scoff at that, as if he didn't have a hope in hell of ever owning a place like this. Didn't know he could buy and sell her family ten times over. Only said quietly, sincerity shining in her eyes, "I hope you do that some-day. You'd be amazing at it."

He thought then that perhaps first impressions hadn't done Cecily Hargrove justice. That if he curved his fin-gers around her neck and drew her to him for a kiss so he could taste that delectable mouth, she wouldn't protest, she'd meet him halfway. That if he did, he might be able to banish some of those dark shadows from her eyes for just a few minutes.

Why all of a sudden it was the most unbearably tempt-ing proposition when it was the last thing in the world he should ever do was beyond him.

He pushed to his feet before madness ensued. "A few minutes of that every day will help him stretch out, trust himself a bit more. It might help."

She rose to her feet beside him, any hint of an invita-tion gone from those blue eyes. If he saw a flash of regret there, she masked it just as quickly.

"Thank you, Colt," she said quietly, brushing her palms against her dress. "He's in excellent hands. Y'all have your-self a good night."

Oh, my God. Cecily dragged in a deep breath as she ex-ited the stables on weak knees, the earth feeling as if it was shifting beneath her feet. *What had just happened?*

You didn't invite a complete stranger to kiss you when he'd clearly barely been tolerating your presence and didn't even *like* you. And yet, her dazed brain processed, for a second there, she'd thought he'd been thinking about kiss-ing her too before he'd replaced those barriers of his and put her back in her place as surely as she'd put him in his earlier today.

Had she imagined it?

She pressed her palms to her heated cheeks. She shouldn't be interested in kissing *anyone* right now. It was the last thing she should be doing with her career hanging in the balance.

Skirting the floodlit natural water grotto her father had spent millions building for her mother, she took the path to the house. Perhaps she should go stick her head in *there*. It might inject some sense into her.

Hadn't her disastrous engagement to Davis taught her a lesson? Good looking men were trouble. A disaster waiting to happen. She was better off sticking with males of the four legged variety. They never broke her heart.

CHAPTER TWO

CECILY SPENT THE next few days steadfastly ignoring sexy, elusive Colt Banyon and putting all her focus into her practice sessions. But it seemed the harder she tried, the worse her times became—as if desperation was setting in and Bacchus could sense it, feeding off her nerves in all the worst ways.

By the time Friday rolled around, her event three weeks away, she was at her wit's end. She could continue to pound away at the fruitless efforts that were getting her nowhere or she could follow Colt's suggestion and take a step back.

She couldn't afford to give up on her hopes for the season, but perhaps she might be able to rewire her horse's brain with a total change of pace. Maybe Bacchus just needed a mental breather, an escape from the pressure cooker. *Just like her.*

An idea filled her head over tea in the thankfully deserted breakfast room. Except she knew her father wouldn't allow it unless she took someone with her and since having company along for the ride defeated the purpose of obtaining some peace, it wasn't an option.

Unless she took the less than talkative Colt with her, she mused over a sip of tea. She could pick his brain about some of his techniques along the way. While keeping her head in sane territory, of course, something that shouldn't be hard because Colt would clearly give her the brush off again if she did something dumb like invite him to kiss her, which of course, she wouldn't.

Her mouth curved. It was a plan. She finished her tea, collected her things and went off to execute.

* * *

Alejandro dropped the package off at the courier office in town on his mid-morning break. Containing a sample of Bacchus's mane hairs, it was now up to Stavros's high tech lab to confirm the Hargroves' crime.

He texted Stavros from the truck.

Package has been sent. Obrigado amigo, I owe you one.

Forget it. I'm feeling generous. I am, after all, soon to be a married man.

Alejandro almost dropped his phone.

Sorry?

You heard me. Details to come. Got to run.

Got to run? Alejandro eyed the phone as he threw it on the seat of the truck. *Antonio with an insta-family? Stavros married?* What the hell was going on? It was… *insano.*

Stavros, he bemusedly processed as he started the truck, didn't even sound panicked about it. He sounded almost… *cheerful.*

The sense of relief he'd been feeling about having netted this particular challenge magnified ten-fold as he drove back to the farm. No chance of any of those emotional attachments with him. He didn't need to acquire a wife as Stavros did, had no undiscovered children lying around— he'd made sure of that. And Sebastien knew his feelings on marriage.

When the day came for him to make a match to deliver the Salazar heir, it would be at least a few years down the road with a woman he'd handpicked as a sensible selection. He would research her just as he would an expensive car, making sure she ticked all the right boxes for the rational, practical match he had planned. Because he knew from personal history, impulse purchases, matches made out of passion never lasted. His parents were a perfect example of that.

He reached the stables five minutes after his break officially ended. Putting his mind blowing conversation with Stavros out of his head, he went directly to the tack room to collect the gear he needed to exercise one of the three horses he had to take out that afternoon.

Checking the gear over, he let the easy rhythm of the stables slide over him. The clip clop of hooves on concrete, the whinny of horses talking to each other over their stalls, the clink of metal on metal as an animal was shod filled him with a sense of peace he hadn't felt in months.

If he wasn't consumed with the thought of the hundreds of emails piling up in his inbox back in New York, the two massive deals his brother Joaquim, director of Salazar's European operations, was stickhandling for him, it would almost be idyllic.

"Hey Hollywood." Tommy, one of his fellow grooms, stuck his head in the tack room. "Boss's daughter wants to see you."

Uh-oh. He'd done such a good job of avoiding Cecily after that moment they'd shared in the stable. Was pretty sure she'd been avoiding him too. So why seek him out now?

He joined a group of grooms congregated in front of the tiny kitchen, Cecily holding court in their midst. Dressed in jeans and a sleeveless shirt that hugged her lithe curves, her hair caught up in a ponytail, she was a tiny, delectable package a man might want to eat for breakfast. Just not him, of course.

She turned to him once she'd finished her conversation

with the others. "I want to go for a hack up to the lake. I'd like you to come with me."

Oh, no. He recognized a bad idea when he heard one. "I still have three horses to exercise," he demurred smoothly. "Perhaps you can take someone else."

A female groom gaped at him. Tommy's brows rose. Cecily lifted her chin, training those vibrant blue eyes on him. "I would like *you* to come."

An order. Back to being mistress of all she surveyed, clearly.

He inclined his head. "Let me gather up a few things."

"Don't worry about food and water. I have that figured out."

He saddled up Jiango, a big, black stallion he'd had to exercise anyway. Tommy elbowed him as he walked the horse toward the yard. "Making an impression, Hollywood? A hundred bucks says you can't get past the ice cold exterior."

"Not looking to." He nipped that one in the bud. Rumors were the quickest way to blow his cover, particularly when they involved him and the boss's daughter.

Cecily eyed him as he brought Jiango to a halt in the yard. "I asked you along because I decided to take your advice and spend some downtime with Bacchus. I would have preferred to go by myself but my father won't let me ride up there alone. You will be the least talkative of the grooms."

So he was supposed to provide silent companionship to her highness? That he supposed he could do.

"Fair enough." He attempted to keep his eyes off her curvaceous rear as she turned, stuck her foot in the stirrup and climbed on Bacchus.

Usually, he went for tall, leggy women who matched him in physical attributes, but in Cecily's case, his mind immediately degenerated into all sorts of creative possibilities.

Bad Alejandro. He gave himself a mental slap and mounted Jiango. "How long a ride is it?"

"About an hour. It's gorgeous, you'll love it."

He did. Jiango, a powerful, Belgian-bred stallion, one of the Hargroves' up-and-coming young horses, more than kept up with Bacchus as they rode through pastures so green they looked frankly unreal, bounded by mile upon mile of picturesque white fence.

Aristocratic flowering trees with vibrant magenta and white blooms lined the track they rode on, providing shade to the long legged, elegant horses who dozed beneath a sky of the deepest blue.

The sun moved high in the sky as midday closed in. They left the pastures behind and entered a shady, light-dappled forest. Cecily turned to him, a mischievous glint in her eyes. "Want to show me what you've got, *Hollywood*?"

"If the prize is you not calling me that," he responded dryly, "I'm in."

"Done." A wider smile, a dazzling one that lit her face. "A race then, to the end of the road. First person over the creek wins." Her mouth pursed. "I will warn you—there are obstacles. You need to keep a sharp eye."

He'd gone cliff diving in Acapulco, bungee jumping in Thailand. He and the boys had even taken on sumo wrestlers in Japan. *This* would be a piece of cake.

"You're on," he said laconically. "You want a head start?"

Fire lit her gaze. She dug her heels into Bacchus and was flying down the road at breakneck speed before he'd even registered she'd moved. Kicking Jiango into a gallop, he gave him his head. Crouched low over the stallion's withers, he did his best to avoid the branches and obstacles that appeared out of nowhere, the odd one snagging him good.

Cecily held the lead. She was an insanely good rider, glued to the seat, but his horse had a longer stride than Bacchus's, helping him to make up ground. He was almost even with her when they neared what appeared to be the end of the road, the track growing steeper, plunging downhill to the creek. It took every bit of his experience to keep Jiango steady as they flew down the incline and headed for the water, the two horses even now.

He crouched forward in the saddle. Jiango jumped the water in a smooth, powerful movement. A gasp rang out behind him. Out of the corner of his eye, he saw Bacchus dig his feet in at the last moment, coming to a screeching halt on the rocks, nearly catapulting his rider over his head.

Somehow Cecily stayed in the saddle, regaining control as her horse skittered away from the water. He turned Jiango around and jumped back across the creek, bringing him to a halt beside Bacchus. Cheeks flushed, frustration glittering in her eyes, all the joy had gone out of Cecily's face.

"Guess that makes you the winner."

He frowned at the false bravado in her voice. "He normally jumps the creek?"

She nodded. "He loves it."

"Did your accident involve a water jump?"

"Yes, but he's jumped them since. His behavior isn't making any sense."

"Fear often doesn't make sense." He bunched his reins in one hand and sat back in the saddle. "A horse I worked with once had a bad crash on a really unusual fence that spooked him. He recovered, but the same thing happened to him that's happening to Bacchus. He wasn't just refusing on jumps that were new to him, he was refusing on jumps he had always been comfortable with—as if he didn't trust his rider anymore. Because, in his eyes, he'd led him astray."

"You think Bacchus believes I let him down?"

"I'm saying it's a possibility."

She chewed on her lip. "What did you do to make the horse right?"

"I gained his trust back."

"How?"

He lifted a brow. "You sure you want to learn from the 'school of psychobabble'?"

She gave him a reproachful look. "Yes."

He dismounted and walked over to Bacchus. "Get off," he instructed. "Take off your scarf."

"My scarf?"

"Yes—off."

She dismounted. Slid her fingers through the knot of her scarf and untied it, pulling it from her neck. Colt tied it around Bacchus's head, covering his eyes. The horse pawed the ground nervously, but stayed put.

"Take your shoes off and walk him across the stream."

She pulled off her riding boots and socks. Colt did the same. Boots in hand, he went first with Jiango. The water wasn't deep, but it moved fast. Jiango hesitated at the edge, but a firm tug on the reins had him moving forward.

Cecily and Bacchus followed. The moment Bacchus's hooves hit the running water, her horse jammed on the breaks and came to a grinding halt. Mouth set, Cecily walked back to him, stroked his neck and talked to him. By the time Alejandro and Jiango had reached the other side of the stream, Bacchus was cautiously making his way across.

"Take the blindfold off," he instructed when the pair walked up onto the bank.

Cecily removed the blindfold. Bacchus eyed the stream, sniffed the water, ears flickering as he registered he was on the other side.

"He knows he can trust you to get him to safety," Alejandro explained. "Now take him back across without the blindfold."

Horse and rider picked their way across the stream, then back again, Bacchus's confidence building with every step.

Cecily stopped Bacchus at his side. "What now?"

"We'll give him some time to think about it. See if he'll jump it on the way back."

She nodded. "It's just so strange. This is his favorite place."

"He's got something stuck in his head. Also," he added, eyes on hers, "he's absorbing your tension. I've been feeling it all week watching you ride. You've got to loosen up—change the dynamic between you two. Rebuild the trust."

She pushed her hair out of her face. "My coach doesn't believe in any of this. You're supposed to *make* the horse do what you want them to do."

"And that's working for you?"

Her eyes flashed. Lifting her chin, she nodded toward a path in the woods. "Lake's this way."

Cecily attempted to recapture her good mood as they walked the horses to her favorite picnic spot on the bank of the lake, but she was too agitated to manage it. For Bacchus to refuse a jump on his favorite ride was sucking what little hope she had left out of her that she would be ready to compete against the top riders in the world in just three weeks. It didn't seem possible.

She knew Colt was right, knew she needed to change the dynamic between her and Bacchus—she just didn't know how.

The sun at its midday peak, hot as the devil as her Grandmama Harper used to say, they tethered the horses in a shady spot under a tree. A mile wide, the lake was a stunning dark navy blue, bounded by forests of the deepest green. Quiet—eerily quiet except for the odd call of a bird or the splash of some water creature, it made her suddenly, inordinately aware of how very alone she and Colt were.

Perhaps this hadn't been such a good idea.

She retrieved the picnic lunch she'd had a farm hand drop off earlier while Colt spread the blanket out on a flat stretch of grass. He sprawled on top of it, taking the containers she handed him, a visual feast for the eye in his threadbare jeans and navy T-shirt.

Her thoughts immediately ventured into X-rated territory. She attempted to wrestle them back as she sorted out the lunch, but it proved almost impossible. He was a gorgeous male in the prime of his life, all coiled muscle and tensile strength, the effect he had on her core deep.

Heart ticking faster, every inch of her skin utterly and irrefutably aware of him, she sat down on the blanket and served up the lunch of fried chicken and potato salad the cook had provided.

Colt demolished it with a cold beer. Her appetite seemingly not in attendance, whether because of her misery or her intense awareness of the man beside her, she pushed her plate away and nursed the wine cooler she'd brought for herself, eyes on the water.

Colt rolled up a towel from the basket and propped it behind his head, stretching out with feline grace in the baking sun. She noted the careful distance he kept between them, the wary glint in his eyes whenever he looked at her. And suddenly, felt like a fool.

"I'm sorry I strong-armed you into coming up here with me."

He paused, beer bottle halfway to his lips. "I'm enjoying it. You were right—it's amazing up here. I was surprised, though, you didn't want to bring a friend."

"I don't have any." She gave a self-conscious shrug.

"At least no real ones. My best friend, Melly, decided we weren't friends anymore after I won the junior championship. I'm on the road so much, there's really been no opportunity to make any new friends other than the people I compete with and those relationships only go so deep."

"That must get lonely."

"I'm better off with companionship of the four legged variety. Horses are endlessly loyal and they don't talk back to me."

His mouth quirked. "They also can't provide anything in the way of strength and solidarity."

She tipped her head to the side, curious. "Is that what your friends mean to you?"

"A big part of it, yes. We go back to college, my best friends and I. We've been through some pretty amazing times together—both good and bad. There's a bond there that's unbreakable even with the distance between us. One of us needs something—the rest of us jump."

A pang went through her. She wished she had that. Someone who knew you so well you could just be yourself rather than what everyone else thought you should be. But she'd never been good at fostering those types of relationships.

"That would be nice," she said quietly, "to have friends like that."

He studied her for a long moment. "So Melly turned out to be a dud. Find someone else who deserves your friendship. You can't spend every waking minute riding a horse."

"According to my coach that's exactly what I should be doing."

"No," he disagreed. "You shouldn't. Success in life comes from opening yourself up to new horizons. *Balance*." He lifted a brow. "What about boyfriends? You must have them."

"Too busy."

"Surely men pursue you?"

She took a sip of her drink. Cradled the bottle between her hands. "My parents want me to marry Knox Henderson. He owns half of Texas. They keep throwing us together, but I have no interest."

"Why?" An amused glitter filled his gaze. "Is he unattractive? Too old? Too boring?"

"He's young, attractive and rich. And he knows it."

"What's not to like about that? A woman needs a strong, successful man."

She rolled her eyes.

"Did you even give him a chance?"

"Define 'give him a chance'."

"Did you kiss him?"

"Yes. No spark." She gave him a considering glance, having overheard Tommy's earlier remark. "I know the bet the boys in the barn have going."

"What bet?"

She waved a hand at him. "You don't have to play dumb. They think I'm a cold fish. And maybe I am."

He rubbed a palm over his jaw. Eyed her. "Was this Knox even a good kisser?"

"I'm sure many women would say yes. Not me. He's coming to the barn party on Friday night. You'll get to meet him then."

"About that," he murmured. "It's very nice of you to invite the staff but I have nothing to wear. I actually *am* Cinderella."

"You get paid today. Buy something in town." Somehow the comparison of Colt and Knox in the same room was far too intriguing to resist.

"It was my mama's idea to include the staff," she told him. "She always loved the family atmosphere it created. Kay, my stepmother, wanted to cut the tradition out when she came here. A needless expense, she said." Her mouth twisted as she brushed a stray hair out of her face. "I ve-toed it. It set the tone for our tempestuous relationship."

"It's a very nice tradition." Colt took a sip of his beer. "You must miss your mother. You lost her very young."

Her smile faded. "Every day." She looked down at the bottle in her hand. "She died up here. That's why Daddy doesn't like me coming alone."

He sat up on his elbows. "I assumed she died while she was competing."

She shook her head. "She and Daddy had an argument. I know, because the whole house heard it. It was a bad one—worse than usual. Daddy flew off to New York on business, Mama left the house in a state and came up here without telling anyone. When I finished my lessons with my tutor I went looking for her. I knew she'd be up here because it was her favorite place.

"I found her hat on the ground. I knew something was wrong. We searched for hours but we couldn't find her. We were on our way back to the house when we found Zeus, her horse. Mama had gotten thrown from him and he was dragging her by the stirrup." She pressed her lips together, a throb pulsing her insides. "He was taking her home."

"I'm sorry," Colt said quietly. "That must have been awful."

The worst day of her life. Her heart squeezed. What she wouldn't do to have her wise, kind mother here now to help her sort out the mess she was in.

She studied the play of the sunlight on the water, a dancing, rippling pattern that continually changed form. "I don't think my father's ever forgiven himself for it. I'm not sure *I've* forgiven him for it. I mean I know rationally, it wasn't his fault, but I miss her so much."

"Did you ever find out what they were arguing about?"

She shook her head. "Daddy won't talk about it. One of the maids told me she heard them arguing about Zeus, but that doesn't make any sense. Daddy never interfered in Mama's horse stuff."

He took a swig of his beer. "Isn't the rumor Zeus was sired by Diablo?"

She laughed. "Oh, that's not true. Everyone likes to make up these crazy stories about him. Demeter, Zeus' mama, was bred with a French stallion named Nightshade—an equally impressive match. Nightshade was a three-time European champion, that's where Bacchus gets his jumping ability from."

He inclined his head. "Funny how rumors get started."

She watched a loon sail elegantly across the glass-like surface of the water, its haunting cry echoing the dull throb inside of her. Being here it always hurt ten times worse, her emotions already far too close to the surface.

"She wasn't just my mother," she said quietly, heat gathering at the back of her eyes. "She was my best friend. My coach, my confidante, my *hero*. She taught me to ride before I could walk, took me to all the shows with her. We were inseparable. I wanted to *be* her when I grew up."

A silence fell between them. "And you want to win for her," Colt said finally.

She nodded, the tears stinging the backs of her eyes threatening to spill over. "I want to do what she didn't have time to do."

Suddenly all the pieces of the puzzle that was Cecily Hargrove were falling into place. Alejandro studied her over the rim of his beer bottle, heart squeezing despite his attempts to remain unmoved. How could he?

He'd watched her kill herself over the past week, wondering what ghosts drove her. Now he knew. But beating herself and Bacchus into the ground over and over again until there was nothing left of either of them wasn't going to fix the problem—wasn't going to fix *them*.

He'd seen glimpses of the real Cecily on the way up here today. Her spirit. Her joy. What she must have been like as a competitor when her demons weren't chasing her. Watching her now was like watching light turn into dark.

Setting his beer bottle down, he turned to face her. "You know what I think," he said softly, studying those beautiful, haunted eyes. "I think you don't know who you are anymore. Who you're riding for. I think you're riding for everyone *but* yourself."

She frowned. "The accident—"

"Was just the tip of the iceberg." He tapped his head. "When *this* gets messed up—when what you want, what everyone else wants, when too much damn pressure starts to build—*no one* can perform."

Her eyes widened. "Bacchus is a problem."

"Yes," he agreed, "he is. But *you* are the bigger problem. Until you figure *you* out, until you decide who you're doing this for, you have no hope of making that team. You might as well pack it up and throw in the towel right now."

Her gaze dropped away from his. She was silent for so long he realized he had gone too far. "I'm sorry," he murmured. "I shouldn't have—"

"No," she said, lifting her head, eyes glazed with unshed tears. "You're right. I have no idea who I am anymore. I've spent my whole life doing what everyone else expects of me. Giving up a normal life—leaving school, traveling eight months of the year every year so I can make this team…" She sank her teeth into her bottom lip. "What if I don't? It's all I know—it's my entire *identity*."

His throat tightened. "Then you find something else to be. But I don't think that's going to happen, Cecily. You clearly have the talent. Now you need to find the *reason*."

A tear slid down her cheek. Then another. A curse left his lips. He pulled her into his arms, his chin coming down on top of her silky hair, her petite body curved against his.

"You need to take control," he murmured. "Decide what you want. This has to be you, Cecily, no one else."

She cried against his chest. He held her, stroking his hand over her hair. How could he do anything else when she had no one, literally no one, to confide in?

He murmured comforting words against her silky cheek. Discovered her hair smelled like lemons and sunshine—that she was far more intoxicating than he'd ever imagined she would be, curled so tightly in his arms.

She finally pulled back, tears slowing. "Thank you," she said. "No one is ever honest with me. Everyone tells me what I want to hear rather than what I need to hear. Except my parents. They just give me orders."

He tucked a chunk of her hair behind her ear. Ran his thumbs across her cheeks to brush the tears away. "Then maybe you need to change that too. You're old enough to own your own decisions—your own successes and failures."

She nodded, eyes on his. Her lashes lowered, sweeping across her cheeks as the temperature between them changed and suddenly everything was focused on the fact that she was in his lap, her arms wrapped around him and really he should be disentangling himself *right now*.

"Colt?"

Distracted, he brought his gaze back up to hers. The reminder he wasn't who he'd said he was, that this *couldn't happen*, should have been enough to have him ending it right now, but the hesitant look in her blue eyes commanded him instead.

"That night in the barn—was I imagining that you wanted to kiss me?"

Por amor a Deus. How was he supposed to answer that? Lie and he would hurt her, something he wasn't willing to do. But telling her the truth wasn't an option either.

"I don't think I should answer that question."

"Why?"

"Because I work for you. Because it isn't appropriate."

"This is already past appropriate," she murmured, eyes on his mouth. "And you've already answered my question by not answering."

"Then we should consider the subject closed." He reached up to disentangle her arms from around his neck. She kept them where they were.

"I think I should test my theory out."

"What theory?"

"That you will be a better kisser than Knox."

Oh, no. He shook his head. "I think we should leave the answer to the theoretical realm."

"I don't." She curved her fingers around the back of his neck and drew his mouth down to hers. He should have stopped it right there, should have exercised the sanity he should have had, but he wasn't going to reject her—not in her ultra-vulnerable state. And, if the truth be known, he wanted to kiss her. *Badly.* Had since that night in the barn.

Lush and full, not quite practiced, the brush of her lips against his sent a sizzle over every inch of his skin. *This was such a bad idea.*

He relaxed beneath her touch, allowed her to play. He'd give it a minute, make it good and get out of Dodge.

"You have an amazing mouth," Cecily breathed against his lips. "But you aren't kissing me back."

"Self-preservation," he murmured before he splayed his fingers around her delicate jaw, angled her mouth the way he wanted it and took control.

Her sweet, heady taste exploded across his senses. As good as he'd imagined it to be—maybe better. Fingers stroking over the silky skin of her cheek, he explored the voluptuous line of her mouth with his own, acquainting himself with every plump, perfect centimeter.

When skin against skin didn't seem to be enough, he

brought his teeth and tongue into play, nipping, stroking, lathing. A gasp escaped her lips. He took advantage of the opportunity and closed his mouth over hers, taking the kiss deeper, mating his tongue with hers. Twining her fingers into the hair at his nape, she followed his lead, sliding her tongue against his, turning the kiss into an intimate, seductive exploration that fried his brain.

Santo Deus, but she was responsive, the taste of them together perfection. He fought the desire to explore the rest of her curvy, hot body with his mouth and tongue. To discover how sweet she really was.

In his world, kisses like this led to hot, explosive sex. In *this* world, however, it absolutely, positively could not happen.

His rational brain kicked in. He broke the kiss, sank his fingers into her waist and lifted her off him and placed her back on the blanket.

Cheeks flushed, eyes on his, Cecily pushed a hand through her hair. "That was—"

"Proof you aren't a cold fish," he said, pushing to his feet. "Now we forget it happened."

She eyed him. "Colt—"

He shook his head. "You know my MO. Here today, gone tomorrow. You don't want to get involved with me, Cecily. Trust me."

CHAPTER THREE

FORGET IT HAPPENED? Cecily couldn't do anything *but* think about that kiss with Colt in the days leading up to the Hargroves' annual summer party. It infiltrated her thoughts, her dreams, her practice sessions, rendering her concentration less than ideal.

To know that kind of passion existed, the explosive kind she'd felt with Colt, had turned her world upside down. Not even with Davis, as crazy as she'd been about him, had she experienced that kind of chemistry. And yet rationality told her Colt was right—the best thing for them to do was ignore it. She had to focus on making this team and Colt would move on again soon.

She put her focus, instead, on her new approach to fixing her and Bacchus's relationship. On fixing *her*. She was twenty-five years old. It *was* time for her to take charge of her life and career. If she didn't start directing things, figuring out who she was and what she wanted, everyone else was going to do it for her. And that was unacceptable.

With Dale's coaching getting her and Bacchus nowhere fast, she began working with Colt in the afternoons, exploring some of the techniques he'd used on his case similar to Bacchus's. Given her horse had, in fact, jumped the creek on the way home from the lake, she thought there might be something there.

They were making baby steps—tiny amounts of progress. Now if only she could make herself immune to the man giving the instructions.

Kay caught her as she walked into the house to get ready for the party, insisting she come greet the Hendersons who would stay the weekend. Toeing off her muddy boots in the entrance way, she walked into the salon. Knox was as flirtatious as ever—she as uninterested as ever. Exercising the briefest of social niceties, she excused herself to go to her room.

Her father intercepted her before she could, pulling her into his study. "Dale tells me you're still working with Colt Banyon," he said, shutting the door. "Why?"

She lifted her chin. "Because I want to. Because I think it's going to help Bacchus."

Clayton Hargrove leaned back against his desk, tall, cool, southern elegance in gray trousers and a white shirt. "What you're doing is wasting your time. That stuff is nonsense he's teaching you."

"I'm going to decide what's right and wrong for me from now on."

"Excuse me?"

She crossed her arms over her chest. "I am twenty-five years old, Daddy. I'm not a child. I need to start managing my own life and career."

Her father scowled. "Colt Banyon is a drifter. He wanders from stable to stable. You don't know anything about him or his credentials."

"I know I trust him. And he comes with impeccable credentials. Cliff wouldn't hire anyone with anything less."

"I could fire him."

A surge of fury rose up inside her. "You fire him and I'll withdraw from the Geneva event."

"You wouldn't do that."

"Try me."

"Dammit, Cecily," her father bellowed. "See some sense here."

"I am seeing some. Finally." She bit the inside of her mouth, deciding to go for broke now that she was knee deep. "What were you and Mama arguing about the day she died?"

Her father frowned. "What does that have to do with this?"

"Nothing. I just want to know."

A stony expression consumed his face. "Nothing that concerns you. It was a private matter between your mother and I."

"After which she broke the cardinal rule and went riding by herself?" Her lips set in a tight line. "She knew better than that, Daddy. Isabella said she looked knocked sideways after you left. What happened between you two?"

He shook his head. "It's ancient history. Let it go."

"I've tried. It hasn't worked." She fixed her gaze on his. "You pretend you don't miss her, but you do. You pretend it never happened, but it did." She pushed a stray hair out of her face with a trembling hand. "I'll never stop wondering what happened that day. What made her do something so stupid. And I'll never stop missing her. Because, apparently, I'm the only one in this family who has a heart."

Spinning on her heel, she stalked to the door.

"Cecily."

She wrenched the door open, walked through it and slammed it shut. Kay and the Hendersons gave her a bemused look as she stalked through the salon and headed for her room. She ignored them all.

"You ready to go?"

Colt opened the door to his cabin to find Tommy, decked out in a checked shirt and jeans, lounging against the doorframe, a pink Kentucky sunset staining the sky behind him.

He shook his head. "I was thinking I might skip it."

Tommy waved his hat at him. "You can't skip it. It's the social event of the season. All you can drink beer and beautiful women… What's not to like?"

The fact that one gorgeous woman in particular was

finding her way beneath his skin—a woman he couldn't have. That he was a day away from completing this challenge of Sebastien's. He wasn't about to blow it now.

Antonio's phone call this morning appealing for a stay on his private island as the paparazzi chased his family for photos amidst a scandal cemented the need to get out of here unscathed. He'd given the Italian the green light to spend his honeymoon on the island and counted his lucky stars it wasn't him.

He rolled his shoulders. "I pulled a muscle carrying that beam today. Think I'll hole up here and read a book."

"Oh, come on, Hollywood." Tommy flashed him a yellow-toothed grin. "You're tougher than that. Get your boots on and let's go. We'll find you a gorgeous woman to work that shoulder of yours out."

Deciding resistance was futile, Alejandro pulled on the new blue shirt and jeans he'd bought in town, applied some aftershave and tugged on his boots.

The party was in full swing when they arrived at one of the bigger thoroughbred barns that wasn't in use. The cavernous space had been done up for the occasion with fairy lights strung from the vaulted ceiling, a bar in one corner and a well-known country band playing in another. High cruiser tables scattered about the space offered the hundreds of guests a lounging spot to enjoy the food and drink being circulated as they enjoyed a lazy, exceedingly warm Kentucky night.

True to Tommy's promise, there were dozens of beautiful women in attendance, clad in pretty summer dresses. Alejandro had always appreciated a southern woman's charms—the big hair, the ultra-feminine way they dressed, the soft, seductive voices—he found it sexy as hell. But tonight only one of those women caught his eye and it was the one who could flay a man's skin with her razor sharp tongue one minute, then slay him with a husky, vulnerable drawl the next.

Cecily wore a burnt orange dress that seemed to have been painted on, its short skirt ending at mid-thigh, exposing smooth, toned legs he couldn't take his eyes off. When he finally managed to, a plunging V-neckline revealed more delectable curves. It took very little of his imagination to imagine what the rest of her would look like without clothes. *Utterly sensational.*

He pulled his gaze away from temptation and up to her face. Unfortunately, there was more of it there. Her hair set in big, loose curls, a smoky eye makeup and vivid red lip color making her look less angelic tonight and more irresistible siren, she was jaw-droppingly beautiful.

She turned her head, as if sensing his perusal. A charge vibrated the air between them, sizzling his blood in his veins in a hot, restless purr. He sucked in a breath, the need to have, to *possess* something that was off limits to him an experience he was unused to having.

He wanted her. Up against a wall would be nice, those fabulous legs wrapped around his waist, his mouth buried in her silky hair while he gave her everything he had. But, really, he was fairly certain any position would do.

"Pretty boy's back," Tommy murmured. "Wonder when he's finally going to get the message she isn't interested."

Alejandro didn't respond. He was too busy sizing up the tall, muscular male at Cecily's side. His dark blond hair slicked back from his handsome face, an air of supreme confidence surrounding him, Knox Henderson wore the look of a man who knew what he wanted: the woman standing beside him in a very sexy red dress whose smile was not at all right.

Not my problem, he told himself. *You can't have her.* He'd been telling himself that all week.

He should have stayed away tonight just like he'd planned. Should have listened to his instincts.

Cecily swallowed hard as she stared at Colt. Knox could have told her one of his oil wells was spouting twenty-four-carat gold and it still wouldn't have penetrated her brain. Her skin shimmered with an awareness that seemed layers deep, her pulse ratcheted up a notch and her breath lodged in her throat as she took in the man she'd told herself she hadn't been waiting for.

Dressed in a pair of dark jeans and a light blue shirt rolled up at the sleeves, the color a perfect foil for his dark, dreamy good looks, Colt was God's gift to women and that was all. But it was the unguarded look on his face that had her complete attention.

Open and direct, *hot*, he'd forgotten to assume that mask he always wore. The horse was most definitely out of the barn and it sent a shiver up her spine.

"We should dance," Knox murmured in her ear. "I haven't managed one with you yet."

Because she didn't want to lead him on. Because he'd already knocked back a couple of stiff bourbons and Knox got handsy when he drank. Because the only person she wanted to dance with was Colt.

Knox, however, was already setting his empty glass on a cruiser table and pulling her onto the dance floor. To compound her problem, the band launched into a slow tune, allowing him to pull her close.

"Why do you play hard to get?" he murmured. "Come on Cecily, give me a break. What do I have to do?"

She tipped her head back to look up at him. "I am hard to get. I've told you more than once, I can't see us together, Knox. It just isn't there."

"Why not?"

"It isn't the kind of thing I can explain. It just is or isn't."

"You won't even try." His hand dropped lower on her hip, dangerously close to her bottom. "You wear a dress like this, what am I supposed to do? Name your price, sugar. You want a stable full of the best horses in the world? They're yours. A place in the south of France? I'll give it to you. Some extra money for upkeep? It'll be in your bank account."

She eyed him. "Upkeep?"

"Well you know, most women I know like to do a nip or a tuck here or there. Keep up appearances." He shrugged. "I'm good with that. It's like tuning up a car every once in a while. I'd consider it part of the maintenance budget."

Her jaw dropped. "I'm twenty-five, Knox. What kind of maintenance do you think I need?"

"I didn't say you *needed* it. I said the option was there if you wanted it."

Lord have mercy. This was going to get ugly if she didn't keep her mouth shut. Chin lifting at a defiant angle, she eyed his handsome, superior face. "The fact is…I'm interested in someone else."

A glimmer entered his blue gaze. "Who?"

"It doesn't matter."

"Sure it does. I am more than a bit curious to see who's penetrated that frigid exterior of yours. I was starting to think it an impossible feat."

Her insides contracted at the direct hit. It was her Achilles' heel that no one would ever want her for who she truly was. Her biggest fear that she would only ever be valuable for the legacy she carried. Davis had made sure of that.

She gave him an unflinching look. "Quit acting ugly, Knox. Bow out gracefully."

His mouth twisted. "*You* could have bowed out gracefully. I flew hundreds of miles to see you, Cecily. I blew off a client to be here. You could have at least given me a heads-up."

Damn Kay and her meddling. A tense silence fell between them as the song dragged on. The near bullet she'd dodged became vividly clear. As Knox's wife she would have been a high-priced possession, bought for her looks and poise. Another ornament to add to his mantelpiece. He would never have *understood* her like Colt did.

She searched for him in the crowd. Found him in a group of stable hands who were fraternizing with some of the locals. Sharp knives of jealousy lanced through her as a beautiful brunette who lived in town pulled him onto the dance floor.

Slim with stunning green eyes, her mother would have called her a tall drink of water. The brunette said something to Colt that made him laugh as he drew her into his arms, a lazy, sexy laugh she'd never heard him utter before.

Her skin stung. The old Cecily would have pretended she didn't care. Would have continued to deny how she felt—closed herself off behind her walls. The new Cecily found she couldn't.

Alejandro threw back a long, cool beer after a few sets on the dance floor, the brunette glued to his side. She was stunning, absolutely his type, but he abhorred meaningless chatter, the only kind, it seemed, she knew.

A scan of the space determined Cecily was still missing. Had been for the better part of a half-hour. Her smile, the not quite right one he'd been trying to ignore, flashed through his head.

"Will you excuse me?" he drawled to the brunette, setting his bottle down on a table. "I need some fresh air."

Winding his way through the crowd before she could invite herself along, which he was sure she would, he exited the barn. It was deserted outside, the faint sound of music and chatter spilling out into a sultry, warm Kentucky night.

He almost missed Cecily. He caught her on his second scan, arms folded over the top of the fence, face lifted to a star-blanketed sky. His steps soundless, he joined her, slinging his elbows over the fence.

She turned a storm-tossed gaze on him. "Leave your fan club inside?"

He ignored the jibe. "You going to tell me what's wrong?"

She sighed. Pushed a hand through her hair. "I had a fight with Daddy. A good one. Then Knox and I tangled just now."

"About?"

"I told him it's never happening between us." Her mouth tightened. "He's not good with taking no for an answer."

"In what way?"

"He was angry. He wasn't very nice about it."

"Let him be angry. You made your decision."

"I know. It's just our families are good friends. And—" she bit her lip.

"What?"

"He called me frigid."

His fingers curled tight around the rail. Now he wanted to kick the guy's teeth in. Damn good thing it was a sure-fire way to get his cover blown or he would.

"He's frustrated," he rasped. "Forget about him. What were you arguing with your father about?"

"You." She turned to face him. "Daddy doesn't want me working with you and Bacchus. I told him too bad, I'm taking charge of my life and career now."

Cristo. Shining a light on himself was not what he'd had in mind when he'd agreed to help her with her horse.

"You might consider taking baby steps," he counseled. "Give yourself time to think. Blowing your whole life up right now isn't a good idea with everything you have on your plate."

Her lashes lowered. "I just feel like I've wasted enough time."

He shook his head. "You are so young, Cecily. You have your whole life ahead of you."

The band began to play a new song, the notes wafting along the breeze that rustled the leaves of the aristocratic magnolia tree above. It was their most notable tune—the lead singer's raspy, deep voice crooning out the plaintive notes of the angsty ballad.

"I love this song," Cecily said quietly. "It's about a girl who only ever gets what she doesn't want. How it's her curse to walk through this world alone." She pressed a fist to her chest. "It gets me right here."

His heart stuttered. She didn't have to explain why the song affected her so much. It was *her*.

He held out his hand. "Dance with me then."

Her beautiful blue eyes fixed on his. Stepping away from the fence, she laced her fingers through his, slid her other hand around his waist and moved into his arms. It was a mistake, he knew it, as he pulled her close. But her damn vulnerability got to him every time.

They danced in the moonlight, in perfect sync, silent as they enjoyed the song. Even the cynic in Alejandro knew it for the rarity it was—to be so in tune with someone, talking was unnecessary.

She drifted closer, eliminating the respectable distance he'd forged between them. Her perfectly proportioned curves brushed the length of his body, her silky hair caressed his jaw, her breath teased the bare skin at the open neck of his shirt—heating his blood in all the most dangerous ways.

"Cecily…" he murmured.

"This isn't working."

"What isn't?"

"Trying to ignore this thing between us."

His jaw set. "It's the right thing to do."

"Why?" Challenging. *Provocative.*

"I've already explained that."

"You want me," she said pointedly. "I saw it on your face tonight when you walked in. That kiss we shared was amazing, you know it was."

"And that's as far as it goes."

She stepped even closer, lifting up on tip toe to bring her mouth to his ear. "I can't concentrate. All I can think about is that kiss. *You.* The entire time I was dancing with Knox I was thinking about you."

Blood pounded his temples. He was about to shut it down, to tell her no more kisses were happening when a smooth drawl drifted across the air.

"So this is where you're getting it from." Knox Henderson stepped out of the shadows, a puff of round smoke from his cigar rising up in the air. He set his gaze on Cecily. "If I'd known you like to get down and dirty with a stable hand I would have lost the suits along with the kid gloves."

A cold fire flared in Alejandro's gut. He set Cecily away from him, stepped forward and faced the man casually puffing away on the cigar. The glazed look in Henderson's eyes said he'd had more than a few drinks.

"I think you need to take that back," Alejandro said quietly, "and go back inside."

"Oh, but I'm curious," the other man demurred. "She leads me on, lets me fly down here, only for me to find she's screwing someone else. Can't blame me for wanting to check out the competition."

Alejandro took a step closer, fingers curling into fists at his sides. "Now you have. Accept that she isn't interested and step inside."

Henderson lifted a brow. "Accept she wants to bang

a stable hand? Sorry if I can't stomach that. It's just too much."

Alejandro moved so quickly, Henderson was still drawing a puff of his cigar when he wrapped a fist around his shirt collar. "I'm giving you one more chance," he snarled. "Apologize."

The other man's mouth curved in a mean smile. "I don't think so."

A fist connected with Alejandro's jaw in a lightning fast punch Alejandro never saw coming. A white-hot sting radiating through his head, he swung his fist in an upper right hook. A fractured cry escaping her throat, Cecily jumped between them, Alejandro barely managing to pull his fist back before it connected with her instead of Henderson.

"*Stop it*. Both of you. *Stop*."

Fury consuming him, Alejandro was almost past the point of listening. Only the panicked look on Cecily's face pulled him back from the edge.

Cecily glared at Knox. "Inside," she ordered, pointing toward the barn. *"Right now."*

Knox looked down at her, a derisive smile curling his lips. "You know what? You're right. You aren't worth it."

Cecily escorted Knox back to the party, not trusting him not to instigate something else if she didn't. Seeing him safely to a group of friends, she took some ice from one of the coolers in the serving area and left via the back entrance.

Taking a circuitous route to the staff accommodations so no one would see her, she knocked on the door to Colt's cabin. He opened the door a moment later. Her gaze flew to the red mark on his jaw, some swelling already visible in the moonlight.

"Oh, God, Colt, I am so sorry."

He put a hand to his jaw. "It's fine. No big deal."

"It's swelling already." She held up the bag of ice. "We can put this on it."

"I can," he corrected, reaching for the bag.

She held it behind her back. "Let me come in and do it. I feel so guilty. I can't believe Knox was such a buffoon."

He fixed a dark, unyielding stare on her. "Give me the ice, Cecily. You know you coming in is a bad idea."

She firmed her mouth. "Let me come in and make sure you're okay, then I'll leave."

They stared each other down. "Fine," he said, stepping back.

She slipped through the door and kicked off her shoes. Extremely basic, the cabin consisted of a queen-sized bed, a chest of drawers, an armchair by the window and a tiny cooking area. Colt hadn't personalized the space, in keeping with his drifter persona.

When that struck a raw place in her throat, she shoved it from her head and moved to the kitchen area to wrap the ice in a towel.

"Sit," she said, pointing to the chair.

He did. She perched on the arm and pressed the cloth full of ice to his jaw, making him wince.

"He hurt you."

He gave her a grim look. "You might have let me retaliate."

"It would have cost you your job." Knox would have made sure of it.

A silence fell between them in the intimate stillness of the cabin. "I asked Daddy about Mama today," she finally said to break it. "About what they were arguing about the day she died."

"What did he say?"

"He wouldn't tell me. He said it was between him and my mother. That I should let it go."

"Maybe you should." He eyed her. "Marriages get rocky. Trust me. It's a fact of life."

"Was your parents' marriage difficult?"

"My parents don't actually *have* a marriage." Cynicism stained his voice. "They have an open-ended partnership they draw upon when needed—utterly dysfunctional and scarily efficient all at the same time."

"Oh." Maybe that explained some of the closed-offness of him. Why he never settled down. "I'm sorry."

"Don't be. I'm sure it works better than a great percentage of American marriages."

She had no doubt it did. Except she knew the magic did exist, because, despite the fiery nature of their union, her parents had loved each other. *Adored* each other. She just hadn't found that magic yet.

A dark hollow dug its way through her insides, Knox's words ringing in her ears. Maybe it was true. Maybe she wasn't capable of love—of giving herself to someone else. Maybe she would never have it.

She adjusted the ice higher on his jaw. "I know I should let it go—what happened that day—it's just Mama's behavior was so off. Something never felt right about it. I think maybe if I understood what happened I could let go."

"And maybe it would only confuse you more."

"Maybe."

His sexy scent wrapped itself around her. No point in wearing that in the barn, she conceded, but she couldn't help but absorb how perfectly the spicy, masculine scent highlighted this more urbane version of Colt. How utterly incapable she was of ignoring either version of him—the sweaty, earthy male she encountered in the barn every day or this drop dead gorgeous version of him. Both were irresistible.

And suddenly she didn't want to ignore it. Suddenly, she didn't care about what was wise or smart anymore, about maintaining concentration on the end goal. Perhaps it was Knox's cruel words or Davis's humiliation of her that drove her—but she needed to know that kiss with Colt hadn't just been a flash in the pan. That she was *worth* something. That Knox was wrong.

"Colt?"

"Mm?" She could see the dark glitter of attraction staining his amazing eyes. *That* he couldn't hide.

"Let me stay."

"No." Hard. Implacable.

She bit her lip. Swallowed her pride, because sometimes it got in the way of expressing what her heart truly wanted—this inability of hers to be vulnerable.

She set her gaze on his. "I'm not good at this—you know I'm not. I'm an expert at pushing people away, at avoiding intimate relationships. Maybe it's because I've been hurt too much. Maybe I'm simply not *capable* of it. But with you," she said solemnly, "with the chemistry we share, it's innate, it's just there. And I need that tonight. I need to be with you."

An emotion she couldn't read flickered in his eyes. "Cecily—"

She held up a hand. "What I'm saying is I want this one night. I know you're going to walk away—it's good that you are, because my career is the most important thing in the world to me right now. But this, *us*, I want to know it."

CHAPTER FOUR

ALEJANDRO'S HEART JOLTED in his chest. He could have taken just about anything she'd thrown at him and put the breaks on this insanity—but *that*—that was like a kick to the teeth.

He ran a hand over his jaw, unfamiliar wiry stubble scraping his palm. How could he say yes? *How could he say no?* What must it have cost her to expose herself like that? And yet she had.

Reason battled with madness. So he gave her that one night she was asking for? Showed to her, *proved* to her for one night of her life that she was special, that she was worth more than that jerk Knox Henderson. That she should hold out for everything she wanted and deserved. Was that really so crazy?

And really, how much worse could this get? He'd already gotten so involved, made such a mess of it, that nothing short of him walking away from here in a day's time was going to fix it.

He raked a hand through his hair. "I'm not sure your head is on straight right now. That you're not going to wake up tomorrow with a massive 'seize the moment' hangover and regret this."

She shook her head. "I know what I'm doing."

Alejandro considered himself an honorable man. A good man. But as Cecily slipped off the chair and moved her fingers to the side zipper of her dress, he knew he wasn't a saint.

Eyes on his, she slipped the sexy red dress off her shoulders and let it slip to the floor. His throat went dry. The lacy underwear she wore beneath it was a rich garnet that contrasted deliciously with her honey gold skin, the body the lace encased so perfectly formed it surpassed every one of his earlier fantasies.

"You should lock the door," he rasped.

Her eyes glittered. She kicked the dress aside, walked to the door and locked it. As she turned and moved back to him, her stride smooth and unashamed in her nakedness, a switch flicked inside of him and he was completely and irrevocably lost.

He pulled her onto his lap, her legs straddling his thighs. Cupping her nape, he exerted a light pressure to bring her mouth down to his. Open mouthed and hot, their kisses inflamed his senses. His hands at her hips, he held her in place for his delectation, each kiss unlike any he'd experienced before—so pure and real they stripped him bare. As if they were uncovering layers of each other that had yet to be explored.

Wanting, *needing* to touch her beautiful body, he ran his palms up the hot, smooth skin of her back, luxuriating in her silken perfection. A sigh slipped from her lips, a decadent, hedonistic release of air that made him smile.

"You like my callused hands?"

She pushed back to look at him. "I have this fantasy…"

His blood heated. "Which is?"

A self-conscious shimmer invaded her brilliant blue gaze. "The night we were in the stables…when you were giving Bacchus that massage." Her silky long lashes shaded her cheeks. "I was imagining your hands on me. How they would feel…what you would *do* with them."

The warmth in his blood deepened to full-fired lust. He lifted a brow. "You want my hands on you, *querida*? It would be my pleasure. *If* you promise to submit to a fantasy of mine."

Her eyes widened. "Which is?"

"You'll find out in a few minutes," he murmured, scooping her off the chair and heading for the bed.

"Spanish," she murmured as he set her down. "Is that your heritage?"

Damn, he hadn't even registered the slip. "Yes," he lied, thankful the word was the same in Portuguese and Spanish. *He might well go to hell for this.* He truly might. But his intentions were good.

Cecily watched him as he stripped off his shirt, eyes darkening to a deep slate blue. "You have an amazing body."

He threw the shirt on the floor, his fingers moving to the button of his jeans. "Strip shows are on your list of fantasies?"

Her mouth curved. "If it's you, yes."

He slipped the zipper down, her admission turning him hard as stone. Stuck his fingers in the sides of his jeans and dispensed with them in one quick movement. Kicking the denim aside, he straightened to find her eyes glued to his close-fitting white briefs. More than a bit aroused by the whole show, by the thought of having her, his erection was thick, straining against the fabric.

"I might switch fantasies," she murmured.

"Oh, but that's not how this game is played," he drawled. "Lie down and roll over."

A flush touched her cheeks. Then she obeyed. He drank her in, testosterone sizzling every nerve ending. She had the most amazing backside he'd ever seen. Firm and curvaceous, toned by hours in the saddle, it was the best part of her by far.

He swallowed past the lust clogging his throat. He intended to show that part of her anatomy his deepest idolatry.

He knelt on the bed beside her. Placed a palm on the small of her back and settled her as he would a nervous filly. A shiver moved through her. Tracing his palm up over her back, then down over her bottom and legs, he absorbed every dip and curve of her beautiful body.

Need gnawed at the edges of his self-control, goading him on. He straddled her. Set his mouth to the back of her neck and took a long, deep taste of her. She arched beneath him, a low moan leaving her throat. "That's not hands."

He ran his tongue along the curve of her shoulder. "I made no promise about the exclusive use of hands."

Not a word in response.

Down her body he went, his touch reverential as he explored every inch of her, kneading her silken flesh. Her whimpers, the way she came alive beneath his hands, fired his hunger. His erection thickening, growing with every low moan, he leashed himself with superhuman effort.

Finally, he reached her amazing backside. The silk thong barely covered the twin smooth globes. Cupping her in his hands, he squeezed and shaped her. Absorbed the hitch in her breath when he slid his palms down to her satiny thighs and pushed them apart.

"Colt—"

"Shh." Pressing a kiss to the small of her back, he slid his fingers underneath the sides of her flimsy panties and stripped them off.

Her breath grew shallower, her muscles tensing. "Relax," he whispered, stroking the inside of her thighs with a feather light touch. When she softened beneath his hands, he slid a pillow underneath her hips to raise her up. Spreading her thighs wider, he ran his knuckles along the soft, silky hair that covered her most intimate flesh. She shuddered, fingers grasping hold of the comforter.

He parted her with gentle fingers. Stroked her hot flesh from bottom to top.

She jerked beneath his hand. *"Colt."*

"Easy," he whispered in her ear, ghosting his thumb

over her. Again and again until she sighed, sank into it and pressed into his touch.

She grew softer, moister beneath his hand. Coating his fingers with her slick arousal, he eased two inside her. Her mewl of pleasure pushed him close to the edge.

He set his mouth to the hollow between her shoulder blades and pressed kisses to her skin while he worked his fingers in and out of her, keeping up a smooth, deep rhythm that had her climbing the rungs of a ladder he knew would lead to her release.

"God, Colt, please—"

Her body clamped tight around his fingers. Shifting lower, he spread her wide and put his mouth to her. Licked her with provocative, leisurely strokes while he worked her with his fingers.

"More," she begged.

He closed his mouth over the swollen nub at the center of her and sucked. *Devoured* her.

"You're so sweet," he rasped, drunk on the taste of her. "Come for me, angel."

She whimpered and lifted her hips. He drove his fingers hard inside her tight, hot warmth, his tongue nudging her core. She screamed, burying her face in the bedding, her earthy sounds of pleasure as her climax rode her the most arousing thing he'd ever heard.

He didn't stop until he'd made her come twice.

Her body racked with a series of aftershocks, Cecily stared up into Colt's beautiful dark eyes as he flipped her over.

Bracing a corded, insanely strong arm on the mattress beside her, he ran a finger down her cheek. "Live up to your expectations?"

Words stuck in her throat. She couldn't be droll in that moment. It had just been too…*earthshattering.*

His thumb slid to her mouth. He exerted a sensual pressure on her bottom lip until she opened to his caress. "Want to know what my fantasy is?"

Unsure she could take anymore, she forced herself to nod.

"You riding me," he murmured. "With all of that superior control and concentration of yours."

Her heart thudded in her chest. Dropping his hand from her mouth, he slid off the bed, stripped off his boxers and threw them on the floor. Her chest went tight. Full, heavy, so insanely masculine, just looking at him made her throb deep inside her core.

"I might like to redirect this fantasy," she murmured, eyes hot on him.

He pulled his wallet out of his jeans and extracted a foil package. "No," he said, coming back to her and tossing the condom on the bed. "You get yours," he murmured, sinking his fingers into her hips and lifting her on top of him, "and I get mine."

Twining a thick, golden curl around his finger, he brought her mouth down to his for a hot, devastating kiss that wiped any alternate plans from her head.

"You can put this on," he murmured when they came up for air. Curling his fingers around the foil package, he handed it to her.

"Oh." She gave him an uncertain look. "I'm not so good at that. My ex-fiancé and I—we—I was on the pill."

He didn't make fun of her. Didn't look down on her as Davis had for being so inexperienced. "Let me show you then."

He ripped the package open and took the condom out. Rolling it part way up his heartstoppingly virile length, he paused, capturing her fingers in his. "Now you."

Carrying her fingers to his shaft, he closed his hand over hers. Eased the condom up his pulsing flesh. Her breath hitched as he jerked beneath her touch. It was the most erotic thing she'd ever experienced.

"You're beautiful," she murmured, heart in her throat.

"Not like you," he said, shaking his head. A sensual promise lit his gaze. "Now get on me."

The stark, sexual command, the promise of oh, so much more pleasure, sent her pulse skyrocketing.

Lifting up on her knees, she curled her fingers around his shaft and brought the lush wide crest to her center. Empty, aching, the desire he inspired in her almost frightening in its intensity, she lowered herself onto the thick column of flesh, a moan tearing itself from her throat as she absorbed the power of him.

"Slowly," he murmured, eyes hot on hers. "You were made to take a man, angel."

Her stomach fell apart. Lost, immersed in a storm of her own making, sure nothing would ever compare to this moment, she had no choice but to surrender to it.

Slowly, gradually, her body gave around his, making way for his possession. When he was finally buried to the hilt, when she'd taken all of him, he uttered a curse, the hard lines of his face a study in concentration.

"Cecily," he murmured, his voice a rough caress, "*querida*. I need you to move, before I lose my mind."

He was holding back. On the edge. She dug her teeth into her lip, a flash of heat careening through her. That she could turn him on this much, that he desired her this greatly, healed a part of her she hadn't been sure would ever mend. It was a soul shaking moment she had to pause and fully absorb, bracing her palms on his rock-hard abs. For in that moment, they belonged to each other.

"Cecily…" Hoarse. Desperate.

She started to move, watching the pleasure explode in his eyes. The intimacy seemed too much, clawed at her to look away, but she couldn't, wouldn't, because if this was going to be her one night with Colt—she was going to remember every last second of it.

Her body fully aroused, drowning in the pleasure he was giving her, she took him easily now, sliding up and down his staff. He impaled her, touched her deeper every time she came down on him. Another orgasm built, this one slow moving and slumberous, radiating out from her core.

Colt tugged on her hand and pulled her forward. A palm at the small of her back, he arched her toward him and closed his mouth over a lace-covered nipple. She gasped, pushed herself deeper into his mouth. His cheeks hollowed out as he sucked her deep, sending more pleasure coiling in her abdomen.

"That feels so good," she moaned, moving faster on him now.

He switched his attention to her other nipple, teeth rasping across the tip as he drove up inside her, pushing so deep he set off a soul-shaking burst of pleasure that tore her apart.

Oh, dear God.

He cleaved his fingers through her hair and brought her mouth down to his. "I want your beautiful lips on mine when I come, angel. Your body is so sweet, you blow my damn mind."

Holding her bottom in his hands, he took her with sensual, mind blowing thrusts that sent more aftershocks of pleasure spiraling through her. Capturing her bottom lip between his teeth, he came with a throaty growl that reverberated right to her toes.

Seduced by his guttural sounds of pleasure, the hard stroke of his body, another wave of white-hot pleasure pulsed through her, rending her boneless and brainless, sprawled across his chest.

And then there was nothing but a dark, delicious abyss.

* * *

He woke her before dawn. Cupping her breast in his palm, he nudged her thigh forward and slid into her from behind.

"You wanted one night," he intoned huskily in her ear, "you get more."

His finger caressed the hard nub at the centre of her with smooth, delicious circles that soothed her sore skin. Rousing her desire all over again, he stroked her flesh until it was wet and pliant beneath his fingertips...until a low moan left her throat and she arched back against him, demanding his deeper possession.

He was in total control in this position. Exquisite and leisurely, as unhurried as the night before had been urgent, he made it last forever. A deep, delicious orgasm sliding over her, she curled back into his arms and slept.

When she woke again, her arms and legs tangled with Colt's, dawn had arrived. Hating to leave, but knowing she should before her absence was noticed and rumors spread like wildfire, she untangled herself and slipped from the bed.

Dressing in the pink-lit room, feeling like a very different woman than the one who had walked in here the night before, she let herself silently out the door and closed it behind her.

Shoes in her hand, feet soaked by the early morning dew, she ran up the path to the house.

All of a sudden, one night didn't seem like nearly enough.

Alejandro woke with a heavy head and a stinging jaw. Hitting the snooze button with the back of his hand, he pried his eyes open to find Cecily gone, the delicate floral scent that clung to the bedding the only evidence she'd even been there.

"Better like this," he muttered, dragging himself out

of bed and into a shower. He made it a practice never to let a woman sleep in his bed, which made awkward good-byes a non-issue.

Returned to the land of the living with a hot shower, he found a text from Sebastien waiting for him when he got out.

Only a few hours left until you've successfully completed your challenge. The jet will be on the tarmac by eight o'clock this evening. You are leaving for personal reasons you must attend to immediately. Looking forward to hearing the debrief.

Santo Deus. He pocketed the phone and headed out the door. He needed out of here and *now.* Before he did something else he'd regret. Because surely what had happened between him and Cecily last night had been unwise. The problem was, he thought he might do it again if presented with the same situation, because watching that sexy confidence take up residence on her face as they'd blown each other's brains out in bed had been worth it.

He went about his daily chores, relieved to find Cecily and Dale had driven out of state to look at a horse after Knox Henderson's abrupt departure this morning. It was better he leave without goodbyes or explanations, because he had none to give.

No matter how real his feelings for Cecily—no matter how unfinished things between them seemed—*they* could never be. He had nothing to offer a vulnerable woman like her except what he'd just offered—a temporary boost to her ego.

The women in his life were well aware of who he was—knew they were temporary fixtures, to be pampered, enjoyed, then replaced as required. *Everybody won.* Cecily didn't fall into that category.

And then there was the fact that he was about to destroy her family's reputation. He was now convinced Cecily knew nothing of her horse's origins or the Hargroves' transgressions. But the crime still had to be punished. As soon as Stavros handed him the proof, he would secure justice for his grandmother just as he'd promised her he would.

Bacchus would be the only exception from the Salazar's revenge. Because on that point, he refused to break Cecily's heart.

CHAPTER FIVE

CECILY REACHED FOR the iron control she was famous for as she cantered into the ring in Geneva for her world championship qualifying event. She found herself deluged by nerves instead, her stomach churning like a rollercoaster ride.

Saluting the judges, she breathed in deep, gathered the electric charge of the crowd and used it to propel her around the course in a very fast, clean round—the final in the jump off.

She pulled Bacchus to a dancing halt, her horse sensing he'd been a star today. Staring up at the clock, heart in her mouth, the roar of the crowd echoed the numbers on the screen.

She had finished in third place.

It wasn't until Dale had pulled her off Bacchus in the collecting ring and engulfed her in a huge hug that it sunk in. *She'd done it.* Her world championship dream was still alive.

It wouldn't erase the lacklustre year she and Bacchus had had, nothing could do that, but it would go a long way toward convincing the committee she should be in the running for a spot on the team. And right now, that was all she could do.

All due to Colt who'd found the key to her and Bacchus. A low throb pulsed through her as she pulled off her hat to greet the press. Colt who'd been gone when she'd returned from Maryland, a 'personal matter' drawing him home.

She'd been worried at first, asking Cliff for his phone number so she could make sure he was okay. But he hadn't left one. *As if what they'd shared had meant nothing to him.*

She kept the smile determinedly plastered across her face as she did half a dozen media interviews, wishing he were here. Which was ridiculous. She'd known he would leave. Had prepared herself for that. What had hurt the most was he hadn't even said goodbye.

Her stomach gave another ominous churn as she finished her last interview. Bile climbing the back of her throat, she barely made it to the washroom before she was violently ill.

It wasn't until she was on the jet flying home that pieces of the puzzle began sorting themselves into dizzying place. In the crush getting ready for Geneva, she hadn't had her period. She'd attributed it to stress, but *oh, my God.* Her heart seized as a sea of blue flew past outside the window. *It couldn't be.* Colt had worn a condom both times they'd made love.

A trip to her doctor, however, proved the impossible possible. She was pregnant with Colt's baby, a fact that threw her whole life—her career—into disarray once again.

Few top performing riders ever competed while pregnant. The risk wasn't worth it. Which meant there would be no world championships for her and Bacchus this year, the last thing she ever would have thought would derail her.

Shock and crushing disappointment consumed her as she fought her way through the next couple of days. What was she going to do? Her single, coherent thought was that Colt needed to know about his child. He might not want *her*, but it was his right to know they had conceived a baby together.

Finding him a preferable next step than telling her father she was pregnant with Colt's baby, she hired a private investigator who had tracked a fellow rider's birth mother down. Forty-eight hours later, Victoria Brown arrived at the coffee shop in town where Cecily had arranged to meet her, a manila folder in her hand.

Cecily lifted her gaze expectantly to the attractive brunette as she sat down, knots tangling her stomach.

"Did you find him?"

Victoria nodded. "There was a slight issue, however. Colt Banyon does not exist."

Cecily shook her head, confused. "But you just said you found him."

"I found the man who was posing as Colt Banyon." Victoria set her gray-blue gaze on Cecily. "There are no Banyons in New Mexico with any connection to the man who worked here. The man who worked for you fabricated his identity. A very sophisticated fabrication I might add."

Bemusement wrapped her brain in a gray haze. *Why would Colt do that? What had he needed to hide?* There had to be a logical explanation for it.

"I ran the photo you gave me from the party through my database," Victoria continued, "minus the facial hair. Colt's real name is Alejandro Salazar. He—"

The crash of china reverberated through the café, attracting stares from the clientele. Cecily looked down at the broken pieces of her cup littering the floor, then back up at Victoria, her brain frozen. *There must be some mistake.* It was not possible Colt could be Alejandro Salazar, the billionaire heir of her family's greatest rival. He could not have been working at Esmerelda.

There was no mistake, Victoria assured her as the girl from the shop came by with a broom to clean up her mess. She'd tracked Alejandro Salazar's movements during that time. He'd been in Kentucky. Colt *was* Alejandro.

She sat there in a daze after Victoria left, the world tilting on its axis. She was pregnant with *Alejandro Salazar's baby*. It was utterly, completely incomprehensible. She'd seen pictures of him of course, years ago, but he'd been clean shaven at a society event, nothing like the man who'd worked at Esmerelda.

Clasping her fingers around the new cup of tea the shop girl had insisted on bringing her, she fought to make sense of it all. What had Alejandro been doing here? Why had he been posing as a groom?

She'd never understood the ridiculous feud their two families were embroiled in. Had asked her parents about it multiple times only to be told the crazy rumors that Zeus's line had somehow been stolen from the Salazars were all in Adriana Salazar's delusional head.

Her heart dropped, fingers curling tight around the cup. Had Alejandro's presence here had something to do with that? Was he out to hurt her family?

Betrayal, hot and debilitating, slid through her. She'd thought she'd known him. That he'd cared about her. That he'd wanted her for who she was. When was she going to learn?

Davis had convinced her he'd wanted her too. She'd been so sure, so convinced he'd loved her she'd swanned all over town picking out china patterns, sending out rose-embossed wedding invitations, before she'd found out three weeks before the wedding from his drunken best man that her fiancé had a mistress he intended to keep. That instead of being the love of Davis's life, she had been a politically advantageous match chosen for her name and fortune.

Don't be so naïve, he'd raged at her when she'd broken things off. *Marriages have nothing to do with love.* Apparently she *had* been that naive, because it turned out she was the only one who hadn't seemed to know about her fiancé's dalliances.

Her teeth sank into her lip, the salt tang of blood staining her mouth. She'd promised herself she'd never let anyone hurt her that badly again. Use her that way. She'd let

Colt—*Alejandro*—in for the precise reason she'd believed he was different.

Once again, she'd been a *fool*.

She moved a numb gaze to the manila folder on the table. She should go home right now and tell her father. God knew what Alejandro Salazar's intentions were. But she couldn't do that—not with the explosive secret she carried. Not when her entire future depended on finding out what the truth was.

The only place she was going to find that was in New York.

CHAPTER SIX

"I HAVE YOUR PROOF."

Alejandro unfolded himself from his chair, stood, cell phone pressed to his ear and prowled to the floor-to-ceiling windows of his Manhattan office, a spectacular view of the Hudson River spread out before him.

"How accurate are your results?" he asked Stavros.

"Indisputable."

Satisfaction warmed his veins. "Courier them to me?"

"Already on the way." His friend took a sip of what was undoubtedly a double espresso served extra hot by his ever efficient PA. "Does this mean you'll have more time to devote to your friends now? At this rate it'll be Sebastien's thing before I see you."

Alejandro scowled. "It's his fault I'm so snowed under. If this damn party was anything but his anniversary celebration, I'd be saying thanks but no thanks."

"Aren't you even the least bit curious to meet my wife?"

Immeasurably. Meeting the woman who had somehow maneuvered Stavros into marriage was at the top of his personal priority list. Unfortunately, his hellish work schedule was derailing that plan.

"My curiosity will have to wait a couple of weeks."

"Kala." His friend took another sip of java. "I have a name to run by you. Guy by the name of Brandon Underwood—an old acquaintance of my wife's. He's in the race horse business."

Alejandro's lip curled. "Old money. Brandon's a spoiled rich boy with aspirations to follow in his senator daddy's footsteps. The Underwoods keep the rug swept so clean, you know there's dirt underneath."

"Good to know."

"You jealous of boy Underwood?"

"Hardly." Stavros shrugged the inquiry off as he always did anything that went more than surface deep. "You planning on bringing a plus-one to Sebastien's thing?"

He hadn't decided that yet. Given he was the only one flying solo, it had been tempting to pick up the phone and call the lawyer he'd met at the gym a few weeks ago, a beautiful brunette who'd made it patently clear she was waiting for his phone call. But he couldn't seem to do it.

Not even a vision of Brigitte's chic, chin-length bob, svelte figure and endless legs could strip his head of a certain voluptuous blonde who'd ridden him to within an inch of his life and left him wanting more. His body still seemed programmed for tiny, stacked females with an attitude.

"Might fly solo," he murmured absentmindedly, as his PA, Deseree, stuck her head in his office and gave him a five-minute signal. "I have a board meeting, I have to go. See you next week."

Stavros signed off. Pocketing the phone, Alejandro rifled through the papers on his desk. A frown creased his brow. "Des—" he called, walking to the door, "I can't seem to find that European market report. Can you scare up a—" the words froze in his mouth as he recognized the woman standing in front of his PA's desk.

Clad in a cream dress made of some soft material that hugged every memorable curve, a sky high pair of stilettos, her honey blonde hair a smooth silk curtain that fell over her shoulders, Cecily looked every bit New York chic. *Gorgeous.* But it was the icy glitter in her beautiful blue eyes that commanded his attention.

Por amor a Deus. She knew.

Dust in his throat, gravel in his mouth. *What the hell was she doing here?*

Deseree stared at them with unabashed fascination. He

snapped his stunned brain back into working order. He needed to defuse this…fast.

"Tell my father to start the meeting without me."

Deseree's jaw dropped. Salazar board meetings were a sacred thing. His father, Estevao Salazar, the Chairman of the Board, was known for his legendary temper tantrums over the tardiness of its members to his strictly laid out quarterly meetings. A true professional, however, Deseree didn't miss a beat, simply picked up the phone and started dialing.

Alejandro gestured toward his office. "After you."

Cecily turned on her heel and stalked inside. Her back a band of pure iron, fire sparking from every inch of her tiny frame, her amazing backside set off to perfection in the form fitting dress, she sent a wave of lust coursing through him that defied rationality. Now was *not* the time.

He closed the door with a soft click. Faced the firebrand in front of him. Hands clenched by her sides, a flush staining her cheeks, she was clearly furious. He thought he might start with an apology.

"*Eu sinto muito*, Cecily," he murmured, holding her gaze. *I'm sorry.* "I never intended to hurt you. I tried to take a step back, you know I did."

Eyes darkening, she lifted her hand and slapped him across the face. *Hard.*

"I deserved that," he said evenly, jaw reverberating with the force of it. "I deserve your anger. Now let's sit down and be rational about this. Let me explain."

"*Rational?*" She planted her hands on her hips. "You would like me to be *rational?* You came to work for my family under false pretenses. You lied to me and everyone else who trusted you, *cared* about you. You're lucky I haven't gone to the police."

He forced himself not to smile at how cute *police* came out in her feminine southern drawl. That would not help matters. "I haven't broken any laws," he returned smoothly. *Well, maybe one or two small ones.* "I applied for a job, was accepted and carried out my responsibilities."

"Why? What were you doing there?"

He leaned a hip against his desk. "Your family stole something from mine. I came to get proof."

She frowned. "Are you talking about *Zeus?* Does this have something to do with that crazy rumor you mentioned on our picnic?"

"It's not a rumor. Your grandfather illegally bred his mare Demeter to Diablo when Diablo was on loan to an American breeder, which means the whole backbone of your showjumping line is based on a lie. I have proof."

The color drained from her face. "What kind of *proof?*"

"I had Bacchus's DNA tested. He is irrefutably of Diablo's blood, not Nightshade's."

"I don't believe it," she whispered, skin a chalky white. "My parents told me it wasn't true."

"The testing was done in an internationally respected lab. There is no doubt as to its veracity."

She turned and walked to the window. Palm pressed to the glass, her slight shoulders stooped, body vibrating with emotion, he had to bite back the urge to touch her, to comfort her, because he couldn't do that anymore. He was the *enemy.*

She turned and leaned against the sill, those dark bruises in her eyes he hated. "Even if this is true, it happened *decades* ago. It's ancient history. Why can't you let it go?"

"Because your family stole something from mine and built a legacy around it. You profited immeasurably from it not only financially but in reputation, while I might add, throwing it in my family's face. It was a crime. It needs to be paid for."

Her mouth twisted. "Adriana is operating on bitterness. She and my grandmother had the biggest rivalry in the business. Adriana could never accept that my grandmother ended up on top. But she is *dead* now, Alejandro. There is no more skin to flay."

He lifted a shoulder. "Your family is still profiting from what it stole. My grandmother should have owned that glory. She will never rest until history is corrected."

"Why didn't she just move on?" She shook her head. "She had as many opportunities to breed Diablo as we did. Maybe we just did it better."

He flinched at the typically superior Hargrove response. "Diablo fell ill when he returned to Belgium." The words left his mouth on a scalpel's edge. "He was never able to sire any more offspring. Zeus was his last."

The blue of her irises expanded. Clearly she hadn't been privy to all the history—the depth to which her family had so completely destroyed his grandmother's legacy.

"What do you intend to do?"

"Take it to court. Extract all the damages my grandmother is due. Make it known the Hargrove legacy is built on a lie."

Her eyes darkened. "My father will never allow it. All it's going to do is create a media furor and drag both our family's names through the mud, only to be left with a truth that no longer means anything."

His blood heated. "It's a question of *honor*, something your family would have little idea of."

"Honor at what price?"

She looked so small, shaken, *vulnerable*, his heart contracted. "I've insisted Bacchus be left out of it. I will not see you two separated. That's the best I can do."

"How big of you." Her mouth curled. "You will save Bacchus while you destroy my family."

He studied her. Noted the dark shadows underneath her eyes. They were new—making her look even more bruised. Since he knew she'd finished in third place in Geneva, had checked the standings, he wondered why they were there. Why did she look as if a burst of air might blow her away?

"Why are you here?" he asked softly. "How did you know?"

"I hired a PI." She stared at him for a long moment, as if waging an internal battle, then losing the war as a breath escaped her. "Was any of it real? Who you are? The way we were together?"

It was his chance, he knew, to restore sanity to the situation. To cut this off now. To let her think it hadn't meant anything to him to make it easier for both of them in the long run. But he was as incapable of hurting her now as he had been from the beginning.

"Yes," he said matter-of-factly. "What we had was real, Cecily. But it was a mistake on my part. It never should have happened."

"That's right," she countered, hurt radiating in those big eyes. "I *begged* you to take me to bed and you are such a *man,* you kindly obliged me."

He took a step toward her. "That's not how it was."

She held up a hand, stopping him in his tracks. "Just to set the record straight—in case you think I was pining away for you, so *love struck* after that memorable night you gave me, I couldn't stay away—perhaps I should tell you the reason I hired a PI to find you. I am *pregnant,* Alejandro. How would you like to deal with that? How does that fit into this revenge plan of yours?"

His stomach dropped. "That's not possible. We used condoms."

"Condoms *fail.*" Her expression was utterly flat. "Clearly they do because two pregnancy tests and a doctor have now confirmed it *is* possible."

His knees went weak. He wasn't about to question if it was his because he knew it was. Knew *her*.

The room swayed around him in a dizzying array of colors, his life as he knew it unraveling so fast it was like he'd lost control of the delicate rigging on his boat and was plunging fast toward a murky bottom.

"This is clearly a development we need to discuss."

Her eyes morphed to a deep, dark blue. "You think so? You intend on destroying my family, Alejandro. You lied to me from the first moment I met you. Why in the world would I have a civilized discussion with you about our baby? Seems to me, this conversation is over."

"Cecily—"

She backed up, eyes on his. "I don't even know who you are. How can I trust you with anything?"

Face shattering, she turned around, flung the door open and left.

Feeling as if a stiff whiskey was in order, Alejandro took himself to the executive conference room down the hallway instead, where the board meeting was in progress. But not before he dialed his driver and told him to follow Cecily when she left the building. Letting the little spitfire loose in New York with her explosive news wasn't a risk he was willing to take with a potential scandal in the making.

His father held court delivering the opening remarks as he slipped silently into his seat. Estevao Salazar stopped talking as he did, his piercing dark stare directed at his son. Alejandro ignored it and motioned for him to continue, head spinning too much to contemplate delivering the agenda.

"Soliciting unnecessary grief?" Joaquim murmured from beside him.

He gave his brother a black look, the irony of the remark sinking deep. *How could he have been so stupid to have risked something like this with Cecily?* He had told himself it wasn't a good idea to get involved with her. Had known the thin line he was walking. And what had he done? Let his lust and weakness for a blonde with big blue eyes and a vulnerable streak a mile-wide override his better judgment.

Maldita sea. Damn it to hell.

His father moved on to the first agenda item. He sat back in his chair. *This was a disaster.* Not an exaggeration when his grandmother refused to step foot in a room with a Hargrove. When Stavros had just delivered him the proof he needed to bring Cecily's family to its knees.

What was his family going to say when he casually announced he'd fathered a child with a Hargrove? What was Clayton Hargrove going to say when his daughter revealed she was pregnant with his child?

If he was in a mess, Cecily was in a worse one. She couldn't ride in the world championships now—at least she wouldn't if she were wise. A massive blow when she'd finally made it back to where she needed to be.

He wondered how she was handling it. Not well, he ventured, recalling her pale face. Those dark shadows ringing her eyes... She'd been carrying this around with her, no doubt trying to figure out what to do, his deception compounding the problem.

He shifted in his chair, the room feeling excessively hot. Loosened his tie. They would have this baby, of course. He might be one of the most commitment phobic creatures ever to roam this earth, but this was his *flesh and blood.* His heir. Becoming a father was a responsibility he would never shirk, particularly given the poor example his own had been.

Estevao Salazar had only ever been interested in raising a successor, not a son. His insatiable lust for power and the adulation that came with it had torn his family apart, his father's affairs driving Alejandro's mother across the ocean to pursue her riding career when their marriage disintegrated, leaving he and Joaquim to fend for themselves in their American boarding school.

His child, he knew with a bone-deep certainty, would have the love and stability he and Joaquim had never had in those early years before his grandmother had taken them in. They would never know a moment of the alienation and fear he had. Never doubt how much they were *valued*.

Which, he acknowledged, meant the right thing to do would be to marry Cecily. To provide his child with that stable environment he'd never had. It would cause waves, no doubt. His grandmother would lose her mind. But what else could he do?

He *liked* Cecily—admired her courage and strength. Their chemistry was undeniable. And since he'd never intended on marrying for love, since his vision had always been about practicality, about making that leap when the time came—well that time had clearly come.

Which didn't necessarily ease the haze enveloping his brain…the apprehension gripping his insides at having his life plan sped up by about five years.

His father pulled him aside on the break. Tall, still handsome at sixty with the smooth good looks he'd parlayed into a career of mistresses, Estevao Salazar's dark eyes snapped with irritation as he regarded his son.

"Nice of you to join us."

"My apologies. I had something urgent to take care of."

"Well see that it's taken care of before tonight. We have dinner with the Scandinavians. I want this deal done."

"I can't make it."

His father's gaze narrowed. *"Com licença?"* Excuse me?

Alejandro lifted a shoulder. "Take Joaquim. It's his deal. He can handle it."

A ruddy flush lit his father's cheeks. "What the hell is wrong with you, Alejandro? Where are your priorities? First your impromptu two-week vacation during our busy time, then *this*? What could be more important than this meeting?"

Avoiding a family scandal. Finding Cecily before she got on a plane.

"A personal matter." He met his father's fury with an even look. "Since you've had more than your fair share of those, I'm sure you'll understand."

Cecily paced her hotel suite, wondering what to do.

Perched high atop Madison Avenue, the luxury boutique hotel's Champagne Suite gave its occupant the impression of utter invincibility. But invincible was the last thing she felt at the moment. In fact, she was highly unbalanced from her showdown with Alejandro.

She should have come here with a plan. She needed a plan. But the fact was she had *no* plan, a problem when she was dealing with Alejandro Salazar, one of the world's most powerful men. Utterly in command of his domain today in his sky-high office, inherently sure of the power he wielded, he was clearly a lethally purposeful creature capable of doing whatever he needed to do to achieve his goal. *Which was to destroy her family.*

Not in the least bit hungry for the dinner she'd ordered, she crossed to the slate of windows that made up the entire front wall of the suite. Manhattan in all its glory sparkled back at her—a glittering spectacle so different from her beloved blue grass, she was usually entranced by it. But not tonight. Tonight nothing seemed to penetrate the numbness encasing her.

Her entire legacy had been built on a fabrication. Her parents had been lying to her this entire time. What it could mean for her family, her career, scared the hell out of her. To lose all her horses but Bacchus, to have the Hargrove name left in ruin. But there was another emotion present too…an insidious one that lingered at the edges. *Disappointment.*

She crossed her arms over the hollow feeling in her stomach. *What had she expected?* She'd known Alejandro wasn't *Colt*—the man she'd fallen for. Had known he was going to tell her something she didn't want to hear. She'd been through this before—the crushing disillusionment of finding out someone wasn't who they'd pretended to be. So what was the problem?

She'd wanted him to be that man who'd held and comforted her? Who'd made love to her so passionately as if it *meant* something? She'd wanted to be *wrong* about him? *God she really was a fool.*

His words echoed against the walls of her mind. *I tried to take a step back, you know I did.*

He was right. He had made every attempt to stay away from her—to demonstrate this thing between them wasn't wise. Had tried to cut things off time and time again. It had been *her* that had pursued him—*her* that wouldn't leave it alone—*her* that had seduced him.

He might have deceived her, but she held responsibility for this mess too.

A plan would have been helpful.

The peal of the doorbell jolted her out of her reverie. *Her dinner.* Pushing away from the window, she crossed the cream colored carpet on soundless feet, unbolted the door and pulled it open.

Alejandro, his sophisticated three-piece suit replaced by a pair of dark designer jeans and a red polo shirt, stood leaning against the door frame. Her heart hammered in her chest. His jaw smoothly shaven, sensual, forbidding mouth relaxed, dark eyes focused on her, he was no less intimidating than he'd been in the suit.

Pulse skittering, every cell affected by his blatant masculinity, she swallowed past the fist in her throat. "How did you find me?"

"I had my driver follow you."

Of course he had. She lifted her chin. "I told you, I'm done talking to you."

"If you were done talking you would have flown home this afternoon." His eyes glittered with a purposeful, black velvet cool. "We're having a child together, *querida*. We need to discuss what comes next. Or," he drawled, lifting a brow, "will you go home and casually mention to your father you're pregnant with my child with no game plan at all?"

"I hate you," she hissed. Particularly this new version of him.

"Go right ahead," he agreed in that smooth, reasonable tone. "But we still need to talk."

He was right. She stepped back, antagonism tightening every inch of her body. He strode past her into the suite, kicked off his custom-made Italian shoes and surveyed his surroundings.

"Nice suite."

"It was all they had to choose from." She watched as he walked to the bar and poured himself a whiskey. "Why don't you help yourself?"

"This is about six hours overdue," he murmured, picking up the glass, swirling its contents and taking a long gulp.

She wrapped her arms around herself as he lowered the glass and subjected her to one of those intense, utterly focused perusals of his. "Did you eat?"

"I have dinner on the way."

"Good. You look pale. You need to keep up your strength."

"Because I'm eating for two?" she scoffed. "You don't

have to pretend you care, Alejandro. My eyes are wide open now."

He cradled the glass in his palm, a ghost of a smile curving his lips. "I do care, Cecily. Thus the situation we find ourselves in. I told you that before I knew about the pregnancy. In fact, everything I said to you in Kentucky was true, every emotion I expressed real. The only thing I lied about was my identity and that I had to do."

Her stomach curled with the need to believe him. To believe *something* in all of this was real—that what they'd *shared* had been real. But she'd be a fool to take what he was saying at face value—even more of a fool than she'd already been.

He gestured toward the cream sofa that faced the spectacular view. "Why don't we sit down?"

"I'd prefer to stand."

"Fine." He lowered himself onto the chaise, splaying his long legs out in front of him. "We are keeping this baby, Cecily."

"Of course we are. *I* am," she corrected. "I would never do anything else."

"Good. And just to clarify," he drawled, eyes on hers, "when I said *we* are keeping this baby I meant *us*. We are both going to be parents to this child, which means we need to be *together* to do that."

She frowned. "What do you mean *together*?"

"I mean we will marry."

Her knees went weak. She slid down onto the sofa, a buzzing sound filling her ears. "You can't be serious."

"Oh, but I am." An amused smile twisted his mouth. "That's why I suggested you sit down."

Her heart beat a jagged rhythm. "You think we can base a marriage on a *lie*?"

"What we had wasn't a lie. We had something good—

you said so yourself…an organic connection it's impossible to manufacture."

"A connection you destroyed with your lies."

"A connection I *damaged* with my lies. I think we can repair it."

"How?" She lifted her chin. "I gave *Colt*—the man I thought I knew, my trust and *he* threw it away."

"I will earn it back," he countered. "The fact that you are carrying my baby changes everything, Cecily. I don't intend to give up my rights to this child and neither do you, which means we need to make this work. And since making this work means we need to smooth the way with our families, find a way to defuse this feud, *I* will begin the process."

"You said earlier your grandmother will never rest until she has her pound of flesh."

"If we present our relationship as a *fait accompli,* she will have no choice but to give." He frowned. "Perhaps she will be happy with an apology on the part of your family—some kind of public nod to the crime committed."

She shook her head. "My father will never agree to that. He would rather drag it through the courts for all eternity than tarnish the Hargrove name."

"Then he's a fool," he said harshly. "The Salazars could buy and sell your family ten times over. He would fight himself into the ground, only to lose."

She pressed her lips together. "You could make this concession regardless of whether we marry. We could find some peace between the two families and co-parent this child together."

His jaw hardened. "This child is a Salazar, Cecily. My heir. He or she will not be illegitimate."

The utter implacability behind that statement made her shoulders sag. "Even if we can negotiate our way through this family feud," she offered, "we hardly know one other. What's to say we can even make this work?"

"Chemistry is ingredient number one for a good relationship." His gaze speared hers, so familiar and yet so foreign. "We have proven we have that, both in bed and out of it. We have also proven we can be a great team. What more could you ask for?"

Love? That elusive thing she craved but wasn't sure actually existed. For her at least.

"Practicality," Alejandro murmured, sensing her hesitation, "is the thing to base a marriage on. Not this creative storytelling everyone is trying to sell these days of happily-ever-afters that don't exist."

"My parents were in love," she said quietly. "That's why he is the way he is, my father. Because he's never gotten over her."

"Isn't it better to avoid that completely? To base a relationship on pragmatism and affection instead?" He shook his head. "I won't lie and promise you things I don't believe in, Cecily. But I do believe we can make this work. Think about how good we were in Kentucky."

She didn't want to think about that because she wasn't sure if any of it had been real. That he wasn't playing her right now to get what he wanted in his child. Except, she acknowledged, swallowing past the tightness in her throat, it was impossible to forget how patiently he had helped her and Bacchus reconstruct their relationship. How he had helped her reconstruct *herself* in those difficult weeks they'd spent together.

She studied the hard, uncompromising lines of his face. Could he really have manufactured the depth of caring he'd displayed? Why would he have when really, there'd been no reason for him to do it—every reason to do the opposite in fact?

"Why did you help me with Bacchus?" she asked.

"I couldn't stand to watch you hurt," he said quietly. "Even though I told myself it was a bad idea, even though I tried to make myself immune to you, you got under my skin."

Her heart contracted. Emotions, feelings, she'd convinced herself had been a figment of her imagination, a product of her naiveté, flooded back in a storm of confusion. She would have preferred the cold, hard truth to this gray area she couldn't process.

She pushed to her feet and walked to the windows, staring out at the lights dripping from the skyscrapers like tear drops hanging from their tall, imposing perches.

"This is insanity."

"You aren't in this alone, Cecily. I'm here."

He who had never intended on saddling himself with a wife in this revenge plan of his...a notorious bachelor by anyone's standards.

She turned around and rested her palms on the sill. "What about all the women you seem to possess for every different social occasion? I'm supposed to believe you will simply give up your bachelorhood to marry me because of our baby?"

He smiled, that whiskey-colored glimmer that did funny things to her insides lighting his eyes. "I find I like the idea of you as a wife. We would never be short of fireworks. I'm sure it would be more than enough to prevent me from straying."

His arrogance hit her right in the solar plexus, right where Davis had torn her heart out. "*If* I am crazy enough to agree to marry you," she stated icily, "which is doubtful at this point, I will not tolerate infidelity. Any hint of it and I walk."

His gaze narrowed. Rolling to his feet, he covered the distance between them. "It was a joke," he murmured. "My father is a serial affair artist. I would never do that to my own relationship."

"That was the truth then, what you said that night about your parents' dysfunctional relationship?"

"All of it was the truth." His gaze held hers. "Now do you want to tell me why you have that look on your face?"

She shook her head. No way was she offering him her truths when he had withheld his.

"Fine. But you *will* tell me, Cecily, because we are going to repair these trust issues of ours."

She sank her teeth into her lip, feeling far too vulnerable, fragile like glass. "If I were smart," she breathed, "I would be getting on a plane right now and flying home, because *this* is not rational. I should not trust you."

"But you do," he countered softly. "You have from the beginning. You know *me,* Cecily. Trust me now. Do this with me."

A haze of indecision clouded her brain. "I need time," she rasped. "To process this. To figure out what to do."

"Fine. You have a week."

"*A week?*"

"It's too explosive a situation to prolong. My grandmother wants action taken. Plus," he added, "I am due to attend an anniversary party in England at the end of the month. If we are to be married, you should be the woman on my arm."

"You mean you don't already have one lined up?" She hated the sharp claws of jealousy that scored her insides. "I would have thought they'd be chomping at the bit to be at your side."

"Funny that," he murmured, eyes on hers. "I was having trouble getting a certain blonde out of my head. I kept remembering how she wrapped herself around me and took me for the ride of my life…those sexy moans she made when I took her apart…how *sweet* she tasted when I did." His eyes were hot, black velvet now. "I find I want *more*."

Her insides fell apart, a wild heat invading her cheeks. A satisfied smile curved his mouth. "We are good together, *querida,* you know we are. Now you just need to admit it."

She lifted her hands to her burning cheeks. "I am not going to make a decision based on our...*sexual compatibility*. That would be foolish."

"Then make it based on rationality. Your life has imploded around you, Cecily. You need me to take control and fix this. *We* need to make a home for this child. It is the only solution."

A flustered denial bubbled to her lips. It died in her throat when he picked up his glass, drained its contents and walked to the door.

"Make a decision," he said, swinging around to face her, "and let me know."

And then he was gone.

CHAPTER SEVEN

CECILY FED A chilled-out Bacchus the last handful of his favorite breakfast treat as she stood perched on the bottom rung of the pasture fence on a gorgeous, sun-soaked day at Esmerelda.

Clearly enjoying his sojourn from his intensive training schedule, her horse was utterly content grazing with his pasture mates. His mistress, however, was still fighting the crushing disappointment of watching her dream go up in smoke.

This morning, she'd called the head of the decision making committee to let him know about her pregnancy—that she wouldn't be competing for a world championship team spot. It had killed her to do it—worse when he'd given her no idea if she'd have been chosen or not, a nudge of confidence she'd sorely needed in that moment.

And still she hadn't told her father.

A whisper of apprehension fluttered in her belly. She needed to do that today, because today was the deadline Alejandro had given her to make up her mind on whether she would become his wife. A *Salazar.*

She knew what her decision had to be—she'd just been too afraid to voice it.

She couldn't bring up this baby alone, not after she'd lost her own mother so young. Not when that void would always be with her and she wouldn't do that to her child. Nor could she simply stand by and watch her legacy destroyed, her beloved horses taken away, everything her mother and grandmother had accomplished wiped away in a red stain of disrepute. Because Alejandro would win this battle—she knew he would.

Which left her with only one option: to marry him. He'd already been as good as his word, flying to Belgium this week to convince his grandmother to accept a public apology on the part of the Hargroves as compensation for her family's crime. Then he'd followed that up with a call to sweeten the pot. Marry him and he would buy them a property in upstate New York where she could build her dream stables away from the oppressive presence of her father.

A generous gesture of goodwill, a tempting one at that, but it couldn't buy her trust. That he would have to earn.

She bit her lip as she considered a brilliant, clear blue Kentucky sky. Her choice might be clear but none of it negated her fears of picking up her life and plunking it down in New York as Alejandro's society wife. The thought of leaving her home was unbearable. She simply didn't think she had any choice.

She gave Bacchus a final scratch behind the ears and headed for the house and the inevitability that lay ahead. The door to her father's study was closed. About to turn away, deep male voices raised in anger froze her feet in place.

Alejandro's voice.

He couldn't have. Wouldn't have.

Breaching the social etiquette that had been drilled into her since birth, she turned the handle on the door and let herself inside the leather and cigar-infused room. Her father, dressed in casual slacks and a shirt, stood toe-to-toe with Alejandro who looked gorgeous in a navy suit and ice-blue tie.

Her heart thumped wildly in her chest as her father turned a freezing gray gaze on her. "Tell me it isn't true," he rasped.

She swallowed hard, knees weak. "What isn't true?"

"That you are pregnant with his child."

She wrapped her arms around herself, throat tight.

"Yes," she said quietly, looking her father in the eye. "I am. I was going to tell you today. Alejandro clearly beat me to it."

"Today?" her father bellowed. "You knew he came here under false pretenses. Knew what he was planning and you didn't tell me? What were you—so caught up in him you were blind?"

Her anger caught fire. "*You* knew about Zeus. About Bacchus… You lied to me, Daddy."

"I was protecting you from *their* lies," he roared. "How could you be so stupid as to do this? I thought I raised you with some sense in your head."

Alejandro stepped to her side and slid an arm around her waist. "I think you should watch how you're talking to your daughter," he said evenly.

"Stay out of this." Her father kept his gaze trained on her. "The Salazars are out to ruin our name and you are playing right into their game."

"Granddaddy already did that. He broke laws doing what he did. He *stole* from them."

"It never happened. Adriana has never been able to get past her jealousy at Harper's success, at *our* success, so she chooses to try and tarnish our name with her crazed ramblings."

"Alejandro has proof. The truth needs to come out, Daddy. No more lies."

Her father turned to Alejandro. "I want you off my property. *Now*. We will settle this in court."

"You are being shortsighted," Alejandro drawled. "Take what my grandmother is offering… It's the best you're going to get. Make a public apology and put this all behind us."

Her father scowled. "You think I would risk a century-old dynasty offering the Salazars an apology for something that never happened?" He shook his head. "I will tie this up in legalities forever. It will never see the face of a courtroom."

Cecily's heart sank. If it wasn't true what her grandfather had done, there would be no need to stall a court case because the truth would come out.

What else had her father been lying to her about?

Alejandro's fingers tightened against her back. "You are willing to trade your daughter's happiness to perpetuate a lie? If you keep this up, Clayton, there will never be peace between our two families and your grandchild will be stuck in the middle."

"No it won't," her father disagreed. "The courts will give Cecily custody. They always rule in favor of the mother."

"That may be the case," Alejandro rebutted coolly, "but it's inconsequential because Cecily is going to marry me."

Her father's face went a deep shade of gray. "That can't possibly be true."

Furious at both men, Cecily would have loved to have told both of them to go to hell. But she'd made her decision. This baby was going to grow up with both its parents.

"It's true," she confirmed. "I am going to marry Alejandro. So you, Daddy, need to wrap your head around ending this feud."

Clayton Hargrove's jaw hardened. "No daughter of mine is marrying a Salazar. You walk out that door with him and you cut your ties with this family."

Her stomach lurched. "You don't mean that."

Her father crossed his arms over his chest. "Stay and we'll work through this. Leave and you are on your own."

Alejandro lowered his head to hers. "Go pack a bag. You can send for the rest of your things later."

She blinked. "You want me to leave with you *now*?"

"Do you want to stay?"

One look at her daddy's face convinced her that no, she did not. She'd made her decision. She needed to go.

* * *

Alejandro spent the flight back to New York stickhandling the two deals he had up in the air after his whirlwind trip to Belgium and Stockholm—the Scandinavian tie-up he'd been negotiating with Joaquim and the acquisition of a twenty-five billion dollar Columbian coffee company Salazar had been lusting after for decades.

He thought it a good thing Cecily had some time to cool down with a parade of drivers, passport officials and flight attendants providing a buffer between them. She was clearly furious with him, in one of her patented snits, when all he'd been trying to do was help given how wary she'd sounded about approaching her father.

Having scaled three countries in forty-eight hours cleaning up the mess *she* had had an equal hand in creating, he was not in the mood. Not after his confrontation with his grandmother in which she had accused him of a lack of judgment, of *loyalty,* when he'd told her about his relationship with Cecily.

His knuckles gleamed white as he snapped his laptop shut with more force than necessary. They had cut right through him those words, coming from the woman who had taught him the meaning of honor—who'd been the guiding force in his life. For her to question his loyalty had both gutted and infuriated him, made worse by the fact that he'd been forced to lie to her about being in love with Cecily in order to bring some sanity to the situation.

His grandmother had, nonetheless, grudgingly agreed to make the compromise he'd asked of her—the offer Clayton Hargrove had so foolishly rejected. He could only hope Cecily's father had the sense to come around.

His fiancée, unfortunately, was no calmer by the time they got home. She turned on him the minute they'd walked through the door of his architecturally striking, five-story Upper East Side townhouse, blue eyes blazing.

"Why did you do that?" she erupted. "You just made everything worse."

"It's going to be fine," he murmured soothingly, shutting the door. "I promise you. Your father will cool down, I will bring your horses to New York, we will find a place to keep them and we will have a good life together."

"I just don't understand," she raged, as if she hadn't heard him. "Is your head so thick you didn't think I'd know the right way to handle this?"

His jaw clenched. "Then why haven't you? What were you doing, waiting for divine inspiration…for the muses to give you the green light? Perhaps if your father had already absorbed the shock of your pregnancy, he would have been better able to consider my offer."

"I was going to tell him after I talked to you. I would have *eased* him into it. But no, you had to fly in like a big hotshot and call all the plays."

"That's not what I was doing," he said silkily, temper beginning to fail. "I'm stretched to the limit as I seek to solve our dilemma, *querida*. I was trying to help. Forgive me if I neglected to use the finesse you so clearly desired."

She blinked. "How could you possibly be *helping*?"

"You sounded unsure about telling your father. I thought if we handled it together it would be better."

"You handled it by *yourself*," she growled. "You have no sensitivity. A typical male."

Por amor a Deus. He ran a hand through his hair. Was this what his marriage was going to be? One argument after another? The very thing he'd promised himself it would never be.

He understood she was upset, that her life had been blown apart, but so had his. *He was marrying her, for God's sake.* He was going to be a *father.* If he wasn't so busy he might be experiencing a severe case of "free market pre-withdrawal" withdrawal.

"And then," she bit out, on a roll now, "you had the audacity to assume I was going to accept your marriage proposal before I even gave you my answer."

"But you *were*," he came back evenly. "Just out of curiosity, why did you?"

She crossed her arms over her chest. "My mother died when I was fourteen. I spent my most formative years without a female influence. I will never deprive my child of its father."

"Then we both agree that putting our child first is what this is all about."

She gave a reluctant nod.

"Along that vein," he suggested pleasantly, "let me give you a tour of your new home. I think you're going to love it here."

"I will never love New York," she said flatly. "Not like I love Kentucky. I mean it's exciting and all, but I feel like I can't *breathe* here."

"You can, I assure you. I do it every day." He flicked a wrist toward the living room. "After you…"

He gave her a tour of the luxury residence he'd paid twenty-three million for—through the dramatic, double-height living room with its twenty-foot ceilings, exposed brick walls and fireplace, to the magnificent dining room built to entertain.

He thought perhaps the private nanny quarters, the yoga studio or the multi-level roof garden might win her over, but Cecily remained stone-faced throughout the tour. He abandoned his enthusiasm when they reached the top floor master bedroom suite with its massive arched windows and wood burning fireplace, leaving her to freshen up before dinner.

He must've been insane to ever contemplate this marriage. Not only was his soon-to-be wife *persona non grata* with his family, she was so far from the practical solution he'd envisioned, it was like ending up with a custom-made, extremely temperamental sports car when all you'd really wanted was a sleek-looking sedan.

Cecily knew she was being a shrew, but she was so angry at Alejandro for what he'd done, so sideswiped by the events of the day, she thought it better to say nothing at all than let loose with something she shouldn't.

By the time they sat down to dinner on the terrace, she thought she had gotten her emotions firmly under control. A serene, stunning oasis with its hidden nooks and vibrant landscaping, the outdoor space was a slice of heaven in the middle of New York City.

It went a long way toward soothing her raw edges, a good thing because sitting across from Alejandro dressed in jeans and an old Harvard T-shirt, his hair mussed, feet bare, didn't exactly put her in a relaxed frame of mind. He was just *that* gorgeous and looked far too much like the man she'd fallen for in Kentucky.

"Why this?" she asked, waving a hand around them as his housekeeper, Faith, removed their salad plates and brought them coffee and tea. "Why a home instead of some big shot bachelor penthouse from which you can rule the world?"

His ebony eyes sparked with warning. "I think that's enough with the big shot comments, *meu carinho*. You are twenty-five, not five, no?"

She sat back in her chair, cheeks hot. Maybe she hadn't quite reacquired her powers of control.

"The house," he elaborated, "was a surprise for me. I was planning on buying something easier to maintain, then my agent showed me this." He lifted a shoulder. "Maybe it was so many years spent in boarding schools, being shuffled between Brazil and Belgium with my parents living apart. I found I liked the idea of a home."

She absorbed the information about the man she really knew nothing about, which was disconcerting to say the least when he had been privy to her most intimate thoughts and feelings.

"Where did you go to school?" she asked, in an attempt to rectify that.

"New Hampshire." He sat back, coffee cup balanced on his thigh. "My parents sent me to an elite boarding school when I was six. The plan was always to build up Salazar's US operations, so having me and my brother in the States made sense. My father was always traveling and my mother spent most of her time on the road pursuing her equestrian career in Europe."

Six. Her heart contracted. She'd always thought the boarding school concept was inhumane, but that was *so* young.

"It must have been difficult to live so far away from your family."

"It was all Joaquim and I knew. Life at home was hellish—we preferred to be at school. We had each other. And in the summers and on school holidays, we'd be at the farm in Belgium with my grandmother."

She sank her teeth into her lip. Absorbed the hard, impenetrable lines of his face. She had the feeling the emotionally closed-off Colt she'd come to know in Kentucky was very much the man sitting across from her—one shaped by his earliest, most painful experiences.

She took a sip of her tea. Regarded him from over the rim of her cup. "What happened with your parents' marriage? Were they ever in love?"

"Madly so, according to my grandmother. It was a passionate, wild, emotional rollercoaster of a ride until my father's attention wandered a few years after Joaquim was born. Not an unusual occurrence in the society we lived in, but my mother, as you can imagine from her ambitious career, was not the type to turn a blind eye.

"She raged at him, threatened to divorce him and when neither worked, embarked on a series of affairs designed to win him back. But none ever did. Eventually she gave up and moved full-time to Belgium for her riding career, neither dissolving the marriage nor pursuing it because the arrangement worked."

Leaving her children behind in the process. "What's your relationship with your parents now?"

"My father and I have never been close. His focus has always been on the business to the exclusion of everything else. My mother—" his face assumed a neutral expression, "is…delicate. She withdrew into herself after the separation, focusing on her riding and her teaching. It would not be a stretch to say she knows some of her students better than she knows Joaquim and I."

Her chest tightened. She knew that sense of alienation— the pain that came with being distanced by someone you loved. Her father had withdrawn into himself after her mother's death with nothing, it seemed, to give to her.

"That couldn't have been easy," she said quietly, "having such a childhood."

"Thus my deep, dark, damaged views on love?" His mouth twisted. "It was actually a relief when my parents separated for good. My mother was happier that way. Things became civil. The tension was gone. It made me see how a practical marriage like the one you and I are about to embark on can work. Everyone's happy…no one gets hurt."

She wondered if that could be true. If the practical union she had agreed to with Alejandro was a better choice than her deeply held desire to be loved? After what she'd gone through with Davis, she couldn't be sure it wasn't.

"Practical, however," Alejandro continued, "will not do for my grandmother. The only way I could extract the concession I did from her was to make her believe we are madly in love—that *we* and this child are a foregone conclusion. She is anxious to meet you and hear about our wedding plans. I told her we'd stop in on the way home from England."

Wedding plans? Meeting Adriana? Her stomach folded in on itself. "I can't even think about a wedding until my father comes around. I always imagined it would be at Esmerelda."

"Then an early October date will give him incentive to see reason."

Her jaw dropped. His expression remained firm. "I'm not so concerned people will know our child has been conceived out of wedlock. I do, however, intend for us to be married when it happens."

A tumble of words rose to her lips. "But that's two months away," she finally managed. "We can't plan a wedding that quickly."

"You will have people to do it for you."

Dear God. She stared at him. "And how are we to handle the news of our baby in public? At this anniversary party, for instance. I think it's too soon to talk about it."

"Agreed. Removing it from the equation also increases the likelihood people will buy this is a love match. Which," he underscored, "is something we need to accomplish in England. It will be a very high profile party—anyone who's anyone will be there—lots of paparazzi. As our public debut together, it will be our chance to send a clear message to everyone, including your family and mine, that this union is real. That they have no choice but to accept it."

A knot formed in her chest, all of it much too much all of a sudden. Perhaps it was the whirlwind wedding he was demanding…the baby she wasn't ready for…the emotionally explosive day it had been. Or perhaps it was that only a few weeks ago she'd been head over heels for the man she'd thought he was. When acting as if she'd had feelings for him—carrying out this charade—wouldn't have been an issue—it would have been a reality.

"Speaking of babies," he said, pouring himself another cup of coffee from the carafe, "my PA has made you an appointment with the best OBGYN in Manhattan. Better you initiate that relationship now so you can build on it as you go."

So he could ensure the Salazar heir was healthy and well protected more likely. It was, after all, the reason she was here.

She fell quiet as a violet light descended over Manhattan, such a different canvas from the star-infused, inky-black sky she was used to, she was suddenly, achingly homesick.

Alejandro set his cup on the table. "It's late. You look exhausted. You should go to bed. I'll join you in a few minutes after I send a couple of emails."

Her shoulders stiffened at yet another order, but she *was* exhausted. She climbed the stairs to their bedroom, barely able to put one foot in front of the other.

Did he expect her to share his bed? She thought the answer might be yes as she arrived in the sumptuous master suite to find Faith had put her clothes away in the armoire while they had eaten, her toiletries laid out neatly in the opulent, marble and limestone en suite.

She stared at them, not sure she was ready for this. Sure, in fact, she wasn't.

Immersing herself in a cool shower, she attempted to regain her equilibrium. But her nerves grew with every moment that passed. Eventually she *would* have to share that bed with Alejandro—to get to know the complex, intimidating male she'd agreed to marry on every level. But she needed to trust him again first.

She understood from their conversations the deep sense of honor that drove him, *why* he'd done what he'd done, could even accept he'd tried not to hurt her, but he'd damaged them in the place she was the most vulnerable by deceiving her and that was not going to be easy to forgive.

Clad in her favorite pale pink nightie, she brushed her hair in the black stone mirror that lay as an accent piece against the wall in the bedroom, her pulse a staccato drumbeat in her throat.

Alejandro walked in moments later. Eyes wary, face lined with fatigue, the same dark stubble shadowing his jaw he'd worn at Esmerelda, he undid his sleek gold watch and set it on the dresser.

His visible exhaustion unearthed a twinge of guilt. "I'm sorry," she said quietly, "for my behavior today. I'm not myself. I'm overwhelmed, turned upside down. I don't know which way is up anymore."

His expression softened. Dropping his cufflinks on the dresser, he moved behind her, setting his hands on her hips. She jumped, the heat of his touch burning into her skin. He settled his hands more firmly around her. "Try and relax," he said softly. "I never renege on a promise, Cecily. I will make this right."

"What if he never calls—my father?" Her gaze met his in the mirror. "What if he doesn't come around? Things haven't always been good between us but he and my horses are all I have."

"He will. He loves you. And," he murmured, "you have me now—the life we will build together. Think of this as your chance to be something other than a Hargrove, to be what *you* want to be—everything we talked about in Kentucky. I said I would back you one hundred percent and I will."

Warmth surged through her. For the first time today, she almost believed it, that everything would be okay, because this man's will would accept nothing less.

This was the man she'd fallen for in Kentucky. Was *he* somewhere within this arrogant stranger she'd agreed to marry?

He took the brush from her hand and laid it on the dresser. "You were right," he said softly, "that I didn't wait for your answer—that I simply assumed you would become my wife. That said, I hope this will make up for the lack of a romantic proposal."

Her throat went dry as he captured her left hand and slid a ring on her finger. Perched on a delicate platinum band, the round, brilliant-cut diamond was cast in a halo setting, accented by hundreds of tiny diamonds that flashed in the light.

It was the most beautiful thing she'd ever seen.

"I thought it fit your vibrant personality," he murmured. "But if you don't like it, I can have Jovan make something else."

Didn't like it? He'd had it made for her? She melted.

"It's perfect," she said huskily. "Exactly what I would have chosen. Thank you."

He feathered a thumb across her palm, keeping her hand tucked in his. "You need to be wearing the appropriate rock when you walk into that party with me. I think this will do the trick."

She stiffened, the glow inside her evaporating. *For goodness sake, Cecily, get a grip. Remember what this is.*

"It's perfect." She pulled her hand free, channeling the ice princess persona she did so well. "I think you're right, actually. I need some sleep. I'm sure I'll feel better in the morning."

"Why not now?" His throaty rejoinder unraveled a curl of heat inside her as he bent to bring his mouth to her ear.

"We're engaged now, *querida*. There's no reason to hold back."

A flood of seductive, heady memories swamped her senses. She pushed them ruthlessly away. She was his *convenient* wife—the one bearing him his child—nothing more. Just like she'd been for Davis. Paramount to surviving this relationship was going to be keeping her head where he was concerned.

"Yes there is." She twisted out of his arms and turned to face him. "We need time to ease into this, Alejandro. For me to learn to trust you again. For me to get to know *who* you are."

He frowned. "You *know* who I am. We've talked about intimate things…deep things. That *is* who I am."

"I *thought* I knew you," she corrected. "Now I'm not sure what to believe."

He stared at her for a long moment, jaw tight. "Fine. Take all the time you need. But the image we present in public is non-negotiable. We *will* look madly in love at that party even if you have to channel your best acting job to do it. Are you clear on that?"

"Crystal," she murmured. "I'll start practicing right now."

CHAPTER EIGHT

ALEJANDRO SPENT THE next two weeks working day and night to free himself up for his trip to England, his multibillion-dollar acquisition occupying the lion's share of his time. Aware that his fiancée was swimming in the deep end and doing her best to stay afloat, he brought work home with him and had dinner with her each night rather than cast her adrift in Manhattan.

Which also allowed him to work toward his other goal of proving to Cecily she could trust him. That he was that man she'd known in Kentucky. He found himself sharing pieces of himself he rarely did in an effort to have his fiancée do the same with him. It was going to take time, but slowly, ever so gradually, she was letting down her guard. He was beginning to see glimpses of the woman he'd first gotten to know—the open, vulnerable Cecily she was at the heart of her.

It infuriated him that her father hadn't called with an olive branch. As if he truly meant to take the Hargroves' crime to the grave with him rather than allow it to tarnish the family name. As if he cared more about his legacy than the daughter he'd disowned.

It was tearing Cecily apart—he could see it in her expressive blue eyes when her vulnerability shone through. Seeking to provide her with a distraction, he pushed ahead with his plans to buy them a place in upstate New York. While his real estate agent searched for the ideal property, he had Cecily work with an architect to envision what her dream stables would look like. Not only had it occupied his fiancée, it had put a sparkle back in her eyes and given them a project they could work on together.

By the time they boarded the Salazar jet for the anniversary party, they had developed a workable rapport between them. Her continuing to freeze him out was another matter. It wasn't going to work this weekend with the façade they had to perpetuate, nor was it going to close the gulf that had grown between them. And since eliminating that tension, putting his life back into its pre-Kentucky order, was his number one priority right now, he needed to solve *her*.

Watching her now, curled up in a chair beside him as the jet leveled out into a smooth sea of blue, he felt that familiar tug of desire. Dressed in leggings and a sweater that emphasized her soft curves, her legs curled beneath her as she reviewed the architect's revamped drawings, it was as if she flicked some internal switch inside of him just by being in the same room.

What would she look like when she started to show evidence of their child? He imagined those lush curves grown ripe with his son or daughter, a powerfully possessive feeling assailing him, one he couldn't even begin to articulate. She would be even more desirable, if that was possible.

He ran a palm over his jaw. Sexual frustration was not, he was discovering, a state of being he enjoyed.

"Happy with them?" he asked, nodding at the drawings.

She nodded. "They're getting there."

"Bring them over. Show them to me."

She uncurled herself from the chair and perched on the arm of his, walking him through the drawings. They were impressive. She'd thought of everything: roomy, loose boxes for every horse in the barn, extra wide aisles for grooming, a bathing area done in tile as well as multiple indoor and outdoor schooling rings that took into account the cold New York weather. Eventually, he knew, she wanted to be a coach, helping younger riders just as her mother had done.

He pointed to one of the outdoor rings. "You might want

to put that one next to the ring for the more mature horses. The novices tend to pick up their good habits."

She chewed on her lip. "That's a good idea." She made a note. Asked if he had any more thoughts. Because he loved the subject, he did, suggesting small refinements here and there. When they were done, she rolled up the drawing and stayed put.

"Tell me about your friends," she prompted quietly, "so I'm not walking into this cold."

Something he should have done already, but hadn't in his preoccupation with everything on his plate. He captured her hand in his, smoothing his thumb over her palm. "I have three close friends. Sebastien Atkinson founded the extreme sports club we all joined in college. It's he and his wife Monika's anniversary party we're attending.

"Stavros," he continued, "is in pharmaceuticals, based here in New York." His mouth curved. "He's a piece of work. You'll see what I mean when you meet him. He recently married a Greek woman named Calli I haven't met yet, so you won't be the only new face."

"Did they elope?'

"Something like that. Antonio," he concluded, "owns one of the world's largest construction companies. Italian, very charming, easy to like. He recently married the mother of his son. A child he didn't know about," he qualified, "until just a few weeks ago."

She frowned. "Why is that?"

"Leo is the product of an old affair between he and Sadie. Why she didn't tell him about his son, I don't know. I expect I'll find out more when I see him."

She nodded. Shifted her weight to stand up. He sank his thumb deeper into the flesh of her palm to keep her there. Heat darkened her eyes, that always on electricity pulsing between them, but there was a wariness there too, a seemingly permanent state of affairs he was beginning to hate, particularly when he'd been the one to put it there.

"I will clearly have to kiss you this weekend," he said huskily. "Perhaps we'd better get back into practice?"

She froze, the hesitancy written in every bone of her body making him curse beneath his breath. He was demonstrating she could trust him in every way he could. *What the hell more could he do?*

"Alejandro…"

"Forget it." He pushed the drawing back at her. "I've got work to do."

He was in a fairly antagonistic mood then as they arrived at Sebastien's glorious Waldenbrook estate in Oxfordshire, situated on two hundred acres of lush, green, forested land.

Perhaps Sebastien would offer up one of his sadistically cruel, military-inspired obstacle courses this weekend… some target practice with a powerful gun. *That* could burn off some frustration.

"Not this weekend." Sebastien dashed his hopes as he stood on the front steps of the impressive Georgian manor, his arm wrapped around his wife. "My niece, Natalia, is mad about show jumping. We're hosting the Oxfordshire County Show this weekend as a show of support."

Alejandro scowled. *A horse show?*

His disappointment evaporated when he saw Cecily's pale face. *Meu Deus. Of all the weekends.* Sebastien moved his gaze between the two of them. "Of course." He bumped his head with his hand. "How bloody stupid of me. Of course you should ride, Cecily. I should have let you know. Borrow one of Natalia's horses."

Cecily pushed a smile to her face. "I'm taking a break from riding. Just for a short while with the engagement and my move to New York."

"Well you must come out and cheer for Natalia. She'd be so thrilled."

His fiancée didn't flinch even though they'd announced the American world championship team today, the papers full of the news, rife with speculation as to why she hadn't made it. Instead of focusing on her brilliant comeback in Geneva, the press had noted Cecily's less than stellar year. He knew it was killing her but she didn't let it show.

"I would enjoy that," she murmured. "Of course."

Sebastien sent them off to get settled in their room before cocktails, a staff member carrying their luggage.

"I didn't know," Alejandro said in a low voice.

Cecily lifted a shoulder. "It's fine."

It wasn't fine. Cecily attempted to readjust her bearings as she and Alejandro were shown to a gorgeous suite on the second floor of the manor, decorated in pale blue and silver with a lovely balcony and luxurious en suite bathroom.

Part of her mental preparation for this weekend had been to promise herself she would not think about her career or family—the gaping holes inside of her threatening to tear her apart. Instead, she had been plunged right into the center of the world she was trying to avoid just as she was slated to put on a performance of adoring fiancée in front of Alejandro's closest friends.

How was she supposed to do that with a horse show going on under her nose?

She walked to the window and took in the sprawling English countryside. Even now she could see them setting up the show course in the distance, the lush surrounding forestland providing spectacular scenery.

"This is for you."

She turned to find Alejandro holding out a cream-embossed envelope. Swallowing back the jagged edge inside of her, she crossed to him, took the envelope and tore it open, reading her hostess's sophisticated script.

> *Cecily,*
> *I hope you will join me in the Rose Room for break-*
> *fast at eight tomorrow morning. I've invited Sadie*
> *and Calli. I'd like to take this opportunity to get to*
> *know all of you better.*
> *Monika*

Alejandro peered over her shoulder. "That's nice. You'll like Monika."

She nodded. "I should have a bath so we aren't late."

She attempted to collect herself while immersed in lemon-scented bubbles up to her chin in the luxurious marble tub. Her interaction with Alejandro on the plane wasn't helping.

He had been a rock in the center of the storm this past couple of weeks, there for her in every way. Sensing how disoriented she was, he'd given her carte blanche on her dream stables and worked side by side with her on the plans, an attempt she knew, to distract her, but one that had also thrown her into confusion.

She'd gotten to know him over those quiet dinners they'd shared talking and working through the plans. Had been able to see beneath some of those complex layers of his. Yes, he was tough and ruthless when it came to ac-quiring what he wanted, but she'd also seen more than a few glimpses of the man she'd met in Kentucky—the bru-tally honest, empathetic side of him with the strength of character she'd gravitated to. Leaned on.

If, as she was starting to believe, he *was* that man she'd met, why then was it so hard to take that next baby step in trusting him? Was she so afraid of being wrong again about someone after what Davis had done to her she didn't trust her own judgment anymore, a fear Alejandro's deception had exacerbated? Because she knew she couldn't afford to be wrong in the decisions she was making right now with her life disintegrating around her?

Or was she more afraid of what it would mean if Alejandro *was* that man she'd thought he was? How powerfully drawn she was to him. That she could easily lose her head over him all over again, the one thing she could never do in this convenient arrangement of theirs.

She knew the next step was hers. She simply had no idea what to do.

She felt frozen. *Paralyzed*. Utterly unsure of how to proceed.

Cecily was too quiet. Alejandro had heard enough *I'm fines* uttered by females who were anything but in his lifetime to know she wasn't fine. But she wouldn't tell him what was wrong. He assumed it was the horse show on top of today's announcement, but *who knew?* The guesswork was making him crazy.

He gave her some space as he took a shower and dressed in trousers and a pale blue shirt in deference to the evening's casual attire. Space was what he needed when he was off balance. Maybe that's what Cecily needed too.

Heading to the sitting room just as the clock struck seven, he stopped in his tracks at the sight of his fiancée, dressed and ready to go.

The sapphire silk dress finished far too high on her thighs in his opinion, a pair of sky-high silver stilettos setting off her toned, magnificent legs. There was only one thing a man wanted to do with a dress like that and you couldn't do it in public.

She murmured something about being late. He tore his gaze away from her legs and found his shoes.

"You're stiff as a board," he said as he laced his fingers

through hers and they walked down the massive, center staircase to the mezzanine.

"Not to worry," she said stiffly. "I won't disappoint you. I'm channeling madly in love as we speak."

A slow curl of heat unraveled inside of him. He shouldn't engage—he should keep this thing sane between them— but he was too annoyed to heed his own advice.

He pulled her to a halt in the hallway that led to the terrace, just before they stepped outside. Resting a palm against the wall, he eyed her. "What's wrong?"

A tilt of her chin. "Nothing."

He *hated* that calm, even tone of voice. "Is it the show tomorrow? Today's news?"

"I'll deal with that."

"Then *what is it?*"

"Nothing." She stared at him. "What's the matter with *you*? You've been a bear all afternoon. You keep impressing on me how important tonight is, how much these friendships mean to you, then when I try and focus and be what you need me to be, you look annoyed."

"I *am* annoyed," he growled. "You're driving me crazy."

Her eyes widened. He stepped closer, the first time he'd allowed himself anywhere near her in weeks. Noted the fine lines of strain bracketing her mouth, the wary cast to those blue eyes. "If you are stressed," he murmured, "you need to talk to me. You *used* to talk to me. Why can't you do that?'

A flicker in those blue eyes. "I—I don't know."

He shook his head. "This isn't going to work unless you let me in. Unless you start trusting me."

Confusion, indecision, wrote itself across her face. "I'm trying. Alejandro, I—"

A thread inside him snapped. He took the last step between them, flattened his palm against the wall. Color rode her high cheekbones, her pupils dilating. "What are you doing?"

He cupped her jaw in his fingers and lowered his head to hers, their breath mixing in a seductive, heady heat. "Solving this impasse."

She didn't move away. He considered that progress. Slanting his mouth over hers, he took her lips in a leisurely, persuasive possession designed to melt those icy defenses. She didn't move for a moment, frozen it seemed, then a sigh tore itself from her throat as she relaxed beneath his hands. Soft and pliant beneath his, her mouth was heaven. Her response—that particularly rare combination of innocence and passion that had slayed him from the very beginning nearly brought him to his knees.

She moved closer, her soft curves brushing against the length of him. Unable to resist temptation, he curved his fingers around a bare stretch of toned, sexy thigh and pulled her even closer, his teeth catching the tender flesh of her lower lip in his.

Santo Deus, he wanted her. Had wanted her for weeks. Ever since he'd had that first taste.

"I would say 'get a room,'" a low voice intoned behind them, "but since you already have one, perhaps you should use it."

Cecily stepped back so fast, she tripped over her heels. Alejandro wrapped an arm around her waist to steady her, directing a grin at Stavros. Dressed casually in a white shirt and gray pants, an attractive, black-haired woman at his side, his friend's dark eyes were dancing with amusement.

"Then I would not be here to greet your passably handsome face," Alejandro drawled, slapping him on the shoulder. *"Ola."*

Stavros was, in fact, more than passably handsome. *Swoon-worthy* as some women liked to call his surly, dark good looks. Alejandro wasn't a fan of how he turned that charm on his fiancée now—darkening Cecily's cheeks to a deep shade of rose.

And that was new. Considering his good friend a threat. Particularly since Stavros's new wife was standing at his side.

He studied her as his friend introduced them. Calli wasn't his usual type. Stavros dated worldly, vivacious women who matched his colorful personality. Calli was quiet and unassuming. Pretty—yes. A killer figure, absolutely. But what was it about her that had convinced Stavros to take the plunge into marriage?

It claimed his thoughts as they found Antonio and his new wife, Sadie, on the terrace along with their hosts Sebastien and Monika. Antonio he could understand. You find your son, you claim him—much like his own situation with his unborn child. Stavros, however, had *chosen* to marry this woman from the vast array of females he had at his beck and call in what he suspected might be a convenient marriage. *Something* about her must have stood out.

And maybe, he acknowledged, as the four couples sat down for dinner together on the torch-lit terrace, this was just him trying to understand his preoccupation with the woman on his arm. How Cecily had defied his usual rules of detachment from the very beginning.

He watched her carefully over dinner to make sure she was comfortable, but amidst the good conversation and laughter at the table she relaxed and was much more herself. He relaxed then too and made a good study of Antonio and his new wife.

It was clear the Greek was enamored with the elegant English brunette. In fact, if he wasn't mistaken, he thought Antonio might be in love with her their connection was so strong.

He caught Cecily's gaze drifting to the newly married

couple more than once during the evening, a wistful expression in those sapphire eyes. Guilt gnawed at his edges. He cared about her, he knew that, but he could never give her that love she craved. He'd known it from the very beginning—why he'd been content to walk away. He'd buried that knowledge when he'd persuaded her to marry him because she was having his child. Sacrifices were necessary.

He sat back in his chair and swallowed a mouthful of the legendary Tuscan Cabernet Sebastien was serving. His inability to forge open, loving relationships was something he'd long ago acknowledged. Somewhere along the way, he'd flipped a switch inside of himself, one of self-preservation. Love wasn't something he was ever going to expose himself to—as unreliable as it was intransient. It wasn't something he could reverse engineer for Cecily's sake even if he wanted to. He was just going to have to find other ways to give her what she needed.

Guilt pushed aside, he focused, then, on the excellent conversation between old friends and the entertaining night it turned out to be, but the woman at his side continued to claim the lion's share of his attention.

There was a connection between them tonight, an invisible barrier that had fallen with that kiss they'd shared. An *energy* that drew him like a moth to a flame. *That* he told himself, was what was going to sustain them, because he couldn't imagine that chemistry fading anytime soon.

He kept an arm across the back of her chair, fingers toying idly with her silky blonde curls as darkness fell across the English countryside and the torches burned bright into the night.

When dinner finally concluded, the women elected to turn in early given their eight a.m. breakfast with their hostess. Alejandro tucked Cecily into his side for the walk back to their room, a chill permeating the late-night air. She shivered and moved closer. Heat stoked low in his belly. Snooker—a late night ritual with the men—was not what he had in mind.

The suite was cast in shadows when they entered. Alejandro flicked on a lamp, his eyes never leaving his fiancée.

"Can you help me with my dress before you go?" she requested huskily, turning her back to him.

Her delicate scent wrapped itself around him, filling his head. He moved his fingers to the hook at the top of her dress. Tiny, almost invisible, he managed to undo it then slide the zipper slowly down her back. He thought it might be the most exquisite form of self-torture invented as he uncovered inch after inch of perfect creamy skin, right down to the dip at the small of her back, his second favorite spot on a woman.

His body hardened as he remembered that night in Kentucky. How he'd made her come apart with his hands and mouth on that perfect skin. This time, he knew, he wanted her just like that on that bed, his arm beneath her hips, but with his aching body buried inside her instead in an animalistic possession that matched his mood.

He set his mouth to her nape.

"Alejandro—" she murmured, a strangled note to her voice.

He turned her around in his arms, reading the conflicting emotions in her eyes.

"One step at a time," he said softly. "That's how we do this, *querida*."

Indecision wrote itself across her blue gaze. He was leaning down to kiss her when Stavros pounded on the door.

"Ouaou." Wow. "You are in a filthy mood." Stavros gave Alejandro a sideways look as they made their way downstairs to the billiards room. "Doesn't that ring on her fin-

ger mean you get guaranteed sex, because you resorting to hallways is a desperate measure my friend."

"We weren't in the hallway," Alejandro countered. "We were in our bedroom. And I was on the way."

"No you weren't," Stavros said complacently. "I was merely helping you along."

Alejandro scowled at him. "Instead of us talking about your bad timing, why don't you tell me what's going on with this marriage of yours?"

A deceptively innocent look back. "Meaning...?"

"You come back from Greece with a *wife?* How does that happen?"

"The same way you arriving here with a fiancée does." Stavros lifted a shoulder. "I married her for custody of my company. As good a reason as any."

His friend's response was just a bit too casual, a bit too blasé for him to buy it. It was a surefire sign there were things smoldering beneath that dark façade of his. *Did he have feelings for his wife?*

"What about you?" Stavros gave him a pointed look as they hit the marble mezzanine and headed toward the entertainment wing. "*I* need to be married...produce an heir. Antonio has a child. What's *your* excuse for breaking the eleventh commandment?"

"Have you *looked* at her?"

The Greek pursed his lips. "Am I seriously allowed to answer that question?"

"No."

"Just like I thought," Stavros murmured, pushing open the door of the billiards room. "You are in trouble. Deep trouble."

Alejandro could have told him he was wrong. That a couple nights of hot sex, the transformation of his relationship into the rational, civilized union he'd envisioned would cure what ailed him. But the ritual of opening a

seventy-year-old bottle of whiskey distracted him as Sebastien made a toast to the three of them winning the bet.

His usual cryptic self, the Englishman acted as if he'd
won the wager, making Alejandro even more sure their
challenges had never really been about subsisting without their wallets.

Antonio, looking far more introspective than he had
earlier, waded in to suggest his had been about finding his
son. Sebastien only inclined his head, saying that had been
a bonus, but he needed to look deeper than that.

The Italian laughed it off, as did they all because who
knew where Sebastien's head was really at? Who *cared* as
the evening devolved into a series of bloodthirstily competitive games of snooker.

Deep into the fifth frame, Sebastien stood by Alejandro's side, eyeing the table while Stavros and Antonio re-
filled their glasses.

"How was Kentucky?"

"Successful." Alejandro lined up a shot in his head.
"Your cover was brilliant, *obrigado*. My grandmother will
be happy now."

"And your soon-to-be wife?" Sebastien lounged back
against the table. "I like her, Alejandro, a lot. She's exactly what you need—a woman strong enough to stand
up to you…to *challenge* you." He lifted a brow. "Are you
really prepared to detonate your relationship over an ancient feud?"

"I'm working on a solution to that." Alejandro took a
sip of his whiskey, tilted his head back to absorb its mel-
low burn.

"And if you don't find one?"

"I will." He pointed his glass at the Englishman. "Why
did you send me to Kentucky? It wasn't about the wallets,
I get that."

Sebastien set his dark gray gaze on him. "There's more

to life than proving you are a better man than your father, Alejandro. Justifying your net worth every single second of the day. Sometimes I think you get so caught up in that you forget who *you* are. What you are capable of."

His skin bristled. "I'm not trying to *prove* I'm a better man than my father, *I am*."

"No one would argue that." Stavros inserted himself into the conversation as he and Antonio returned with their drinks. "Far too serious a topic," he reprimanded Sebastien. "I leave for five minutes and look what happens. Tonight is about the game."

Alejandro couldn't disagree. Stavros had dragged him away from his room at the worst possible moment. He was damn well winning this match.

He did. His luck, however, had run out when he clambered up the stairs in the early hours of the morning to find Cecily, her silky blonde hair splayed across the pillow, curves plastered into a tantalizing piece of cream silk, fast asleep.

CHAPTER NINE

ALEJANDRO WAS UNCHARACTERISTICALLY still asleep when Cecily woke the next morning for her breakfast with the ladies. Still singed from their encounter of the night before, she averted her eyes from all the toned, olive-skinned muscle exposed right down to where the sheet cut across her fiancé's lean hips and pointed herself in the direction of the bathroom instead.

That would not help her composure, something she needed today. The pretty rose-colored dress she slipped on *would*. She did her hair and applied a light coat of make-up, then left Alejandro to sleep and descended the intricate, hand-carved, dark wood staircase to the main floor of the manor.

Besieged by the sights and sounds of today's festivities, her new-found composure was rattled before she'd even reached the bottom step. Horse caravans emblazoned with the rider's names were arriving in the yard, sound systems crackled as they were tested and caterers flitted throughout the house, preparing for the lunch Monika and Sebastien were hosting for the riders and dignitaries—a lunch she and Alejandro had been asked to attend.

Event day buzz had always energized and excited her. Today it tightened her stomach into a ball that refused to unwind. It felt as if the world, *her* world and everything in it was passing her by and there was nothing she could do about it. She wanted to be out there walking the course, thinking through strategy, chatting with her fellow riders. Instead she would merely be a spectator.

Determined to master the day in spite of its wobbly start, she pasted a smile on her face and entered the Rose

Room. She was the last to arrive, Calli looking lovely in a floral print dress while Sadie was elegant in yet another print that hugged her slender curves.

Never the best at these feminine gatherings, she was happy to play with a piece of toast she didn't really want and drink her tea while Calli regaled the table with an amusing tale of Stavros ending up in the pool the night before recovering a priceless bottle of sauterne Sebastien had tossed in.

Monika laughed softly. "That's the sort of thing they do. They thrive on challenging each other. Of course, this most recent challenge takes the cake."

That was when Cecily realized it wasn't just Alejandro who had been undercover. So had Antonio, posing as a mechanic in the garage where Sadie had worked and Stavros, dispatched as a pool boy to the villa in which Calli had lived. The assignment, Monika reported, clearly assuming they'd known all about it, had ostensibly been for the men to go two weeks without their wallets, but Sebastien's wife seemed sure there had been a deeper meaning to each of the individual challenges.

To ruin her family. Cecily set her cup down with a rattle. *This had all started as a game?* She was too dumbfounded to speak. Guessing from the looks on the other women's faces, she wasn't alone.

"What were the stakes in the bet?" she asked Monika.

"If Sebastien won, the men would give up one of their most prized possessions. Alejandro's private island, for instance. If Sebastien lost, he promised to donate half his fortune to charity."

"And all three men completed their challenges?"

Monika nodded. "Sebastien will be making the announcement of the donation in a few weeks' time. He plans to set up a global search and rescue team with it, something that's close to his heart given his near miss last year."

Cecily's head spun as Monika told the story of how Stavros, Antonio and Alejandro had dug Sebastien out of an avalanche. It was a gut-wrenching story, a noble endeavor Sebastien was embarking on, to be sure, but her brain was still caught up in the wager that had brought Alejandro to Esmerelda.

She was trying so hard to get past what he'd done, how he'd deceived her. Had just begun to trust him, *them,* again. But to find out this had been part of a silly bet as her life fell apart at the seams? It made her head want to explode.

Alejandro eyed his fiancée over lunch on the terrace. She looked like some kind of pink confection in the dainty little dress, one he wanted to consume inch by inch. The smoke coming out of her ears, however, suggested the idea of a trip back to their room might not be well received.

Biting back his impatience, he bent his head to hers, keeping his voice low given the dignitaries at their table. "I know that look. What are you so angry about?"

"Your bet came up as a topic of conversation over breakfast."

Ah. He took his sunglasses off. Eyed her. "I didn't tell you about it because it only complicated an already complex situation."

"You don't say." Her eyes flashed a brilliant blue fire. "Do you know how blindsided the three of us were? I felt like a fool."

He rubbed a hand against his pounding temple, the after effects of the whiskey lingering. "I should have told you. But it changes nothing about us Cecily—everything I've told you is the truth."

"The truth," she derided, "is a subjective state of being for you, Alejandro."

Heat seared his belly. "It was an *omission,*" he said curtly, "not a mistruth."

"It was *juvenile,* ill thought-out and ill advised. Although Monika," she added, voice dripping with sarcasm, "was quick to point out there was some deeper lesson you were all supposed to be learning. What was yours...*revenge is sweet?*"

"Maybe it was that *you* are sweet, angel, as I seem to have acquired a high-maintenance fiancée along the way."

She made a sound at the back of her throat. Fixed her gaze on his. "And to *think* I was considering being intimate with you again. *Trusting you,* when life is just a joke to you."

"I assure you," he returned in a dangerously low voice, "I take all of this very seriously. I've done nothing *but* since our impetuous night in bed together landed us in this unfortunate...*situation.* It was an expensive move for both of us, *querida,* and the costs keep rising."

Her sapphire eyes snapped with fury. She put her nose in the air and began a conversation with a judge sitting across the table. He slid his sunglasses back on, muttering a curse beneath his breath. No way was he letting her derail them again—destroy what they'd begun building. *This* was ending *now.*

He laced his fingers through hers as they left the lunch and headed for the show jumping ring to watch Natalia ride in her junior class. Cecily tugged on his hand. "We don't need to be joined at the hip."

"Yes we do," he replied evenly. "There are photographers everywhere. Now is not the time to regret your impulsive behavior, *meu carinho.*"

Her chin came up. "And I expect you do?"

"In this moment, *sí.*" He flashed her a blinding smile as a photographer pointed a camera at them.

Her smile slipped as Natalia bounded up to them, wearing cream colored breeches and a red riding jacket. "Will you walk the course with me?" she asked Cecily, breathlessly. "I always get so nervous before a class I want to upend my stomach."

His fiancée dropped his hand and gave him a victorious look. "Sure. Jump on Sappho and show me her stride."

Cecily walked the course with Natalia, focusing on the technical aspect of the test ahead of the young rider rather than the familiar, almost ritualistic routine she would have done anything to be a part of. She'd thought she might feel better contributing. Instead she felt more ragged inside with every step she took. More *undone*.

When was it going to stop hurting so much? Because right now it felt like never.

She managed to avoid the familiar faces she came across, including Virginia Nelissen, her arch rival on the Dutch team who was competing in a later class. Slipping out of the ring after wishing Natalia good luck, she went to watch in the VIP area with Alejandro and the rest of their group.

The strategy she and Natalia had devised paid off. Cutting the corner at precisely the right angle, Natalia turned in a clear round with a very fast time and placed second in her class. Sebastien, radiating with pride, insisted they all join him and Monika for a celebratory drink in the tent he'd had erected for refreshments.

It was über-hot in there, with the soaring afternoon temperatures, far too many people packed inside far too small a space. Cecily's head throbbed, a band of tension encircling her skull. She really should have eaten more today but her stomach had been so off.

She would find Natalia, congratulate her and leave. But that, of course, proved impossible. She and Alejandro got caught up in an endless round of chit chat with her old social set. Wrapping herself in an impenetrable shield, she allowed nothing and no one to permeate it, including her fiancé she was still furious with.

She was discussing the course with a jubilant Natalia, intent on extracting herself imminently, when Virginia Nelissen tracked her down.

"Cecily." The current number six rider in the world enveloped her in a cloud of perfume and air kisses, causing Natalia to melt away into the crowd. "How did I not know you were going to be here?"

"I'm not riding."

"Why ever not?' Virginia, the circuit's biggest gossip, gave her a speculative look. "It's a fabulous course."

"I'm taking a break," Cecily said woodenly. "That's all."

"Oh," said the Dutch rider, hazel eyes wide with feigned innocence, "I was worried the rumors were true."

Don't bite, don't do it, Cecily. She's poison. But she couldn't help herself.

"What rumors?"

"I heard the powers that be on the American committee were worried you'd lost your edge after the accident. That they didn't think you were a good bet for the team." Virginia lifted a shoulder. "I'm sure it isn't true."

Or was it? Her stomach twisted as she remembered the closed-off conversation she'd had with the team chief. *Did they think she was damaged goods?* Was her career on the rocks? Once you had a reputation for being a broken rider, it tended to stick.

Alejandro joined the two of them. She gave him a frozen look, remaining stiff under the arm he wrapped around her waist, the thick air in the tent closing in around her with every minute that passed.

Confused, shattered, the heat pressing down on her lungs, it was all she could do to function on auto-pilot until Alejandro excused them and pulled her aside.

"This whole routine is getting old," he murmured in her

ear. "You freezing me out, me trying to make this work. It was a bet, Cecily. Get over it."

Perspiration broke out on her brow. She swallowed hard as a wave of nausea rolled over her, noticing the curious looks Sadie and Antonio were directing their way. "Can we get out of here?" she asked sharply, biting back the bile that climbed her throat. "Your friends are watching us."

"When we're finished here." His ebony eyes blazed with heat. "You *know* you can trust me. I'm not going to let you derail us again, just when we're finally getting somewhere."

A cold sweat enveloped her, a clammy film covering her skin. She dragged in a breath, but the air felt too thick, too heavy to speak.

"Cecily." Alejandro's voice sharpened. "What's wrong?"

Darkness swirled around her, everything dissolving into a thick, gray fog. She swayed into him. "I—I can't breathe."

Alejandro cursed and slid an arm around Cecily's waist. He couldn't even see the exit through the crush of people. A glance back at her ash-colored face made his heart pound.

Sinking his fingers into her waist, he hoisted her slight frame into his arms, and elbowed his way through the crowd. Shock guests gaped at them. Alejandro threw a laconic smile in Antonio's direction. "Lovers quarrel," he said loudly enough that everyone in the immediate vicinity could hear. "Only one way to solve this problem."

The crowd parted like the Red Sea. A blast of fresh air hit him as soon as he walked outside, making him realize how oppressively hot it had been in there for his *pregnant fiancée*. Furious at himself for being so insensitive, he carried Cecily up the hill and into the house. He didn't stop until they were inside the cool, quiet confines of their suite, away from prying eyes.

He set her down on the edge of the bed and made her put her head between her knees. "Breathe," he instructed, sitting down beside her. She took a deep breath, then another. He made her continue until she was taking regular, even inhales of air.

"I can't believe you did that," she said when she sat up, still pale but far less gray.

"Would you have preferred I let you pass out in front of everyone?

"No." Her chin dropped. "But what are they going to think?"

"That we are having sex." He was amused to see that brought her full color back. "Why on earth didn't you tell me how you were feeling?"

"I thought it would pass. It usually does…but it was so hot in there. And," she admitted, eyes on his, "I was angry with you."

His gaze darkened. He stood, walked to the sideboard and poured a glass of water from the crystal jug. Carrying it back to the bed, he handed it to her and sat down.

She took a sip of the water. Exhaled with a deep sigh. "I told myself I was going to be tough today—prove I can get through this."

"You were tough. You walked that course with Natalia. You faced what must have been a difficult day head-on."

She shook her head. "I let Virginia get to me. She told me she'd heard a rumor—that the selection committee might not have picked me for the team. It…upset me."

"You can't listen to that kind of conjecture," he reprimanded. "She's playing with your head, Cecily. You of all people know how cut throat the competition is."

"But she's connected. What if it's the truth?"

"If it is, there's nothing you can do about it except prove them wrong. Focus on what you *can* affect rather than what you can't." He arched a brow at her. "Remember what we talked about in Kentucky? *You* are the master of your own destiny. No one else."

"That's just it," she said quietly, "I can't *prove* anything right now. I'm scared of what this year off—this baby—is going to do to my career."

His heart tugged at her vulnerability. "Your mother had you when she was young and remained highly competitive. You will do the same because you are just as fiercely competitive. You are a *Hargrove*."

A hint of her trademark stubborn defiance crept back into her blue gaze. "Use the year to get your stables up and running," he advised. "Find another couple of horses to back up Bacchus and Derringer so when you come back, you come back even stronger than before. That's what winners do. They build on their setbacks. They use them to make them stronger."

She eyed him. "Why do you always know exactly the right thing to say?"

"Because I know what it's like to be on top. What it's like to be surrounded by people whose mission in life is to tear you down. Protect yourself by having an unshakeable vision. Don't give the Virginias of the world the opportunity to steal your joy."

Her gaze darkened. She looked down at the glass she held balanced on her lap, the afternoon sun arcing off its finely cut crystal edges. "You asked me once who I was doing this for. I thought about it a lot after you left. I know now it's for me. Of course it's for my mother too," she acknowledged, "but this dream, the dream to be the best that I have, comes from *me*, not from what I'm *expected* to be. Riding is who I am, Alejandro. It's what I love. I can't imagine doing anything else."

"Then tune out the noise," he said softly. "Follow your heart."

She nodded. A play of emotion moved through those

beautiful eyes. "What you said about trust... I have trouble trusting because of what happened with a previous relationship of mine. I was engaged to a man named Davis Hampden Randolph when I was twenty-three—of the banking Randolphs. My father does business with him."

He tipped a brow. "An arranged match?"

She shook her head. "I was mad about Davis. I was about to marry him and move to Savannah when I found out weeks before the wedding he was mad about his mistress too—he just wasn't going to marry her."

Shades of his father. "I'm sorry," he said quietly. "That must have been difficult."

A shadow whispered across her gaze. "I was a political choice for him. Funnily enough, when I gave him the ring back, it turned out I was the last to know."

His stomach hollowed out. He knew that humiliation. Had watched his mother go through it more times than he could count. And he, *he* had not made the situation any better by deceiving Cecily, then walking away.

He curled his fingers around hers. "I promise I will never hurt you like that. You will get honesty from me but never pain."

Her chin dropped. "Every time I've invested myself in someone in my life I've gotten hurt, Alejandro. Melly, Davis, losing my mother, my *father's* lack of caring..." She shook her head. "I know this is a practical thing between us—exactly as I was for Davis. That we are doing this for our child. But I need to know if I put my trust in you, that trust is inviolate. That *you* are willing to invest in us too."

He almost laughed at the unnecessary nature of the request. He'd been invested in her from the beginning—far more than he ever should have been. He thought it might be that extreme vulnerability of hers—how it tapped into a part of him that remembered all too vividly what it felt like to be at the mercy of the world. To have those who should have protected you fail in their promises.

It made him wonder about Sebastien's analysis of him. If perhaps he was capable of more with Cecily because he did care about her. Maybe *that*, he ventured, was what he could offer her beyond the love he couldn't give her. He could be the one person who never let her down. Who taught her she was worthy of that promise.

He set his gaze on her. "I *am* invested," he said quietly. "I've always been invested. I proposed marriage between us because I thought it could work, because we are good together. Because you have many of the qualities I admire in a woman, not just because you are having my baby. But *you* need to believe it can work too, Cecily. You need to trust me again."

She nodded. "I'm learning to. But there's only so many of these landmines I can take and still do that, Alejandro." She arced a brow at him. "Is there anything else I should know? Because you should tell me *now* and not later."

"Yes," he said silkily, running a finger down her cheek. "I have a date with Antonio at the shooting range in twenty minutes. Which means *you* have time to rest up for our date tonight and find a sexy dress to wear, because *we*," he added deliberately, "are picking up where we left off last night, *querida*. No distractions, no manufactured dramas and no interruptions."

Her eyes widened. He lowered his mouth to hers, giving in to the lush temptation in front of him. "And if Stavros comes knocking," he murmured against her lips, "I swear I will kill him with my bare hands."

CHAPTER TEN

CECILY HAD NEVER been so nervous in her entire life. She had changed her dress three times while Alejandro had showered and shaved after his shooting date with Antonio and still she wasn't convinced she'd made the right choice.

Champagne with a definite hint of pink, the sultry dress hugged her body like a glove, plunging at the neckline to show off the curves of her breasts, dipping in to highlight her tiny waist then flaring out over the full line of her hips. Very Marilyn Monroe, she'd thought as she'd purchased it on Madison Avenue last week. Sexy as Alejandro had requested. But was it too much?

"Oh, no," murmured Calli as they stood under the elegant marquee set up on the Waldenbrook grounds. "You look like an angel. A very *wicked* angel. Alejandro can't pick his tongue up off the ground."

Her gaze slid to her fiancé who stood speaking with Sebastien and Antonio. He looked gorgeously sophisticated and untouchable in a black tuxedo, dark hair slicked back from his face. As far removed from the man she'd met in Kentucky as it was possible to be. And yet tonight she was sure she knew him. That she'd always known him. What was terrifying was what that meant.

The night she'd spent with Alejandro in his cabin had been a forbidden assignation with no consequences attached to it. Tonight there were so many consequences involved her stomach was doing backflips.

She was about to place herself in the hands of a man she hoped wouldn't shatter the last piece of heart she had left. To fully trust him as she hadn't yet let herself do because she needed to in order to make this marriage work. For the child they were going to have.

That didn't mean it wasn't terrifying. Because it was. Keeping that level head she'd promised herself was going to be key, banishing those feelings she still harbored for him to restricted territory, except keeping a level head was almost impossible to do as the man in question executed a subtle seduction over dinner in the beautifully set up marquee.

Seated with Stavros, Calli, Antonio and Sadie at one of the round tables dressed with white linen, candles and fresh roses, it was all she could do to keep her mind on the conversation with Alejandro's eyes and hands on her the entire evening in an orchestrated campaign meant to drive her mad.

Her composure was in shreds by the time they got up to dance, Sebastien and Monika kicking things off. The Englishman and his wife had eyes only for each other, the deep love they shared patently obvious. It led to dangerous thinking on Cecily's part. If Sebastien, once a confirmed bachelor, as steadfastly opposed to marriage as Alejandro had once been according to Monika, could change so much with the right woman, perhaps Alejandro could too?

And that, she castigated herself as Alejandro took her hand and led her onto the dance floor to join Sebastien and Monika, was the kind of thinking she needed to avoid if she was going to survive this relationship.

Heart hammering in her breast, pulse beating so fast she felt like she was in a drag race, she allowed him to pull her close, his fingers wrapped around hers, her head tucked beneath his chin.

Their fit was so perfect, so right, it sent her spiraling back to that night in Kentucky when he'd held her beneath the stars. When she'd given up fighting the attraction between them because it was simply too powerful to resist.

His heart beat a steady, staccato rhythm beneath her ear. A sigh left her lips.

Alejandro drew back, his gorgeous, inky black eyes glittering with amusement. "Are you all right, *querida*?"

"Fully recovered," she murmured, "from this afternoon at least. This campaign you are waging has me distinctly on edge."

The grooves on either side of his mouth deepened. "You seduced me last time. Surely turnabout is fair play?"

"*I* seduced *you*…the operative words. I knew what I was doing then."

"And now?"

"Now I have no idea what I'm doing."

"Yes you do," he said softly. "You know this is right. Why so nervous, angel?"

"Because," she whispered, so caught up in him she was a lost cause, "it was…*magical*."

His gaze darkened. Tightening his arm around her waist, he brought his mouth to her ear, his stubble rasping the sensitive skin of her cheek. "I will make it magical. *Trust me*."

She melted, her insides dissolving into liquid honey. He pressed a kiss to the sensitive spot behind her ear, sending a shiver through her. She arched her neck to give him better access, tiny bolts of electricity exploding across her skin as he tasted her with an open-mouthed caress.

"Oh," she said, jolted out of her reverie. "That's odd."

"What?"

"Sadie just walked off the dance floor."

He straightened, his gaze flicking to Antonio who stood at the side of the dance floor, looking a little dazed. "That is odd."

She watched Sadie hurry toward the house, her heels sinking into the grass. She stopped, removed her shoes, then ran the rest of the way, stilettos hanging from her fingers. *As if she couldn't move fast enough.*

"Should I go after her do you think?"

"No." The curtness of Alejandro's tone claimed her attention. The banked fire in his eyes held it. "No distractions, no drama and no interruptions," he said meaningfully. "Let them handle it."

Her stomach curled. When the song ended, her fiancé had a quick word with Sebastien and Monika, wrapped his arm around her waist and walked her across the lawn toward the house. Her heels kept sinking into the grass just as Sadie's had. Pulling to a halt, she bent and tugged them off.

Alejandro increased his pace, Cecily half running to keep up with him. When they reached the cobblestoned walkway he swung her up into his arms and carried her up a set of back stairs she hadn't even known existed.

"Could be glass," he said blithely.

"You just like carrying me," she teased.

"Yes," he agreed, "I do. And it gets us there faster."

She clung to him as he walked down the hallway toward their suite. Outside their room, he paused and shifted her weight to open the door. She wrapped her arms around his neck, bringing his mouth down to hers for a kiss. The hot, open-mouthed caress was wild and delicious, sizzling the blood in her veins.

Muttering an oath, he broke the kiss. She made a sound of protest, twining her fingers tighter into his hair. He ignored her, turning the handle and carrying her inside.

His eyes were like burning coal as he set her down. "Stavros already thinks I'm out of control when it comes to you."

"And are you?" she asked archly.

"Not yet," he murmured, walking her backward until she collided with the hard surface of the wall. "We are, after all, on the other side of the door. But there's still time yet."

Oh, my. Her shoes clattered to the floor as he buried his fingers in her hair and kissed her—slow, drugging caresses that made her sag weakly against the plaster. *Good Lord the man knew how to kiss. How had she even resisted this?*

Lost in him, in the wild scent of pure, aroused male, she obeyed when he nudged her legs apart and stepped between them. Heat in the air, so thick she could taste it, she gasped as he settled his hips against hers, imprinting her with a hot, hard masculine demand she could feel right through the fabric of his trousers.

"Alejandro," she whispered.

Palming her thigh, he pressed his thumb to the hollow where hip met leg and spread her wider apart. She flattened her palms against the wall as he thrust against her with a slow, erotic focus that stole her breath.

Dark, sensual eyes met luminous blue. "You want me, angel? I want to hear you say it."

Her tongue seemed glued to the roof of her mouth. He moved closer, resting his hands on the wall on either side of her, letting her feel every hard, pulsing inch of him.

"You're punishing me," she breathed.

"*Sim,*" he agreed. "I can't focus. I can't think anymore for wanting you. So say the words, *querida. End this.*"

She closed her eyes. Rested her forehead against his chest, bones too weak to hold her. "Make love to me, Alejandro," she whispered. "I want your hands all over me."

He picked her up and carried her to the massive, king-sized bed with a speed that made her dizzy. Sitting down with her on his lap, he ran his thumb over her trembling bottom lip before he took possession, his kiss a shimmering, sensual meeting of the mouths that promised only exquisite pleasure.

Her skin felt cool as he slipped the straps of her dress

from her shoulders and pushed it down to her waist. Bare under his gaze, body vibrating with tension, she felt her nipples harden in blatant invitation. The lust in his eyes as he drank her in coiled her insides tight. Her heart slammed in her chest as he bent her back over his arm and sampled one rosy tip, then the other, the erotic flick of his tongue, the hard suction of his mouth driving her wild.

She moved restlessly beneath him. Lifting his mouth from her flesh, he set her on the bed, stretched her out like a feast for his consumption. Her eyes were glued to his as he placed a warm hand on her thigh, pushed her dress up to her waist.

"Alejandro."

"Shh." His big palm scaled the taut, trembling skin of her abdomen. "We're both wound up. I'm going to give you some relief first, *meu carinho*. Make you feel good. If I take you now, it won't be good for you."

She could almost guarantee it would be, but she wasn't about to argue when he sank his fingers into the sides of her panties and stripped them off. Her teeth dug into her lip, palms went damp as he pushed her thighs apart with gentle hands and settled himself in between them.

She tensed as he slid his palms beneath her hips to lift her up.

"Let me," he murmured, breath hot against her most intimate flesh.

And then there was only the delicate slide of his tongue against her overheated, aching body. Light so light, it was just enough to tease, to make her crazy. She arched into his touch, a desperate plea on her tongue. Deeper he delved, his sensual, leisurely enjoyment of her as he stroked and tasted her making it clear he loved to do this to her.

It turned her on to watch. Made her crazy. She cried out when he closed his mouth over her sensitized flesh and sucked gently. Shoved a fist in her mouth as she absorbed the waves of pleasure that rolled over her. Slow and languorous at first, they gathered in intensity as he consumed every centimeter of her as if he couldn't get enough.

She begged him hoarsely for relief. He captured her swollen nub between his teeth; razed her sensitive flesh. A flash of white lightning chased through her, fleeting, *almost there*. And then his mouth was back, the delicious lap of his tongue speeding up in intensity and she tipped over the edge, falling headlong into a shimmering river of pleasure so intense it locked her spine.

Alejandro moved up Cecily's beautiful body, nuzzling her damp, velvety skin, absorbing the tremors that racked her limbs. He was shaking, so into her reactions he was hovering on the razor's edge.

Leaving her bathed in the aftershocks, he rolled off the bed, stripped off his clothes and slid on a condom, his flesh so sensitized, so swollen, he had to grit his teeth to do it. Cecily watched him from the bed, looking so sexy and disheveled, half-clad in the golden dress, having been thoroughly consumed by him, he was tempted to take her like that. *Like a fallen angel*.

But he wanted her naked more—all of her lush curves bare beneath his hands. And he knew exactly *how* he wanted to take her because he'd been dreaming about it for weeks.

Stepping back to the bed, he wrapped his fingers around hers, drew her up onto her knees and unzipped the back of her dress. Sliding it over her head, he exposed her delectable, hour glass figure.

His eyes held hers. "I want you on your hands and knees," he murmured. "Can I have you like that?"

A flush crept into her cheeks, her eyes huge, glittering sapphires against pale honey skin. There was shock there, yes, but also a deep pulsing excitement that pushed his own higher. Dropping a kiss on her shoulder, he placed her on her hands and knees. She was trembling, anticipating his touch as he joined her on the bed, caged her legs between his and found the sexy hollow of her back with his mouth.

She arched into his touch with a low moan. His blood fizzled in his veins. Trailing his hand over the slope of her beautiful bottom, he slid his fingers between her thighs and rubbed at her damp, silken skin with the heel of his hand. A gasp escaped her. He bit down on his lip, leashing the urgent demand of his body as she pushed back against his hand, riding his touch.

He waited until she was wet and more than ready for him before he covered her body with his; rested his throbbing length in the curve of her buttock.

It was hot and erotic to have her like this, utterly at his mercy. Her fractured, shallow breathing said she felt it too.

"Cecily," he murmured, pressing his mouth to her back, "you with me?"

She nodded. He ran his hand up the inside of her thigh and widened her stance. One hand on her hip, he guided the crest of his erection to her slick, wet flesh.

Her breath hitched. "I'll take it so slow," he murmured. "I promise you. Trust me."

Her body was silken and welcoming, wrapping around him like a hot, velvet glove. It took every bit of his experience, his self-control, to move slowly, allowing her body to adjust to his. Finally, he was buried inside her, hips flush with her buttocks. Tipping his head back, he exhaled. She felt impossibly tight, impossibly good—like heaven on earth.

"Alejandro," she murmured, reaching a hand back to him.

"Shh." He set a palm against her stomach, anchoring her, holding her in place as he stroked deep inside her. It was more intense for her this way, he could feel it in the tension of her body, in the low sounds she made at the back of her throat. Relaxing as her body melted around his, she met his thrusts with an eagerness that threw all his composure out the window. Shredded his self-control.

"Angel," he murmured, flattening his palm against her stomach, feeling the tremors that raked through her. Blood pounded against his temples as he took her hips in a firm grip and stroked into her with hard, soul-shaking thrusts that threw him right to the edge.

When he reached between her legs to take her with him, she made a broken sound. "Alejandro—"

He froze, buried deep inside her.

"I need to see you. *Please*."

The desire to carry his fantasy to its insanely good conclusion crumbled at the emotion in her voice. Pulling out of her, he picked her up and wrapped her legs around him so they were face to face, his heat buried inside of her in a single, smooth movement that made her gasp.

"Better?"

She dug her nails into his shoulders, beautiful eyes fixed on his, bright and unclouded. "Yes," she breathed.

He had his doubts in that moment he'd ever be able to deny her anything if it meant he could keep those eyes bruise-free, the spell she cast over him was so complete. His need to protect her, to *have* her, had always been far more powerful than his common sense.

He distracted himself with her lush mouth, pushing that far too telling thought from his head. Her mouth against his, his hands under her buttocks, he brought her down on him again and again, the intimacy of their position, the caress of her silky flesh as he slid in and out of her a perfection he couldn't describe.

His head nearly exploded when she reached between her legs to pleasure herself, throwing her head back and giving herself to him unconditionally.

"*Meu Deus*, that is sexy," he murmured, heart stuttering in his chest. Her lashes fluttered down over her cheeks. Heat singed his skin as he watched her stroke herself to the edge. When her silken muscles clenched tight around him, squeezing him in a vise-like grip, he closed his eyes and gave himself to her in a shuddering release that seemed to go on forever.

Her blue eyes were full of questions when he opened his. *Hope. Expectation.* Gathering her in his arms, he avoided them all, murmuring quiet words into her hair until she fell asleep.

Nowhere near possessing the ability to do the same, he spent twenty minutes staring at the wall then slid out of bed, threw on some sweats and walked out onto the terrace with a cold glass of water.

Bathed in the light of a spectacular orange and gold harvest moon, he stared down at the abandoned marquee, flapping in the breeze. Told himself it had just been good sex—perhaps the best of his life. That she was to be the mother of his child—of course he would *feel* something for her. But he knew it for the mistruth that it was. He'd never been able to flip a switch with Cecily like he had with every other woman in his life—to separate his emotions from his lust.

She affected him—no question about it. Watching her walk out there today to help Natalia, into a world she loved, one that was making her bleed inside she missed it so much, had affected him profoundly. Her strength and her courage always had. But allowing himself to bring that emotion into this relationship wasn't something he could afford to do. He would only let himself feel so far, then he would cut it off and Cecily would be the one getting hurt.

He took a long draw of the water, absorbing the cool slide of the liquid down his throat. He'd finally gotten his relationship with Cecily back on track. Now he needed to ensure it became the rational, even keel affair he'd envisioned for the sake of the child they were having. Particularly given what lay ahead.

He'd heard radio silence from Clayton Hargrove, something he'd have to deal with when they got home. He had a feeling with Clayton's supreme arrogance in play this might all get worse before it got better—yet another reason to keep an already complex relationship from going places it could never go.

CHAPTER ELEVEN

"Relax," Alejandro murmured as they stepped off the jet outside of Brussels, deep in the heart of Salazar country. "My grandmother has promised to be on her best behavior."

Cecily gave him a long look. *Relax? She was walking into enemy territory.* About to meet the woman who refused to be in the same room as a Hargrove. How was she supposed to accomplish that?

He slid an arm around her waist and tugged her into his side as they walked across the tarmac toward the jeep that waited, a silver-haired, diminutive figure standing beside it.

Cecily had met Adriana Salazar once when Alejandro's grandmother had presented her with a rosette at a show in Germany. A tiny powerhouse, she'd struck Cecily as having an iron spine. Proud. *Regal.*

All those qualities met her now as they came to a halt in front of the hawk-eyed eighty-three-year-old, La Reve's glorious seventy-five acres spread out behind her like a vibrant green picture postcard.

"You remind me of your mother," were the first words out of the matriarch's mouth as she stepped forward to take Cecily's hands in hers. "You could be twins."

Unsure if that was a compliment or not, Cecily brushed a kiss to both of Adriana's lined cheeks. "Lovely to meet you," she murmured. "We met in Germany of course, but it was very brief."

"Yes," Adriana said. "You had a hell of a ride that day. You are gutsy, just like your mother was."

She chose to take that as a compliment. "Thank you."

Alejandro's grandmother gave her grandson a warm hug, the deep affection between them obvious. "Come," she said, gesturing toward the jeep. "I have lunch waiting."

The lovely meal in the Spanish, hacienda-style house was utterly civilized as Alejandro had promised, only the three of them in attendance with Alejandro's mother, Luisa, off at a show. It was when Adriana took Cecily on a tour of La Reve after the meal, as Alejandro caught up on work, that the more probing questions came.

She was clearly being vetted as Alejandro's choice of bride as they explored the lush Belgian countryside in the jeep. Prepared for it, Cecily answered Adriana's curious, sometimes blunt questions with honest, straightforward answers…and fell in love with La Reve along the way.

The sprawling countryside was magnificent, the architecturally complex indoor schooling rings the work of a master, but it was the stunning, dark wood stables with their cathedral ceilings and beautiful chandeliers that stole her heart.

It was there that Adriana housed her center for equine therapy where horses and riders from around the region came seeking her expert help. It had been in her head ever since Alejandro had helped her heal Bacchus that she might someday provide those same facilities in her own stables. She listened with rapt fascination as Adriana talked about the program, asking question after question.

"You're interested in that type of work," Alejandro's grandmother commented when they finally concluded the tour in the late afternoon with a glass of lemonade on the porch.

Cecily nodded. "Bacchus and I had a bad accident in London. Alejandro helped us to get past it. I'm not sure we would have without him."

An assessing look from those hawk-like eyes. "You care for him."

She nodded. "I had no idea who he was when I met him. I fell for the man with all the trappings stripped away."

Adriana's gaze moved back to the activity in the yard, a young groom leading an impressive black stallion toward the barn. "Alejandro tells me you didn't know about Bacchus's lineage."

"No," she said evenly, "I thought he was descended from Nightshade. That's what I was always told."

Adriana rested her head against the back of the chair, a frown drawing her brows together. "I never understood it."

"Understood what?"

"Why your mother didn't know." She looked over at Cecily. "Luisa and Zara had an argument after the world championships the year your mother won silver. A big blow-out. Luisa lashed out, calling Zara a coward for refusing to admit Zeus was stolen property. Zara said it was all lies."

Cecily shook her head. "My mother *didn't* know."

Adriana lifted a shoulder. "I had no proof. DNA typing wasn't available then. But there was a groom who had worked at the stables where Diablo was studded. We had him ready to testify in a court case—until your father's money got to him."

Her skin stung. "Did Luisa tell my mother about the groom?"

Adriana nodded. "Luisa told her not to be so naïve. She said Zara seemed flattened…that she left after the awards ceremony and never went to the party."

Confusion consumed her. That would have been weeks before her mother died—before that awful argument with her father. But surely her mother would have told her if she'd known? They had never kept secrets from each other—not even the smallest ones. Especially about something like this.

But if that was true, what *had* her parents been arguing about that night?

She shook off the uneasy feeling that ran through her. "I'm sure she didn't know," she said to Adriana.

"Even if she did," reasoned Alejandro as they walked out to the pasture after dinner to enjoy the spectacular sunset, "does it really matter now? Perhaps she was protecting you."

She shook her head. "She would never have done that. We told each other everything. We were building our careers on those horses."

And another lie would destroy her right now. Alejandro laced his fingers through hers as they walked down the cobblestoned path that lined the pastures, voluminous, silver-leafed chestnut trees swaying overhead.

It was a stunning night, the sunset painting streaks of orange, yellow and pink across the sky, the grazing horses silhouetted against the blaze of color. But his fiancée's attention was elsewhere, her face creased with her current preoccupation.

"So what did you think of La Reve?" he asked. "Pretty impressive?"

"Yes." A smile lit her face. "The equine therapy center is amazing. I was blown away by the work they do. I peppered Adriana with so many questions she was likely glad to get rid of me."

"I'm sure that isn't true." He'd watched his grandmother softening up to Cecily all day, no more immune to her charms than he was.

"I was thinking," she said, shooting him a sideways look, "of asking you to teach me what your grandmother taught you so I could offer those services in our stables. It helped Bacchus so much, I think it could do the same with others."

And her. He didn't miss the subtle psychological cue. "It's a big time investment. You will have your career and a new baby to think about."

"I have a year before that happens. We could train the grooms so I have back up when I'm busy."

The sparkle in her eyes was irresistible. She'd clearly been thinking about this. "It's a great idea," he conceded. "But you should ask my grandmother to teach you, not me. And that should wait until we get this issue with your father sorted."

She nodded, a shadow moving across her gaze. He bit down the antagonism that rose inside of him. He was dealing with Clayton Hargrove as soon as they got home.

"Do you think she'd say yes?"

He nodded. "My grandmother has always been a teacher first. It's her great love."

She fell quiet then as they walked in silence to their destination, a lush, green pasture in which a dozen horses grazed.

"It's so gorgeous," Cecily murmured as they stood watching the horses cavort and play before they came in for the night. "I can see why you were so happy here as boys." Her eyes were bright as she looked up at him in the fading light. "There's this air about it here, this *spirit* I can't describe. More like when my mother was alive at Esmerelda."

He nodded. "It comes from my grandmother. She's competitive, she likes to win, but nothing comes before her horses. They are her lifeblood."

Her lashes swept down. "It must have been great therapy for you boys to be here, surrounded by all of this. I can see why your grandmother means so much to you."

"She was the glue," he said simply. "She insisted we come here instead of being exposed to the toxic environment at home. She knew the grounding effect being around the horses would have on us." He rubbed a hand over the stubble on his jaw. "Those first few summers, Joaquim and I were broken. We had no conception of what love was. My grandmother gave it to us. She was the one thing that made sense when nothing else did."

A wet sheen blanketed her eyes, turning them an iridescent blue. "Sometimes that's all you need," she said quietly, "that one person who believes in you—who gives you that unconditional love."

Something unraveled inside of him. *Santo Deus,* she tore him apart.

"Yes," he agreed huskily, "sometimes that's all you need." He pressed a kiss to the top of her head, dangerously close to a host of emotions that were strictly off limits to him.

She pulled back to look up at him. "How do you feel?" she asked. "About our baby?"

The question caught him off guard. He thought about it for a moment, realized his feelings had morphed from shock into something deeper he couldn't describe. "Hopeful," he finally said, "that I can do things differently. That I can give our child all the things I never had…that *we* can give he or she a happy childhood."

Her eyes darkened. "I think you will be a better parent for your experiences, Alejandro. You will *know* what's important for our child because you have been there."

Perhaps. And perhaps he might severely disappoint her with his inability to foster a deep, open relationship with their child, exactly what he couldn't offer her.

"What I do *know*," he said quietly, shaking it off as he tucked a lock of her hair behind her ear, "is that we are going to do this together. If one of us falters, the other one will pick them up. It will be a team effort."

"Yes," she agreed huskily, "it will be."

He directed her toward the fence with a hand at her

waist. "Would you like to see your engagement present now?"

Her brows pulled together. "I didn't know we were doing that."

"Not officially no." He pulled an apple out of his pocket. Made a clicking sound with his teeth to catch the attention of a striking, chestnut-brown Belgian warm blood grazing a few feet away. The horse lifted his head, saw the apple in his hand and trotted over, tail held high.

They climbed up on the bottom rung of the fence. "This is Socrates," he said as the stallion butted his head playfully against his closed hand, looking for the apple. "I know he's not Bacchus and I *will* get you Bacchus back, but Socrates's lineage is nearly as impressive. He's my grandmother and I's progeny. We think he's going to be a brilliant jumper."

Cecily stared at him, then at the handsome horse with the white blaze down his face. "What are you saying?" she breathed.

"He's yours."

Her eyes widened. "You can't give him to me."

"Why not? You need a back-up horse. I can't think of a better way to cement the ties between our two families. It's the perfect symbolic union."

She bit her lip. "Your grandmother is okay with this?"

"Yes." He handed her the apple. Socrates pursued it, butting Cecily's hand now. She laughed and opened her palm, the stallion burying his muzzle in her hand and disposing of the apple in two big bites.

"Why Socrates?" she asked.

"I'm a football fan. Soccer," he elaborated, "for you. Socrates was a great Brazilian midfielder."

A smile tipped her lips. "Socrates it is, then."

The stallion stayed for a little more attention then wandered away. Cecily climbed off her perch, stood on tiptoe and kissed him.

It was the sweetest, simplest kiss they had ever shared and it drove a stake right through his heart.

Cecily didn't know what to do with her heart on the walk back to the house. It thumped in her chest in the strangest of ways and refused to stop as she and Alejandro climbed the stairs to their suite of rooms that overlooked the lake.

He murmured something about having to work and plopped himself down in front of his computer in the sitting room. She showered and pulled on a filmy blue nightie, her mind still caught up in the very personal, undeniably special gift he'd just given her.

He kept doing these things that melted her heart. Coming on the heels of last night's passionate, explosive encounter between them, it put reckless thoughts in her head. Like maybe they *could* be more, because she was sure he felt something for her.

Or maybe, she conceded, running a brush through her hair in a ruthless stroke, she was just seeing what she wanted to see. If she were smart, she knew, she would ignore this pull between her and her fiancé just as he was doing right now. Give them both time to breathe. But there were too many questions raging through her head for her to think straight.

Had her mother known about Zeus? What had her parents been arguing about the morning she'd died?

A vice gripped her chest. She couldn't stand for one more thing to not be as it seemed…for one more piece of her life to come careening apart, because her memories of her mother were all she had.

She tried to tell herself how fragile she was. How much Alejandro was coming to mean to her. How *dangerous* that was to her. But right now he seemed like the only real thing in a sea of uncertainty. Nothing could seem to stop her feet from moving as she put down the brush and walked into the sitting room where he was working.

To hell with the consequences.

Slipping behind him on the sofa, she ran her hands up the taut, muscular skin of his back. The heat, the masculinity of him, singed her fingertips beneath the well-worn material of his T-shirt. Sent her pulse racing.

She set her mouth to his nape.

A tremor ran through him. "Cecily—"

She trailed open-mouthed, sensual kisses over the hot, salty skin exposed by the neck of his shirt. Slid her arms around his waist, imprinted her breasts against the muscled skin she'd just been touching. "You sure you want to work?"

"I need to get this report finished before—"

She dropped her hand to the hard length of him beneath his jeans. A curse left his mouth. He was steel beneath the denim, sizzling her blood in her veins.

Suddenly she was upside down, thrown over his shoulder, Alejandro heading toward the bedroom before she had a chance to breathe. And then it was her battling to regain her equilibrium as he deposited her on the bed, took her mouth in a series of hot, hungry kisses in between which he ripped off his jeans and pulled his T-shirt over his head.

"You are killing me," he murmured, eyes holding hers in a suspended, searing moment she felt all the way to her toes, "slowly but surely."

She sucked in a breath as he rode her nightie up her body with his hands and pulled it over her head. *This* was an Alejandro she didn't know, the intensity in him bubbling over the edges, seeping into her skin.

She felt the burn of his gaze on her bare skin seconds before he pushed her back on the bed and braced himself on his elbows above her, a solid wall of sheer male power that made her mouth go dry.

He ran a possessive hand down her body, lingering on the dips and curves he found. Her pulse stuttered, then took off at a dead run. This wasn't going to be a languid, leisurely seduction. It was going to be something else entirely.

Cupping her breasts, he traced his fingertips over the velvety points. Rolled the sensitive peaks between thumb and forefinger until she moaned and moved restlessly beneath him. Satisfying her demand, he palmed the curve of her belly with his hand, then drew his fingers down over the sensitive crease of her thigh.

She opened instinctively for him, eyes on his as he slid a hard male thigh between hers, moving against her in a sensual, breathtaking rhythm. She reached up, curled a hand around his nape and brought his mouth down to hers for an intensely erotic, open-mouthed kiss.

The friction achingly good, her body beyond ready for him, a low plea left her lips. Releasing her mouth, he slid a hand beneath her head to fist in her hair, sliding his other hand down her leg to urge her thigh up and over his hip. With a single, hard thrust he was buried inside of her, her breath escaping on a harsh gasp.

He kissed her through the slow, deep ride he took her on, stroking into her body with deliberate, sweet slides until her insides were a hot shimmer and all she could feel was him. Every inch of her catching fire, she shattered apart, nails digging into his biceps. He came with her, his powerful body swelling, expanding, spilling his scalding heat inside her.

She'd never been so lost and found all in one moment. So sure she'd made an irrevocable choice she could never take back.

CHAPTER TWELVE

ALEJANDRO PACED THE floor of his lower Manhattan office the morning after his and Cecily's return from Belgium, managing the delicate threads of the Columbian acquisition while simultaneously castigating himself for allowing his relationship with Cecily to devolve into the emotional affair it had become.

Clearly he couldn't be trusted not to sink into that realm with her, which necessitated a cooling off period while he figured out how to handle his vulnerable, irresistible fiancée. Because that couldn't happen again between them—another of those charged encounters guaranteed to push their relationship off the track.

His conference call droned on, digressing into legalese he couldn't be bothered to follow. Stopping in front of the windows, he braced his palms on the sill and took in a gray, stormy-looking view of the Hudson. Most people would welcome that level of emotion in their relationship, he acknowledged. For him it was a place he would never go because he knew where it led.

No matter how good he and Cecily were together, no relationship retained that shiny, newly purchased glow. Whether boredom, friction or simply like turning to dislike, all good things came to an end. He'd watched his parents reenact that vicious pattern over and over again and it never ended well, passion and happiness turning to anger, then to hatred and back again until he'd been begging for them to end it. It wasn't something he'd ever subject himself or his child to. Nor would he raise Cecily's expectations as to the type of relationship he could provide.

Better to take his own advice and focus on the things

he could affect such as attacking the root cause of all of his problems.

His conference call mercifully came to an end. Discarding his headset, he sat down at his desk and messaged his lawyer.

Is the letter ready?

Just finished. Want me to bring it over?

Please.

Sam Barton knocked on his door just as he was taking a sip of his espresso. Waving him into a chair, Alejandro scanned the document his lawyer pushed across the desk.

The letter, addressed to Clayton Hargrove, recapped the terms of the public apology the Salazar family was willing to accept from the Hargroves as compensation for the financial and reputational losses it had incurred as a result of the theft of its property.

Should the Salazars not receive a written response by the date indicated on the letter, the family would proceed with its plans to prosecute the Hargroves to the fullest extent of the law, exposing the lies and criminal business practices the Hargrove dynasty had been built upon.

A very persuasive letter. Satisfied with its contents, Alejandro strengthened the language in a couple of sections, then pushed the document back across the desk to Sam.

His lawyer scanned the edits. Raised a brow. "That will get his attention."

"That's the point."

"And if he doesn't respond?"

"We cross that bridge when we come to it."

He was hoping that day never came. That Clayton Hargrove's lawyers would take the letter for the warning it was and advise their client accordingly. Because *this* had to end, this piece of history that was tearing his fiancée apart. This daily hope her father would call when the bastard clearly couldn't care less, because it was dismantling him too to see her this way.

It needed to be over.

Cecily resumed her life in New York determined to cultivate that unshakeable vision she had promised herself. She tuned out the newspapers and the gossip, focused on the future she and Alejandro were building together and refused to look back, only forward.

Controlled the things she could.

The week after they returned, their real estate agent found them a property in upstate New York that was everything they'd been looking for. Sitting in the shadow of the Catskill Mountains, Cherry Hill Farm, a two hundred and fifty acre spread being sold by its polo ground owners, was spectacular.

Cecily lost her heart to its scenic views across the Hudson Valley, acres of riding trails up into the mountains and its elegant, eighteenth-century ranch-style house.

"You love it," Alejandro said, flicking her a glance as they made the drive home after viewing it.

She nodded, excitement brimming inside her at the potential of such a special place. Warmer than the grand Esmerelda she'd grown up on, she knew it could be a wonderful home for her and Alejandro's family, plus a great base for her business. Something as special as La Reve.

And if that brought with it a host of questions as to where her relationship with Alejandro stood after that explosive night they'd shared together in Belgium, she ignored them just as she'd been doing all week.

She didn't want to examine the depth of feeling she had for him. How much she was coming to depend on him. The fact she'd unwisely allowed herself to care for a man who'd had no trouble playing by the rules ever since they'd returned to New York.

Maybe it was the way he made love to her with such passion, then walked away afterward as if he'd been untouched by it. As if he could turn his feelings off and on for her as he pleased while she felt as if the world was shifting beneath her feet. As if whatever brakes he'd been attempting to put on them that night in Belgium were firmly in place and he was keeping him there.

Or maybe it was because the very thing she'd been afraid of happening—that she would fall into love with him—was exactly what she'd done.

Bottom lip caught between her teeth, her attention was captured by the phone call Alejandro was having with their real estate agent. *Buying the farm.*

She gaped at him when he'd finished. "Did you just do that?"

"*Sim.* He was going to put it on the market tomorrow. Better not to take chances. Plus now we have a location for our wedding. We can get the invitations out."

Her stomach plummeted. Given the simple ceremony they'd envisioned and the wedding planner they'd hired to execute it for them, six weeks was more than enough time to execute it. It was not having it at Esmerelda that ripped open the jagged hole inside of her. The fact that there had still been no word from her father.

"*Don't,*" Alejandro murmured. "I am going to fix this, Cecily. I promise you."

How? Both sides were so deeply dug in, their pride ruling them, she didn't see any way around it.

She turned her head to stare out the window. Perhaps Alejandro had been right. Perhaps her father *would* see reason once he received their wedding invitation and acknowledged it as the inevitability it was. Because he wouldn't let her walk down the aisle without him, would he? As rocky as their relationship had been, she loved her father and deep down, she thought he loved her too.

* * *

Fortunately, she was too madly busy over the next few weeks to ruminate about anything except getting the renovations done at Cherry Hill Farm so the wedding could go on as planned.

The ceremony was to take place in the lovely wild flower garden at the back of the house, the reception, a barn party Alejandro had suggested as apropos for them. Which meant her priority was making sure the main barn—the showpiece of her new stables—was ready in time.

The days passed in a flurry of frenzied activity, a small army working at the farm. It was surreal, *magical,* to watch her dream come true. Her stomach swooped with butterflies every time she thought of saying her vows to Alejandro in the beautiful garden. Dancing her first dance with him under the sparkling Murano chandeliers inspired by La Reve.

If she worried she was committing herself to a man who might never love her, that those walls of his showed no signs of coming down, it was a reckless ride she couldn't seem to stop because he was becoming everything to her, this man who always kept his promises.

If she got too carried away, hot on its heels came the reminder her father had not yet responded to the deal Alejandro had offered him, nor to their wedding invitation. Neither had the better portion of the Hargrove clan for that matter—as if her father had orchestrated a family-wide boycott of their nuptials.

If this kept up, there would be only Salazars at her wedding.

It ate away at her insides, corroded her happiness. But she refused to show it.

An unshakeable vision.

Two weeks before the wedding, she arrived home well after dinner, so exhausted she could hardly move, but bubbling over with enthusiasm with the progress of the day. Curled up in the chair beside Alejandro's desk, she gave him a recap.

"It sounds as if you're almost there," he said, leaning back in his chair, coffee cup in hand.

"We are. It's going to be amazing." She set her gaze on the man who seemed intent on doing everything he could to help her rebuild her life alongside his. "Thank you," she said huskily. "For this. For all of it."

He shook it off. "It's nothing. It's what I promised you."

"It's everything and you know it."

An enigmatic look claimed his face. He took a sip of his coffee, set the cup down. "I have to go to Colombia tomorrow."

"Colombia?" She blinked. "Our wedding is two weeks away. We have the ultrasound tomorrow."

"It's the acquisition...unavoidable, I'm afraid. I'll do the ultrasound, then leave for the airport from there."

"When will you be back?"

"Friday."

Friday. A week.

"Okay," she murmured, lifting her chin. She could hold down the fort for a week. She'd been doing it all along with his insane schedule.

They discussed a few urgent wedding items. She lost the plot somewhere along the way, her eyes drifting closed. Alejandro took her cup from her hand, placed it on the desk and pulled her to her feet.

"Bed," he instructed.

She stood on tiptoe, curved a palm around his nape and brought his mouth down to hers. "Come with me," she murmured against his lips, "and I will."

He pressed a hard kiss to her mouth. Set her away from him. "I have to get ready for this trip," he said quietly, "and you're dead on your feet. You should get some sleep."

Her skin stung. He'd hardly touched her over the past few weeks. She'd attributed it to the pressure he was under with this deal that was making the papers, the crazy amount of work he had on his plate. But she knew in that moment she hadn't been imagining the distance he'd put between them—it was a very real thing she'd been willfully avoiding. Testimony to his promise love wasn't ever going to be on offer from him even if he did feel something for her.

Too tired to face it now because she knew she was already in far too deep—she immersed herself in a long, hot bath, hating the hollow feeling inside of her. Hating that she'd come to need him so much.

Curling up in bed, she picked up her tablet. Eyes blurring, emotions too close to the surface, she checked her email before she turned out the light. Everything on track with the wedding, she flipped to their RSVP inbox. Froze at the email from her father.

She pressed a shaking finger to the screen to open it. It wasn't from her father, it was from his assistant, Claire.

Your father regrets to inform you he will not be able to attend your wedding.

No explanation. No elaboration. He hadn't even sent it himself.

A tear slipped down her cheek. Then another, until they were a steady, inexorable flow.

She had to go see him. She had to know the truth.

She and Alejandro attended the ultrasound together the next morning at her doctor's plush Upper East Side clinic. Everything thankfully on track, their baby healthy and thriving with a vibrant heartbeat, Cecily found herself left with a remarkable sonogram and a whole host of emotions after her fiancé departed for the airport.

Anticipation about her and Alejandro's baby had replaced fear as her dominant emotion as she put her faith in the future. With it had come a desperately strong hope her baby would be a girl—that she would develop that same unbreakable bond with her child that she'd had with her mother and maybe it would fill some of the void still left inside of her.

She flew to Kentucky the day before Alejandro was due home, the finishing touches on the barn almost complete, last-minute wedding tasks in her planner's capable hands. Cliff, bless his heart, met her at the airport.

She gave him a hug. "Thank you for coming."

"It was a good escape for me. How is New York treating you?"

"Just fine." She gave him a wary look as she drew back. "How's father?"

"Missing you," he said bluntly, "although he refuses to admit it. The place hasn't been the same without you."

"Kay?" She wrinkled her nose to hide the sharp stroke of pain that cut through her. "Left to her own devices, she'll spoil everything."

"Yes," Cliff said with meaning. *"Kay."*

They drove out to the farm. The familiar lush beauty of Kentucky's horse country hit her like a brick to the chest. *How had she survived without this?*

A vision of Cherry Hill Farm with its spectacular canopy of pink cherry blossoms and soaring views up into the mountains filled her head. *That* was why. Because she wanted that life she'd envisioned with Alejandro so badly it hurt.

She gave into the impulse to go see her horses when they arrived, which didn't help her level of emotion as she rapped on the door of her father's study.

What if he wouldn't speak to her? What if he threw her out?

She let herself in at her father's curt command. He sat

behind the solid, cherry wood desk in a pose imprinted from childhood, head bent over the document he was reading, brow furrowed in concentration.

Swallowing past the lump that formed in her throat, she took in the newly imprinted lines bracketing his eyes and mouth as he looked up at her.

"Daddy."

His expression softened for a moment, a warmth entering his cool gray eyes, before his face closed over into an expressionless mask. "You didn't say you were coming."

She crossed her legs at the ankle, wrapped her arms tight around herself. "I got your RSVP. I wanted to talk to you."

"You made your choice, Cecily. You chose to marry a Salazar."

She pressed trembling lips together. "So your pride means more to you than I do?"

He rested his head against the back of the chair and regarded her with a hooded look. "I gave you everything… your career handed to you on a silver platter, the best coaches and horses in the world, every advantage you could ask for. You could have married a fine man like Knox, instead you chose to jump into bed with the man who is trying to destroy us. What do you want me to say?"

Her temper caught fire. She moved forward until she stood flush with the edge of the desk, hands clenched by her sides. "I would like you to care for me like a father should. And for the record, *I* made my career, not you."

An emotion she couldn't read flickered in those wintry gray eyes. "What I *want* from you, Daddy, is the truth. I want to know why you can't make this apology and put it behind us so I can be happy."

He got up from his chair and rounded the desk. "You think Alejandro is going to make you happy? He's marrying you to secure the Salazar you're carrying, Cecily.

He is *loving* taking you away from me, paying me back by stealing the one thing I value most, but he does not *love* you. Don't be so damn naïve."

Her insides curled into a tight little ball. "It was *me* who pursued Alejandro. And I do trust him. He's the only thing I *can* trust at the moment because you keep lying to me."

He gave her a stone-faced look. "Then you're being a fool."

She swung away to the window, a wet heat blurring her eyes as she stared out at the perfectly manicured gardens. She blinked the tears back, fighting the show of emotion, but they fell unbidden down her cheeks.

"Cecily," her father rasped, placing a hand on her shoulder. "You're making me make impossible decisions."

"Why?" She swung around. *"Tell me why* so I understand."

He raked a hand through his hair. Rested a palm on the window ledge. "My father, in a severe lapse in judgment, made a deal with Paul Macintosh to stud Diablo to Demeter while Diablo was on loan to him. Your grandmother, as you know, was obsessed with beating Adriana, convinced if she had a horse as good as Diablo she could. So my father made it happen. No one was ever supposed to know."

"But the groom talked."

He frowned. "How do you know about him?"

"Adriana told me. She said we bought him off."

"Unfortunately, yes. My mother was terrified of what would happen to her career if anyone found out…that she could be blacklisted or worse, stripped of her titles. So my father paid him off."

"How did you know about it?"

"The groom came back years later, short on money, threatening to spill the story. I gave him more money hoping that would be the end of it."

"But it wasn't." She bit the inside of her mouth. "Was

that what you were arguing with mother about the day she died?"

"Yes." The single word dismantled her insides. "I thought it was better she didn't know. That *neither* of you knew. That you focused on your careers." He shook his head, eyes bleak. "In hindsight, I should have known it was the wrong thing to do. Your mother was so emotional. She'd built her career on those horses. It was," he said heavily, "my fault."

Her heart pulled loose, anger and confusion clawing at her insides. All these years she'd wondered why her father couldn't love her the way she needed him to…why the aloofness he had always carried had suddenly grown so much deeper, when it had been guilt driving him all along.

"I was trying to protect you," he said quietly, eyes on hers. "I've always been trying to protect you, Cecily, to do what's best for you, even when it hasn't always appeared that way."

She got that. She even believed it. But she wasn't sure she could forgive him for sending her mother off in emotional distress while he went and did business in New York. For taking away her best friend.

Heat flashed in her father's eyes. "Don't you think I wish I'd done things differently? I miss her too, Cecily. Every single day. But I can't change history. It's the one thing I *can't* do."

Her nails dug into her palms. "You could apologize."

"A public apology would stain your grandmother and mother's reputation. *Yours*. Dismantle everything we've built. I won't break the promises I've made."

Even if he broke her heart keeping them.

She pressed her palms to her temples. "The Salazars will level you. Alejandro is a powerful man, Daddy. He's not just going to walk away from this."

Her father's mouth thinned. "He's made that clear. Perhaps you should remember that yourself. He *is* ruthless, Cecily. Have you read the letter he sent?"

What letter?

He walked to his desk, came back with a piece of paper he handed to her. She skimmed the letter. The last paragraph sucked the breath from her lungs.

Should you not respond to this communication by the date indicated, expressing the Hargrove family's intent to make the public apology outlined above, the Salazar family will proceed with its plans to prosecute to the fullest extent of the law, exposing the lies and criminal business practices the Hargrove dynasty has been built upon.

The blood drained from her face. She'd thought it would never come to this. She'd thought her father would make the apology. And perhaps, she acknowledged grimly, she'd thought Alejandro might bend given the growing feelings between them. *Because she didn't think he would do this to her.*

Her father trained his gaze on hers. "You think you know him, Cecily…that you can *trust* him…that he *cares* for you? Tell him to back off…to leave ancient history where it belongs."

CHAPTER THIRTEEN

ALEJANDRO ARRIVED HOME late on Thursday evening, his Colombian acquisition complete. He'd left the post-deal celebrations to his legal team and flown on to Kentucky in an effort to talk some sense into Clayton Hargrove, only to have a series of thunderstorms send him home instead.

Unfortunate with his wedding a week away and his schedule jam-packed. But he'd also been anxious to get home to Cecily. She hadn't sounded right on the phone when he'd talked to her last night—hadn't sounded right all week.

He knew he'd hurt her before he'd left, but giving in to his weakness for her, allowing their relationship to slide back into what it had been was not something he was going to do—not now when they'd developed exactly the kind of safe, solid partnership he'd been looking for. Knowing a confrontation with her father was on the horizon had also been extra incentive to keep his head clear.

Dropping his briefcase in the living room, he shrugged off his jacket and flicked on a light. Cecily must still be up at the farm. He poured himself a drink and wandered over to the floor-to-ceiling windows to take in a floodlit view of Central Park while he waited for her.

He'd been giving Clayton Hargrove time to come around—*to do the right thing*—so he didn't have to make decisions he didn't want to make. To choose between the two loyalties rapidly tearing him apart. But Clayton had backed him into a corner instead.

He couldn't ask his grandmother to give anymore than she already had. His only remaining option was to call

Clayton's bluff, a card he was loathe to play given what he really wanted was Cecily's father at the damn wedding.

Twenty minutes passed. Thirty. Visions of Cecily stranded by the side of a busy highway filled his head. He had put down his empty glass, was about to call her and give her hell for not texting she'd be late when she walked through the door.

His senses settling, he crossed to greet her. Setting his hands on her waist, he bent to kiss her, but she turned her cheek at the last minute, the kiss landing on her jaw. He frowned and set her away from him. Surveyed her pale face and stiff demeanor. "What's going on?"

She threw her purse on a chair. "I flew to Kentucky yesterday to speak with my father."

Meu Deus. He'd been hoping to get to him first. "Why didn't you tell me?"

"Because I was trying to handle it myself." Her gaze was a wintry blue as she trained it on him. "Because *you* told me once that I'm in charge of my own happiness, so I went to him to get the answers I was looking for."

And they hadn't been the ones she wanted. "What did he say?"

"He told me the truth. That my grandfather did what we all think he did. That it was a mistake he's been covering up ever since in order to preserve the legacy of three careers."

"Is that what your parents were arguing about the day your mother died?"

She nodded. "The groom showed up the night before asking for more money. My mother was terrified it would ruin her career when she found out."

"At least you know she wasn't keeping it from you."

"But it was unnecessary," she bit out, mouth trembling. "All of it. If my father had told my mother the truth, if she hadn't been so upset that day, it never would have happened."

"You can't know that," he murmured, brushing a thumb across her cheek. "Your father isn't responsible for your mother's death, Cecily. No one is. I know how much you loved her, what a special bond you had, but she's gone. You need to let her go."

"I do," she agreed, fire glinting in her eyes, "and so do you. This *devastation*," she said, waving a hand at him, "this badly miscalculated mistake my grandfather made— it needs to end, Alejandro."

"Tell your father to apologize and it will."

"He won't do it. He promised my grandmother and my mother he would never sully their legacies. He'd rather you strip him of every cent he has than break his promise."

He clenched his hands by his sides. "So he elects to use you as a pawn instead? He knows exactly what he is doing, Cecily. By putting you squarely in the middle, by tearing my loyalties in two, he won't have to sacrifice anything. It's the same insane arrogance your family has been perpetuating for decades."

"Funny," she said quietly, "that's what he said about you. That *I* am *your* power play. That you are only marrying me to secure your heir...that you are enjoying taking away the one thing he values most."

"That's ridiculous," he bit out. "You know what you mean to me."

"I thought I did." Turbulent emotion swirled in those blue eyes. "Now I'm not so sure."

He narrowed his gaze. "Explain."

"My father showed me the letter you sent him. You were supposed to be getting him to see reason, Alejandro, not threatening to annihilate him."

That made his skin sting. "I *gave* him time to see reason. I *hand delivered* him a generous compromise—a much more generous one than most would offer. I was on my way to talk sense into him today when my flight was diverted—time I don't have. But sometimes, *querida*, the only thing a man like him understands is the bottom line."

"And that worked well didn't it? You are like two stags engaged in a fight to the finish. There will be no winner in this."

He threw up his hands. "What would you have me do?"

"Drop this," she said quietly. "We can heal this wound together if we refuse to perpetuate it. You said so yourself when you first proposed marriage."

"That was assuming your father was a reasonable man."

She regarded him silently. "Is it really so different what he is doing than what you are? He is trying to preserve my family's honor just as you are yours."

"A crime was committed, that is the *difference*," he growled. "Don't make me make impossible decisions, Cecily."

Exactly what her father had said. Cecily turned away, arms wrapped around herself, feeling like a patchwork quilt she was knitted into so many pieces, the stitches barely holding.

She'd left Kentucky battered and broken over her father's refusal to *choose her* over a decades-old feud. Over the realization his love and duty toward her mother, something that had always been so passionately strong, had superseded his feelings for her. But it had also answered the question she'd asked herself at the very beginning of her and Alejandro's relationship.

"Cecily?" Alejandro curved his fingers around her arm and turned her back to him.

She lifted her gaze to the frustration tangling in his. "I thought I could do it," she said huskily. "A practical marriage to you for the sake of our child. I thought that what we could have together was better than this secret desire I've always had to be loved, because who knew if that even existed for me?

"And then," she said, taking a deep breath, "you made me believe in *you*. You were the one thing in all of this I could hold on to when everything else was crumbling beneath my feet. You were my *person*."

His gaze darkened. "I still am. That hasn't changed."

"No," she agreed. "*I've* changed. I allowed myself to fall in love with you. I started buying into this dream we were building together and once I started, I couldn't stop. I want it all, Alejandro. I want that unconditional love we talked about that night at La Reve. I want you to *choose me* over this feud that is tearing us all apart."

He looked as if he'd been sucker punched. "I did choose you. I'm marrying you. We are building a life together."

"No," she said, "you're marrying me because I'm carrying your child. And maybe because on some level you care for me, because I believe you do. But ours will never be a real marriage. You will never let yourself love because your past has made you too afraid to do it."

His face shuttered. "I'm not *afraid* to love, I *refuse* to go there because I know it will mess up a perfectly good relationship. Because we have more to consider in this than just us—we have a child on the way."

She shook her head. "Allowing yourself to feel won't mess *us* up. It will make us *better*."

"It's inconsequential," he said curtly. "Love is not a capacity I have, Cecily. I've been clear about that from the beginning. I'm not trying to be obstinate, I'm telling you the truth."

Her heart dropped at the utterly closed off look on his face. *She'd known this was coming, hadn't she?* That she'd been letting her feelings run away with her in the hope the caring she sensed in him might turn into the love she needed. The love she now knew she *deserve*d. But to hear him say it, to reject it so completely, was like a knife to the insides.

"So what will you do?" she asked quietly. "Take my father to court? Put our child in the center of this war between two families, exactly what your parents did to you?"

"We will shield them from it," he rejected. "Ensure that never happens. Your father has a choice, Cecily, let him make it."

"So do you. You have the power to make this decision and yet you won't. *I* am expected to give up everything for a marriage with a man who will never love me."

His hands fisted by his sides. "Cecily—"

She swiped her purse off the chair. "I think we both need time to think."

"*About what?* We are getting married in a week."

"About whether I can do this. Because the man I fell in love with wouldn't do this to me. He wouldn't make me make this choice."

She turned and stalked to the door. He followed, his face a dark cloud. "Stay and we'll talk this out. You can't just walk off into the night like this. You're clearly emotional."

She pivoted to face him, eyes flashing. "I am *emotional,* Alejandro. So give me the space I'm asking for."

"Where will you go?"

"I have no idea." She yanked the door open before that last stitch gave. "Given the two males in my life have managed to so thoroughly disappoint me, I feel the need for some distance."

Gluing his feet to the floor, Alejandro resisted the urge to go after her. It might push her over the edge in the mood she was in. But the thought of her out there alone in New York, even with his credit cards, made him crazy.

He traced a path back to the bar instead and poured

himself another glass of Scotch, his fury growing with every breath. She couldn't just change the rules of the game at the eleventh hour. *Decide* she loved him, then walk away. Break the promises she'd made to him and his child.

Because as much as she'd enjoyed throwing his emotional unavailability at him, he had invested in her too…in this future they were building together. He had trusted her to stick—not to walk out that door in an eerily similar scene to one he'd been privy to far too many times in his life.

He collapsed in a chair. *I want it all, Alejandro. I want that unconditional love we talked about. I want you to choose me over this feud that is tearing us apart.*

He scowled at the amber liquid in his glass. *He* was the good guy here. He'd been honest about what he was capable of from the very beginning. It was Clayton Hargrove, the arrogant bastard, who was intent on breaking his daughter's heart.

He rested his head against the back of the chair. An envelope on the table caught his eye. Picking it up, he pulled out its contents. *The sonogram.* Living, breathing proof of the child he and Cecily had conceived together, it knocked the air from his lungs all over again.

It had all become too real. Too easy to envision the family he and Cecily could have together. How complete the idea of it made him feel. Tempting—too tempting to want to have it all—everything he'd never had.

Cecily made him want things he knew he couldn't have. He didn't have the inherent trust in him to subscribe to that kind of a vision—an unconditional love. He'd given that up a long time ago.

And hadn't she just proven his instincts right by walking out that door?

He woke the next morning with a viciously heavy head. Canceling his meetings, he flew to Belgium.

"I take it this isn't a social visit," his grandmother said over coffee the next morning on the porch, eyeing his combustible demeanor.

He shook his head and gave her the recap, finishing with Cecily's departure.

Adriana looked pensive. "What a mess," she murmured. "Can you really blame her? She feels as if she's been betrayed by the two men she loves."

"Yes," he bit out, "I can. You don't walk out on someone when you're having a disagreement. You talk it out. *Work* it out." He lifted a brow. "And who's side are you on anyway? This is *your* battle I've been fighting."

"Yes," she agreed softly, "and maybe Cecily's right. Maybe it's time it ended."

Blood pulsed against his temples. "You're telling me this *now?*"

His grandmother took a sip of her coffee. Sat back in her chair. "There's more to the story of Harper and I than you know. The rivalry we shared was epic, fueled by our mutual ambition. We pushed each other, made each other *better*. You might even have called us friends in the beginning. But somewhere along the way, it turned toxic, this need to win."

"Harper decided Diablo was the key to it all. When I wouldn't agree to allow her to stud him with Demeter, she lashed out, tried to hurt me. We were at a show in Barcelona when I discovered she was having an affair with your grandfather."

With Hugo? The most honorable man he'd known?

"It was a mistake," his grandmother acknowledged. "Harper was beautiful. *Irresistible* to men. And partly," she conceded, "it was my fault. My mindless obsession with my sport hurt your grandfather—he felt I loved it more than him at times. And maybe I did."

The remnants of a long-ago pain stained her dark eyes.

"The affair was over by the time I confronted him about it. I think he knew she had been using him. But it nearly cost us our marriage."

Alejandro attempted to absorb the chink in a relationship that had seemed bullet proof. "You forgave him."

"I loved him, so yes I did. Marriage is never perfect, Alejandro. It's messy and complex, but your grandfather and I built something strong enough that it withstood the difficult times. He was the love of my life."

He took a sip of his coffee. Considered the message she was sending. He could have that with Cecily. He knew it in his heart. All he'd ever wanted from the beginning was to protect her—to take away the shadows. To *keep* her.

So why was it so hard to make that leap she was asking of him? Was the survival instinct that had driven him for so long simply too strong? And yet, he knew even as he thought it, that he loved her. That she'd found a way beneath those defenses of his from the very beginning until she'd crawled into the very heart of him.

He'd spent every minute since denying what he knew to be true because she made him feel so alive, so complete, he couldn't contemplate ever losing her.

Except where had that gotten him? He would lose her now if he wasn't careful.

His grandmother set a gnarled, weathered hand on his. "Go find Cecily. Tell her it's over. I've spent far too much time and emotion chasing my pride, Alejandro. Enough is enough."

He nodded. "I'll go talk to Clayton."

"No," Adriana said, fixing her dark gaze on him. "Leave Clayton to me."

CHAPTER FOURTEEN

ALEJANDRO RETURNED TO New York intent on finding Cecily and making things right. Except his fiancée had turned her phone off and wasn't returning his calls.

She was not, according to her father, in Kentucky, apparently having followed through on her vow to achieve distance from both of them. Nor was she in Manhattan according to the private detective who'd worked on the Hargrove file for him. Which left him precisely nowhere—five days before his wedding.

The calls started then. First the wedding planner with one urgent item after another, then the contractors at the farm with some last minute snags on the finishing materials. With no capacity to sit on a phone all day advising them on things he couldn't see, he moved up to the Cherry Hill and managed his business from there.

His fiancée would, he assumed, come talk to him when she was ready. *Which needed to be soon.*

He personally supervised the unloading of Cecily's horses as they arrived from Kentucky—his other surprise for her. He even went out and bought a box of that crazy-looking American cereal for Bacchus who was now missing home as well as his mistress.

He could identify. A piece of Cecily haunted him everywhere he looked. Taunting him with his own stupidity—reminding him of what he stood to lose.

He woke the next morning to a text from Cecily saying she was fine. That she needed more time to think. No clue to her whereabouts. No time frame on the thinking.

He left another message for her. Told her he needed to talk to her. No reply.

Was she trying to make him sweat? Or was she reconsidering marrying him?

And then it was the day before his wedding. All the renovations complete, the main barn a gleaming masterpiece of wrought-iron and mahogany, he wrote a massive check to the construction manager and thanked him and his team for their hard work.

Watching them leave, a very real fear consumed him that Cecily wasn't coming back. That he had hurt her so badly by not putting her first, by letting her down like everyone else, he'd ruined everything.

But she'd left him for God's sake. How the hell was he supposed to fix it if he was talking to himself?

"In case you've forgotten," Stavros drawled that evening in the Great Room at Cherry Hill, pool cue in hand, "a wedding does require a bride. You need to make a call on this, Salazar."

Alejandro was well aware of that. It was a fact his groomsmen had been dancing around all evening, but with two hundred guests set to descend here tomorrow, it was a reality he could no longer ignore.

"How about this?" Stavros suggested, lifting the cue. "I sink this shot, you call it off. I miss—we keep it in play for another twenty-four hours and hope she shows up for a *Concerto in E*."

Antonio grimaced. "This is no time for your warped sense of humor."

"On the contrary," the Greek drawled, "some humor is desperately needed here."

"Not that kind," Sebastien interjected. "Maybe we should determine what we're going to tell the guests if we do call it off."

"A permit issue with the renovations," Antonio suggested.

"Not bad," Sebastien pondered thoughtfully.

"Or you could call it off *now*," Stavros said. "Before half of New York gets into their cars and drives up here."

If he were smart, Alejandro conceded, that's what he would do. But he had signed on for this future he and Cecily had built together. He had promised to never let her down. *He* wasn't going to be the one to bail on her.

"I'll make a decision in the morning."

Cecily paced the veranda of the rustic cabin she'd rented in the Catskills as the sun made its way into the sky.

Her wedding day.

Her heart climbed into her mouth. She had to make a decision. She was supposed to marry Alejandro in hours. But nothing seemed clear.

This idyllic paradise, buried deep in the heart of the mountains had seemed the perfect place to think. *To lick her wounds.* Because both her father and Alejandro had cut her deeply.

She knew it was Alejandro's sense of honor at work, knew her history was at play here too, but she wanted, *needed* that unconditional love from the man she married. She couldn't settle for less.

And yet, she conceded, leaning against the pillar of the veranda and looking out at the splendor of the red and gold leaves, all this beautiful place had done was remind her of the home she and Alejandro were building—the place where her heart was.

And so—her impossible decision. Marry Alejandro and grow to hate him for what he was doing to her family. To *her.* Don't marry him and deprive her child of a home and herself of the man she loved.

She watched the sun rise high above the trees. A long-ago conversation with her mother filtered through her head. *"You don't choose who you love, Cecily. How and when you love. You just do."*

Something unraveled inside her. And suddenly she knew.

The yard at Cherry Hill was a beehive of activity as Cecily pulled the car into the parking lot.

She sat in the car and watched it all flow by, fear gripping her bones. What if Alejandro hated her for doing this to him? What if he didn't want to marry her now?

Paralyzed, she sat there until the wedding planner, Mariana, flew by in a panic. Pulse pounding in her throat, she stepped from the car.

The morning sunlight lit the façade of the main barn. *Her vision come to life.* But there was something new—a sign the crew had affixed above the main doors.

Hargrove-Salazar.

A knot tied itself in her throat. Her feet moved without conscious decision, carrying her through the massive mahogany doors. The whicker of a horse greeted her, then a frenzied whinny and a stamping of feet.

Bacchus. She flew across the cobblestoned floor, fumbled with the latch on the door of his box and stepped inside, throwing her arms around his neck.

Had her father relented?

Deciding he'd received enough love, Bacchus nuzzled her pockets. She laughed. "I'm sorry. I don't have any right now."

"There's a box of your scary-looking American cereal in the feed room," Alejandro said quietly.

Her heart thumped against her chest. She turned to find him standing outside Bacchus's box. He looked so gorgeous in dark jeans and a white T-shirt, his hair mussed beyond redemption, she ached to throw herself in his arms. But she didn't because he also looked mad. *Furious*.

"I was coming to see you."

"And you left it until *now?*" He shook his head, fire lighting his eyes. "You left the ball in my court, Cecily. How the hell was I supposed to respond if I couldn't find you?"

She crossed her arms over her chest, stomach sinking. "I needed time to think. You are a force of nature. I was worried if I let you in, you would steamroll me into making a decision I wasn't ready to make."

He rested a palm against the stall door. "So have you?"

She stepped out of the box and latched the door. Braved all that suppressed male fury as she stepped into his space. "Yes," she said, lifting her gaze to his. "I love you, Alejandro. We are going to find a way to make this work."

A flicker of something in those dark eyes—the faintest softening she hoped might be a positive sign. He caught her hand in his and tugged her closer until all she could feel was the heat vibrating from him.

"I have some things to say to you too," he said huskily, eyes on hers. "First of all, I let you down, Cecily. I promised you I would always be there for you—that I would make this right and I didn't. That will never happen again.

"Secondly, Adriana went to Kentucky to see your father. It's over, this feud between the Salazars and the Hargroves. Your father and Kay are here for the wedding."

Her father was here? Adriana had gone to Kentucky? Her head spun. "What happened between them?"

"I have no idea and I don't care. Thirdly," he said eyes on hers, "I chose *you* the night I crossed the line and made love to you at Esmerelda. I chose you when I asked you to marry me. I chose *you* the night you gave me that damn speech about unconditional love." He brushed a thumb across her cheek. "You break my heart, *querida*. You always have."

Her breath caught in her chest. "What are you saying?"

"That I love you. I fell in love with you that night in Belgium, Cecily. That's why I pulled away. Because nothing good in my life has ever lasted. I couldn't stand for that to happen to us."

Her heart leaped in her chest. "It won't," she said fiercely, cupping his jaw in her hands. "What we have is special, Alejandro. *Powerful*. Look what we've done… we've ended the longest-running feud in equine history."

A smile curved his lips. "I want to chase this dream with you," he said softly. "I want that unconditional love you talked about. But I am not perfect. I'm going to have my moments. Which doesn't mean I won't always be there for you because I will."

That completely undid her. Throat too thick to speak, she grabbed a handful of his shirt, stood on tiptoe and kissed him—a sweet, shimmering, soul affirming kiss that promised forever.

The hint of uncertainty in his eyes as he drew back made her frown. "What is it?"

"I thought I might have ruined it."

She melted. "You can't ruin love, Alejandro. It just is."

It wasn't something he was going to accept overnight. It was going to take time. Luckily she had the rest of her life to prove it to him.

The afternoon dawned a picture-perfect, unseasonably warm, fall day in the Catskills—as if some higher power had decided Cecily and Alejandro had already defeated enough of the elements and today was reserved for the bright, shiny future they would have.

Her elegant chignon in place, the stylist slipped Cecily's romantic, spaghetti-strapped, ballerina-style dress over her head, the gown settling over her hips in a whoosh of silk. With its elaborate, scalloped bodice, plunging back and floral embroidered lace overlay, the only adornment required were her mother's drop sapphire earrings.

That final grounding element in place, she descended the central staircase of the ranch house to where her father stood waiting at the bottom.

A flash of emotion stained his gray eyes as she took his arm. "You look beautiful."

"Thank you."

He frowned. "Cecily—"

She shook her head. "This is the beginning of a new chapter, Daddy. We decide where it goes from here."

He was silent for a moment, then nodded, walking her outside into the sunshine.

Somehow Alejandro had managed to keep the hordes of photographers circling the estate via helicopter away from the private affair they had wanted it to be. Cecily ignored the distraction as she entered the garden on her father's arm, the fall blooms a riot of red and gold around them. Her focus was firmly on the man who waited for her at the end of the aisle, a look of pure possession on his face.

Alejandro's three groomsmen, Stavros, Antonio and Sebastien all looked devastatingly handsome in dark suits and silver ties, but Alejandro was the only man who would ever make her heart beat this way—as if her whole world revolved around him.

Stavros gave a low whistle, eyes on Alejandro's bride. "Well I'd say she's worth the merry tune she has you dancing."

Antonio eyed him. "And you aren't dancing one yourself?"

Stavros lifted a shoulder as if to concede the point since

everyone knew he was mad about his so called 'convenient wife'. "Salazar, however, is *love struck*."

Well, yes he was. But Alejandro wasn't fighting it anymore. Not when he'd almost lost the woman who had come to mean everything to him. He kept his eyes on Cecily as she negotiated the long row of seats on her father's arm to the strains of a classical Bach piece. And then suddenly she was there by his side, her father giving her away.

He brushed a kiss against her cheek. "You okay?" he murmured. "You look very focused."

Her lips curved in a winsome smile. "Yes."

"Marry me then."

And so she did.

"Well that's the last man down," Stavros concluded, saluting Alejandro with his beer as the barn party moved into full swing. "You must be feeling good about yourself," he said to Sebastien.

The Englishman lifted a shoulder. "It's good to see you three happy."

"A toast then," Alejandro said, tipping his glass toward Sadie, Calli, Monika and Cecily who looked up to no good whispering at one of the tables. "To the women in our lives and our luck in finding them."

The men lifted their glasses in a salute and drank, all of them, Alejandro was sure, aware of how lucky they were.

"Apologies," Stavros said to Sebastien when he'd lowered his glass, "that Alejandro and I can't make the press conference on Monday. It's an admirable thing you're doing, Sebastien, giving away half your net worth."

"You're forgiven," Sebastien allowed, "since I've put you all on the Rapid Response board of directors."

"Oh, no," said Stavros, lifting his hands. "No bandwidth here."

"Me neither," said Alejandro.

Antonio frowned. "Yeah, I—"

"Excuse me." Mariana arrived to pluck Alejandro out of the group for the first dance. "I need him."

"Saved by the wedding planner," said Stavros.

"You have no capacity for that," Cecily observed as they waited for the band—*their* band from that night in Kentucky—to finish up the upbeat tune they were playing. "You have no time as it is. We're having a baby."

"I know," he said, lacing his fingers through hers. "But Sebastien tends to get what Sebastien wants."

The band introduced them to the crowd with a flourish. Cecily took Alejandro's hand and they walked onto the dance floor under the sparkling Murano chandeliers. A hand laced through his, the other on his shoulder, her head tucked under his chin, they danced to the same ballad they had that night in Kentucky.

Time fell away and suddenly she was back under that star-filled sky, dancing with the man she'd fallen madly in love with. Except this time, it wasn't just for one night— it was for forever.

"Alejandro," she murmured.

"Mmm?"

"It's not my song anymore. I *got* everything I wanted. Well," she added, a wistful note to her voice, "almost everything."

He leaned down to kiss her. "You will have that too. Remember the rule?"

An unshakeable vision.

EPILOGUE

World Championships of Show Jumping,
Normandy, France.

VIRGINIA NELISSEN GALLOPED out of the stadium having compiled four faults in a lightning-fast round that had the Dutch team sitting in first place with only the last American rider to go.

"Boo," said Alejandro to his eighteen-month-old daughter, Zara Rose, sitting on his lap with a front row seat to the action. "We don't like her. She was mean to Mama."

"Boo," said Zara, imitating his scowl.

"Excelente," he murmured, pressing a kiss to the top of her head. "Now," he whispered as Cecily cantered into the ring, "you have to cheer for team Hargrove-Salazar. Because *this* is going to make history."

"Salazar-Hargrove," Adriana corrected tartly. "And I really don't like how nervous Cecily is. She was wrapping enough fences in the warm up to bring the whole course down."

Because this was his wife's dream. Because ever since her return to riding she'd been anchoring the American team on Socrates and been brilliant while doing it.

If there was pressure here today, it was on the woman riding into the ring, hair caught up in a sleek chignon beneath her velvet helmet, navy coat and crisp white shirt perfectly pressed. But if there was anything he knew about his wife by now, it was that she was a fighter. A survivor. She would leave it all in the ring today.

Cecily brought Socrates to a halt in front of the judges

and took off her hat in a salute. The applause and buzz of the crowd died down until you could hear a pin drop in the stadium. And then there was only the sound of Socrates's hooves pounding the sand as Cecily pushed him into an easy canter with a touch of her heels to his sides.

His smooth, glorious stride ate up the ground as Cecily guided him to the first jump, a high, complicated juxtaposition of poles Socrates eyed as unfamiliar then proceeded to rap hard as he cleared it.

Not an auspicious start. Adriana was right—both rider and horse were nervous.

An easy turn to the next jump and Socrates was taking off too late, clearing the jump by the skin of his teeth, then roaring toward the next, where Cecily placed him at the jump too early, forcing him to exert a superhuman effort to make it to the other side unscathed.

"Lord have mercy," said his grandmother, covering her eyes. "I can't watch."

A nice long gallop to the next oxer, he watched Cecily visibly collect herself and her horse. *Good.* They cleared the wide, imposing jump with perfect form. Then it was a quick turn to the triple combination that had felled every single rider thus far including Virginia, the jumps trickily placed off-stride to test the riders.

Cecily attacked it with military precision, placing Socrates perfectly for the first jump, then sailing over the next two with shortened strides that efficiently addressed the challenge.

His wife glanced at the clock with four jumps to go. She was close to time faults. She needed to avoid them and go clear for the American team to win. His stomach dropped as Cecily whipped Socrates around at a near suicidal angle and galloped toward the next combination at a speed that made Adriana gasp.

"Dear God," she said. "That's a bad call—that's—"

Socrates whipped over the first jump, galloped flat out toward the second and annihilated it too.

"—brilliant," said his grandmother.

She's retiring, thought Alejandro.

A sharp turn to the right and his wife was thundering toward the last jump. The crowd was on its feet now, caught up in the gutsy ride, its home team already out of it.

One more jump, Alejandro whispered. *One more jump, angel, you can do it.*

And then she did.

Cecily rode into the collecting ring where the media was assembled for the post competition interviews.

She had nothing left for them. Had gone through every facet of the emotional spectrum out there on that course, her mother's riding pin attached to her chest. When she caught sight of Alejandro waiting for her, Zara in his arms, a sob rose to her throat.

Her husband set Zara down. Cecily kicked her feet out of the stirrups and slid off Socrates's back and into his arms—the man who had never failed to catch her each and every time she'd stumbled over the past year: as she'd become a new mother, as she'd resumed her career, as she'd walked the tenuous road of balancing both.

Alejandro cupped her jaw and kissed her. "No tears, *meu carinho*. You were magnificent. Your mother would be so proud."

The tears came then in a great big flood. For the things she'd lost. For the things she'd gained. For what was still ahead.

A reporter from an American sports network descended on them, noting Adriana's legendary presence. "Perfect.

Can I have an interview with the complete team Hargrove-Salazar then?"

"Team Salazar-Hargrove," Adriana corrected. "And yes you may."

* * * * *

If you enjoyed Jennifer Hayward's contribution to
THE SECRET BILLIONAIRES *trilogy*
don't forget to read the first two stories

DI MARCELLO'S SECRET SON
by Rachael Thomas

XENAKIS'S CONVENIENT BRIDE
by Dani Collins

Available now!

MILLS & BOON®

MODERN™

POWER, PASSION AND IRRESISTIBLE TEMPTATION

0717/19

Join Britain's BIGGEST Romance Book Club

- **EXCLUSIVE offers every month**

- **FREE delivery direct to your door**

- **NEVER MISS a title**

- **EARN Bonus Book points**

Call Customer Services

0844 844 1358 *

or visit

millsandboon.co.uk/subscriptions